S.E. SCHAEFER

I0670485

TRIALS OF THE ORDER

Cover design © Fantastical Ink

Edited by Caitlin Lengerich

ISBN: 979-8-218-58759-8

Content Warnings

Trials of the Order is a adult fantasy novel. It is written with the intent of being read by adults only. Many difficult topics are discussed when talking about the character's past and motivations, as well as while they do what assassins do best.

This novel contains:

Graphic depictions of murder and death, Domestic violence, Child abuse, Assault, Sexual abuse (mentioned but not described on page), Vomiting, and Profanity

Contents

To everyone putting in the work to better themselves despite your own trials.

I see you. I AM you.

Keep your head up. You're doing great.

PROLOGUE

I mmortality had grown dull—monotonous even. Nothing motivated Zylah to continue in this horrid, neverending existence beyond her desire for power. She hungered for it like an animal with a craving that could never be sated, forever longing for her fill. Even the omnipotent and eternal yearned for a higher purpose beyond simply existing. She knew the magic the mortals held could be the key to unlocking her true potential.

And Zylah wanted it all.

She stood amongst the other gods in a circular room, open to the outside air and surrounded by white, towering pillars. This place existed in paradise, with lush green fields and a never-ending ocean encircling the palace. Despite the near utopia in which they dwelled, it had grown lonely. Only the gods and their loyal servants resided here, leaving the rest of this plane of existence cold and uninhabited.

Her footsteps echoing her frustration as she paced the marble floor. Time and time again, she had tried to convince the others, but just as in all the previous arguments, her plight was ignored.

"They are undeserving and unappreciative of everything we have given them. Why should I stand by, feeling my power slowly wither to nothing to benefit the mortals? There are better uses for my magic—our magic. And far better uses of our time than the decaying flesh sacks—"

Pilean lay upon a red satin divan, his long, golden hair draped over the back, flowing in a curling cascade. He raised a hand, silencing her. "Enough, Zylah. We have voted and decided in favor of the mortals," he stated dismissively.

His muscled, bare abdomen gleamed with sweat at the rising temperatures of a new day. Sunshine streamed into the room, highlighting every curve and contour of his tanned skin.

Pilean's blithe reaction only frustrated Zylah further. She hated each of their beautiful faces, believing their alluring appearances were just a way to lure them into complacency. The mortals on worldly planes knew nothing of their true form; the statues erected in the gods' images were only based on distorted visions and never the truth.

"We are wasting our birthright," she insisted, crossing her arms over her chest. "With the power we hold, we could conquer worlds—entire realms. And yet, you all sit here," she spat, motioning around the room to the other gods draped across their plush lounges. "You all sit here and allow yourselves to waste away."

A sharp laugh sounded from behind her, echoing through the open room. She turned on her heel, narrowing her eyes at a half-naked Helka being fanned by a servant. "Speak for yourself. I am far from wasting away," Helka stated, motioning to the thin sheets of gold draped haphazardly across her body. "We want for nothing. Our entire purpose is to live benevolently, to be wanted and worshiped. The very least we can do is remain in infamy forever with the undying love of those . . . what did you call them?" She paused, pressing a finger to her perfectly painted red lips, pretending the term Zylah had used evaded her instead of amused her.

Zylah rolled her eyes at the motion.

"Flesh sacks," Helka continued brightly, barely hiding her smile.

Zylah's near-white hair flowed around her in the unnatural wind created by the sentient palace, but it did nothing to dampen the heat within her. Most days, this palace felt like a prison, a cage to contain and control her, though she blamed the people inside more than the house itself.

Through the centuries, she had grown tired of the whims of fickle gods and wanted more than the life she had been given. She would never be content with doing so little, existing only to be worshiped by mortals a universe away or spending her days on plush couches with nothing to look forward to.

She had to have more.

More.

More.

It was all she could think about these days—a thought that refused to leave her head, slowly driving her mad with its repetition.

The house sensed something was wrong before Zylah even noticed herself. It began providing her with entertainment and distraction through never-ending rows of books, paintings, and servants who wanted nothing more than to bed a god. It was a beautiful diversion for anyone who did not plan to conquer this universe and every other one.

Despite the house's efforts, Zylah was slipping further into madness, carelessly dancing on the point of no return.

Sitting in the corner, a book propped in their hands, Aradia listened to the argument but stayed decisively quiet. Locks of their short mahogany hair fell into golden eyes, but they ignored it, too enthralled in their reading and too used to the petty squabbles to bother.

Infuriated by their silence, Zylah turned on them. "Have you nothing to add?" she snapped, baring teeth that were sharpened to points. She wanted to snatch the book from Aradia's hands, toss it into the burning hearth at the center of the room, and watch Aradia's anger match her own as it turned to ash. At least then she would know they felt something, anything.

She tapped her foot impatiently, awaiting an answer that did not come. "We could rule more than just this universe." Zylah continued to the silent room. "We could conquer worlds and be worshiped by uncountable mortals. You sit here and tell me that you wish for none of that? You wish for life to continue as it is for the rest of eternity?"

3

Silence, nothing but silence.

"Answer me!" she demanded. "I will not believe it unless I hear it from all of your lips."

Zylah's temper was brewing, power bristling through her body in electric waves. The house shuddered in anticipation, preparing to repair whatever she broke in her anger. That was the benefit of having a home that caters to your every whim; anything broken was repaired with just a thought.

Her knuckles turned white, teeth grinding together. When she felt like she was going to burst, a soft voice sounded out.

"Yes."

"Yes?" Zylah repeated, incredulously, stalking toward Aradia. "Yes?"

"That is what I said," Aradia stated, balancing the book upon their chest and tapping it with the fingers of their right hand. No longer able to contain her anger, Zylah's power lashed out, the wall behind Aradia turning to rubble with a flash of light. A shimmering iridescent bubble, courtesy of the palace, surrounded and protected them from falling debris. Aradia huffed a sigh, annoyed by the inconvenience, and brushed dust particles from their book.

"Yes?" Zylah repeated. "I cannot stand to be in the same room, let alone the same universe as you lot. You have no dreams, aspirations, or desires beyond the next meal you take in." She spun around, eyes flashing with rage. "And I am stuck here, doomed to be nothing more than this. Meanwhile, the mortals you so love gain more and more power. All because you voted to give them our very essence. I've seen the way the special ones walk through universes while we are trapped here. Trapped and doomed to fade away to nothing. The more they reproduce, the more I feel the power leaving my being."

"We are not trapped," Aradia said with a snort. "We have always had the ability to leave; you have never asked the right questions."

"Aradia," Pilean warned, his face stern. "Is this true, Zylah? I have felt nothing of the sort."

"She's being dramatic, Pilean," Helka jeered. "No one's powers are fading. They cannot take more from us unless we gift it; that is how it was designed. The magic on their planet is simply reproducing. You are just angry that you do not possess it. Tell the truth and stop burdening us with your worries."

"Do not speak for me, Helka. I can feel my powers fading each moment of every day. If you all are so blind to it, you deserve to be powerless," Zylah snapped. Helka had always been an unwelcome adversary, and she could think of no worse fate than spending eternity with her.

Zylah knew she needed to change tactics and appeal to a different side of them. Taking a deep breath to calm herself, she lowered her voice and continued. "If you all are so content to become mortal, I should take our magic back and begin something new—benefit a new universe. Let me take back what is rightfully ours if they no longer need it. They are weak and foolish. We could find a better lot to worship us," she said with false sincerity.

Pilean shook his head, summoning a servant before whispering in the male's ear. Zylah waited for someone to answer her, the silence burning her from the inside out.

She watched the red-haired servant stoop closer to Pilean, leaning in to hear his every word. He let out a breathy chuckle, running a finger down Pilean's chest, coming dangerously close to the thin cloth that barely covered his lower half.

Unable to watch the flirtation before her any longer, Zylah released an exasperated breath and narrowed her eyes at the motion. "You all are useless."

Aradia slowly set the book on the seat before rising to their feet. "You have no idea what it is to be powerless. The mortals were accomplished long before we gave them anything. I have grown tired of this argument. Must we have it every day for eternity?"

"Yet they would be nothing without us!" Zylah shouted. "They would be nothing without my magic. You may have given them a little gift, but they would be but a speck in existence if I had not breathed life into them. My magic creates worlds, not just party tricks. They would be nothing without me. Same as all of you."

"Let's find out, shall we?" Aradia crooned, stalking toward her. Zylah stepped back, unsure of Aradia's objective in advancing toward her. Death did not exist in the In-Between, but pain still thrived, and Zylah had no intention of finding out what Aradia was capable of. "Why don't you spend time as one of those powerless mortals to give you some perspective?"

Aradia began tracing symbols in the air, twirling their fingers with expertise far greater than Zylah had anticipated. Aradia looked deeply into her eyes, stopping just one stroke from completing the next glyph. "Let this be a lesson in humility. While your power creates worlds, we have created life from your debris."

Zylah's lips curled back, exposing shiny white teeth. "You wouldn't dare," she snarled.

Aradia looked over their shoulder, smiling at the other gods, still seated in luxury. "We will all enjoy the silence for once. And," Aradia added, "it will do you some good."

She opened her mouth to protest, but Aradia had finished the glyph, stealing the air from her lungs and binding her tongue. Zylah was falling through an endless sea of black, a nothingness, unlike anything she had ever known. There was no beginning or ending; just ceasing to exist in the blackness that consumed her.

CHAPTER 1

T he Simulation began as it always had. The rain patter against thin glass panes soon replaced the deafening silence of the Simulation room. The cool leather of the padded chair beneath me faded to the warmth of the soft fleece nightgown I had worn when I was only fourteen.

No matter how many times I practiced, I never got used to the feeling of not only witnessing my worst memory but reliving it as the scared child I had once been.

The creature's magic took less than a minute to pull me under, the sea of my unconscious state floating in ribbons of color until I was no longer Varine of the present. I was no longer an assassin training for the Trials, free to move about and live how I wished. I was once again the girl being suffocated by the alabaster walls in a house that was really just a cage.

I was aware of the faux reality taking shape, but only in the way that a nagging thought breaches the back of the mind. The memory was so intoxicating that I craved it the moment it dissipated. Addiction was a side-effect of repeated exposure that made it increasingly difficult to break free. Each time I entered the Simulation, it became harder to escape.

Sharp details filled my vision, and my parents' angry voices drifted up the stairs, only muffled by the closed door of my bedroom. They were fighting about me again.

These days, it was always about me.

In a family of immensely powerful Witches, magic was passed down to the first-born daughter on their thirteenth birthday. But not to me. I was an anomaly, an abomination, a disgrace to my familial line.

The day of my thirteenth birthday had passed without so much as a drop of magic emanating from my fingertips. Each glyph, every magical symbol I had drawn, had only been in vain. Even now, a year almost to the date later, I could hear the words my mother had spat.

"Cursed."

"Shameful."

"Useless."

"Dangerous."

A never-ending loop of her disappointment.

For weeks before that horrible day, I had studied the book of glyphs that had been passed down from Witch to Witch. When the time finally came to demonstrate what I had learned, nothing happened. Mother's silence was almost more painful than her words. I begged the gods to allow even a spark to come forth, but I was left with nothing but heartache and defeat.

Foolishly hoping that I had just not studied enough, Mother locked me in my room for days, only allowing me to leave to eat and relieve myself. But with each failed glyph drawn and erased, both of our frustrations only grew.

All I had wanted, dreamed of even, was the magic that was promised to me. Magical ability increased through each generation—at least in the Crestin family—slating me to be the most powerful Witch of an entire generation. This magic would allow me to travel to far-off places, go on incredible quests, and be revered everywhere I went. But when thirteen passed and fourteen inched closer to its end, my dreams and my mother's aspirations felt more and more out of reach.

My name was a curse on my mother's lips—the argument below growing louder. I flinched at the sound as I traced the glyph for flowers in the condensation left on the window from the evening storm. The sun was preparing to sleep, giving way to an orange sunset over the mountain lake. Dark clouds built in the distance, threatening to turn the light patter of rain into a violent tempest.

When nothing happened, like always, I angrily swiped the markings away, leaving nothing but my reflection staring back at me. Anytime they spoke of me, I was quickly ushered into my room with promises of sweets and stories of my father's grand adventures. Though I loved his stories, I was growing tired of being cut off from the conversations that were very obviously about me.

Creeping toward the rising voices, I tiptoed around the floorboards that would squeak beneath my feet and reveal me to my parents below. My door slid open on a whisper just as my father began shouting. I left it ajar in case a mad dash to the safety of my room was needed.

"She's only a child, Ursa!" His rage-filled features came into view as I stood on the tips of my toes to peer over the half-wall that shielded the upstairs hallway. "You are talking about sending our daughter to war before it even begins to look for her."

Mother wore a beautiful cream and cerulean dress, attire much too elegant for lounging around the mountain house. Her ash brown hair was tied in a knotted braid around her head; strands broke loose when she shook it in dissent.

Before I became a reminder to her of all that she had lost, she was the shining star of my admiration. I wanted nothing more than to be and look like her, as she was the perfect example of what my future would hold.

Over the past year, she had morphed into someone unrecognizable, and now I was thankful that I inherited far more traits from my father than from her. The eyes of my bloodline, one blue and one green, that marked us as different, blessed even, were the only similarities between us. Luckily, my thin, straight nose and hair the color of my father's favorite wine, came from him.

Where my mother had high, commanding cheekbones with a slim face, my cheeks remained decisively round. Mother had a beautiful tan despite the season, and I inherited my father's pale tones. I was like my father in every way, from my love of gardening to my distaste of reality—preferring to daydream instead of existing in the present, much to Mother's chagrin.

"I am well aware of my child's age," Mother snapped. "It does not matter. She will be hunted every day for the rest of her life. The best thing we can do is give her a fighting chance."

I pushed up on my toes further, unsure that I had just heard her correctly. I couldn't imagine a safer place for me than here. The entire property was warded specifically to keep intruders out—and to keep me in.

Father's eyes filled with fury, the fiery tendrils of his hair writhing with his anger. "Do not pretend," he spat, punctuating each word, "you are making this decision for her. You are making it purely out of your hatred and contempt for those of us who do not possess magic. Would you be making this same decision if her magic had presented itself? If she had been born with powers?"

My hand flew to my mouth, trying and failing to cover the sound of a gasp before it left my lips. I crouched down, using the wall to hide my spying, and prayed to the gods that they had not heard me. It upset me that my father might have worried I would feel the same way. That *I* might have looked down upon him if I had magic, in the same way he now accused my mother of.

"Everything, Odell, *everything* I have done and will do will be to protect her. We are moving in circles and having this same argument on repeat with no way forward. I wouldn't be asking you this if I did not think it was best for her." Her words were no more than a rushed whisper. "I love you for who you are. I knew when I met you that you did not have powers. I did not care then, and I do not care now."

Poking my head back over the wall, I watched Mother step forward, reaching out to him.

"There is a way forward. Let me protect you both as I have always done," he pleaded, grabbing her hands. "You can strengthen the wards around the house and glamour us from sight. She will be safe," he insisted when Mother shook her head. "We'll *all* be safe."

She freed one of her hands and gently placed it on his cheek. "That's the problem, my love, she already knows. They will take her, and when they discover that she possesses not even a single drop of magic, they will kill her."

Having heard enough of the jumbled information I didn't understand, I decided it was my turn to ask questions. Father always came when I asked; I knew this time would be no different. Would he give me answers to who wanted to find me and why I wasn't safe in this secluded and protected place?

He opened his mouth to argue further, but I couldn't wait even one more moment. "Father?" I called, ducking down so that I would not be seen.

"Coming!" he called back. His whispered words to Mother were barely audible. "We'll finish this conversation later."

I half crawled, half ran toward my bedroom, hoping I would be quick enough to reach my room before he could ascend the stairs.

The soft click of the latch sounded behind me as I launched myself into my bed and under the covers. Only seconds later, the rapping of our secret knock sounded against the door—three knocks, followed by one, and another a few seconds later.

I smiled as the door slowly crept open, his fingers wrapping around the door frame, and his head appeared from behind it. "Can I come in, Flower?" he asked sweetly. I barely held in the giggle at how silly he looked—just a floating head without a body.

All traces of anger and sadness from only moments prior had evaporated from his voice. When I nodded, he closed the door softly behind him, his shoulders shuddering slightly before turning around, as if he had to take a breath to steady himself.

"Was that about me?" I blurted before he could make it to my bedside. My blanket was clenched tightly to my face, hiding my embarrassment that I had just given myself away. He sat at the edge of the bed, smiling softly at me. His knowing eyes practically yelled, "I know you were listening."

"Your mother just worries, my little Flower. She always has."

11

I reached out to interlace our fingers, my small hand swallowed by his large, calloused grip. Dirt clung to the underside of his nails, his skin rough from working in the garden.

"Then why do you look so sad?" I asked.

His other hand reached out to tug on the curls that hung loosely around my shoulders. "I worry too. Mostly about you," he said with a wink that faded to a forced smile. "Your mother worries about who might come to seek you and the power you are supposed to have. I told her—"

"But I don't have any magic," I insisted, interrupting him. Just as I had suspected, Mother was being ridiculous and overreacting. She had always treated my lack of magic like the end of the world. Choosing to resent me for what I could have been instead of loving me for who I was.

"I know that, Flower. But the world doesn't. Even if they knew, they would not believe it. A powerless, first-born Crestin has never happened." He sucked in a deep breath, looking toward the closed door, and then the floor. "I worry for the world we live in and what that might mean for the future. Your future . . . our future."

"So, you *were* fighting about me," I pouted, dropping his hand and covering my eyes with my palms. "Why does Mother hate me? Haven't I always been good? I've tried my very best to impress her. I excel in everything but magic."

He exhaled loudly, obviously saddened by my words. "She does not hate you. She is—" He paused, presumably trying to think of the right thing to say. "Disappointed." He continued. "But not in you, in what she thought the world might have looked like if you had come into your power."

"She hates me," I repeated. Colorful starbursts had begun coating the back of my eyelids from where my hands pressed firmly into them; I pushed them harder into the sockets to distract myself from the stinging pressure of my tear ducts and the lump lodged in my throat.

"Varine, look at me," he said sternly. When I did not move my hands, he removed them, finger by finger, careful to keep his touch gentle, light as a feather. I squeezed my eyes shut, refusing to open them, fearing the tears might spill out if I did.

Father chuckled, causing an involuntary smile to form across my mouth that I tried and failed to bite back.

His voice softened. "Flower, please open your eyes."

I peeked a single eye open, looking into the deep, burning embers of his golden-brown gaze.

"Your mother does not hate you. And I promise you that I will spend every day of the rest of my life fighting for you. You have nothing to worry about."

"You won't send me away?" I sniffled.

He shook his head. "You're not going anywhere," he promised, crossing his finger over his heart.

The gesture brought a smile to my face, the burning lump that had threatened to choke me soothed by my father's love. "Good."

An involuntary yawn escaped, giving away the late hour. I tried and failed to stifle it but it was already too late, Father had already seen it.

He smiled down at me. "Good," he repeated. "Now, let's tuck you in; you need your rest. And where is Caylina?"

Throwing the blankets from my body, I clambered from the bed and dropped to my knees to peer under the wooden frame, hoping to find her there. "Caylina! Bed time!" I called to the room in a sing-song voice when I failed to locate her under the bed.

A plump, tawny tabby flounced out from the open closet and leapt onto the duvet. Caylina stretched her claws out before curling onto the pillow I had placed next to mine, just for her. Father held the blanket open for me, the fresh scent of lavender and eucalyptus laundering soap soothed my weary head.

He tucked the smooth fabric of the comforter around my body snugly, ensuring that I was fully encased in cloth. I giggled to myself, as I imagined I was a caterpillar, cocooned and awaiting a transformation. Father leaned down, brushing loose tendrils of hair from my forehead before placing a kiss where they had just been.

Bracing a hand on the mattress, he prepared to stand, but panic seized me at the thought of him leaving the room. I scrambled for a reason to keep him here for just a moment longer.

"Wait!" I exclaimed, looking around the room desperately before settling my gaze on the cat. "What about Caylina?"

He smiled at me, the corners of his eyes crinkling with amusement. Gently, he kissed the white spot between her eyes. She purred loudly before resting her head on her paws. I sank further into the plush mattress, another yawn sneaking its way out as sleep began to consume me.

"Sweet dreams, my precious Flower. I'll see you in the morning," he promised. Pausing in the doorway, he blew me one final kiss before shutting the door behind him.

A chill breeze drifted in from the cracked window, dousing the oppressive heat of the summer day. Snug under my blankets, the rain pattering against the glass lured me away from any thoughts of my parents' argument. The answers to my questions could wait. Caylina snored softly as my breathing deepened and sleep claimed me.

CHAPTER 2

M y father's earthy smell and the cool softness of the duvet still filled my senses as the Simulation room came back into view. I rubbed at my bleary eyes, the memory lingering on the outskirts of my vision and imprinted on the back of my eyelids.

"What was my time?" I asked groggily, the remnants of the strange magic taking its time to withdraw from my system, leaving me in a stupor that resembled the aftermath of a night of drinking.

It was exhausting, both mentally and physically, to not only relive the memory but also to fight my way out as it clung on desperately. Facing it wasn't the most significant threat, though; becoming trapped was.

Once you enter the Simulation, the only person who can get you out is yourself. If you can't face the memory and overcome it, you're forced to relive it on an endless loop for eternity, being slowly driven mad until your body succumbs to death. If you're lucky, someone might take pity on you and end your suffering.

Acceptance was the key to escape. Looking deep within oneself and acknowledging the repressed memory as it truly was, no matter how difficult, was the only way for the magic to recede.

The further I pushed into the echo of what was, the more it felt like a punishment instead of preparation for the Trials.

The Simulation room was nearly sterile, devoid of furniture except for the chair I lay upon. The smell of antiseptic filled the air, washing away any remnants of my father's lingering scent. A long wall of mirrors reflected the dull, colorless room to me. Everything was white—the walls, the floor, the pale creatures standing unnaturally still and watching my every move.

"Four minutes and sixteen seconds in the Simulation," the Time Keeper stated to the Record Holder. Even though they answered my question, I knew the words were only spoken for the benefit of the other. No matter how hard I tried, I couldn't convince them to speak directly to me. Rather, they refused to speak to anyone.

The Record Keeper nodded, not needing to write down the time because of its impeccable ability to recall details, or so the belief was.

Bracing my hands on the silver-colored plush chair, I sat up, tossing my long red braid over my shoulder. "Fifteen seconds faster than yesterday," I declared with a smirk.

Standing before the mirrored wall, I fixed the strands of hair that had wandered loose while keeping one eye on the creatures as they moved in unison from where they had stood over me, to the back wall.

Thick, draping robes shadowed their faces from view. Despite their towering height, the fabric puddled around them in an ominous crimson pool. Long, bony fingers hung from their sleeves, jutting out at unnatural angles and protruding from pale, veiny hands like gnarled tree branches. The humanoid outline of their bodies beneath their cloaks was their only comforting trait.

Despite their ability to wield magic, these creatures were not Witches drawing glyphs, Shifters changing their forms, or Conjurors shaping elements to their whim. The history of where they had descended from was a mystery, and how they had ended up in the keep, assisting the Order of Assassins with the Trials, was an even bigger one. Their species was nameless; the only way to refer to them was by using the title given to them.

Utilizing magic was dangerous in a world ruled by Queen Desma. Luckily for the creatures residing here, she seemed only interested in mortals with power. Unlike the human wielders who we were forced to hide their abilities in fear that their neighbors would sell them out, they roamed free, practicing with abandon, unafraid of the queen's desires.

It hadn't always been this way. I was old enough to remember a time before her rule, when magic wielders used their powers for even the most mundane things, like washing laundry or enchanting a field to grow quicker. Since Desma's reign began, the continent had grown more poor. Our trade routes had been cut-off from the other lands, and crops died quickly without the spark of life that magic gave. A growing number of wielders willingly turned themselves over to provide food for their starving families. But even those who chose to hide were frequently found and taken away by a cadre of specially trained guards.

I had never watched a creature be torn from its family, but I had watched many wielders dragged from their homes, never to be seen again. Her rise to power was the sole reason my family had retreated to the mountain house, locking me and my freedom away in a disillusioned attempt at protection.

Luckily, here in the keep, residual minor magics like the floating lights above me and the warming fires igniting of their own accord still existed, as they were only remnants of magic and not power itself. It was created only for convenience and had no ability beyond what it was initially designed to do. It was morbid to think about the people that had made them, those wielders either long dead or stolen away.

Satisfied that I had groomed the flyaway hairs back into their rightful position, I studied the creatures behind me, their stillness eerie. Leaning toward the mirror, I looked for any sign of their chests moving but found no evidence that they were even breathing.

I had searched the library for information on their species and abilities but could not locate anything close. Their magical ability to trap a person in their worst memory, even repressed ones, was undocumented. I even searched libraries and bookstores when given the opportunity to travel. The more I could learn about these creatures, the better off I would be in the Simulation.

A shiver ran through me as I imagined what other beings with undocumented powers were likely running around the continent of Kalahvin. Were they hiding in the forests or the mountain range that cut directly through the land? If the two before me were any indication of what might be lurking, I would be better off leaving the others undiscovered.

A deep, silken voice jarred me from my unintentional staring contest with the Record Keeper. The pounding and ache in my head kept me from hearing the door swing open.

"Stop glaring at them; they don't like it when you do that," the voice jeered. "Your time is good, but not good enough to put you on top."

Amias Ronin, self-proclaimed King of the Order of Assassins, leaned in the doorway, arms crossed across his broad chest. Shaggy, chestnut hair was plastered to his forehead, and his bronze skin gleamed with the remnants of sweat from the training he did every morning.

The skintight fighting leathers he wore accentuated the defined muscles in his arms and thighs. His appearance was that of a man in his mid-thirties, though I did not know his actual age. Despite only appearing ten or so years older than me, I had looked up to him as a father figure since my initiation.

Shaking my head, I attempt to clear the fog from my mind. "Four minutes and sixteen seconds puts me far ahead of the other Journeymen," I stated. "And I don't need to be fast, I just need to get out."

He ran a hand through the mop of hair, smoothing back the stragglers to reveal his intense almond-shaped, hazel eyes. He apprised me with a downturned mouth. "That was only a small taste of what the Courage Trial will contain. Even though you have forgotten the memory, it is still there. You'll face the entire thing during the Trials," he warned. "And it will not be easy or painless."

I rolled my eyes. "I know, I know. Courage, Intelligence, Physical Strength, Determination, and Resourcefulness. The five traits revered and trained into your assassins and represented in the Five Trials." I mocked, having heard that

18

line from his mouth more times than I could count. "Why are you even here? Don't you have something better you could be doing?"

The Simulation fell under the Courage Trial and was the only one we could know of and practice beforehand. Spectators were strictly forbidden from viewing another's Simulation practice; something about it being a culmination of who we are at our core and not being fair for another to know until the Trials officially commenced. The Order liked the whole equality thing—as if death cared about fairness.

Amias, however, had been making appearances at many of the Journeymens' training sessions lately, typically arriving at the very end. Had his presence not made me anxious, I might have been flattered by the extra attention. Though I did not appreciate the intrusion, he made no indication he had witnessed any part of my memory. But that didn't stop me from growing suspicious of his intentions.

The memory I had just relived was extremely personal and contained information I was not yet ready to share—secrets I had even promised not to tell—specifically, that of my lineage.

Amias and the other apprentices were unaware I was a descendant of the famed Crestin line, which I would continue to keep close to my chest for as long as I was able.

Mother had done me one favor before sending me away, though I suspected it was more to protect herself than it was for me. That was glamouring my distinctive eye color. Tattooed into the bottom of my right heel in ink to match my skin was the glyph that colored my eyes a muddy brown. My promise to hide my identity relied solely on the dainty swirls embedded in my skin.

Secrets were a currency among the assassins, knowledge being a powerful commodity. Amias was not exempt from this; if anything, he was the biggest gossip of them all, hoarding information like a dragon with its trove.

He shrugged nonchalantly. "I can check up on whomever I want. Perks of being in charge," he said with a wink. "You're a far cry from the scared child you were eight years ago, but you still have much to learn before you're ready to compete."

Making a show of my confidence, I crossed the room until we stood face to face. Amias's tall form loomed over me as he had at least a half-foot of height on me.

I shifted on the balls of my feet, silently checking that the daggers I had slid into the sheaths at my thighs and in my boots were still in place. He tended to turn every interaction into a lesson, and I was not in the mood to fight today, nor would I willingly be caught unprepared.

"You better watch yourself, or someone might think you're worrying about me."

He raised his eyebrows, his lips drawing into a thin line. "My motivations are none of your, or anyone else's, concern."

That was the problem with our leader, his desires beyond making money were unclear. Unless serving a purpose for him, he took little interest in the thirty assassins that lived in this keep. Ignoring us was how he drew us in, always resulting in a fight for any scraps of attention he might send our way.

Amias was a collector of things—powerful, broken, damaged things, whether that be a person, animal, or creature. Anything that made him appear better than or feel like the king of the continent instead of the king of misfit assassins.

His collecting proclivity was awfully similar to that of the queen's, though we were prisoners to the Order in a different way than those she held. When I had told him as much, he had been appalled at the comparison and even threatened to throw me out.

As a member of the Order, I had many freedoms, and even more to come once I completed the Trials, but the vow of loyalty we swore upon our ascension through the ranks chafed restrictively.

"When the time comes, I'll be ready," I promised, moving to push past him. He grabbed my arm gently, stopping my exit.

His eyes searched every inch of my being for a sign of weakness; head tilted in the way it often did when he surveyed his next mark. "Don't wander far, I require your assistance on an errand."

My ears perked up at the word, a smile crossing my face. "An errand?" I asked, trying and failing to hide my giddy excitement. *Errands* were Amias's way of downplaying the horrible acts we commit—making it sound as if we were running to the market for a fresh loaf of bread.

The name had always amused me, which I knew deep down was a terrible thing to find humorous. The further you progressed into the Order, the more detached you became from the actions you performed; it was easier that way.

Amias smiled back at me, releasing my arm from his grip. "Unfortunately, this one is an actual errand, a quick trip over to Dexmore. No death . . . at least not that I have planned currently. I do appreciate the enthusiasm, however."

My smile dropped, and I rolled my eyes. "I'll pack a bag," was all I said before pushing past him, careful not to turn my back fully on the King of Assassins as I strode down the hallway.

CHAPTER 3

T he keep was nearly empty as I walked through the winding hallways designed to confuse and ensnare anyone who made it past the intricately woven wards that protected the property. I could still remember my awe at the way they had parted around me, revealing a towering fortress instead of an unkempt farm surrounded by grain fields like the glamour suggested.

Despite the protection from outsiders, the occupants inside were far more dangerous than any other. Within the keep's borders it was survival of the fittest; murder between apprentices was not unheard of or even uncommon. Amias was far more dangerous than he looked, going as far as to eliminate an entire class of Journeymen before they could even begin the Trials just because he deemed them unworthy.

That first day, I was greeted by a sprawling, multi-level castle with lush courtyards and an impressive reflection pool. Grandiose, stark white columns framed the entranceway, fanning out along the length of the structure. Each pillar was wrapped in climbing greenery, sheathing it in stark, contrasting color.

Two imposing onyx ravens stood watch at the precipice of the grand staircase, guarding the entrance. Their beady red eyes seemed to follow my every movement—fuck, I hated birds. I didn't care that they were a symbol of the Order, they should have chosen a less creepy animal to represent them.

I paused my wandering in the main foyer, too busy lost in my mind to give a thought to the direction I was heading. I knew I should return to my room and pack for whatever trip Amias insisted I accompany him on, but I found myself staring at the double staircase in front of me. One led to the senior apprentices' sleeping quarters, and the other to the training rooms. Two directions to travel, but neither took me to a place of purpose.

It seemed to be a coincidence that I found myself standing before the two staircases every time I contemplated what had brought me here. Of the two paths I could have chosen, entering the Order was not the one I thought I would follow. But I was left without a choice, and here I would rot until the Afterworld claimed me.

Sighing, I ran my hands along the cool wooden banister, taking the path toward the training rooms. It wasn't that I was avoiding this trip with Amias, I just needed to get out of my head for a few more minutes. Packing alone, in the silence of my room, was the last thing I felt like doing.

As I passed each classroom, I looked casually into each one-way window, watching for only moments before moving along until I found exactly who I was looking for. I watched my best friend, Melba, lecture a room full of Novices on foraging and utilizing nature's resources. She exuded confidence with each flick of chalk on the board. The apprentices diligently took notes, undoubtedly marking every detail of the fruits, nuts, and flowers she had drawn. Not a single student looked bored or disinterested; they all sat fully engaged, lapping up each word she fed them.

Melba's smile was infectious, and I returned it without a thought, despite not being visible to her.

She was becoming a strong leader on whom the Order depended. She didn't hesitate to teach others and improve our little organization. I had never been more proud of her.

I promised myself I would only watch for a few more moments. Amias was not a patient man, and keeping him waiting much longer would likely mean I would be left behind or punished in whatever way he saw fit.

Before I could decide how to proceed with my time, footsteps and nervous-sounding small voices echoed from down the hallway, drifting easily in the otherwise empty area. Turning toward the noise, three people emerged from around the corner.

"Oh, Varine! How lucky that we found you," Ewelyn said with a smile. She stood barely over four feet tall but was one of the most feared Masters the Order had. Her black hair was pulled back into a bun so tightly she resembled the ravens guarding the keep. "I was just showing these two new Novices around since they both just recovered from their initiation."

I looked at the two children before me, both standing behind Ewelyn as if she were the last shield between them and their enemies. Based on the pained faces of the new apprentices and the way they flinched at the word "initiation," they had been just as naïve as I had been to think that freedom and indoctrination into the Order would come without any pain.

Amias had swept me into the foyer that first day, smiling as he sold me promises of what my future might hold. At the conclusion of his sickly sweet words, he signaled to the other apprentices that it was their turn to teach me. Their lesson, however, was taught with fists instead of words. I became a dummy to their will, a pell to practice combat upon.

Hiding my horror with a smile, I took in their small builds. My body, like theirs, had been painted in ribbons of black and blue, my eyes swollen shut for several days. They appeared to have healed quickly, with only minor cuts and bruises remaining from the inhumane right of passage. "What are your names?" I asked.

I wished someone above my status had taken an interest in me the way Ewelyn seemed to be with them. It would have been nice to have a guide in this backward place.

The smaller one spoke first, tucking short, blonde curls behind her ear and casting down her eyes. "I'm Ella."

"Rune," the fair-haired boy next to her grunted. He didn't look away from me submissively like Ella had. I could see a fire building in his eyes, a fierce protectiveness of the young girl beside him.

Looking between them, I noted similar facial structures: short, stubby noses, round eyes, and thin lips. "Are you two related?"

"Siblings," Ella said, a shy smile crossing her lips. She looked up at me with sparkling brown eyes for only a second before turning away again. Rune cut her a glare that she didn't see. He was right to distrust me, that attitude would get him far here.

Despite the cruelty Amias allowed to take place and even trained into the very fabric of our beings, I believed that he might genuinely care for me and some of the others. I wondered if Amias had visited them during their recovery as he had with me. It was an all-encompassing solitude, spending an entire week recovering from being beaten to a pulp.

A new place, a new world, really. At least Ella and Rune had each other and didn't have to experience the icy hand of loneliness that chilled to the bone.

Not giving me a chance to respond, Ewelyn continued. "Would you mind finishing their tour while I take care of something? I know you're busy and leaving soon with Amias, but I could really use the favor," Ewelyn asked, even though I knew it was a command. Telling a Master "no" was just as frowned upon as telling Amias "no," and I couldn't afford any missteps this close to the Trials.

Even though I didn't have time for this, I nodded, pursing my lips. "Make it quick. Amias will have all of our heads if I make him wait." The last part was a joke that only Ewelyn and I found amusing. The Novices seemed to cringe at the thought—too soon, I guessed. They'd get over that.

Ewelyn quickly departed, waving over her shoulder. "Meet you in the courtyard in fifteen!"

When we were alone, I looked down at Ella and Rune. They were young, too young to be in this messy business, but it was not my place to shame them for the same decision I had made. "Well," I said, turning on my heel. "Come on then, let's make this quick."

They nearly ran down the hallway after me, their short legs barely keeping up with my long strides. Waving a hand toward the classrooms, I indicated what might be taught in each. I didn't have time for an in-depth lesson about every intricacy of the Order and the keep, so I kept it simple.

"Thirteen Novices, well . . . fifteen now, with you two. Seven Dilettantes, six Journeymen, five Masters, and obviously, you have met our King." Looking back over my shoulder, I watched their small nods. "Every apprentice enters the Order as a Novice, works their way to Dilettante, puts their blood, sweat, and tears into becoming a Journeyman, and competes in the Trials to become a Master. You'll either rise to the rank of Master after your training, or you'll die trying."

"Morbid," Rune muttered under his breath.

I cleared my throat while trying to hold in my laugh at his comment. "Tell me about it."

Keeping up the speedy pace, we were nearing the end of the training hallway. I turned around, ushering them back the way we had just come.

"Our ages range from twelve to twenty-eight, excluding Amias, who is very likely much older than we all suspect, despite his young appearance. However, he refuses to disclose that information as it is irrelevant to our duties. With that being said . . ." I paused. "How old are you two anyway?"

"Twelve," Ella whispered.

"And a half," Rune clarified.

I looked between them, noting how close to identical they looked. "Both of you?"

"Yes," Rune grunted.

"Twins. Nice," I said. Two years younger than when I came to the Order—practically babies. "Anyway, our numbers are very high at the moment. Don't get attached to anyone, even each other."

They looked alarmed, but I continued. I was quickly running out of time, and the more time I spent with them, the more I wanted to tell them to run—run far, far away, and never look back. "It seems the more desperate people become under the Queen's reign, the larger our ranks grow."

Rune eyed me suspiciously; I could just about hear the question hanging on the tip of his tongue. *Why? Why are you here?*

It was no one's business, especially not this child's. Or maybe that was just the weight of all my secrets building in my gut, creating my unease.

Stepping down into the foyer, I motioned to the right, facing the doorway. "Younger apprentices live on the first floor that way, Journeymen and Masters on the second floor. To the left is Amias's wing; stay out unless told otherwise. The dining area and kitchen are straight behind you, your entire class will attend all meals, unless someone is away on an errand. And directly behind this staircase is a set of hidden steps that lead to the basement. Got it? Any questions?"

"What's an errand?" they asked in near unison. Ella glared at her brother this time, who stuck his tongue out in return. She reminded me of little Varine so many years ago. Shy, quiet, withdrawn, but also fiery, passionate, and full of life. I hoped she would make it through without losing everything I had.

"That's what we call 'murder' around here." I could have sworn I heard Rune yelp at the word.

"Oh," was Ella's response.

As we entered the front courtyard, a slight wind blew my hair behind me. Ewelyn was nowhere to be found, so I led the way toward the fighting rings and shooting ranges. "Each movement in rank will cost you," I stated, making eye contact with them. "The first thing you'll lose is your innocence, and based on your solemn faces, that part has already been stripped from you. The second is your life, which I mean *mostly* metaphorically."

Two Dilettantes fought with wooden swords in the contained ring—dirt from their moving feet clouding the air. The loud clatter of their weapons colliding repeatedly almost covered Rune's response.

"Great." Rune groaned, followed by an angry "Hey!" when Ella elbowed him in the ribs.

Bored of the show, I continued, leading the group to the archery range, which was just long lanes of cut grass leading to wooden targets mounted on bales of hay. It was empty, but the racks, full of different bows and uncountable amounts of arrows, widened their eyes.

"Upon swearing your loyalty to the Order and Amias himself, you will now and forevermore be the property of the Order of Assassins. No running, no hiding. Your only escape is death, so I hope you chose well." I paused, waiting for a reaction that didn't come from either of them. I guess they were firm in their decision. "The day you become a Journeyman is when you'll receive the mark of the Order, effectively giving up whatever is left of your bodily autonomy."

Rune reached out to touch the feather soft fletching of the arrows, while I remembered the painful scratch of the needle down my back that made the now healed skin burn and itch.

A phantom hand retraced the dagger, wreathed in clematis, the bite of pain nothing but a lingering memory. On either side of the dagger's guard balanced a golden scale. The tattoo was a sign, or warning, of who we now belonged to and what we had sworn to do.

"Clematis symbolizes mental strength, cleverness, and mischief. It's also poisonous—a good reminder that pretty packages are often deadly." I winked at Ella. "The scale for balance, order, fairness. All traits essential for the Order to run as a cohesive unit. The dagger itself reminds us to dominate through the difficulties."

"Does it hurt terribly bad?" Ella asked, her face filled with pure admiration that I was wildly undeserving of.

"That depends on how much pain you can handle."

Her face turned fierce and determined. "I can handle anything. I'm going to be tough."

My lip tugged up just a fraction, and a small laugh escaped. Whether she knew it or not, she would be finding out how much she could handle very soon, and I hoped I could witness her succeed.

I stopped the tour, sitting on a marble bench tucked into the courtyard pathway. Ella and Rune stood before me, watching and waiting. "The last thing you'll give up is your past. Every tragic memory, every happy thought, every fleeting moment, given over to the Order to do with it what they want. This is how they keep us in line. We're shamed into silence and essentially blackmailed to prevent betrayal. Such is the only way to ensure the Order's secrets stay hidden."

I smiled at them, hoping my rushed descriptions were enough and they could understand the true weight of what they had sold their souls for. "Well, that's our tour," I said cheerfully, waving a hand at the keep behind us. "I, for one, think you're going to love it here."

My voice bordered on sarcastic despite my hopes that they would be happy. I hoped it was worth whatever they had given up.

Rune looked contemplative momentarily before asking, "So, just to be clear, we are basically going to die no matter what, right?"

Ella looked like she was about to cry.

I should have felt guilty for scaring them, but this was their new reality, and they deserved to know the truth.

"Train hard and do what you're told, and you'll do just fine," Ewelyn answered for me, rounding a large hedge in the expansive courtyard. She patted Rune on the head before smiling at me. "Thanks for doing that, Varine. You should hurry up to your quarters to pack. I passed Amias and told him what you were doing, and he was less than thrilled."

"On it, boss," I responded, not wasting any more time. "See you two around," I said, waving to the new apprentices. "Come find me in a few days if you need more information about what you volunteered for. You'll both be fine."

"Wait!" Ella called to my back. "You never told us how to advance in rank. I know we have to give things up, but how exactly do I move on to the next step? How do I prove I'm worthy and be like you?"

I didn't want her to be like me. I was bitter, angry, and without humanity—something I wouldn't wish upon anyone. I was merely a shell of the person I once had been. But I was happy too, wasn't I?

"Oh, you're going to love this," I said with a laugh, trying to hide how startled I was by her comment. "There is no set way to 'move up,' no list of tasks to complete, and certainly no step-by-step instructions. Simply impress a Master, and you will be rewarded. Make a small mistake, and you'll be pushed back several steps. A truly frustrating and never-ending battle of back and forth." I nodded my head toward Ewelyn. "Better be on your best behavior, she's watching."

Even though I was walking quickly toward my room, Ewelyn's voice still carried to me. She retold the rumor of how Amias became King, describing how he sold his soul to an ancient, powerful Witch, who granted him immortality and anonymity in exchange for a favor.

The group's laughter at the tale drifted to silence as the heavy door shut behind me.

In the quiet of my chambers, I stuffed clothing and weapons into a small bag. Black, ruby, and silver adorned almost every surface in the keep, and I mean *everything*: my duvet, the chaise in front of the stone fireplace, the linens in my bathing suites—everything. They were the preferred colors of Amias and the Order.

Each apprentice's room was nearly identical and surprisingly spacious. My room, however, was just a little special. Because it was at the end of the hallway, I had the luxury of a small balcony overlooking the courtyard.

As the weather turned warmer and the snow began to melt, I had a lovely secluded area to store plants and spend my free time, even if it was rarely longer than a few moments.

When the days began to grow longer, Amias had finally announced that the Trials would commence this year. But the catch was that he only planned to welcome three new Masters. Meaning our six Journeymen would be cut down to only three.

At the end of each Trial, we would be ranked according to how well we competed and whether we received any assistance.

The more assistance you need, the lower your score. Disqualifications were rare but still a possibility. In the past, they had only resulted from an apprentice trying to awaken another from a Simulation; in the end, they both died.

Even if we all completed the Trials, only the top-scoring three would be allowed to move forward. And if I knew anything about Amias, the winners would be cleaning up the loose ends.

Once the Trials began, they could not be paused or delayed. Unsurprisingly, in Amias fashion, we were not informed before the Trials began. Instead, we were to be prepared every moment for the remainder of the year. The heat of the summer was at its peak, and the tension among Journeymen was only growing.

A sharp rap sounded at my door, stirring me into action. I packed one more dagger into the leather bag before zipping it closed.

Impatient as ever, another knock sounded before I could reach the door. "I'm coming!" I snapped, ripping the door open. No one stood outside, the hallway completely empty. I threw an obscene gesture toward where I was sure he had stalked off to. With my bag slung over one shoulder, I slammed the door behind me.

If I wanted to survive, I wouldn't just have to succeed; I would have to be the best.

CHAPTER 4

The idea of killing another human being had made me incredibly uneasy and downright nauseous at first. But after so many years of bathing in blood, it was all I knew. Funny how something so sick could grow on a person.

It had been several weeks since I had been given an actual errand, and I was craving my next adrenaline high. During the day's trek to Dexmore, I kept my eyes peeled for any signs that this was a test, an actual errand Amias was using to evaluate my readiness, but no such thing occurred.

Amias didn't speak to me for most of the trip, and I grew annoyed by his obvious avoidance. I was moments from snapping at him, demanding what his problem was.

He had invited me and practically insisted I accompany him, but the words I had been stewing over died in my mouth when we rounded the corner and entered the city's foothills.

Our pace quickened until we passed through the metal archway of the town's entrance. My mouth watered as the scent of deliciously sweet pastries filled my senses. Breathing deeply, I was transported back to the kitchen in the lake house. My eyes fluttered closed, and the memory of my mother's flour-covered apron drifted into view. She smiled down at me, holding my hand in hers, guiding me through each cut of the pastry dough we molded.

I had been so young then, young enough that my magical ability wasn't even a thought in her mind. My lips curled up at the memory, but it was lost too soon when Amias's rough voice jolted me from it.

"Pay attention, Varine."

My eyes flew open, and I tossed him a sheepish grin before looking at my feet to avoid his stern gaze. The past few days had been uneventful, but I should have known better than to let my guard down. For days after the Simulation, it felt like my mind was mush, and I hated how distracted I felt. I knew it was my brain reprocessing the information it had received, but working with only half a mind would likely ruin my reputation as a dangerous assassin to the one person it mattered to most.

The smooth, brown slippers I wore were so different from the black boots I had been wearing for training. I wiggled my toes, savoring the soft fabric that brushed against my skin, silently thanking the gods that I didn't have to spend the day in my heavy training boots as we roamed the city.

I was more agile in these shoes anyway; they would be suitable for running if necessary, though I would have to be careful not to roll an ankle on the uneven streets.

"What can you smell?" he asked without looking at me.

I breathed deeply before letting out a sigh of contentment. "Besides the incredible delicacies coming from that bakery?"

"Yes," he answered flatly.

"Dirt."

He let out an exasperated sigh, dragging his hand down his face and shaking his head. I grinned up at him. I had always loved getting under his skin. He hid it well, but it was comically easy. For a man with such a young face, he acted centuries older.

"I'm going to fail you for the day if you don't start taking this seriously."

"Smoke, rot, your bad attitude," I grumbled. "Not like it matters as long as I pass the Trials."

He ignored me, arms swinging loosely at his sides as we walked side by side through the cobblestone streets.

To any suspecting eyes, he looked like an average man accompanying a woman to the shops. But I knew about the daggers hidden expertly at his side and how he noticed every little movement around us. An insect couldn't sneeze without Amias knowing.

I had to nearly run to keep pace with him, his long strides eating up the distance between us and the small apothecary we were approaching on the corner. He pulled ahead, leading the way when I stopped to remove a stone that had tumbled into my shoe.

That shop was why we were here, in Dexmore. Amias had received word of a new, undetectable poison from one of his contacts, and the shopkeeper had saved him a vial of it. Even on a trip to gather supplies, it was unsurprising that Amias was turning it into an opportunity for a lesson.

I had never been to Dexmore, the coast town at the continent's tip. A roaring ocean flanked it on one side and a beautiful cove on the other. The perfect spot to vacation. Except it wasn't. Everything here was dreary and dingy as if a large fire had spread ash across the entire canvas of the city.

The intoxicating smells of the market almost overshadowed the stench of decay lingering in every alleyway, but not quite.

The townsfolk weren't much better. We had dressed modestly, without extravagance, but the people, like the streets, were coated in filth. Our attire pinned us as outsiders at first glance. Had I known Dexmore was so impoverished, I would have used my time before the trip thinking of ways to help them instead of playing tour guide to the newest killer twins.

"What exactly are you looking for with that question? What should I be smelling?" I asked, breathless from chasing after him.

He stopped so abruptly that my feet skidded to a stop, and I nearly slammed into his back. His face was filled with only one emotion: annoyance—my favorite.

"You shouldn't have to ask."

"But I *am* asking. How am I supposed to learn if you're unwilling to teach me?" He looked up at the wooden sign above us that hung precariously from rusted chains—a hand-drawn bubbling cauldron with dripping white ooze down its sides.

A large, black bird looked down at us with its beady eyes, perched perfectly on the sign as if awaiting our arrival. Its near-human eyes blinked at Amias before it turned its gaze on me. I eyed it suspiciously before determining it was an unlikely threat, unless it shit in my hair.

I shooed it away, pushing past Amias to enter the building. Better to get this over with so I could spend more time collecting new plants for my balcony.

A bell rang, indicating our entrance, but no shop owner or worker emerged. Shelves lined with bottles of liquids and powders surrounded us, causing the shop to feel more crowded than it actually was.

Dust covered all the surfaces in a thick sheet, indicating that this wasn't a commonly visited place. I reached out to run my fingers over a delicate-looking green glass bottle, but Amias snatched my hand away before I could make contact. Shaking his head, he lowered his lips to my ear.

"Touch *nothing* in here."

Swallowing hard, I tried to dislodge the lump in my throat from the quiet reprimand. The hairs on my neck stood at attention, my skin prickling with goosebumps. Nothing seemed out of place; no evil lurked among the shelves, but I couldn't shake the overwhelming sense of wrongness emanating from the shop itself.

Amias, seemingly unfazed, navigated through the shelves toward the back of the room. Refusing to be left alone, I rushed after him, careful not to let so much as a hair brush against the narrow shelves.

A small wooden counter with a glass display case below it blocked a back entrance shrouded by a faded, threadbare red curtain. Behind the protective glass, assorted animal bones, laid on delicate cloth, were presented in a decorative manner. I bent down to get a better look, hoping to identify what animals they had been taken from, but Amias yanked on my arm hard, bringing me back to a fully standing position just as the curtain moved aside and a small, elderly woman with thick spectacles pushed through.

The woman's eyes crinkled in obvious delight as she looked from Amias to me. Amias's hand, still gripping my upper arm, tensed, sending pain up into my shoulder.

My lip stung from where I bit into it, resisting the urge to rip myself from his grasp. Something about this woman told me she would take too much pleasure in seeing my defiance, likely hoping for more pain at my expense.

It must have been the way she eyed his hand on my arm, like a scavenger awaiting a predator's next kill. Or it could be how she licked her lips in anticipation, making my skin crawl.

She grinned at us, revealing rows of missing teeth. Only a few remained, but those that did were jagged and sharp as if she had taken a file to them herself.

"Did you bring me a treat?" she asked, narrowing her eyes at me and smacking her lips together. Her voice was hoarse and grave—a dying man's voice in a hot desert.

The hairs on my neck that had raised upon our entrance now threatened to flee of their own accord. The uneasiness had grown into fear of this unknown woman. Every instinct in my body told me to run, but Amias made no indication that he was worried or frightened in any way.

He chuckled, releasing my arm and stepping around the counter. "A friend, Tully. We don't eat our friends."

My mouth hung aghast, and I nearly bit my tongue as I snapped it shut when Tully raised her eyebrows at me in challenge. She *did* want to eat me. Who was this woman? If one could even call this creature that.

Before I could voice my concern, she turned, reaching for the curtain behind her. "What a pity. This way, please."

I lingered back, hesitant to follow the pair to who knew where, but they didn't wait to ensure I was behind them, and I did not want to be left alone in this creepy shop of horrors. Though Tully might just be the strangest and most dangerous thing here.

The hallway was dark and shrouded in cobwebs that caught in my hair and wrapped around my hands when I brushed them away. When the narrowing hallway felt small enough that the walls might just collapse, it finally opened up into a small round room. Despite the appearance of the rest of the shop, this room was surprisingly clean and dust-free, smelling faintly of citrus cleanser.

A lovely and comfortable sitting area greeted us, but it felt wildly out of place. Wooden floor-to-ceiling cabinets were built into the rounded walls and contained bottles and jars identical to those at the front of the shop. A basin and mirror were tucked between shelves, both shining in gold.

My eyes narrowed on the splash of color against the washing bowl. From this distance, I could not differentiate the crimson dots from rust or blood.

Tully motioned to the couches, grinning with her empty mouth. "Sit, sit. It will be just a moment."

Without pause to ensure her guests' comfort, she began rummaging in the bottom drawer of one of the cabinets.

"We're kind of in a hurry, Tully. The Queen's guards have been reported to be in the area, and I have no interest in mingling with them. We would rather take our leave sooner than later," Amias stated flatly, sitting on the couch and spreading his arm across the back in a lazy gesture.

I stood in the doorway, eyes darting around the luxurious and too-small place. Anywhere in that room was too close to Tully.

It had been a long time since I had felt fear toward another person, but she looked like the embodiment of evil, and I didn't want to find out what she was capable of. My fear of Tully and my annoyance toward Amias's lackadaisical way of addressing such a horrid place only made my anxieties grow. Everything here felt wrong.

Disgusting, dirty, and wrong.

The rough sheath at my thigh rubbed against my skin, providing me a little comfort.

"You'll leave when I've gotten my payment," Tully replied, the words laced with sinister promise.

Her eyes darted to where I stood and then away again. I was going to kill Amias if he thought he could use me as some sort of bartering piece—an object to be traded to this monster. Widening my stance, I braced for a fight, hands tensing at my sides. If Amias thought that I would go willingly, he was dead wrong.

He smiled, a hint of something I didn't recognize flashing in his eyes. "As promised, Tully. When have I ever gone back on a bargain?"

I opened my mouth, a retort to Amias's statement on the tip of my tongue, but the words left in a rush of air as I watched her pull a curved and dangerously sharp blade from the drawer she had been rummaging through.

In an instant, my own was in my hand, but she made no move to come near me. Instead, she presented the blade to Amias, along with a small vial of green cloudy liquid.

She said no words but smiled a horrible, toothless smile. My tongue unconsciously flicked over my teeth, ensuring she hadn't stolen mine to replace hers.

Amias nodded toward the vial. "Just that today, thank you," he said sweetly, the way you would speak to a child who had brought you a toy covered in sticky sweets and drool.

Instead of stepping away to put down the blade, I watched in horror as she began to raise it, as if she would plunge it down into Amias. I made it all of one step before I could feel the slice of the air beside my head and the loud hollow sound of the blade embedding in the door frame beside me.

My eyes widened at how incredibly fast she was, moving so quickly that I barely had a chance to react.

"What the fuck was that?" I demanded. The tip of my knife was sharp between my fingers, seconds away from a toss that could end the vile creature.

Tully threw her head back, letting out a loud, throaty cackle. I lunged for her but was halted by Amias's raised palm, stopping me from slicing her throat and showing her who the real threat was.

I bared my teeth but kept my distance. "Watch yourself," I spat. "You don't know who you're dealing with." One wrong move, and I would gladly make it her last.

She smirked at me, eyes narrowing. "Oh, I think I know exactly who I'm dealing with. The question is, does he?"

My jaw clenched so hard my teeth felt like they might shatter. She was bluffing; she had to be. There was no way she knew anything about me.

"Perhaps this is a conversation for another time? We really are in quite a hurry. Though the Queen and I have a mutual understanding, being caught with anything from your shop will likely put a bad taste in her mouth."

She placed the vial in Amias's hand and moved back to the drawer she had been rummaging through.

The Order was rarely bothered by guards and never sought out by any authority to stand trial for our crimes, though they would have to catch us and identify us to do so, which was highly unlikely. As long as we didn't kill any of the Queen's guards or interfere with her abduction of wielders, she pretended that we didn't exist. Why would this shop suddenly change that?

"And," she continued, staring directly at me, as if Amias had not just spoken to her. "You'll make an excellent addition to my collection."

"Over my dead body," I spat.

"Oh, wouldn't that be just divine."

I could feel my face paling. Amias really was trading me for a single vial of poison. We sat in silence for one heartbeat, then two. I stepped backward toward the door, drawing another blade into my left hand.

The jingle of coins rattling against fabric drew my gaze from her to Amias. "Your payment," he drawled, tossing a pouch of coins to her. "While I have enjoyed watching you torment my protege, we shall take our leave now. I believe we have nearly overstayed our welcome in this city."

Tully pouted, lip jutting out, her stringy hair falling around her face. "I was just beginning to have fun." She took a step toward me, raising her hand. "She really is an excellent find; a few locks of her hair might just be enough."

I matched each of her steps backward as she advanced. If I could make it into the hallway, I would have the advantage. I always did my best work in the most confined spaces.

The sound of breaking glass and screaming emanated from the front of the shop. Amias and I shared a panic-filled glance as the voices of villagers yelled at the arrival of the Queen's guards.

Tully scrambled for something among her shelves, and a hidden door opened, revealing a stairway that descended into blackness. It seemed the Afterworld itself was our only exit.

Tully waved a hand to us. "Through the back. Now."

CHAPTER 5

S moke filled the air from a fire somewhere several buildings away, but it was the screams of the villagers that coated my tongue with ash.

Children's cries were muffled as parents frantically shushed them. Glass shattered from shop windows; the guards destroyed everything they could—leaving an already broken town beaten beyond repair.

Amias tucked us into an alley that was obstructed by towering boxes and overflowing discarded debris. The stench of trash and waste was overpowering as we crouched in the dilapidation that was the Dexmore underbelly.

One wrong breath and I worried we would be found, dragged out from our hiding spaces to face a judgment we had avoided for years—especially if we had been seen leaving Tully's.

His warm body pressed into mine, offering me protection from the scene unfolding around us. If I hadn't been so worried about what might happen, I would have taken a moment to appreciate the care and affection Amias was showing toward me.

Nowhere in my imagination could I see him doing this for anyone else. I peered around Amias but he let out a low hiss, pressing me further into the alley wall. "Stay hidden, Varine."

"How am I supposed to defend myself if I can't even see what's in front of me?" I snapped, pushing against him, but he remained solidly in place. After several heartbeats of silence, he leaned barely to the side, allowing me a slightly clearer view of the horror taking place around us.

The cacophony of sound was near deafening; absolute fear echoed around us.

I didn't want to hear the devastation as a woman begged for the life of her son, pleading with the emotionless guards to show mercy.

Or the sound of the boy's nails as they scraped along the rough cobblestone, his boots scrambling for any purchase. Trying again and again but failing each time.

The scene before me was a nightmare come to life, but I couldn't look away. I even found myself wanting to see. To know what my future might have looked like if I had inherited the magic of my bloodline. I just didn't want to hear the cries, the screams, the utter devastation. That was too much for me to bear.

The boy looked normal, ordinary even. He was tall but lanky and thin, as if his last meal had been weeks ago. His black, shaggy hair was gripped by the meaty hand of a guard as he was dragged kicking and screaming through the streets.

Flames sputtered from his hands and sparks burned where his feet dragged, the only indication that he possessed any magical abilities.

His flames became frantic, flashing brightly and abruptly spurting out, likely worsening due to the boy's panic the closer he drew to the carriage that would take him away to an unknown future. Yet another wielder, a Conjuror of elements, was being torn from their family to fuel the desires of Queen Desma.

The woman screamed a final time, her voice now hoarse as she dropped to her knees. Tears spilled from between her fingers, her body arching toward the ground in agony. The boy was tossed into a four-sided, wooden box on wheels, and the door was bolted shut from the outside. Townspeople watched in silence, a collective breath being held. The woman didn't dare move closer, likely knowing that her life depended on her submission. There was nothing the woman could do but weep. She would never see her son again.

She whimpered in the streets alone, grieving her loss, as the carriage rolled away, taking the marching guards with it. She crawled on her hands and knees after the carriage, fingernails bleeding as she scraped at the cobblestones.

As the carriage disappeared over the hill's precipice, the woman collapsed and didn't move again. Fires were lit and the sounds of shattering glass and villager screams followed the stampeding group until they had exited the town completely.

After too many silent heartbeats had passed, shutters slowly began to open again. Villagers returned to the streets to begin the cleanup of their ravaged city, but no one approached the woman. It took everything in me to keep from running to her and throwing my arms around her. I knew what it felt like to lose everything and have to start anew, and it burned like acid the entire way.

But I didn't move. And neither did Amias.

The crowds now filling the streets parted around the woman, refusing even to brush her, as if the magic that had gotten her son taken was contagious.

As if they would be the next victims of the Queen's greed.

Amias linked his fingers with mine and squeezed gently—a reassuring gesture I was surprised to receive from him. He tugged lightly on my hand, urging me to move, but I was frozen. Is this what shock felt like? I had just witnessed what my future might have been, and now I couldn't move—could hardly catch my breath. I could feel panic rising like bile in my throat.

He tugged gently again. "Varine," he whispered, "we have to go."

I nodded and allowed him to pull me behind him, weaving our way through the crowded streets.

Looking over my shoulder, I couldn't stop myself from trying to catch one last glimpse of the grieving mother, but she had been swallowed whole by the growing sea of moving bodies.

CHAPTER 6

I was content with the silence that surrounded our trip back. Neither of us wanted to talk about the horrible experience.

Upon arrival at the keep late in the evening, Amias only patted me on the shoulder before going into his office. That night I slept fitfully, the woman's horrible screams replaying even in my dreams.

Now, as I sat around the dining table for breakfast the day after our return, I found myself scrutinizing the other Journeymen, wondering if they would have sold out the boy or if they would have fought for his freedom. Or if they would have done nothing, just as I had.

Tatton, Melba, Xarissa, Gedeon, and Cenric wrapped around the table to end on my left. The table was large enough to fit all members of the Order, but Amias only allowed us to gather on our apprenticeship level. Journeymen with Journeymen, Masters with Masters, and so on. The illusion of one big happy family, as long as we stayed within our rank.

The faces around me, save for Melba and Cenric, would have ratted that poor boy out for a few extra coins in their pockets without a second thought. From what I knew of this lot, they would have done it regardless of the reward, just so they could have an excuse to be cruel.

Amias was smart to have us all eat together. No one at this table would hesitate to stab another apprentice in the back, or the front.

Eating together, from the same dishes, reduced opportunity—too many eyes were watching at once. Violence of any kind during meals or while sleeping was strictly prohibited, and violation of this rule would lead to the immediate death of the violator.

It didn't stop us from watching each other suspiciously every time a dish passed hands, though. Our attentive ears listened for the clink of empty vials or the crinkle of paper containing loose powders.

Xarissa and Gedeon looked too happy today. They murmured among themselves, casting smug glances at the rest of us. I watched them more carefully, stabbing aimlessly at the food on my plate in an effort to keep my eyes on them.

Meals had always been this way. The tension between us had been building from the moment we all met. The Order was a constant competition, but the hostility had been exacerbated by the death of a young Journeyman, Waylon.

I had only been at the keep for a matter of weeks before news of Waylon's poisoning, and the screams of the other Journeymen swept through.

He had sat down to eat with his class, taking only a few bites before he fell from his chair, convulsing as foam poured from his mouth. We had all lined the entryway, watching as Amias carried his lifeless corpse out the front door; his already short statured body appeared so small in Amias's arms.

Icy blond hair had obscured his discolored face, but even in death, a smugness only an assassin could have remained.

At only fifteen, he had progressed through the ranks faster than most, excelling at academics and impressing Amias on every errand. But he was brash, arrogant, and snarky, leading him to be heavily disliked by everyone else.

I was lucky to have had few interactions with him, but the ones I did have were nothing short of unpleasant. His only redeeming attribute was that he had refused to lay a hand on me. When everyone's fists and feet had made me into a broken mess, he had refused to touch me. He barely even looked at me.

Amias supervised his pyre alone while all the members of the Order were punished despite our denial of being involved. This murder was only fuel to the fire of distrust and a good reminder that, in the end, no one will mourn you.

"Can the competition this week be something Varine sucks at? It's not fair that she wins every week," Xarissa whined, shaking her head so that sandy blond wisps of hair fell onto her face. "I want to sit at the head of the table."

Gedeon and Xarissa were Legacies of the Order. Their parents met because of the Order and trained their children to kill from a very young age. Hand-to-hand combat, archery, toxicology, and sword-wielding were just a few of the things they had mastered by age twelve, making them fierce competitors in this fight for our lives.

Xarissa was small, her body nearly resembling a child half her age. Her speed was her only advantage over the rest of the Journeymen. She moved faster than anyone I had ever seen. If you blinked while sparring with her, she would pin you in a second.

"Maybe if you spent less time running your mouth and more time training, you could actually beat me," I jeered, sending a round of laughter bubbling up from everyone except her and Gedeon.

She narrowed her large cobalt eyes at me, attempting to sear a hole with her thoughts. "Maybe if you weren't Amias's little pet, the games wouldn't be rigged."

Gedeon's head snapped to her, eyes wide. "Uh, let's maybe *not* bring Amias into this."

He was much larger than Xarissa and one of the strongest among us. His muscles and sharp jawline were accentuated by the slim-fitting shirts he often wore and the tight bun he tied his long brown hair in.

I would find him attractive if he weren't such a raging asshole at all times. That seemed to be a trend with all of us—pretty to look at, an advantage in our chosen career, but arrogant beyond belief.

"Better listen to your nursery maid before you find yourself in trouble. I like a fair fight, and you need all the practice you can get," I stated nonchalantly, grabbing a pastry from the tray in front of me.

Her face transformed into a sneer. Raising the knife she was using to butter her bread, she pointed it at me. "You better watch yourself. One of these days you just might find your little friends gone. When you're all alone, with no one left, I'll be there."

"Ditto."

The threat on my best friend's—Melba and Cenric's—lives should have made me more upset, but cruelty was the unspoken foundation of the Order, and it was in no short supply among the crowd around me. I knew the dangers. I knew the likelihood of all three of us surviving the Trials.

I would do everything possible to ensure that Cenric, Melba, and I came out on top, even if that meant breaking up the makeshift family I had acquired. It wouldn't be terribly painful to see Xarissa and Gedeon gone.

Toxicology was one of the first lessons taught to Novices as it was one of the most commonly utilized weapons in our arsenal, and more discreet than a sword. Typically, a Master instructed the course, but unfortunately for me, Amias decided to teach it to me himself.

My breakfast turned tasteless in my mouth as I remembered how he had made me touch and taste each toxic ingredient, poisoning myself for what I had felt, at the time, was purely for his entertainment.

I knew better now, though. Without his strict instruction, I might not have valued or respected poisons like I do now. I also might not have had a relationship with Cenric if he had not been waiting outside the classroom that day.

The first words he spoke to me were, "The first lesson is the hardest." He meant it as encouraging, but in my exhausted, poison-addled state, I was only annoyed by the sentiment and concerned that the boy speaking to me was a hallucination remaining from one of the poisons.

He was fifteen at the time and had been with the Order for years before I arrived. We hadn't spoken since my arrival, and I was unsure why he was suddenly taking an interest in me. Now, I knew that he was just as desperate for a friend in this desolate place as I was.

But I had not been friendly toward him. In his snarky tone, he had asked me how long Amias had made me suffer before giving me the antidote and joked that the more he liked someone, the longer the time. I snapped at him in return, storming to my room only to have Cenric follow me. When I attempted to slam the door in his face, he caught it before it could close and smiled at me, a beautiful, enticing smile. He promised to ask me to be his friend again in the morning.

He upheld his promise, asking me every day for an entire week and refusing to give in until I befriended him.

Now, he meant everything to me.

I was no longer a young, frightened girl of fourteen; a girl scared of her own shadow, the world, or even Amias. I had become an expert on combat, poisons, and deception. I was stronger, smarter, and far more clever than I ever could have thought.

I was a force to be reckoned with.

Amias swept into the room, a burgundy cloak floating on an unseen wind behind him. He looked well-rested, while the purple bags under my eyes gave my exhaustion away. We were no better than the guards when it came to taking a life, but at least the people we took from their families were usually deserving. Amias was far better at coping with the evil in the world than I was.

He strode to the table across from me, surveying the Journeymen. "Gedeon and Xarissa, I have an errand for you today. Please meet me in my office when you are finished with breakfast," he said curtly. "Melba, I need you to teach a field survival course, and Tatton, you will partner with the Masters to teach our new Novices some basic combat skills."

Turning to me, his lips pressed into a line. "Varine, you'll spend the afternoon practicing your Simulation. I expect a better performance than last time."

Xarissa snickered at this, and I threw her a glare.

He continued. "Cenric, you are welcome to train as you usually do."

"I'll be in the stables," Cenric declared to the room.

Melba rolled her eyes and exchanged a look with me. "We know, Cenric. You don't have to tell us."

Cenric stuck his tongue out at her in response.

Amias cleared his throat to bring our attention back to him. "Now that that's settled, please finish up and assist Brenla with the cleaning. If I hear from her that any of you left a mess, the Masters will practice their interrogation techniques on each of you. Am I clear?"

"Yes," we all grumbled.

Just like his dramatic entrance, Amias swept out of the room, the swinging door fluttering in his wake.

Cenric turned to me, raising his eyebrows. "You know, Varine, you could join me at the stables since you'll have some free time before you practice."

Melba made a kissing noise next to me and I raised a hand to silence her before Xarissa and Gedeon could hear and catch on to the conversation.

"Uh, yeah, I'll think about it," I said with a small smile, though I wanted to grin ear to ear at the invitation.

He patted my hand before clearing his plate from the table and stalking toward the kitchen.

"When are you going to tell him?" Melba asked when he disappeared from earshot.

"Tell him what?"

"That you've had a crush on him for like ever."

I scoffed. "I don't have a *crush*, Melbs. You're making it sound so juvenile."

"I only make it sound like that because you act like one. I know he feels the same, so just tell him and save us all the stupid tension between you two."

49

Xarissa leaned forward on her elbows, opening her mouth to speak. I jumped to my feet, grabbing my plate from the table before she could say a word.

"Not doing this right now, Melba."

Melba called after me as I disappeared into the kitchen, "Just think about it!"

CHAPTER 7

Before I could stop myself, my feet led the way toward him. Even if I didn't know exactly where he would be, my heart would have found a way to him anyway.

The stables sat on the outskirts of the property. An extravagant building with marble archways and solid wood doors obscured my view of the animals that resided inside. The stalls were decorated with intricately placed tilework rivaling the keep itself. Cenric spent so much time here that Amias threatened to give him a room in the stable.

Stopping just outside the gated riding area, I easily found him. Sweat glistened on his perfectly tanned golden arms; midnight hair so dark it practically ate the sunlight hung loose from a bun and fell into his eyes in the way I loved. It made him appear younger, as if it had been just yesterday when he became my first friend in the Order.

He was alone, save for the massive gray destrier he rode on. Selma, his favorite horse, was young enough to be full of energy and old enough to detest everyone except for Cenric. On several occasions she had tried to bite me, and even tried to kick Gedeon. I didn't mind the second. I leaned on the fence, propping my head up on my hands, taking the rare opportunity to observe him before he noticed me.

Cenric met each movement the horse made, his body moving in time, muscles tensing and releasing with the animals. It was beautiful to watch. *He* was beautiful to watch.

Did I have a stupid crush on him that I had been stewing about since we were children? Absolutely.

Was it a good idea to tell him that?

Absolutely not.

Despite Melba's insistence, ruining a friendship with one of my closest friends was not at the top of my to-do list, especially when I wasn't entirely sure he returned the sentiment. Relationships with other members of the Order were not unheard of since we lacked better options due to our occupation. Still, with the impending Trials, it just felt like terrible timing. I did, however, worry that one or both of us might die without my feelings ever becoming known, but I didn't even know how to broach the subject.

Dirt kicked up, stinging my eyes as they trotted around and around in the enclosed ring. Gods, I would be in so much trouble if he didn't stop looking like that.

The assaulting cloud of dust finally became too much. My nose tickled, causing a loud sneeze that I tried and failed to muffle in the crook of my arm. Cenric pulled on the reins gently, bringing their gallop to a stop. His eyes met mine, a smile gracing his beautiful lips.

I waved to him over my head, ducking down to contain another sneeze that threatened to escape. As he approached me, he whispered to his horse, "Such a good girl. You know you're my favorite, right?" he asked the animal, giving her a loving pat and sliding from the saddle.

"I thought I was your favorite?" I faked pouting, jutting out my lower lip. "I'm here, aren't I?"

Cenric looked at his mare lovingly but answered me. "I'd probably like you more if you weren't afraid of horses."

I slapped a hand to my chest. "I am not afraid of horses," I insisted. "Riding is just not one of my favorite things to do."

When he looked at me skeptically, I repeated myself. "I'm not afraid."

"Let me teach you then."

Scrambling for an excuse, I kicked at a rock with my boot. It bounced into the arena and I could have sworn Selma glared at me. "I actually have someplace to be rather soon."

"No, you don't. You're scared," he said with a wink.

I bit my lower lip to keep from smiling at the way he taunted me. "I'm due to practice the Simulation. We both know I can't be late for that."

Cenric crossed his arms across his chest, drawing my eyes to the muscle peeking out from the open V of his shirt. "As I recall, from less than an hour ago, you are due to practice this afternoon. It is still very much morning." He reached out a hand to me, smiling. "That's plenty of time. Get over here."

I ripped my gaze from the patch of skin at the base of his neck with a gulp.

He was right. I *did* have time; I just didn't want to be anywhere near Selma. But I could really use the lesson. I was a decent rider—not the best, but certainly not the worst.

Horsemanship could very likely be part of the Trials, and I couldn't afford to be found lacking. "Can you show me on another horse?"

"Absolutely not," he said definitively while patting Selma on the neck. "There is no one better to learn on."

"If you say so."

I began walking toward the gate at the far end of the arena, but he called after me. "No way, Varine. You get back here. I don't trust you not to run away."

Looking over my shoulder at him, he smiled, nearly laughing at his own joke.

"I'm not going to run away," I said incredulously.

Walking toward me, he reached both hands over the metal bars. "Up, up," he replied, as if speaking to a child.

With a shake of my head, I gripped the bar, slowly climbing over. This was ridiculous, and I probably looked it, too.

When I reached the top, he held my hand, calluses from our years of training scraping together. My skin bristled where his fingers met mine. My body was nearly weightless as he lifted me over the remainder of the fence.

The moment my feet met the ground I had to dance out of the way, Selma already trying to take a bite of me. "Evil horse," I grunted, brushing remnants of dirt from my black leathers.

"She can sense your fear."

I stomped my foot dramatically and pushed his shoulder. "I'm not afraid of horses, Cenric."

He snorted in response, keeping his hands on the reins of his horse. He stood near her head, likely to keep her from trying to bite me again. "All right, foot in the stirrup and hoist yourself up. I'll come up behind you and show you how to ride this beautiful creature." He finished his sentence with a kiss to her muzzle, luckily missing the way my eyes widened for a fraction of a second.

Behind me? This was a terrible idea.

I was in trouble. Deep, deep trouble.

"Wouldn't it be better if we rode separate horses?" I nearly squeaked.

"No, it will be far easier to show you how to ride properly if we're on the same one." As if sensing my unease, he continued. "I won't let her hurt you," he added.

But it wasn't about the horse, it was the proximity between us. How could I continue hiding my interest with him so close to me?

Grumbling, I muttered, "Okay, fine."

Selma stood seventeen hands tall—an absolutely massive beast of a horse. Despite my best attempts and above-average height, I couldn't quite reach the stirrup with my foot. I must have looked ridiculous, hoisting my leg in the air, keeping it aloft with my hands as I tried and failed repeatedly to close the gap. Selma stomped in annoyance, wrinkles appearing near her nostrils.

Cenric laughed at me, holding his belly as he nearly doubled over. "I should have warned you that Selma doesn't like deranged-looking flamingos."

Curls broke from the binds of my braid, falling in my eyes with each attempted hop. I exhaled loudly, blowing the loose tendrils from my face only to have them fall back again. "I need a stool. She's as tall as a tree."

He dropped the reins, moving toward me. "Oh, come here, I'll help."

"A stool will do nicely, thanks," I said almost too quickly, but he didn't seem to notice, his smile never faltering.

"Don't be ridiculous." Before I could react, I was sitting on the back of the horse having been lifted as easily as a sack of flour.

I sputtered, shocked at what had just taken place. "Uh, thanks."

Effortlessly, Cenric mounted the horse, sliding into the saddle behind me. The moment his body made contact with mine, my spine instantly straightened, his prominent muscles hard against my back beneath his thin shirt.

Gods. Couldn't he have put something else on? Anything. Even a linen garbage sack would do.

Strong arms reached around me, his chest pressed to my back as he reached for the reins. Each moment felt like a lifetime, each movement setting my body on fire. I held my breath until he sat back again, suddenly very thankful that he couldn't see the blush spreading across my cheeks.

"You can lean back a little, Varine. She's not going to buck you off."

"I'm good," I said far too quickly.

He chuckled, our closeness making the sound reverberate through me. If I didn't know any better, I would think he knew exactly what he was doing.

My thighs clenched as the horse jolted into motion with a slight movement of his hands. This was not what I had come out here for. I wanted a reprieve from dangerous acts—a listening ear without judgment when I whined about the Simulation for the thousandth time.

Instead, my stomach was floundering like a fish, and it wasn't because my worst memory was at the forefront of my mind; it was because this was the most treacherous game of them all.

An unneeded distraction, that's what these feelings were, I told myself. It's just another thing to be used against me if anyone but Melba found out about them.

We circled in the arena, gradually picking up speed. With each step, my confidence on Selma grew, though I still preferred the less wild and unpredictable mares. Cenric pressed the reins into my hands, leaning in to bury his face in the space behind my ear. His breath, a warm caress against my bare skin; his boldness a shock to my system. I resisted the urge to throw myself from the horse just to escape the feelings reverberating through me.

"Do you trust me?"

"Wha—" I began, cut off by Cenric nudging the horse into a gallop—far faster than we had been riding before. He reached around, covering his hands with mine, steering us toward the line of jumps in the middle.

I tried to protest but found my breath suddenly taken as we launched over the first pole and the next. Traveling at a speed I would have never dreamed of, I would have thrown my arms out wide and my head back if I hadn't been so perfectly encased in Cenric's arms. All I could do was laugh until my belly ached.

Coming to a stop, Cenric grinned at me wildly. "Should I say I told you so now, or later?"

Making a show of it, I sighed loudly before moving my left leg to accompany the other on one side. "You know, you didn't actually teach me anything."

I prepared to slide off, but his arms wrapped tighter around me, holding me firmly in place.

He squeezed gently until I looked up at him. "I'm willing to bet you learned more than you think you did."

My heart fluttered into my throat.

Wasn't that the truth.

CHAPTER 8

The mirrored simulation room was never comfortable, but it had grown even more cold since I had just left the warmth of Cenric's body. Devoid of any soothing objects, I awaited the strange magic that would send me into a nightmare. I rubbed at my chest with a fist, already feeling the ache the memory would leave deep inside of me.

Behind my closed eyelids, I could feel the jerking movement of my eyes; my body relaxed as it prepared for what would come next. A calm washed over me until I was startled awake by the sound of a door hitting the wall with a loud bang.

But this wasn't the Simulation room. I was back in my childhood bedroom once more.

Darkness still consumed the world, but I didn't know how long I had slept. The door slamming could have been from the wind if it hadn't been for my parents arguing again. Their voices were hushed this time, but I could hear the panicked way they rushed their words.

Kneeling on my bed, I pressed an ear to the cool wall that separated my room from theirs.

"I'm not the one at fault here, Odell," a voice that I knew belonged to my mother said.

"We can be a normal family now. It's a blessing that they agreed to block her magic," my father insisted.

"Have I not shared the prophecy with you countless times?" Mother asked. Her voice drifted off until I could barely hear her. I was sure I had missed some of what she said before her voice rose again. "The worst crime of all though, is that you have made Varine believe she had no powers."

I pressed my ear harder to the wall, wondering if I had misheard.

"I did it for us."

Mother continued as if she had not heard Father. "If you had not convinced the Dragons to put a block on her magic, she would have been the most powerful Witch of the century. She could have fulfilled the prophecy, Odell. Do you even understand what you have truly done?"

"I did it for *us*," he repeated, enunciating the last word.

"At what cost?" she yelled before lowering her voice again. "She was at least useful to Desma if she could produce magic. Now, when she finds her, she will kill her. You saw exactly what I saw. You've left her absolutely defenseless because of your selfishness."

Both my child mind and the consciousness that existed in this memory couldn't comprehend what was happening. I had, in fact, not been born powerless; my father had bargained my magic away. For what? And what prophecy was I meant to fulfill?

I wanted to know it all—scream and demand answers, but I stood in silence, the words refusing to leave my mouth, instead sticking to my throat and threatening to choke me.

"Ursa—" Father began but abruptly cut off.

I pressed my body to the wall until my bones began to ache, desperate to hear more, but all I was met with was silence. Mother must have realized I had been eavesdropping and warded the room so that sound could not escape. A talent I wished I had.

A talent a *Witch* should have had.

A Witch. I longed to be called that, and now the title was rightfully mine. I did have powers, or at least *had* them. If they could be bartered away, there had to be a way to get them back. What I would give for just a single drop of what had been promised to me.

The storm still raged outside, but new sounds began to float through the thin panes of glass. The window had been left partially ajar, the raging storm wetting and blowing the curtains.

Caylina, still curled on my pillow, peaked open a single eye.

"What was that?" I whispered to her.

Her ears twitched, and a yawn escaped her mouth. She jumped from the bed and padded over to the window sill, pressing her pink nose to the glass.

Footsteps crunched on the gravel outside the house, accompanied by muffled shouts. There was a steady *tap, tap, tap* of water droplets hitting the ground. The smell of rain-washed grass floated to me, and I breathed deeply, savoring the wonderful scent. The odor of something odd mixed with the familiar, jolting me forward and out of bed.

Sweat, smoke, leather.

In the distance, small flickering lights emerged as the downpour began to ease. They were odd, their movement so different from the magical orbs I used for reading on dark evenings. Voices rose from below. Mother and Father were outside now, talking intensely again before both running in opposite directions.

Caylina let out a low growl as the lights grew brighter and closer. The fur on the back of her neck prickled, sending a shiver down my spine. My gentle tabby had never made a noise like that, and it sent a wave of fear through me. My fearless, sweet cat was afraid of whatever was nearing the house.

Suddenly, my door crashed open, almost sending me toppling from where I had perched on the small ledge near the window. Mother stood in the doorway, a sword strapped to her back—the hilt peeking over the edge of her shoulders.

"You will lock your door; no matter what you hear, you will not leave. Am I clear?" Mother demanded rather than asked.

I resisted the urge to run for my bed, to throw the duvet over my head and cower from her intense stare, the violence written in her eyes. Instead, I blurted out my questions. "Why? What are those lights? Is that a dragon? What's going on?"

She ignored me. "I do not have time for your questions. Am. I. Clear?"

Behind the anger and violence in her eyes, I could see something new: fear.

"I—I understand," I stammered.

She stared wordlessly at me for several seconds before slowly backing out of the doorway, closing it behind her. "Lock the door. Now."

It clicked closed, and I rushed to my feet, my body hitting it with a thud in my hurry. I threw the bolt into place before running back to the window. I could now see that the approaching lights were torches gripped by five moving figures.

It was already unusual for us to receive guests at the mountain home. Mother and Father led me to believe that only my grandparents knew of our location, but they certainly didn't arrive in the middle of the night on the rare occasion they visited.

Fear bubbled inside as tears burned my eyes. Somehow, I knew everything was about to change.

Baldwin, our groundskeeper, rushed from the tiny guest cottage adjacent to the main house. It was a perfect miniature replica, every detail a mirror of the one I occupied. Stark-white walls reflected the flames as they grew closer and closer. Delicate blue shutters snapped shut with a thud, presumably at his wife Monet's hands, mimicking the sound five pairs of bootsteps made. The sound seared itself into my brain.

I couldn't look away as men in muddy uniforms emerged from the tree line. What was happening? Who are they? I wanted to scream my questions but clutched Caylina to my chest silently.

Baldwin ran, pausing only to rip a hatchet from a nearby stump. He skidded to a halt between Mother and Father. A shiny metal sword I had never seen was pressed into Father's hands.

He held it like a warrior, something I had never thought him to be. He had always been my protector, but now he looked nothing short of bloodthirsty.

Mother, sword still strapped to her back, held a long wooden staff in her hands. They made a fierce pair with their wide stances and eyes on the advancing threat.

The storm raged anew, the eye passing and the torrential downpour returning with vigor. Flames fizzled out, smoke rising in black clouds.

That's when the screaming began.

CHAPTER 9

My breathing was labored and heavy, my throat raw, as if the screaming had been my own.

Slowly, my senses returned to my body until I could open my eyes. My body ached despite only my mind leaving the Simulation room, my head pounding in time with the flickering lights above.

Bile rose in my throat as the memory flashed before my eyes in rapid succession for the final time. I was relieved to find myself alone with only the Record Keeper and Time Keeper, thankful that my secret was still intact and that no one else would witness me lose the lunch Brenla, the housekeeper and cook, had painstakingly made.

She was a constant here among so much change. The deal she had struck with Amias kept her around to cook and clean as long as she kept her mouth shut about the depraved acts we performed. She was treated like royalty among us, and rightfully so. What I wouldn't give for one of her calming tea blends; maybe that would help me come to terms with my new reality.

What had just been revealed to me was dangerous. Deadly even. I would be at his discretion once Amias witnessed the full memory during the Trials. Would he turn me over to the Queen, or did accepting me into the Order mean he would offer his protection?

I struggled to process the new information, unable to believe it was true. The funny thing about memories was that they weren't always reliable. Could what young Varine heard and witnessed be accurate, or had I interpreted something wrong? If I were a Witch with my powers only hidden, what would that mean for my future?

There are too many questions and not enough answers.

Stumbling from my seat, I reached the door and threw it open. I gulped in air, relieved to be free of the suffocation that threatened me in the Simulation room.

Thankfully, the hall was empty.

My hand traced the wall beside me as I used it to remain upright.

There were a few things that I now knew.

One, I was a Witch—a powerless one thanks to the bargain between my father and a dragon.

A fucking dragon.

But still, very much a Witch.

Two, Queen Desma had sent her guards to my mountain house in the middle of the night, likely for some nefarious reason that I'm sure would be just as painful to relive.

And three, there was some sort of prophecy I would have fulfilled if I had magic. A prophecy I had never so much as heard of and certainly did not know how to find.

Realistically, nothing and everything had changed simultaneously, and I now only knew a fraction more than before. But it still hurt—a burning pain in my chest.

Gods. What a mess.

Cenric turned a corner just as I slid down the wall to sit on the floor. He rushed to me, crouching down to meet my eyes.

"Can you help me to my room? I need to lie down."

He held my face softly between his hands, worried eyes scanning every inch of me. "That bad?" he asked.

"Worse."

Pulling me to my feet, he began tugging me down the hallway. "I think I know exactly what you need."

CHAPTER 10

Thunk was the sound Cenric made as he hit the mat.

"Submit," I demanded, straddling his waist and pinning him to the ground with my hips. My weight sat heavy, pushing him into the ground as he tried to buck under me.

Cenric narrowed his eyes and grunted as he tried to throw me off. "Never!"

I smiled down at him. "How about now?" I asked, pulling a hidden dagger from my belt and holding it against his throat, taking care not to draw blood.

He was right. This *was* exactly what I needed to forget.

Cenric raised his hands, palms facing me in clear acceptance of his defeat. "All right. All right. Best two out of three?"

His hair had fallen into his eyes, sweat sticking the strands to his forehead. "You know, it's dangerous to keep your hair that long. It's a distraction." I chastised him but didn't mention that it was almost more of a distraction for me than it was a problem for him.

He tugged on my braid gently, laughing when I batted his hand away. "But the ladies love it, Varine. How could I ever deny them?"

"In my opinion, staying alive is more important than female attention."

"Debatable."

A few months ago, I asked Cenric to train with me more frequently. I was fast, but I couldn't match the strength of those bigger, putting me at a disadvantage. Luckily, he helped me focus on technique rather than muscling my way through the complex sparring movements.

He practically beamed at me when I pinned him for the first time. His lips, perfectly pink and full, had curved up like they were now, revealing a dimple.

His eyes met mine, and I realized that I was staring, staring at his lips and straddling his body.

My cheeks heated, and I swiftly moved to my feet, pulling him up with me. If he noticed the way my eyes bore into him, he didn't mention it.

"You know that's considered cheating, right?" Cenric said as he dropped into a crouch and threw me a grin.

I braced my feet in a defensive posture, ready for his next attack. "Nothing's off-limits in a—" Before I could finish the sentence, Cenric was lunging at me.

Sidestepping his advances, I pushed his shoulder away from me, trying to redirect his momentum. He spun around with supernatural speed, reaching for my leg. I barely dodged him, almost tripping over my own feet.

I quickly righted myself only to catch my foot on the edge of one of the mats and stumble. Cenric grabbed my leg, sweeping me under his body. I swore at my mistake when my back hit the mat. I was never going to hear the end of this.

He crawled over me, agonizingly slow, but with so much of his weight that I didn't stand a chance of throwing him off. Before I knew it, I found myself pinned between his muscular thighs. I thrashed, cursing at him, but he remained a solid force atop me.

Our breathing was heavy, but he grinned down at me, obviously proud of himself. "Your turn to submit."

"And what if I don't?"

"I'll make you."

I bit my lip. "Do it then. Make me."

His gaze darted down to my lips and then back to my eyes so briefly that I would have missed it if I had blinked. My cheeks heated from his attention and I fought the urge to pull him closer, to feel his skin beneath my lips.

In his moment of distraction, I reached a single hand for the knife I had tucked back into my belt.

But he was one step ahead of me and snatched my hand away, gripping my wrist and pinning it to the mat at my side. He let out an exasperated sigh and rolled his eyes. "Didn't we just talk about this? That's cheating, Varine."

"I was never good at listening."

Smiling, I reached for my knife with my other hand, quicker this time, but still not quick enough.

Cenric pinned my other hand to my side, bringing his face closer to mine as he leaned forward to keep my hands on the mat, our chests just a breath from touching. So close I could make out flecks of gold in his intense stare. I licked my bottom lip, hoping to stave off the dryness that had presented from our exertion. He tracked each flick of my tongue, his gaze seeming to heat.

Friends, we're just friends.

"Oh, get a room!" Melba yelled from the open doorway.

We both jumped like we had been caught doing something we shouldn't have been. Cenric turned his head away from me to glare at her.

Seeing the opportunity, I raised my knee behind him and slammed it into the base of his tailbone. He yelped in shock, loosening his grip on my wrists.

Using his forward momentum to push him over and to the side of me, I rolled out from under him and clambered to my feet. He landed with a thud on the mat next to where I had just lay.

He lay face down in defeat. "Bunch of cheaters," he muttered into the mat, throwing up a middle finger on both hands for several moments before rolling onto his back and standing.

Leaning forward, he reached for his toes, stretching his muscles and blatantly trying to ignore us.

The soft skin of his lower back poked out from under his raised shirt, and I imagined running my fingers over it.

"Who? Me? Couldn't be," Melba said, pushing her lips into a feigned pout.

I quickly averted my eyes from his perfectly tanned skin, only to find Melba watching me. She knowingly winked at me, causing heat to rise to my cheeks for the hundredth time today.

She leaned against the wall, arms crossed across her chest. She was dressed in heavy boots, thick leather pants, and a flowing red tunic—not attire designed to spare in.

"Your turn then," Cenric said while slowly stalking toward her. He lowered his stance as he went, aiming to use the move he had just done on me.

When she was almost within reach, she swatted at his hands while dancing away.

"Not a chance. I'm saving my energy for an errand."

"Am I invited?" I asked, trying and failing to hide my excitement. My arms were sore where they met my shoulders. I cradled one across my chest, stretching it out before switching to the other. "Wait. Do you mean *your* errand?"

"Uh yeah, why do you think I'm in here? It's definitely not for the entertainment," she said with a roll of her eyes. "You two are rather boring, actually. Except for the position you were just in; that was kind of hot."

Melba continued before I could formulate a response. "Amias is waiting for us. Hurry up and wipe your sweat off the mats, and let's go."

"Cenric will take care of it, right?" I asked, turning to face him, too eager to leave, knowing Melba was leading.

He waved at us from where he now lay, arm tucked under his head. "Yeah, yeah. I'll be your maid. Get out of here."

"See," I said, striding toward the door. "I can't believe you've finally got your own errand. "

"Have fun, cheaters!" Cenric called. "Can't wait to hear all about it."

"I'm talking to you too, sore loser. The three of us are going."

Cenric's head snapped up, his eyes meeting mine. Both of our faces were a mirror of shock. A smile crept its way onto my face, and he mimicked my expression.

"We never get to go on errands together," I said, filled with giddy excitement.

Amias rarely partnered Cenric and me together or even allowed us both to go when we requested it. Cenric had a bad habit of protecting me above all else and jeopardizing the entire mission. It had been several years since Amias had allowed us to go together because of this.

Amias cared more about his reputation than our survival, and Cenric made him look bad by being sloppy and rash when he was on errands with me. I didn't blame him for the unspoken rule, though it would have been more enjoyable to have Cenric with me more often.

Being able to go on an errand with Cenric wasn't the only exciting thing about this particular mission; it was also a monumental stepping stone in Melba's career.

An apprentice accompanied a Master and even Amias on errands until they were proven worthy and trusted to lead their own. I had been doing so for years, but not Melba.

I could barely contain how proud I was that she was finally being given the opportunity.

Curling my arms around both my friends' waists, I tucked them into a hug, squishing me between them. "This is going to be so great."

I only hoped my sweet, tenderhearted friend would survive it in more ways than one.

CHAPTER 11

"**D**id he say why he finally gave you one?" I asked as Melba led us down to the front entryway.

She shrugged. "He just said I'd earned it after all the time I spent teaching classes for him."

Cenric followed behind us, arms crossed across his chest. "Did he say why both Varine and I were invited?" His voice was laced with suspicion; all traces of the giddy excitement I thought we had shared were now gone.

Melba glared over her shoulder. "Don't ruin this for me with your bad attitude. Just say thank you."

"Fine," Cenric grumbled. "Just seems weird."

Melba's gorgeous, long, chocolate brown coils were pulled back into individual tight braids and combined to drape down her back—a style she wore often and considered "fierce."

I would have agreed with her if they hadn't been swaying frantically back and forth while she nearly skipped down the hallway toward Amias's office.

Her deep bronze skin seemed to glimmer under each light we passed. I had always been jealous of that; how she could lay out in the courtyard with a good book, turning the perfect shade of brown, while all I got was more and more red.

"Little tomato," she had called me during a fit of laughter one evening after I had spent too much time baking in the summer sun.

I wanted to stab her sometimes—with love, obviously.

She was full-figured, whereas I was slender. Where her arms were sleek and powerful, I was all gangly limbs. She even had a picture-perfect round nose with almond-colored eyes as deep brown as her hair.

And as if being physically perfect wasn't enough, she was also a genuinely good person. For an assassin, that is. If she wasn't one of my very best friends, I might fall in love with her.

She skipped ahead, leaving Cenric and me walking side by side. We were so close that our arms frequently brushed, tingles spreading into my shoulder with each touch.

"Remember when you hated me?" Melba said, turning to look at me. "And now you can't stop staring at me. Do you think I can't see you?" She laughed with her entire body, shaking from head to toe at her own humor.

"You're literally in front of me, Melbs. If I didn't look at you, I might run into you. And I think your memory is failing because how I recall this story is very different. You're the one who stabbed me. I never hated you."

That was a lie. I definitely had, but for a good reason.

"*You*," she said sweetly, dragging out the word, "deserved it."

I scoffed and resisted the urge to push her into the wall.

Before my arrival, Melba had been Amias's favorite. Unfortunately, for both of us, Amias had taken a special interest in me, which has caused nothing but problems for me since. Melba didn't like the competition and did everything in her power to remind me that my place in the Order was at the very bottom, even going so far as to stab me in the thigh when I had bested her in a sparring match.

I had been the one punished and reprimanded for letting my guard down.

Two weeks after *that* incident, Amias invited both of us on an errand to Nilth. Our job was merely to observe and learn from him. The trip was just over a day's ride one way—just south of Canlere. This was just the right amount of time for animosity to grow and fester.

When I found an edible flower, Melba snared a rodent for supper. When Melba located a stream to drink from, I built a fire. So on and so forth, as we tried our best to capture Amias's attention. It was a match of wits and wills, neither one of us willing to back down.

Amias, however, spent most of the day ignoring us, unamused by our attempts to gain his favor.

Once arriving in Nilth, things quickly turned for the worst. We became separated from Amias— just Melba and I crashing through the forest, an angry militia on our heels.

I scoffed and resisted the urge to tackle her into the wall. "Remember when *you* almost got both of us killed because you wouldn't cross a little rope?"

Melba stopped walking in the hallway, turning to Cenric at my side. "You're just going to stand here and let her talk to me like this?" She grinned, the motion lighting up her features. She was enjoying this, I could tell.

Melba liked to be teased, especially about the day we had nearly died and became best friends. She frequently told me that she never actually hated me and was just teasing me, but the scar on my thigh said otherwise.

Cenric threw up his hands, "I am not getting involved in this." I nudged him with my shoulder playfully, and he winked in return.

While running from the angry mob, we found ourselves with only one way across a large ravine, a thick rope used to transport goods from one side to the next. I had crossed the precarious rope with only a few death-defying saves, but Melba lingered too long on the other side.

She began walking again, continuing to lead us down the long hallway. "Guess I should have warned you that I'm afraid of dying on precarious ropes."

"That would have been important information to know," I laughed.

Her pace began to slow until Cenric nearly ran into the back of her in his attempt to remain at my side. She continued to walk slower until he had no choice but to trail behind us as she took his spot with a giggle. Her voice turned sincere, "Thanks though, Varine. Thanks for pulling me up."

After convincing Melba to trapeze across the ravine, the mob began to cut the rope. Her leap of faith landed her dangling with only my hands keeping her from the icy rushing water below.

For a second, I contemplated letting go. I almost did. But as she slowly began to slip, both of our hands growing slick with sweat, the sounds of her pleading to live, to travel, and to see the world filled me with remorse.

Those were the exact things I had wanted when I was a prisoner in the mountain house, and I could not take that away from her.

When we both had finally reached safety, we collapsed in a pile of tangled limbs. The screams and jeers of the men on the other side were swallowed by bubbling laughter and tears that fell from our eyes.

After defying death together, a rivalry seemed frivolous. The tension between us had snapped just as easily as the rope across the gorge. A bond forged through mutual trauma was stronger than any other.

I grabbed her hand, interlacing our fingers and giving her a slight squeeze. "Always."

Cenric snorted behind us; when I looked over my shoulder, he raised an unamused eyebrow. "We're about to murder someone, and you two are reminiscing like school girls. Maybe we can talk about something more appropriate, like tactics?"

I shook my head back and forth mockingly. "*Like tactics.*"

"Just because I was so rudely kicked out of my spot, doesn't mean I can't hear."

Melba turned and stuck her tongue out at him, causing a low chuckle to brush over us. The chills that rushed over my skin nearly caused me to shudder.

Some days, I questioned if being *more* with Cenric was worth messing up the friendship we had created. Being around him felt right, as if a force was pushing us together. I couldn't make up my mind whether I should tell him, but I hoped being with me was something he would want, even if I didn't entirely know what *I* wanted.

Our little parade stopped in front of a closed, thick wooden door. Amias's study lay just beyond it. Melba's happy demeanor had been cast aside; a mask of stubborn resolve replaced it. She took a deep breath before blowing it out of her mouth. "Well," she said, "let's do this."

CHAPTER 12

The entire room was immaculate, as always; not a trinket was out of place, and not a speck of dust. Large, mahogany bookshelves lined the walls, framing the expansive picture window in the center. A matching wooden desk was placed on a ruby and black circular rug adorned with whirling symbols.

Upon our entrance, Amias didn't bother to look up from where he sat on a tufted, velvet armchair, sharpening a long knife.

"I was beginning to think you three had gotten lost. It would be in your best interest not to keep me waiting in the future."

"That's my fault," Melba said, jumping to our rescue. "It took me a little bit to find them."

He studied a spot on the blade, gently wiped it clean with a cloth, and then carried on sharpening. "I have a high-profile errand for you tomorrow. As I'm sure Melba has informed you, she will lead. The success . . ." He paused, finally looking at us. "Or failure, will rest on her shoulders. Try not to disappoint me."

"What are the known details?" Melba asked.

"The Duke of Pery will be visiting Canlere proper tomorrow. My sources say he's a man who likes women and drink. We have been compensated handsomely for his failure to return to his city. The less messy, the better, but do as you wish, as long as the job gets done."

I could almost see the wheels turning in Melba's head, sorting through the questions she needed to ask to get the information that Amias would withhold if not asked directly. "Do we know the time and location? Canlere proper is a large area to cover for the three of us," she said.

"My sources report that he plans to be in the square, visiting the market shops for that entire afternoon. What he does after that is left for you to find out."

Cenric scratched his head absentmindedly. "What about guards? Do we know how many he will have with him?" I elbowed him in the ribs, glaring at him, hoping he would catch the hint to shut his mouth and let Melba lead the discussion.

Amias leaned back in his chair, propping his feet up on the desk and folding his hands in his lap. His eyes flitted between the three of us, a sarcastic smile pulling up one corner of his mouth. "Do you expect me to do this for you? Have I not trained you adequately?"

"No—" Cenric began.

"Then do your job and figure it out. My sources can only give so much. Use the skills I've taught you." He waved a hand dismissively at us. "Cenric, you will be the protection detail. You are to remain unseen unless absolutely necessary. Melba, you'll take the mark. Varine, you'll be the distraction."

Cenric's jaw tightened so hard I swore I could hear his teeth grind together. Was that reaction to his assigned duty or mine? I grumbled. "This is just your excuse to force me into wearing an impractical dress."

He tucked his hands behind his head. "I don't need to make excuses. If I say jump, you do so. If I say put on a pretty dress and distract a man with your beauty, you also do so," he stated, sliding a piece of folded paper across the table toward us. "Melba is to take his life. I do not want to hear of one of you doing it for her."

Melba snatched up the note, quickly reading its contents, and shoved it deep into her pocket. "We'll take care of it," she promised.

"See to it that you do."

We turned to leave, using the dismissal in his words as our cue to exit and prepare, but his voice called out to us before we could reach the door. "Cenric, you stay behind for a moment. I have something to discuss with you."

We exchanged startled glances at the urgency that laced his words. The errand together was strange enough, but the fact that Amias wished to speak to him alone was odd. What could he possibly say that he didn't want us to hear?

"I'll meet up with you later," Cenric promised, returning his attention to Amias.

Melba and I nodded.

Before the door could close, I looked behind us one final time, only to be met by Cenric's back and Amias's watching eyes.

"What are you thinking? Why do you think this Duke is the target?" I asked Melba, who had thrown herself onto my bed. She burrowed into the mattress, making herself nearly one with it.

As I had guessed, an impractical dress was waiting for me upon entering my room. Amias had undoubtedly chosen and purchased it for this errand. It dangled from my fingertips as I eyed it with disdain. I didn't hate dresses, I just found them absurd and impractical for errands.

The light green bodice would fit every curve of my waist, the neckline drooping just low enough that it would draw attention. The sleeves, made of some sheer material, would sit slightly off my shoulders. The skirt was beautiful, shimmering shades of emerald.

A distraction I would be, indeed.

"You look like you're going to throw up," Melba mused, sitting up to run her fingers over the layers of chiffon.

I sighed exasperatedly. "Where am I supposed to put my knives?" I whined. "How am I supposed to run in this? I'm going to trip and break my neck."

Melba fell back onto the bed, giggling. "Dresses are perfect for hiding weapons. No one expects the beautiful woman to carry the sharpest blades."

"How poetic."

She laughed, patting the spot next to her. I glared at the dress one final time before tossing it onto the nearest chair. I would have to talk to Amias about the practicality of garments that should be worn; this was getting to be ridiculous.

"You think you'll be okay?" I asked her. She was still optimistic and gentle; I feared an errand would change that, and she would become bitter and jaded like the rest of us.

I loved the Order, it was my escape when I needed it the most, but it turned even the most kind-hearted into monsters.

Her hand balled and released at her sides. "I heard the bastard is a trafficker. I think I might even enjoy killing him."

"Gods!" I exclaimed. "I knew it was getting bad, but the Queen has people of title trafficking magic wielders now, too? I thought she only had her guards doing that."

Melba pushed up onto her elbows. "Oh yeah, she's the worst. I heard they're paying double, so more and more families are giving up their children. I know it's treasonous to say, but I wish she could be one of our errands. I'd like to give her a taste of what she's been doling out to all of us."

I snorted, thinking about being assigned an errand like *that*. "You mean kidnapping her?"

She gave me an incredulous look. "You really think all she's doing is hiding people away in her castle? You've never questioned why they never return or wonder what she does to them?"

"She probably eats them," I joked.

A pillow hit me in the face before I could block it. Melba's lips curled. "You're disgusting. I'm being serious."

Laughing, I threw the pillow back, but she rolled out of the way. I covered my hands with my face, unsure that this was a good conversation to be having. If Melba caught wind of what I had found out, I didn't know how she would react—if she would even accept me.

"I guess I've never thought about it. What would be her motive for killing them?" I asked. "Do you think she's jealous that she doesn't have magic?"

"Maybe she thinks herself a god and is tampering with things she shouldn't."

The gods, Pilean, Helka, and Aradia, had given us mortals a kernel of their magic, imbuing the lucky with powers. Pilean created Shifters, giving them the ability to assume human or animal forms. Helka created Conjurors who drew their power from the elements—lightning, wind, water, and fire. Any magic they performed was created by the natural elements.

And then the Witches were created by Aradia, they drew power from the glyphs, essentially creating anything they wished. Witches were blessed with immense power, which is why Aradia had limited the family lines they blessed. The Crestins were one of the few surviving lines, and one of the strongest, though most of my family had been killed or were as powerless as I was.

A handful of surviving Witch clans lived on the southern end of this side of the range, in Eldreta, but they did not venture from their territory often, nor did they allow outside contact. Their city was so heavily warded that it kept them in and others out. Something I was all too familiar with.

"Maybe she's the lost god, Zylah," I joked.

Melba attempted to hit me with the pillow again, but I caught it and hugged it to my chest.

"Don't even joke about that. You'll anger the gods, and I need their favor as much as I can get right now."

A fourth god, Zylah, existed long ago when magic was created. History holds little record of her beyond her banishment from her home world, referred to as the "In Between." Not quite living, not quite in the Afterword, just between both. The other gods feared Zylah, her lustful hunger for power, and especially her belief that the gods' gifts were wasted upon us humans.

Each god had a relic of their power—an amulet, a sword, a golden coin, and a chalice. Each object contained not only the essence of each god but also had its own innate power. Aradia's amulet had sealing magic that they used to trap Zylah's power within, before she was cast out and doomed to mortality.

Many believed that Zylah had died long ago without ever returning to her home or experiencing magic again. Of course, these were just fables. And their existence, just like the gods, was up for debate.

With such power came a desire to take it—to use it for nefarious purposes. Fearful of who might try to possess their relics, the gods also created dragons they called Endwen to protect them.

Or to strike bargains to steal young girls' magic.

They apparently did that, too.

I shrugged at Melba's fear. I didn't believe the gods cared about what mortals said and did, and even if they did, they certainly wouldn't care about me.

"Well, we better rest up so you can be bright-eyed and bushy-tailed when you become a murderer like the rest of us."

CHAPTER 13

The second lesson taught by the Order was the art of disguise. A conspicuous assassin was a dead assassin. It was far better to blend in with your surroundings, rather than identifying yourself as a threat before you could even close the distance. The concept was the same in all kinds of killing, whether it be that of an animal or a human.

Even if that meant wearing this ridiculously absurd dress Amias had chosen.

This errand had a particular air of danger, as it would take place in the city we most frequented, where we were most likely to be recognized.

Canlere was the closest city to us, the keep residing on the outskirts of the town boundary. Women in our city, and most of the continent, preferred to wear trousers, but the women that the Duke of Pery surrounded himself with were proper— always dressed immaculately. Unfortunately, only the finest would do.

Cenric, Melba, and I, dressed in our fighting leathers with weapons strapped everywhere imaginable, would draw too much attention. Two women heading to the shops with their armed bodyguard would draw none thanks to the muggings that routinely took place in back alleys.

I liked to think that my life would have looked like the farce we were trying to portray if my mother hadn't isolated us and hidden us away instead of fighting back against Desma's reign.

My world might have been filled with magic, pretty dresses, and shopping trips with my best friends. We could have even lived in the castle with my grandmother, Mathilda. And though I would have been treated like a princess, knowing I would never rule was relieving.

Mathilda presided over one of the three Celestial Territories that made up the continent of Kalahvin. Each territory was dedicated to a god—the Temple of the Sun for Pilean, the Temple of the Stars for Helka, and the Temple of the Moon for Aradia.

Because of this, the territory's monarch was a direct descendant of the wielder they had created. Historically, this had typically been a female elected by the masses, though a few males had been voted in in the past.

We lived in beautiful, magical harmony. Agriculture and magic flowed through the continent in abundance until Desma arrived with an army of the powerless. Despite all that wielders offered to society, it was never enough. Jealousy was a stain that could never be cleaned from our world.

My grandmother had held out the longest. She was a mighty Witch but was no match for Desma and her followers. Upon Mathilda's surrender, Desma stormed her castle, laying siege to its entirety, and slaughtered everyone in her path just as she had done to the other two monarchs and their ruling partners.

Towns had been raided quickly, leaving magic wielders with three options: go into hiding, be forced into servitude, or die. Rebellion groups formed and fought for the freedom of magic—the freedom of the people—but they all were put down, one group after another. The rumor around Canlere was that they still existed underground but hadn't been seen or heard from in years. They were either too afraid or building their forces to one day fight back.

I hoped that it was the latter.

My mother was right to be afraid; I was frightened of what would happen when my truth finally came to light. The world we lived in had become lost. Poverty and fear ran like a flood across this land. Would I be dragged through the streets just as that boy had?

Would anyone crawl on their knees after me?

The layers of my dress flowed in the breeze, the city growing closer with every step our horses took. Lush fields greeted us around every turn, and farmers stood in their fields preparing for the abundant fall harvest that would be upon them soon, though it would likely not be enough to support them once the Queen's share was taken.

Cenric hummed to himself as we rode, keeping uncharacteristically quiet. When the brick wall of the town had just come into view, Melba brought her horse next to mine.

"Are you going to be okay with being a distraction? I heard this guy is gross, and I don't want to do anything you're not okay with."

"This isn't the first time I've used my body to occupy a man, and it certainly won't be the last," I said reassuringly. "With men, it's typically over quickly anyway."

Melba giggled. "That's why you should date more women, we're much more . . . attentive."

"Oh, trust me, I know," I muttered.

"Though I wish I couldn't hear you both talking about your sex lives in code, I unfortunately can!" Cenric shouted over the pounding of our horses' hooves. "I beg of you, can we please just talk about the errand, or better yet, we could just not speak at all."

"Technically, we are talking about the errand," I said.

"So, the second option then?" Cenric offered.

Melba and I both laughed as she pretended to button her mouth shut; Cenric didn't find it nearly as amusing.

Towering gates made of cobblestone and metal were thrown open to reveal a bustling square, the market in full swing. Vendors lined the streets, each selling their wares. The aromatic spices of cinnamon and cloves filled the air, enticing patrons to make purchases at the stalls.

Cenric, Melba, and I walked our horses through the crowded streets, weaving through throngs of children playing with sticks and wooden balls, their parents haggling the best prices for supplies and their supper. The dried-up well at the far end of the market was our intended location; it was a good meeting point where the crowds sat to enjoy their meals, and our group would not draw any unwanted attention.

Sweat dripped down my back, the sun cresting its highest point in the sky. While looking for a vendor who sold a cooling fruit drink, a white-haired bladesmith standing before an array of knives caught my eye. A slight tug in my stomach told me to stop at his booth, but it turned insistent when I tried to ignore it.

It was a strange and not entirely pleasant feeling, something I would need to explore at a later time, when I wasn't in the middle of something. My feet stopped moving, townspeople passing around me like a rock in a stream, the tugging ceasing when my movement did. The man before me shined the beautiful daggers with delicate hands, holding each blade with surprising reverence.

My gaze snagged on one that was exceptionally thin. Its hilt was solid gold, but the body of the dagger itself was silver, with golden embellishments trailing down it. Cutouts on each side of the blade left the middle almost hollow, save for a thin line of metal running through the center. It was unique, like nothing I had ever seen before. And it called to me, tugging with urgency for me to touch it, hold it, take it.

Taking advantage of Cenric and Melba disappearing into the crowd, I led my horse to the table swathed in black sheer fabric. "How much?" I asked, pointing to the beautiful dagger that had caught my eye.

The white-haired man appeared to be in his mid-forties. He had the beginnings of wrinkles around his eyes and mouth, as if he had spent most days with his face tensed in disapproval rather than showing joy. He looked up at me as I approached and smiled a toothy grin that didn't meet his eyes. "Ah, the dragon blade. She's a beauty, is she not?" His voice was smooth and lilting in a way that might be reassuring if the hair on my neck wasn't alerting me to some unknown danger.

As he reached for the dagger, I noticed that, despite his young appearance, his hands were marred with age; wrinkles and sun spots decorated his skin. How curious that this part of his body aged far quicker than the rest. He paused momentarily, gently sniffing the air before giving me a curious look. Holding the dragon blade aloft, he slowly twirled it, allowing me a good view and further enticing me to make a purchase.

"I'll give you five silvers for it," I bargained. It was a low price for such a beautiful dagger, but I was confident he would take it if he was desperate enough for coins.

He looked me up and down as if he was just now seeing me for the first time. His eyes drew into thin slits, and his lips pulled back from his teeth. "What would a pretty girl like you need with a blade like this?"

I looked back toward the direction my companions had gone, attempting to peer through the crowd. Something about the man and this particular blade made me want to remain unseen. I was relieved that they had not reappeared to look for me. They wouldn't realize I was missing for several more minutes if I was lucky.

"If you must know, I collect them," I lied. "If you don't want to sell it to me, I'll take my business elsewhere." It was a bluff that I hoped he did not catch on to. I didn't want another blade. I wanted, no *needed*, this one.

My fingers unconsciously reached out to brush what I expected to be cold metal, but I jerked my hand back when heat spread through my body. The man dropped the blade with a hiss, his gaze turning sinister as he sniffed the air again, breathing deeply in through his nostrils. "Why don't you tell me why it calls to you, Witch?" he asked, spitting the last word in disgust. "Do not even try to deny what you are. I can smell it on you."

Doing a poor job of hiding my shock, I lied. "I don't know what you're talking about." Surely, he was mistaken. With my lack of magic, there was no possibility he could smell anything on me.

He let out an inhuman hiss from between his teeth as he tried and failed to retrieve the blade, red welts appearing on his fingertips. I tilted my head, looking the man up and down as the pieces connected themselves in my head. It all added up—his appearance of both young and old, his enhanced sense of smell.

"I am no Witch, but you, you're a Shifter, aren't you?" I questioned, though I already knew the truth. "I thought the Queen would have rounded you all up by now."

His white hair flared brown for a breath before returning to white. "Keep your mouth shut, Witchling. If you alert the guards of my presence, I will make it known who you descend from. A Crestin Witch. I can smell it in your blood."

"Like a dog?" I mocked, despite the panic that raced through me. I kept my expression neutral and willed my racing heart to calm. If he could smell my blood, he could undoubtedly smell my panic. "And as I said before, I don't know what you're talking about."

He shook his head, looking around to ensure we had not been overheard. "So, it is agreed then? You keep your mouth shut, and I'll keep your secret."

I leaned forward on my hand, placing it close to the prize I hoped to claim, my fingers inching toward the blade. "You forgot to shift your hands," I jeered before snatching the dagger from the table and tucking it into my satchel.

The heat of the blade filled my blood, sending sparks from my fingertips through the length of my body. It was an intense warmth that both calmed and startled me. I walked quickly through the crowd, disappearing from the sight of the white-haired man, who didn't even bother to yell after me.

I didn't make a habit of stealing, most citizens of this continent were far too poor, but since he was no ordinary merchant, and certainly not a polite one, I would make an exception.

A shifter in Canlere was unheard of. Due to its proximity to the capital of Eltris, just through the Delisan Pass, it was one of the first cities to be raided. I had visited this market many times and had never encountered the white-haired Shifter, or any other magical being. He would get himself captured or killed if he wasn't more careful with his magic. Petty theft would be the least of his worries.

Melba and Cenric watched me break from the crowd, arms crossed and faces stern. Handing the reins of my horse over to the stable boy who was currently grooming Cenric's mare, I quickly tried to think of an excuse for my tardiness.

Cenric pushed off the wall he had been leaning on as I joined them. "Doing some shopping, Varine?" Suspicion laced his tone, making me wonder if I had given them a reason to mistrust me. I was keeping secrets, but so was Cenric. The words he had exchanged with Amias were still being held captive.

"A little trinket caught my eye," I conceded, offering a half-truth. My hand twitched to touch the blade hidden in my bag, but a little voice warned me to keep it hidden. "But sadly, the shopkeeper wanted a price that was too steep."

"The white-haired bladesmith?" he asked.

How did he know that? I made sure that they couldn't see me before I even approached the table. There's no way he could know that unless he had come back to find me or followed me.

I shrugged. "I like daggers."

Melba slid her arm around my waist, pulling me into her. "Oh, you know us high-class women, always getting distracted by shiny things."

I gave her a silent, mouthed thanks. Her eyes twinkled knowingly. Melba could always tell when I was hiding something, but she was also smart enough to know that I kept my secrets close to my heart, and if I wanted them to know, I would tell them. Melba always accepted that, but Cenric . . . he rarely did. It was something I loved and hated about him.

"Is there a reason you're accosting me about my shopping habits?"

He ran his hands through his hair. "We can discuss whatever you're hiding later."

"And you can tell us all about what Amias wanted later," Melba added.

He ignored her comment and instead turned toward the dilapidated stone building at the opposite end of the square. The wooden sign hung haphazardly from a single chain. The words "The Angry Owl" could barely be read through the worn and peeling paint.

"While you were busy *shopping*, I was able to determine that the Duke entered that tavern early this morning and hasn't come back out yet. Based on some information Melba gained from locals, he's likely to remain there for the day."

"He's a drunk," Melba chimed in, still clinging to me. "I overheard some men in the alley behind the building talking about the Duke losing his temper and kicking them out. This will be even easier than we had thought."

I didn't miss the nervous excitement in her voice, or the way she was hopping from foot to foot in anticipation. Grinning, I waggled my eyebrows at her. "Shall we enter this . . ." I paused, watching a dirty, unkempt man stumble from the open door. "Uh, fine establishment?"

Having spent time drinking away my days in this exact bar, I knew it was anything but fine. The beer was watered down in an effort to earn more coin per glass, and the patrons were just as unsavory.

She reluctantly released my waist, only to link our arms together. "Oh, definitely. This will be fun."

"Right. Fun," Cenric said sarcastically. He pointed toward an adjacent building that offered a view of the tavern's front and back entrance. The sun beat down on the roof, no trees large enough to cast even a whisper of shade. "I'll be up there, if you need me."

"We won't!" Melba said, indifferent to the hurt on Cenric's face as she half dragged me in her effort to skip away.

CHAPTER 14

T he smell of urine and stale ale assaulted my nostrils as we walked through the doorway of The Angry Owl, the filth lingering in the air like an impenetrable wall. Booths lit from above by candle-filled chandeliers lined the outside walls, the glow barely reaching the tables dotting the open area in the middle of the room, leaving them shadowed in darkness.

Half of a door, barely hanging upon rusted hinges, blocked what looked to be a small kitchen in complete disarray. Overflowing pots bubbled on the stove, soot coated the walls in black, and I could have sworn a rat ran from under the door.

Absolutely disgusting.

Next to the kitchen doorway was another, but this one was shrouded in purple, iridescent beads. It presumably led to the back exit and what looked to be a stairway leading up to who knew what else.

The dark atmosphere of the tavern matched the depraved acts that no doubt took place here at all hours of the day and night. Winding our way among the tables to a booth at the far end of the room, I locked eyes with the Duke and quickly looked away when he winked at me. Based on my research on him, he liked timid, demure women who were easy to control. While I was none of these things, I was a great performer.

We slid into the sticky, grime-coated booth. Far enough away to not draw too much attention, but close enough that we could watch the Duke and the two courtesan women who sat on his lap vying for his attention. They were beautiful. He, however, was a disgusting excuse for a man, both in looks and actions.

Two guards stood watch at his sides, halting anyone who approached before they could reach the table. Another guard stood near the front door, scoping out any threats as they entered. It wasn't to our tactical advantage to approach him when we needed to get him into the alley alone, so we would have to wait for him to come to us.

I sipped on a piss colored lager, grimacing when I found it warm and stale. It was going to be a long night if all the alcohol was this terrible.

As the day melted into the first dregs of night, more bodies began filing into the tavern, their sweat from a long day's work making the already musty tavern somehow more unbearable. Melba flirted with the few men and women who brought us drinks, adding their cups to our growing pile of mostly full glasses. To drink nothing would draw too much attention, but to become intoxicated would jeopardize everything.

"Has it always been this easy for you?" Melba asked, casting aside her glass of equally terrible looking beer.

"Has what been easy for me?"

"Errands."

My attention had been elsewhere when she asked, focusing on the Duke and his movements, the way the guards shifted and adjusted the weapons at their sides. But now, my attention was entirely on her. Melba didn't ask about my past often; instead, she let me give her bits and pieces of myself when I felt comfortable enough to do so.

"Are you asking about physically or emotionally?"

Training had been rigorous leading up to my first errand. Amias had spent countless hours making sure that I wouldn't embarrass myself, or him. But the emotional toll had been far greater than a few sore bruises and sore muscles.

"Yes," Melba replied. "I haven't even—" she paused, looking around and lowering her voice. "Completed an errand, and the mental strain of doing so is starting to weigh on me. How do you do it?"

I paused, thinking back to the preparation I had done before my first errand and how I had felt after completing it. Edmond Ashford had been my mark, the son of a well known rebel sympathizer. He was only sixteen, a year older than I had been at the time. Both of us were children caught up in the deadly games played by adults, and just as Melba grappled with what was to come, his death still hung heavy in my heart.

Amias claimed that every kill would be easier and every death would impact me a little less. And they did. Despite my best attempts to hold onto my humanity, taking someone's life had grown less painful after each time, but that didn't stop them from haunting my dreams. Unfortunately, getting used to that feeling meant that I had accepted my new morals and my role in the Order.

"To be honest, Melba, some days are harder than others. Physically, you'll grow used to the strength you'll need to utilize to take down a grown man. Mentally though? I hope that you don't replay them over and over in your head at night when you close your eyes like I do." Her face dropped as she reached for my hand, but I pulled it back. Half because I didn't want the Duke to think something was going on, and because I didn't deserve her sadness, or her comfort. Melba's hurt was evident across her face, but she didn't speak on it.

"You deserve more than this, Melbs. You don't deserve the stain it leaves on your soul—forever a burden for you to carry. It's too late for me, but not for you. You can still change your mind."

She crossed her arms over her chest, leaning back onto the wall behind her. "I would like to remind you that I was at the Order before you were. I am not better than you, and you are no better than me. You have your secrets and I have mine too, so don't think that you know what I *deserve*. I chose this just as much as you did."

Before I could respond and try to explain, her eyes lit up and she leaned forward on her elbows. Her voice was flirtatious as she greeted the brown-haired woman who sauntered up to our table. When she slid into the booth next to me, I watched the Duke's eyes flick to mine. I raised the long ago warmed beer in acknowledgment of his attention and he winked in return.

I was the dangling piece of bait, and he was the circling shark surveying his prey before going in for the kill.

"Your hair is gorgeous," the woman next to me slurred. I had left my hair down, letting the strands curl naturally down the length of my back. Her fingers tangled in the waves, fingertips brushing softly against my spine.

She was a pretty distraction that I might have been willing to get lost in if I hadn't come here for a purpose. Despite my better judgment, I nuzzled into her hand slightly, causing her fingers to drop lower until they played with the strings of my bodice. "Tell me, are you as fiery as your hair color promises?"

I leaned back, whispering into her ear, hoping that playing into her advances might draw out the Duke—make him play his hand before the evening grew too late. "Would you like to find out?"

Grinning wildly she slid closer, our bodies pressing together until there was no space between us, before a large hand gripped her bicep, ripping her from the seat. "Hey! Watch it!" she protested, but her words were a jumbled mess. She turned a glare on the man who had grabbed her only to nearly fall over herself with apologies. I worried her eyes would bulge out of her head when she realized who she had snapped at.

The Duke of Pery stood before me, reeking of smoke, perfume and sweat. "I think you've had enough visitors for tonight," he commanded, deeming me his property already. He was on the shorter side, maybe an inch or two taller than me, but as wide as you could imagine someone who had spent their life gorging themselves on the land while everyone else suffered would be. His skin was pasty, near jaundiced; probably from all the time he spent in seedy taverns like this one.

A long, patchy, untamed beard sat upon his chin. The wiry hairs fanning out in all manner of directions. Beautiful blue eyes were his only attractive feature, though they were now bloodshot and glassy from inebriation. Greasy, ruddy brown hair clung to his forehead, slick with oil.

Sliding over onto the bench, I patted the seat next to me and batted my eyelashes up at him. "Why don't you take a seat?"

"Oh, yes! We would be delighted if you joined us," Melba said eagerly, laying our false adoration on thickly.

He looked me over hungrily, a vulture awaiting its next meal. A shiver ran through my body, and his eyes flared at my movement as he mistook my disgust for anticipation. Wasting no time, he placed a hand atop mine and slid into the booth. I smiled to myself, pleased that all my subtle teasing and flirting had paid off.

His thick leg pressed into me and I urged myself not to just stab him right at this moment and get it over with. But we were being watched, not only by his guards, but by the women of the tavern. Their jealous gazes imagining themselves where I longed to run away from.

"I was thinking we could go outside, get some air," he grunted, inclining his head toward the beaded curtain in the back. The statement verged on a command more than a suggestion. It wasn't surprising that he was rushing the game we were playing, if anything I was relieved that I wouldn't have to play for too much longer.

Pretending to wrestle with my moral values about accompanying a man alone into a dark alley, I chewed on my lower lip. He watched my every movement, licking his lips as his desire built as a result of my coy act. "That sounds like a wonderful invitation, but I couldn't leave my friend alone in a place like this," I pouted.

The Duke wasn't a man used to being refused; the anger that flashed across his face was evidence of that. His hand tightened on mine, squeezing hard enough that a sharp pain radiated from my fingers, but I didn't cry out like he likely expected. Instead, I smiled up at him.

Melba rose in one quick motion. "I'm actually supposed to meet my girlfriend anyway. You go have a good time," she said cheerfully, sliding from the booth. "I'll catch up with you later," she promised.

I watched her weave through the crowd until the front door opened and shut behind her. Now that she had an excuse to be elsewhere, I hoped she was preparing for what would occur in the next few minutes.

Our entire plan hinged on my ability to get him away from the three guards and any other watching eyes. It was evident by the little attention his guards were paying that they did not see me as a threat.

With Melba gone, I brought my attention back to the Duke who had released my hand but was now eagerly running his fingers up the fabric that covered my thigh. Flashing him a meek smile, he continued his advances, his hands climbing higher and higher up the length of my leg.

"That was a problem easily solved." He chuckled, pressing his body closer to mine, nearly suffocating me in his stench.

I bit my lip, looking away shyly. "I don't even know your name."

Instead of answering me, his hand tightened on my thigh before moving back to my hand. He intertwined our fingers, tugging me to stand and leading me toward the back doorway. Beads brushed against my face as he pushed through them, aiming for the exit to the back alley. I let him lead me away from the safety of the tavern and into the darkness, where, if all went to plan, only one of us would survive the night.

"You can call me whatever you want," he purred. He held me so tightly in his arms that he practically carried me from the tavern.

I wanted to throw up.

Shadows darkened the back alley as we stumbled through the door, scaring a couple already in varying stages of undress. They scampered off, arms full of their discarded clothing, when they saw who had intruded on their affair.

The moment the door clicked shut, he abruptly turned me so that my hands scratched against the building's aged brick. The muffled clanging of swords against hardwood let me know that we were all alone now, his guards attempting to give us privacy.

He was not an incredibly strong man, but to keep up the appearance of my feebleness, I let him pretend to control me, though I was confident I could easily break free. The telltale sign of his arousal and desire pressed into me, demanding more than he would be receiving. I could feel every movement of his disgusting body as he writhed against me.

Reeking breath tickled the back of my neck as his hands roamed from my waist down toward my hips. Bile rose in my throat at his touch, but I forced it into a moan of fake pleasure that had him pushing harder into me.

"I've been watching you all night," his voice was muffled, stifled by the hair he had burrowed into. "Was this outfit because you knew I would be in town?" he asked, slurring his words and running a possessive hand up my stomach.

It was challenging to keep my face schooled into a look of desire when all I could think about was throwing my head back into his face and shattering his nose. Death, or Melba, better find him quickly; my patience was already beginning to waver.

"This old thing?" I turned to look over my shoulder, fluttering my eyelashes.

His body pressed further into me, pinning me to the wall as his lips met the side of my neck. His fingers tangled and pulled at the strings of my bodice.

"What was your name?" he asked, each word punctuated between each brush of his lips. My body shivered with revulsion. I clenched my fists, fighting the urge to end his life myself.

I mimicked his words. "You can call me whatever you want."

He hummed against my skin, seeming to enjoy that I repeated him.

Gods. It felt like this was lasting forever.

He suddenly pulled back, causing me to look at him over my shoulder. A smile curled on his lips as he reached for a handful of fabric at the hem of my dress. Growing even more bold, he leaned forward, and claimed my lips, his tongue trying to break through the seam of my lips.

When it broke through, I bit his tongue sharply. He pulled back, reaching a finger up and into his mouth to find that I had left him bleeding.

His expression turned devilish, "Oh, I like them feisty. This will be even more enjoyable than I thought."

As he pressed forward to kiss me again, a welling line of crimson appeared across his throat. Stumbling backwards, he gripped his throat with both hands as blood dripped from between his fingers and down his arms.

Pleading blue eyes looked through me, his weakening body sliding down the far wall until he collapsed lifelessly to the cobblestone ground. The last sounds of his garbling, gasping breaths faded away, leaving the alleyway in silence.

"About time," I grumbled to Melba. "It's going to take a week's worth of baths to get his scent off of me."

"We have to move. Now," Melba demanded, grabbing my hand as she pulled me down the alley. The sounds of our feet pounding against rough stones echoed behind us. "That couple stayed around, and they're likely reporting the Duke's murder to his guards right now."

Hair and chiffon trailed behind us as the door to the tavern was thrown open. The three guards spilled out, their shouts growing closer when I stumbled on the fabric of my dress.

"I knew this dress was a terrible idea," I muttered under my breath while I struggled to remain upright.

"You two, halt!" their voices yelled to us. "Get them! Murderers!"

"You need to run faster," Melba gasped in between breaths.

"Can't you see I'm trying? It's this stupid dress."

They were fast—too fast—and gaining on us quickly. I ripped a dagger free from a sheath I had hidden at the top of my thigh. Melba gripped my arm, allowing me to hold my dress in one hand and the blade in the other. It left my fingertips, hitting its mark with a resounding thud, followed by the louder sound of a body hitting the ground.

One down, two to go.

Seconds were precious, and I lost several when I slowed down to throw the blade.

A second guard rushed us, sword raised in his hands, preparing to strike. I fumbled for another blade, hands sticky with ale and slick with sweat from our run.

Cenric appeared from the shadows, blocking the downward blow the guard meant to deliver. The third guard threw a dagger toward us, but it missed us as we continued our frantic run through the streets.

If we got to our horses, we could limit tonight's bloodshed.

Cenric ran after us, but the guards refused to relent. Turning, he slammed the hilt of his sword into a guard's head, the body crumpling to the ground in a heap. "Forget the horses!" he yelled. "Just keep going!"

Melba swerved left, directing me away from the market square where we had quartered our rides home, and instead led us through the entrance gate and into the forest.

The path was marred with roots making it a slow, treacherous journey. I barely had time to worry about Cenric before the sound of horse hoofs pounded the dirt behind us. He jumped from his horse, face red and angry.

"That could have been more discreet, Melba," he chastised.

She crossed her arms across her chest. "You're telling me you could just stand there and watch that disgusting man paw at Varine for even one more minute?" She threw her hands up in exasperation. "I had to do something, it was unbearable to watch. I thought I was going to throw up."

"You and me both," I muttered, winning a glare from Cenric.

He shook his head, the tone of his voice short and clipped. "We had a job to do and you nearly messed it up. There were witnesses in the alley, Melba."

Melba stepped closer to him until they were nearly nose to nose—the anger building between them. I knew it would devolve into a fight if we didn't get out of here.

I tucked my hand to my chest and the other to my forehead, playing the damsel in distress. "My heroes," I swooned. "My big brave warriors saved me from the evil villain. What would I possibly do without you?"

Their eyes turned to me, the fight winking out as they looked me up and down. I scowled at their change in expression when it was not the humor I had been expecting.

"Shit, Varine," Cenric swore, rushing over to me. He gripped me by the shoulders, holding me at arm's length. "You've got a dagger in your side. Don't move, I'll help you."

The guard's blade hadn't missed after all.

Adrenaline had fueled our escape and dulled my senses, but the ache of pain was now radiating from a spot near my waist. I looked down to see trails of red seeping into my gown. The boning of the dress had deflected the blade from lodging too deeply, but it stuck deep enough that it protruded from my body unassisted.

"I've been stabbed before." I shrugged, ripping a piece of fabric from the hem of my dress.

"It's not like you build a tolerance to it, Varine!" Melba exclaimed, her look of shock matching Cenric's. "Let me help you."

After shooing her away, I carefully removed the blade, tucking it into my now empty sheath.

The dagger wasn't nearly as lovely as the one I had thrown, but with a bit of sharpening and shining, it would be a nice addition to my collection. Blood ran from the wound, dripping down to my feet.

Melba watched as I struggled to wrap it around me and keep enough tension to staunch the bleeding. Without waiting to ask, she took the fabric from my fingers, tightly wrapping it around my waist. I sucked in a gasp of pain and averted my eyes from her, only to meet Cenric's.

"Let me see," he demanded.

I waved them away, reaching for the saddle's horn to pull myself up. "I'm fine. Let's go home." Pain ripped through my side, and a hiss escaped my lips.

Pulling myself up was far more difficult than I had anticipated. Cenric reached for me, but I willed my body to move before he could lift me onto the horse. Blood was already soaking the binding fabric.

Cenric ran a hand through his hair, leaving it on the top of his head. "Amias isn't going to be happy."

"I don't really care right now. Let's go home." I pulled on the reins, leading my horse away. Amias could be as unhappy as he wanted. The errand was complete, and based on my very brief assessment, I would likely only need a few stitches.

Assassins were injured all the time; it was a dangerous profession, after all. If Amias grew angry at every injury we incurred, he would never experience joy again.

Cenric rode beside me on the bumpy, weather-worn roads to the keep. From the corner of my eye, I noticed how his gaze frequently darted in my direction. I kept my eyes straight ahead, willing the journey to end. I tried to hide the way my breathing hissed from behind my teeth, thanks to my clenched jaw. But I knew Cenric could tell. His careful glances gave him away.

"Is it later yet?" he asked, trying to break the tension between us by asking about our conversation from before the errand. He wanted to know about the man at the market. But even if I was willing to spill my secrets, I wasn't in the mood to do so now. I knew he was equally curious and using it as a distraction, but I wouldn't give in so easily.

"Are you going to tell me why Amias made you stay behind?" I countered. "Or why you think he's going to be upset?"

"I can't."

I sighed and pulled my horse forward and away from him. "Then I can't either."

CHAPTER 15

A rrow after arrow hit its mark. The weekly contest for the head of the table was taking place, and I was at a significant disadvantage thanks to the wound I had sustained the previous day. It had been stitched and bound tightly, but each pull of the bowstring had me grating my teeth.

My dreams had been filled with roving hands that pinned me to walls. My screams were soundless as I thrashed but couldn't manage to break free.

The Duke was far from the first errand I had gone on where I had used my body as a distraction. I would do anything for the Order, so I always did so willingly, but this one felt different.

There was something about the intent in his eyes. The way he was going to take whatever he wanted, even if I didn't consent, would haunt me.

I didn't feel bad for the Duke. He was a horrible man who preyed on the weak and the poor, trafficking magic wielders to fund an estate that could contain the entire town of Canlere.

I certainly didn't feel bad for him, but I almost pitied him. What a sad, sorry existence to have nothing and no one—used for only the coin within my pocket.

When my fifth and final arrow hit the target, off-center, to my chagrin, I knew that I wasn't winning this round.

"Nearly messed that one up, didn't you, Varine?" Gedeon sneered from beside me.

I sighed deeply, an unwilling participant in whatever game they were trying to play. "What exactly are you referring to?"

101

Xarissa joined in, bouncing her hip against Gedeon's. "You know exactly what he's talking about," she taunted. I often wondered if the mirrored sneers on their faces were permanently affixed to them.

"The errand was completed, it doesn't matter how it was done." My words were clipped. This wasn't about me. Yes, they didn't like me, despised me even, but they hated Melba more. Something about being the underdog rubbed them the wrong way.

Gedeon loosed an arrow, barely hitting the target at all. His face began to redden, his knuckles growing white. He opened his mouth to speak, but Xarissa's voice filled it.

"It does matter!" she nearly shrieked, pointing a dagger at me. "You bring shame upon the Order when your kills are sloppy. It's the talk of the entire town. You fucked up."

She began to move toward me but was stopped by the tip of the arrow I had notched into place. "For one," I drawled, "it wasn't my kill, so piss off. And two, if Amias thought you could have done it better, he would have asked you."

Her temper flared, red flushing her cheeks as she took another step forward. I drew the bowstring back but Gedeon rushed forward, grabbing onto Xarissa.

"Take another step. I dare you." I was unsure if my words were a threat or a promise.

Gedeon dragged her backwards, trying to pull her away from me as she tried to lunge forward. "Where is little Melba anyway? Couldn't handle her first kill? What a pity she didn't even show up to the challenge. Guess we all know where she stands."

My eyes narrowed at the sound of my best friend's name on her snake-like lips. "Even when she doesn't attend, she somehow still places better than you. How embarrassing that you both are terrible shots."

"She won no points," Gedeon protested, the muscles in his arms flexing as he tried to keep Xarissa contained.

I shrugged. "Neither did either of you."

"You better watch yourself, Varine. Your attitude won't earn you any favors," she threatened. "You should be begging to be a part of our group and for our protection. I'll be surprised if you even make it through the first Trial with how sloppy your work is. Don't even get me started on your little lover boy. He's been sneaking around for ages without you even noticing. You're a sorry excuse for an assassin."

I rolled my eyes and looked pointedly at Gedeon. "Are you going to get your yapping lap dog out of here, or will I have to put it down myself?"

Xarissa screeched and thrashed in his arms, scraping her nails down any exposed skin, trying and failing to escape his firm grasp. Glaring openly in my direction, he threw her over his shoulder and stalked toward the keep. "You're making a big mistake," he called back to me but I only offered a wave of my hand in return.

They were right about one thing: Melba's not participating in the challenge was not a good sign that she was coping well with last night's events. I needed to go find her and make sure she was okay. Turning to place my bow on the rack, I noticed Cenric watching me, arms crossed across his broad chest.

"What?" I asked.

"You shouldn't do that," he muttered.

"What shouldn't I do, Cenric? Put my bow back and instead leave a mess for someone else to clean up?" I knew what he meant, but I couldn't help but antagonize him just a little. "That would be awfully rude of me."

He pushed off the weapon rack he was leaning against, sauntering over to me with a face that was not nearly as amused as I was.

"You know what I'm talking about. Antagonizing them is a bad idea. They've had it out for you from the start and you're far too valuable to m—" He stopped, catching himself on the word. "To the Order."

My eyebrows raised at what went unsaid. He was going to say "me"— that I was valuable to him. "What was that, Cenric?"

He ignored me. "And you shouldn't have been shooting. You're going to pull a stitch and then I'm going to have to listen to you bitch about the injury even more."

"I don't bitch about my injuries."

Stepping closer, a smile on his face, he leaned down to meet my height. "Says the person that doesn't have to listen to it."

Archery had been a sufficient distraction while it lasted, but now my mind swam with a sea of worries.

My position in the Order once the Trials began was precarious, leaving me entirely at the mercy of Amias, who seemed to have ulterior motives and was now keeping secrets with Cenric. Not to mention Xarissa's claim that he had been sneaking around.

I didn't blame him for not telling me what Amias had wanted, if he had been sworn to secrecy, Amias couldn't be denied. And sneaking around was just something assassins did and Xarissa was just a bitch trying to make me suspicious of him.

Maybe I needed to try something else to distract myself from all of it—or *someone* else.

I licked my lips at the thought, forgetting his snarky comments. Cenric traced the motion, eyes darkening in response.

"Don't look at me like that," he growled.

"Look at you like what?"

"Like you're thinking something inappropriate about me."

I scoffed, pressing my lips together, trying and failing to think my next words out carefully. "Would it be a problem if I was?"

"No, the problem would be that I'm probably thinking the same thing."

My breath caught in my throat, delicious heat flooding my body at these words. I took an involuntary step toward him, unable to bear even the smallest distance between us. "So what if I am?"

Alarm bells rang in my head, warning me of the dangerous game we were playing. If we took the next step of admitting our feelings instead of dancing around the truth, everything would change between us.

Maybe it was finally time for us to make a decision, but I was terrified that I would make the wrong one and end up with a ruined friendship that we both needed.

"You're not," he said with a shake of his head. "You're avoiding what's actually going on."

I crossed my arms over my chest, the spell broken. "I am not."

The tension that had been building and winding its way through my body fell like a rock into the pit of my stomach. A war was raging in and around me. I was stupid to think that the timing of this relationship would benefit either of us.

He closed the remaining distance between us, grasping my hands in his. "I know something's wrong. Tell me what happened at the market."

The market.

I hadn't even thought about the Shifter. I was too busy replaying the errand over in my head. As his beautiful green eyes stared into mine, I wanted nothing more than to spill my secrets and unburden myself from all I was hiding. But he was too insistent, almost suspicious of me. When I tried to remove my hands from his grasp, he held firm, unwilling to let me go.

"Tell me what Amias wanted."

His eyes flared as if he was surprised I had remembered that little tidbit of information. "You're not going to like it," he said, dropping my hands.

My skin was cold, the lack of contact seeping into me like a winter's day. I missed the heat already. I sighed exasperatedly. "I usually don't."

He turned toward the stables, looking at them longingly, as if they could shield him from his next words. "He asked me to protect you."

"Why?" I demanded.

Never once had Amias tried to shelter me from danger. In the last eight years he had never stepped in when I had been beaten, never given me a hand when I fell. He'd even gone so far as to put me directly in harm's way. Why would he now be asking Cenric to protect me?

He ran his hands through his hair, leaving them atop his head, a nervous gesture he had done since we were young. "He said—" Pausing, he sucked in a breath. "He said that you were in danger and that someone was looking for you. Did you mess about during an errand and get caught? Who would be looking for you?"

My mouth hung slightly agape and my breathing quickened at the accusatory question. I shoved down the panic that rose in my throat. I hadn't been negligent during any of my errands, there should be no one looking for me, let alone even knowing who I was.

It was the Queen, wasn't it? I could think of no one else who would be looking for me. The very person my mother had sent me away to avoid. Why hadn't she given up?

"Shit," I whispered, the word unintentionally leaving my lips. This was bad. Very bad.

He reached for my hands again, but I snatched them away and tucked them behind my back. "What? What do you know? *Is* there someone looking for you?" he questioned.

I shook my head. "I . . . uh . . . nothing. I don't know who would be looking for me."

Cenric pursed his lips. "You're lying."

I avoided his touch when he again tried to reach out. Hurt and confusion crossed his face. If he touched me right now, I didn't think that I would be able to resist telling him the truth.

"You know how it is," I said, trying to divert the topic away. "Everyone wants to find the famous assassins."

"You really are a terrible liar," he repeated. "Varine, what's going on?"

I backed away another step. "I need to find Melba." I gulped. "I need to check on her."

I couldn't have this conversation with him right now. Not now, and hopefully not ever. The less he knew, the safer we both would be. I turned on my heel, taking hurried steps toward the back entrance of the keep. I expected to hear his footsteps behind me, but when I looked over my shoulder, I found him frozen in place.

CHAPTER 16

Cenric could always be found in the stables, but Melba could be found in the library. She devoured books like a hungry dragon, flying through their pages with supernatural speed. That was the first place I looked, and I was relieved to find her there. Now, as long as Cenric didn't follow me, I could deal with one problem at a time.

I found her curled up on a couch in the back corner of the library. Her head rested against the arm, a book propped up on her knees. She didn't look up as I sat beside her, tucking my legs under me. Her mouth was a thin line that I knew wasn't from concentration, as she silently flipped through the pages.

The library was peaceful—most apprentices avoided it, taking the physically demanding training more seriously than studying. It smelled like dust and parchment, with just a hint of smoke from the crackling fireplace. Floor-to-ceiling bookcases built into the walls lined the sides of the room. Each shelf was filled to the brim with all manner of books and maps.

Novels that had been published more recently could be found at the entrance to the room, progressing in age until they reached the windows at the far end. Stained glass depictions of ravens filled the large window at the back, the multicolored glass illuminated the room in splashes of color.

Romance was Melba's favorite genre. She often gushed and swooned over almost every female protagonist she read about and would give up just about anything to insert herself into the love interest's role.

Melba *loved* love. Her biggest dream, beyond completing the Trials, was finding a partner who would love her just as much as she loved them. I envied her desires, even if I felt so far from them. It wasn't that I didn't want to find someone; the fear of what a relationship would look like in my uncertain future held me back.

How could I ask someone to spend their life with me when it could wink out like a candle in the wind? And then, on top of it all, I would have to trust someone with every intimate part of myself; giving my heart freely without expecting it to be returned in the same condition. I wasn't sure I was capable of doing that anymore, not after Loretta.

My first love was the product of proximity and opportunity. Our relationship had started with simple grazes, a fingertip here, a shoulder brush there, eyes lingering on each other as we passed in empty hallways.

At fifteen, Loretta had been the most beautiful woman I had ever laid eyes on. Her chestnut brown hair was cropped close to her head, and beautifully intricate flowers were carved into the buzzed hair at her temples. She had molten pools of chocolate for eyes that I wouldn't have minded drowning in for eternity.

Our sly touches quickly turned into rushed stolen kisses in the nearest dark corner, which then progressed further into early mornings spent sneaking from each other's rooms. The relationship had been mostly physical. I was secretive and guarded, and she wanted me to open up. The result of which led her to distance herself from me emotionally.

The darkest parts of me whispered that she didn't love me as much as I did her—that she wouldn't believe me or that she might even fear me—a heartbreak in and of itself.

But it didn't matter anymore. Loretta was dead, and fifteen was lifetimes ago.

Melba sniffled next to me. A sad sound that had me reaching out to comfort her, my hand resting gingerly on her knee. "Do you want to talk about it?" I asked.

Melba continued to stare at her book, refusing to look at me. I could tell she had stopped reading and was now using it to hide her face. Her eyes began to line in silver, and her bottom lip trembled.

"I feel ridiculous," she mumbled. "This is exactly what I've been training to do and I feel awful. I asked you about it in the tavern because I was worried this was going to happen. I feel like a completely different person."

Scooting closer, her knees resting against my shoulder, I could feel the shake of her body with each ragged breath.

My eyes stung at her words. "The first death is always the hardest. Trust me," I offered, wincing. "I'm sorry that I didn't warn you better, or at least try to prepare you for what it feels like."

She covered her face with the book, but I knew it was to hide her tears.

"I'm no expert, but I know what it's like to kill," I started, pausing to think of the right words. I leaned my head against the back of the plush couch and closed my eyes. "You will never forget what you have done, but you will find a way to move forward and cope with it."

Her breath came in sobbing gasps as the words hung between us for several moments, the crackling embers in the fireplace filling the empty space. I wouldn't rush her, when she wanted to talk, I would be here. If she needed to cry and grieve her innocence like I had, I would sit here all night.

"What was your first errand?" she asked suddenly, peeking out from the top of her book. Her voice trembled with each word. "I just realized that you've never told me about it."

I made a point not to talk about my errands often. Only reporting back to my assigned Master or Amias at their completion. Some things were better left unsaid, it was easier that way, or that's at least what I had convinced myself.

The first errand was different from my first kill. No one but Amias knew that the first life I ever took was Loretta's.

I had kept the first deaths at my hand close to my chest, but now, as I stared into Melba's grief-stricken eyes, the sister I had chosen for myself when I had none, I knew I owed her. After everything she had done for me, I could at least give her a part of me; she wouldn't even hesitate to do the same.

Thankfully, she had only asked about my first *errand*, and Loretta was never one. No, she was a horrifying, devastating accident that left me a shell of a person—a heartless killer who couldn't love.

"Well," I started, "I was dressed in the most incredible gown that I had ever laid eyes on, let alone worn. It was a deep shade of burgundy and cinched tightly in the back. A matching overcoat made of velvet complemented the dress perfectly—snowy white with embroidered roses," I said with a sigh, remembering the way it had fit me like a glove.

"What does your clothing have to do with your errand?" Melba mumbled.

"Shh. I'm painting a picture for the story."

She laughed through her nose, just an exhale of air, and shoved her feet under me. Physical touch was always something she craved, so if putting her icy toes beneath me gave her even a little comfort, I would allow it.

"Can I continue, or are you going to interrupt the tale I'm weaving again?" I teased.

"Please do."

"Amias had some woman I had never seen come into my room to pin my hair into an elaborate style and secure it with silver jeweled pins. I looked like a princess. Amias even dressed for the occasion, wearing a dark cloak over his fine clothing and black leather gloves to match."

Melba threw her head back, laying it on the armrest behind her. "Gods. I hate his stupid capes." Amias was truly the most dramatic man I knew both in his dress and his actions, but his attire was always impressive.

I raised my eyebrows at her, a small smile on my lips. She waved at me to continue, pretending buttons across her lips.

"We were attending a ball at the Ashford estate, and I was pretending to be Amias's daughter. I even had a fake name—Aranea. It means, 'spider', which I thought was very smart since I was weaving a web of lies and deceit."

Her hand covered her mouth, suppressing another giggle. "Clever."

"Thank you," I said, even though I knew her comment had been more of an insult. I remember my first errand so viciously I could practically see that night in front of me. "Beautiful is the only word I could use to describe the estate. Smooth white stone steps greeted us from the doorway of the carriage, leading us into the largest ballroom I had even seen. Amias gave me until midnight to find Esmond and complete the errand and then he disappeared into the crowd, leaving me to my own devices. Finding Esmond was surprisingly easy, leaving the incredible chocolate tarts was the hard part."

Melba suddenly sat up. "Varine. You did not."

"Hey!" I protested, bumping her knee with my shoulder. "I like to eat. And if you would have seen the dessert table you wouldn't blame me."

"Whatever," she scoffed. "What was Esmond like?"

"Gorgeous."

She rolled her eyes and waited for me to continue. I waited, watching her squirm for more information until she finally asked me, "And?"

"He had red hair that hung to his shoulders, and sapphire gemstones for eyes that looked like they had been plucked from the earth and polished just for him. When he asked me to dance I practically swooned. I even tried to tell him no, insisting that I didn't know how to dance, but he was so sweet, insisting we could learn together."

"And instead of dating him, you killed him?"

I glared at my friend. "You know, this story is supposed to bring us together and show that my first errand was just as difficult as yours, but here you are trying to ruin it."

Tucking her book to her chest, she shoved her feet even farther underneath me. I smiled, thankful that she was relaxing into my comfort, her tears beginning to dry.

The point of this story had been to make her feel better, but in truth, this errand *had* been difficult. I fell hard and fast for a boy that seemed to set my soul on fire. I was young and stupid, and most of all naïve.

His death was nearly as devastating as Loretta's. Though I knew him for only moments, he *saw* me. He saw who I really truly was and held no fear, only love. An acceptance I had craved more than anything, one that even my parents nor Loretta had given me.

"He led me into the back garden," I began again. "And showed me the evening blooms. That's when he told me that he knew I was there to kill him."

Melba gasped, covering her mouth with her hands. "How did he know that?"

"He had witnessed me with a Master in town and had recognized them, connecting the dots when I arrived at the party."

"Shit."

"That's not even the worst part. When the time came, I couldn't kill him. My naïve teenage heart had fallen for him too quickly and I couldn't complete the errand. Esmond told me that he wasn't afraid to die, but I was terrified to kill him." I paused, taking in a ragged breath at the memory. She watched me intently waiting for the horrible conclusion to this story.

I could do this. If I said it enough I might actually grow to believe it. I could tell Melba the secret I hadn't told anyone, how I had almost ruined my career before it even started. "I couldn't do it," I repeated. "But he kissed me and then plunged the dagger I held in my hands into his own heart. A death blow."

Melba was quiet for a long time before she finally whispered, "That's horrible."

Though I had told her the truth, I was still lying. The part I withheld from Melba was how Esmond had recognized me. He never saw me in town, instead he claimed he knew that I was a Crestin. "A savior to the wielders" was what he called me, spouting nonsense about my role in the rebellion.

When I confronted him about knowing my identity, he told me that the rebellion had an object that allowed them to see through any glamour, no matter how strong, and because it was located in his house, it made my eye color visible again to those who had touched it.

When I protested, he held me, stroking my hair gently before he sacrificed himself. He died with the belief that I would save the people of Kalahvin, and with his death he was saving me. How stupid and wrong he had been.

My heart couldn't take much more pain, which is why I hadn't formed any romantic attachments since.

I wiped my eyes with the back of my hand, brushing away the stray tears that had sprang forward during my tale.

"I know our errands were very different, but the point I wanted to make is that it's never easy. You are not alone in this and you are allowed to feel how you are feeling. No matter the intent, killing is killing, and death is death. What matters in the end is that we have each other."

She squeezed my shoulders in a quick, comforting gesture, moving to lean her head against mine. Droplets of water fell from our eyes, mingling in the fabric of my tunic.

The pain of my first errand, and the loss of my first love would remain with me for the rest of my life, just as Melba would remember last night forever.

"Do you regret it?" she asked.

"No," I answered with absolute surety.

Melba took a deep breath. "I don't regret killing the Duke either. Actually, I think he deserved it."

"He would have continued hurting people. If it helps, you could think of all the people you saved by killing him."

She smiled at my words, just a slight lift of her lips. "Thank you for sharing your story with me. I know how difficult that was for you. And, Varine"—she drew my cheeks into her hands, squeezing them gently—"thank you for being my friend. I'm sorry I snapped at you yesterday; it was just the stress of the errand. I knew what you meant, though, that you want something better than killing for all of us."

I closed my eyes instead of answering her, and I sank into her warmth, letting the smell of old parchment and her familiar scent of mint fill my nostrils. We remained in the library for several hours, sitting in content silence. A fantasy novel Melba selected for me in my hands, a romance in hers.

As the sun began to set and the day's last rays disappeared behind the distant mountains, Cenric joined us, carrying trays piled high with meats, cheeses, and slices of crusty bread.

Thankfully, he didn't mention our interaction earlier as we enjoyed our feast in private, breaking the regulation Amias imposed on dining as a group. Sometimes, rules were made to be broken, especially during times like these.

Cenric dozed in a chair next to the fire, his feet hanging over the side of the armrest. I watched the rise and fall of his chest and admired how boyish he looked in such a restful state. His hair had grown long the past few months, falling nearly to his shoulders in dark waves that now obscured most of his face.

Melba's breath tickled my neck from where her head rested on my shoulder. Her book was open in her lap, still turned to the last page she had been reading before she too had fallen asleep.

Time was beginning to run out before the Trials. The days would soon grow short, indicating the closure of the warmer months. Amias had promised they would be held this year, leaving a small amount of time for them to begin.

My eyes drooped from the sleep my body demanded, but I fought their closure, refusing to join my two best friends in slumber. Instead, I found myself watching them, relishing the comfort of their nearness. If anyone survived the Trials, I would ensure it was us.

It had to be us.

CHAPTER 17

A week had passed since Melba's errand, and the wound in my side was healing dramatically thanks to the salves Brenla made. The days were filled with lessons and training, but my evenings were spent in the library, trying and failing to produce any information on the dragon blade in my possession. Its temperature seemed to fluctuate, which I assumed meant it was trying to give me a message, but I had yet to determine what.

Hidden deep within a trunk in my room, with my other prized belongings, it called to me, but I couldn't risk bringing it out. Every other dagger felt wrong in my hands— either too long, too short, too heavy, or too light. It made practicing with them difficult—my aim entirely off from what it was before.

"Amias is looking for you."

Sighing as loudly as I could, I dropped the dagger in my hand so that it hit the table with a sharp clang. "He's going to have to wait. I'm in the middle of something," I told Tatton, who watched me from the doorway.

I picked up another blade and tossed it at the wooden target on the far side of the room. Retrieving the blade, I noticed it had barely embedded into the wood. I ran the edges against the whetstone, sharpening it before tossing it at the target again. Though it had landed too far off the mark, I was satisfied with how far it had sunk in this time.

He crossed his arms across his chest, inclining his head toward the door. "Better get going. You shouldn't leave him waiting."

Tatton was the eldest of the group at twenty-eight years old. He was of average height and build but incredibly strong, evident in the hard lines of his muscles that were barely visible through his form-fitting training leathers.

Inky black coils were clipped short to showcase his broad forehead, and soft coffee-colored eyes were framed with long, dark eyelashes.

Tatton was an unknown. Like almost all of us, he had arrived under strange circumstances. As a young child, he had been found wandering the fields that surrounded the keep, seemingly appearing out of nowhere. Amias quickly adopted him as one of his own and began training him immediately.

That's probably why no one had questioned my sudden appearance either.

Tatton typically kept to himself, never being outright friendly or aggressive to any of us. He completed his errands and trained as hard, if not harder, than the rest of us. I had no complaints about him other than that he was often used by Amias to deliver messages, which is why he was bothering me now.

He tapped his foot impatiently but I ignored it, choosing to clean the blade I had just sharpened instead. Clearing his throat he asked, "Did you hear me?"

"Yes, Tatton, I did."

He huffed. "Then why aren't you going?"

Raising the blade in my hand, holding it with the tips of my fingers, I turned to face him in the doorway and threw my hands out wide. "I'm. Busy. Obviously."

When I turned away from him to continue my work, he moved quickly, snatching the blade from my hand. He embedded it to the hilt in the target, smirking at his handiwork. "Now you're not."

"Too bad I have more."

Stepping forward he tried to snatch the blades off the table. My annoyance now palpable, I raised one of the knives, pointing the tip at him. "Touch one of my daggers again. I dare you," I snapped. "Just because you kiss the very dirt Amias walks on doesn't mean that I have to drop everything the second he needs something."

"That is your ruler you speak of. Show him some respect," he snarled.

Show Amias some respect? I would do so when he returned the favor. Angry didn't even begin to describe how I felt that he had asked Cenric to protect me. He must have taken me for a fool, or a helpless child. Either way, I was tired of being underestimated. And I wouldn't stand here and be bullied by his errand boy when I had much better uses of my time.

"Piss off, Tatton."

Muttering under his breath, he slammed the door behind him.

I stayed in that room sharpening, polishing, and testing each of my blades until I was confident in their ability to slice to the bone. Once I had completed my task, I waited even longer to find Amias, knowing full well that it would irritate him.

He had been acting strange since we returned from our errand and I didn't want to know what that meant. But now that he had summoned me, I knew I was about to find out.

Amias found me before I could find him.

The main floor of the keep was empty, the hardwood floors giving away my location as I tried to swiftly, and silently ascend the stairs to my quarters.

"There you are," Amias called from behind me. My foot was still raised to take the next step when he spoke, his voice appearing from the shadows.

I jumped, clutching the sharpened blades rolled in fabric tightly in my arms. I had hoped to put them away and clean up prior to finding him, making him wait as long as possible, but I had not been fast enough.

Cringing at being caught, I slowly turned around to face him. "I was just looking for you," I lied.

He raised his eyebrows. "Upstairs?"

Several apprentices that had been roaming the hall, stopped and stared at our interaction. I looked between Amias and the stairway that would lead to the safety of my room. "Um . . . yes?"

"Right," he said flatly, obviously not believing me. "I just wanted to check in on your injury after your last errand. Will you join me in my office?"

"Oh." The word left my mouth in barely a whisper and I couldn't stop my jaw from falling open. Asking me to join him to discuss my injury was a strange invitation to receive from Amias. While I had no intention of discussing the events of the errand, especially my interaction with the merchant, I was intrigued by this soft, caring side of Amias. The side of him that I so rarely had the pleasure of seeing, and even more rarely had been directed at me.

He inclined his head toward the hallway, stepping back to release me from where I stood frozen at the base of the stairs. Wordlessly, I followed behind him.

The scent of honey filled the hallway, his hair slicked back giving away that he had recently bathed. I wondered if he had just returned from an errand before finding me.

When he opened the door, and sat behind his desk, I remained in the doorway. He motioned for me to join him in the seat across from him, but I didn't move.

Before entering the room fully, I looked around for any threats and signs that this was a test. Finding none, I shut the door behind me but still did not sit. I had never been trusting of Amias, but his little stunt with Cenric had left an even more bitter taste in my mouth.

A dainty, bone-colored tea set sat upon the desk, tendrils of steam wafting from the pot's spout. The delicate set looked out of place among the stacks of paper, knives, and other baubles, like a dove that had been lured to, and ensnared in a dark cave.

Sighing loudly at my refusal, he again motioned to the chair. "Why do you have to make everything so difficult? Come sit down."

"This is weird. You're being weird," I muttered, refusing to move.

He ignored me instead, inclining his head to the parcel in my hands. "Remember when I gave you your first blade?" he asked. "I was very proud of you that day."

Oh good. Not only was he checking up on me, we were reminiscing now too.

"You nicked your finger within seconds of me handing it to you." He chuckled.

Crossing my arms over my chest, I questioned his reasons for bringing me to his office. If it was simply to talk about the past, I would rather use one of the daggers against myself.

"Is there a reason you asked me to come in here?"

"I told you that I wanted to check up on you. Will you please just sit down? Brenla will be quite offended if you don't try the new tea she made."

The faster I got this over with, the sooner I could escape him. "Fine. Only for Brenla, though."

Plopping into the chair, I crossed my leg over the other, my foot bouncing as I waited for him to continue. He pushed a cup of steaming fragrant liquid toward me and I took it in my hands.

Clearing his throat, he poured a cup for himself, stirring it gently with a silver spoon. "You've come a long way and I'm impressed with your progress. I heard that my combat instruction helped you during your last errand, you're welcome for that. Seems you've improved from the young girl falling on her ass when trying to strike."

Taking a sip of the sweet brown liquid, I fought back the urge to throw it at him. "A lot can change in a few years."

"That it can."

In the darkened hallway I hadn't noticed how disheveled he had become. Though he was clean, his chin now bore dark stubble. The bags under his eyes a bright purple in contrast to his skin, his lids drooping slightly. It was startling to see him in such a way.

"So?" I asked. "You're wondering about my injury?"

Setting down his cup, he rested his elbows upon the desk and steepled his fingers together. "Are you too injured to compete in the Trials? Unfortunately, we cannot postpone much longer due to the circumstances."

The *Trials.* That caught my attention. In an effort to not seem too overzealous, I sipped from the cup and waited a few moments to answer. The stitches in my side still pulled, but only slightly—the pain mostly gone except for a dull ache.

"I'm fine," I stated flatly. Even if I wasn't, there was no way I would be telling him that.

He leaned back in his chair, lifting his cup to his lips. His eyes searched mine over the top of the rim. "I want to impress upon you the dangers you will face. There is no going back. Once the Trials begin, you will either complete them, or you will die. You cannot choose to stop—not for an injury or any other reason. I need you to think long and hard about whether you are in a position to complete them if they were to begin at this very moment."

"I can do it." It wasn't a lie exactly, but my injury was minor and I knew with every part of me that I could outcompete and outlast any of the other apprentices, even being injured. He smiled at that, my answer seemingly appeasing him.

"Good. Now, the errand I sent you on is the first of many that we have been hired to take on. It appears that someone is trying to kill off the Traders."

"Traders?" I asked, the word feeling heavy on my tongue. I took another sip, hoping it would quench my suddenly parched throat.

"Yes." He paused to set down his cup and pour more tea into mine. "That is what the traffickers of magical beings are calling themselves. We will make a large sum if we do our jobs properly."

I coughed, choking on my drink. They rationalized and justified their actions to sleep warm in their beds while thousands of magical beings rotted in the castle.

"Because 'Slavers,' or 'Traffickers,' weren't fitting enough titles for them?" I sneered.

Amias shrugged. "They found those names to be in poor taste."

"And is that what you think? That their actions are in poor taste?"

The sun had begun to set, the rays casting colorful swirls of light around the room. My head was growing heavy with exhaustion from the long day, the beginnings of a headache forming at the front of my head.

"I do not have any respect for their actions, but just like us, we all have a job to do."

My vision was growing red with my anger. If he didn't oppose it, he was in favor of it. Was this what my future would hold when he found out?

"So, you think that it's okay for them to continue selling anyone that has magic into potential slavery?"

"I did not say that."

"*That* is exactly what you said," I retorted, taking another sip of the brown liquid swirling in my cup. His silver spoon clanged against the sides of the cup as he stirred it.

I finished the last of my drink, setting it down on the table before me. Amias immediately refilled it. I hadn't realized how thirsty I had become until the liquid warmed my throat.

The headache that had been coming on was now pounding through my head, creating the illusion that the room was spinning.

"I did not bring you into my office to discuss politics or the intricacies of morality."

I sighed deeply, my body feeling like it was floating.

His eyebrows lifted, a small smile pulling on the corners of his lips. I hadn't realized how tired I was until I sunk back farther into the plush chair, the softness enveloping me like a warm embrace.

The sunlight danced in his hair illuminating the blue and silver undertones in his dark strands. The colors that had swirled gently in the waning light, now arched in a torrent of bright movement around the room.

"Hmm?" Amias asked, snapping my attention back to him. Had he asked me something? He was staring at me intensely, as if he was waiting for an answer to a question that I hadn't known was asked.

"I asked if you were feeling okay?"

My eyelids began to flutter closed, sleep coming to take me into oblivion. "I'm fine." My voice came out wobbly and slurred. Was that even my voice? It was hollow in my ears as if I had been pushed underwater.

I was clearly not fine right now. My vision became fuzzy around the edges. My surroundings became vibrant with color and then faded to muted tones in rapid succession, over and over.

It took all of my energy to focus on Amias. Gods, I was so tired.

He stood, rounding the desk, to lean on the edge directly before me. The smile that had played on his lips was now a full-blown grin. "If you say so."

"I do say so," I slurred. I could barely feel the words as they left my tongue. Something was wrong. Panic raised through my numb body. I looked to where our cups sat on the desk, mine was now drained to the dregs but Amias's had been left full, completely untouched.

"I gotta go . . ." I said, the words not quite taking shape or making sense. My body felt distant, like I was existing separately from it. I tried and failed to rise from the chair.

He stood over me, stooping to look into my eyes that I could barely manage to keep open just a fraction.

"If you're so *fine*," he mocked, "your first Trial starts now."

My eyelids closed, leaving me with a final vision of Amias standing over me, his arms slowly reaching toward me, and a smug smirk across his face.

CHAPTER 18

T his was it.

The Trials had officially begun and I was back in the Simulation. Amias must have poisoned me and carried my body into the Simulation room.

It turns out you don't need to be conscious for the creature's magic to work on you.

My bones felt chilled to the core as the scent of smoke returned to me through the open window of my room. The men I had watched from a distance now stood with their burnt out torches outside my front gate, refusing, or unable to cross onto the property.

Eerie silence hung around me for several seconds—my parents and Baldwin staring down the group before them. Even the wind seemed to have quieted in preparation for whatever was to come.

Mother pointed her staff at the threat, the other hand twitching in anticipation, as if longing for the blade strapped to her back. She was often cold and cruel, but I have never seen her hurt anyone, let alone be armed, outside of hunting or cooking. Mother much preferred her words as weapons, and they often struck harder than any blade.

A tall and broad man stepped forward, towering over the flimsy gate before him. His blond hair was tied in a braid draping down his back's center. In one hand, he gripped the torch, the flames lapping and flaring with each movement. The other hand gripped the handle of a double-sided ax at his belt.

Now that they were close enough, I could see the embroidery of a four-pointed star on their cloaks—the insignia of the Queen and the Temple of the Stars.

"The crown demands the heir." His voice was deep and rough, grating against my skin, causing an unpleasant shiver to rake up my spine.

"Which one?" Baldwin demanded, stepping forward.

The men exchanged looks before the blond spoke again. "The only true queen. Queen Desma, the rightful ruler of Kalahvin."

Mother sucked in a breath. "What of the other Queens? My mother? They will not stand for this."

A smaller brunette man with a bright white scar crossing his left eye, starkly contrasting his dark skin, threw his head back in laughter. "They're dead!" All except the blond-haired man cheered. "We killed them! Those abominations had it coming."

The blond man placed his hand upon the garden gate and Mother took a step forward, raising the staff in her hands. "You are not permitted to enter." Her words were laced with the promise of violence. I shuddered with the thought of what might happen next.

"We do not need your permission," the brunette spat, stepping forward to meet the blond at the gate. He tried to push the gate open but it wouldn't budge. Whining electricity filled the air and a transparent blue shield materialized around the house's perimeter. Intricate symbols were carved into the shield, linking together in a never-ending chain.

I gasped, jerking my head back from where it rested upon the window and placing a hand over my mouth. I hadn't realized how beautiful the wards were that Mother had created. The intricate symbols matched those painted on the walls of the house. I felt admiration for my mother as I realized she had painstakingly warded every inch of this house.

Since my thirteenth birthday, Mother had avoided the use of magic, so it was shocking to see it now displayed so blatantly. I had almost forgotten what it was like—the buzzing in the air and the metallic taste on my tongue.

The blond man ran his hand across the flickering blue shield. He looked up toward my window, a slow smile spreading across his face. I dropped to the ground, flattening myself as best as possible.

"Stop toying with them, Clayton. Let's get the girl and get out of here," the brunette said to the blond man I now knew was named Clayton.

My body shook with terror, threatening to drown itself in fear. The man had seen me and now knew exactly where I was. I heard the words they spoke. They were coming for me. They would take me away from the only place in the world I knew.

I feared what would become of my family if I did not watch as if the world couldn't possibly carry on until I witnessed it. I hesitantly raised my head, just the top sticking above the windowsill.

Clayton continued to stare up at me as if he was speaking directly to me. "The Queen worried that this would be a problem," he mused, running a finger along the wards. "But I don't believe it will be. That blade, if you would, Reedling."

The brunette retrieved and presented a thin golden sword to him. Clayton held it in one hand and cupped the sharp metal with his other, creating a line of red across his palm.

Dipping the tip of the blade into the cut he had just made, he let the blood saturate the metal. The sword seemed to consume it, the gold hue changing to crimson. Once it had drunk its fill, he thrust the sword into the glistening shield, the only thing standing between us.

It shuddered but remained fully intact.

Mother began frantically drawing symbols in the dirt with her staff. Each glyph shining in brilliant blue. When one sputtered out, she drew another, and another.

When the wards did not fall, Reedling took the blade, sliced it across his palm, and dipped it in his blood, before striking the wards once more.

The edges started to fray as each man took turns slicing their hands and plunging the blade. Mother continued to draw glyph after glyph, fighting to keep the protective barrier in place. Father and Baldwin raised their weapons as the last man cut his hand and plunged the blade through.

With a snap, the wards fell.

My mother screamed in frustration, trying and failing to raise them again.

Everyone moved at once. The guards rushed forward, charging through the gate, meeting the steel and shouts of Baldwin and my parents. I could barely stand the sight of the blood and gore that now filled the front yard. This wasn't what I wanted when I wished to be anywhere but here. I didn't want anyone to die because of me, or even *for* me.

Baldwin threw his hatchet as the last man entered the property. It struck true, embedding itself in his skull, the body a broken heap on the ground. Mother and Father grappled with other guards, unaware of Clayton standing at the back. Instead of watching the fray in front of him, his eyes were on my window, on me.

I yelled out as Baldwin bent to retrieve his weapon, unknowingly giving up his back to an approaching guard who had seen his distraction as an opportunity. Sword raised above Baldwin's head, it came down hard, only to be deflected by my father's blade. The guard reached out with a dagger in his other hand, swiping blindly toward Father's leg.

Focusing on the hands of his attacker, he was unable to dodge the blade. Blood now dripped from his thigh, a deep gash that sent him down to one knee. Still, the guard advanced, swiping his dagger with a newfound fervor.

Father yelled as their swords collided. Struggling to rise to both feet, he pressed forward until he towered over the man. I looked away, but the sound of tearing flesh could still be heard. My stomach turned queasy at the horrible things taking place.

The battle went on for what felt like hours, but could have only been minutes. The grunts and yells were replaced by heavy breathing—both sides starting to tire.

Mother and Baldwin fought a man who must have been as large as a tree and took both of them to keep him from hurting the other. Father was exchanging blows with Reedling, whose face twisted with rage with each hit. And Clayton still stood, watching and waiting for his moment.

Death was a promise that lingered in the air.

Blood pooled in my father's pant leg, the brown pants soaked through. He was growing weak due to the blood loss. I could see it in the way his movements slowed, the way he caught an attack just a second before it became fatal. I watched in horror as his eyes flicked to my Mother for a moment too long, giving Reedling the opening he had been waiting for.

A blow to his weapon hand knocked Father to the ground, his sword falling out of his reach.

"I am going to make you suffer for your treason," Reedling spat, standing over him. "Your death will be my reward."

My fists hit the window, resounding through me. I had to stop this. I had to end this battle before I lost everyone. Running to my bedroom door, I frantically turned the handle only to find it was sealed shut. Throwing my body into the sturdy wood did nothing as a glowing blue glyph appeared on the frame. It remained intact, mocking with its light even as I scratched it with my nails.

Helplessly, I returned to the window. Every part of me warned against what I might see, but I promised myself that I would bear witness to the sacrifices being made for me. I did so more as a punishment than out of respect; a reminder when this was all over what magic had done.

What *I* had done by being without.

If I had just been stronger or somehow recognized that there was a block on my magic—its existence buried somewhere deep—maybe I could have prevented all of this.

Father was still on the ground when I found him among the carnage, but instead of Reedling standing over him, the man was now bloody and face down next to my father. Exhaustion consumed Father's every feature. I wanted to call to him, tell him to come inside and be with me, but the words stuck in my throat as Clayton stalked toward the house.

My sweet cat hissed and growled at the man, fur sticking up in jagged spikes along her back. This man was dangerous, I could see it in each footstep, filled with determination and nefarious intent.

"You will not touch her!" Father yelled, his weakened body refusing to allow him to his feet.

Clayton turned to smile at him. "Give up and I'll let you live. The Queen will get back what she desires, as it is what she deserves. If you surrender to me now, I will take her and let you live."

"You will not touch her."

"What a pity." Clayton paused, looking back up at me. "I'm sorry that she'll have to watch you die."

Searching the yard, I prayed Baldwin would come to save him, but I found him lying in the grass next to where my mother continued to fight the monstrous guard. Squinting with my face pressed to the window, I willed his chest to rise, unable to bear the thought of his death.

To my surprise and joy, it did; the movement barely noticeable in the early dawn light. The new morning's colors were too cheerful for what had taken place during the night.

Mother kicked the guard from where he had been impaled upon her sword. Her staff had been cast into the grass long ago; glyphs did nothing to protect us now.

Noticing Clayton's looming figure over my father, she ran for him, only to find herself frozen, midstep. An aggravated scream ripped from her lips.

Clayton had his hand raised, fingers curled inward to touch his palm. I watched my mother's frightened eyes as she could do nothing to prevent my father's death. Tears streamed down my face, my voice now hoarse, as Clayton brought down his ax upon Father.

A pool of crimson filled the blades of grass upon which he laid. I begged and pleaded to any god that would listen, but it did nothing to stop his eyelids from fluttering closed for the final time.

Now that he had taken the one person in this world who meant the most to me, Clayton turned his eyes on Mother. Chuckling, he twirled a lock of her hair between his fingers. "So eager to join your husband, are you?"

Though her limbs were frozen her mouth could still move. She spat in his face, cursing him. "You'll pay for what you have done. The gods will not forgive this."

Clayton's humor turned to bloodlust as he wrapped his hands around her neck and squeezed, her feet dangling off the earth.

Her skin began to change colors, first to a bright red and then to blue, her eyes bulging in her head.

The glass reverberated beneath my fists, making a hollow noise that begged for my mother's life to be spared. Caylina howled next to me, intertwining with my own sobs. Mother's eyes began to flutter closed and I knew this was the end. My parents would both die tonight and I would be taken away.

Blinded by his rage, Clayton didn't see Balwdin rising from the shadows behind him. He stumbled forward, tripping over the mess of bodies before grabbing a discarded hatchet from the ground. The blade met Clayton's neck with such force his head nearly left his shoulders. Panting, Mother dropped to the dirt with a thud, losing consciousness for several seconds. Clayton's body laid lifelessly next to her.

My screams turned to sobs, both in relief that my mother had been saved, but also in anguish at what had been lost. Slowly, mother roused and crawled toward the lifeless body of my father. Her hands caressed his face, brushing hair from where it clung to his forehead.

The sun had broken the horizon, casting glorious light over the picturesque mountain lake. While Mother wept into my father's chest until she drifted to sleep upon him, I grieved alone.

I had been in this memory longer than any of my practices. My consciousness existed both as everything and nothing, in past and present—all at once. The fight had been drained from me. Was this what it would be like to be trapped in my own mind? To be forced to relive this memory over and over until the word itself ceased to exist?

When Mother finally returned to the house, my father having been burned to ashes that scattered in the wind, she was a ghost of her previous self—an empty shell that held nothing but hatred and blame for me.

Day and night mingled, the days passing in a blur of endless loneliness until my door was thrown open one morning. Squinting into the darkness, I could barely make out my mother's features, her body silhouetted in the growing light.

"Only bring the necessities. You won't be allowed to have much more," she commanded.

I stared blankly at her, sleep addling my mind, making it impossible to comprehend what she was saying.

"Why are you just sitting there?" she asked. "Start packing."

"Why?" I whispered.

"Speak up. You know I hate when you mumble."

I jerked back in surprise at her words, my head nearly hitting the headboard of the bed. Mother's eyes were lined in red, as they were most days, and she didn't bother to hide her anger through thin smiles anymore.

"Why?" I repeated, louder, enunciating the word.

She took large steps, crossing the room until she was standing over me. She dropped to a crouch, bringing her face closer—so close our breaths mingled and brushed against my cheeks.

"I can't do this anymore, Varine. I can't protect you any longer. I don't know what your father bargained for the block on your magic. I fear that they will come back for you, bringing more guards and I will not be able to stop them."

Tears built in my eyes and streamed down my cheeks. "I don't want to go. We can ask them to give my powers back and then I can stay!"

Mother shook her head. "It's not that easy."

"I don't want to go."

"There is no other choice. Start packing," Mother insisted. She walked to the doorway, her eyes glazing over and foggy like they had been since that night.

"Father said there is always a choice," I insisted.

She shook her head, gripping the handle of the door until her fingers turned white. "He's dead." Her words were blunt, and sharp enough to sting. Tears sprang to my eyes in response, threatening to overflow.

The door slammed behind her.

I rocked back and forth, sobs wracking through my body. Caylina jumped onto the bed and nudged at my arm, trying to comfort me. "I'm going to miss you," I cried, burying my face in her soft fur. She purred gently, a calming noise that helped my breathing slow.

When it returned to its normal cadence, I kissed her on the head, right on the little white spot that father had just a few nights ago. Mother's patience had been thin before, but now I knew she would not tolerate my avoidance of packing.

Packing had taken almost the entirety of the day, I had paused only to eat a quick lunch that Monet had brought to me. Each item in my room seemed to beg to join me on my new adventure, but only so much could fit into my small trunk.

I looked around what remained of my belongings that hadn't been packed away. My breath caught and lodged in the back of my throat when I noticed the green and black hardcover book laying on the vanity. I was scared to look away from the book now that I had noticed it, worried it would disappear from my life just as Father had.

I ran my fingers over the raised title, *The Trove of Dragons: A Complete History*. His voice still lingered in my mind, the sound of him reading aloud to me each night was one I would never forget. A single tear slipped down my cheek but I wiped it away, focusing instead on my anger.

They had cursed me; blocked my power. I blamed them for his death, and by default, the creator of them. If the gods had wanted me to have magic, they wouldn't have allowed it to be taken so easily.

Mother called for me up the stairs but I didn't join her for dinner. I was unable to bear the thought of sitting at the massive dining table where we had once sat together, with only silence left to fill the empty space.

Instead, I walked to the front porch and sat on the wooden porch swing. The turquoise waters of the mountain lake were rippling in a soft breeze. It was beautiful, it had always been. The sun was just beginning to set below the horizon, washing the sky in spectacular crimson and gold.

Baldwin sat next to me in silence, hands clasped in his lap. The sun dipped below the horizon. Flying, light-filled bugs began to buzz around the yard, flashing on and off in a special song.

"Do you now understand why you were never allowed to leave?" he asked. "You are far too special. Your parents were worried you would be found and hunted."

Hands that had rested in my lap, now clenched into fists. Anger rippled through me at his words. "I was found. I was hunted. People died because of me."

Baldwin's eyes were sad as they reached for my hand. When I pulled them away, he retreated, placing his palms in his lap. "They tried to protect you. *We* tried to protect you." He looked away, the silence lingering with all he wanted but couldn't say. "Odell was a good man that made a tough choice."

Fire rose in my chest, cheeks turning red with fury. They always gave away what I was feeling, unable to hide my emotions, just like Father. "Do not speak to me of my father's choices. You think you all know what is best, but all you do is remove my choice. If someone had bothered to ask me, I would have told them I wanted my magic. I wanted it, Baldwin." I paused, sucking in a breath from the words that had come out in a mad rush. "I feel empty without the power I know should be rushing through my veins. Where a spark should be, there is nothing."

I looked down at my hands, willing any power to come forth. But like always, nothing happened.

"I am sorry."

Remaining silent, we watched the bugs flit and dance around the yard. One landed on my hand and I softly closed it within my palm, looking through a small hole to see it illuminate and grow dark, over and over.

"And I'm sorry that I must ask this of you." He cleared his throat, drawing my attention back to him. His face was serious, the lines of his skin drawn taut. "You must not tell anyone who you are. Where you are going, you will only be safe if they do not know. Everywhere outside this home, they hunt magic wielders. If they know where you are, they will take you. Promise me, Varine. Promise me you will not tell anyone that you descend from the Crestin line."

My hand opened, releasing the creature back into the night. It danced in the air in front of me before flying off to join its partners. "I promise."

"I am truly sorry this is happening to you, Flower," he murmured, putting his large hand over mine.

Jumping to my feet I stormed for the front door. Fury once again raced through me. "Do. Not. Call. Me. That," I spat, enunciating each word. "Do not use the nickname he gave me when there is nothing left in me but thorns."

The world blurred before me, my heart hammering in my chest. Hidden under the security of my blanket, I willed my body to sleep, to ease the ache that raged in my chest, but it evaded me. I knew I needed to rest; the journey to my new life would likely be long, but I was too filled with anger. The conversation with Baldwin repeated in my head, the promises I had made searing into my soul.

Before I knew it, the rage opened a dam to my sadness. I allowed the tears to consume me until I was lulled into a fitful sleep. Caylina snored lightly next to me as my eyelids floated closed.

And snapped open once again.

CHAPTER 19

"Isn't it funny how your own memories can trick you? What the mind will do to protect you?" Amias asked from where he leaned against the wall. "Congratulations. You passed your first Trial. However, I'm not impressed by how long it took you, and I'm not happy the Crestins made you my problem."

Bracing my hand on the arm of the chair, I sat up, finally free of the darkness and the memory it brought with it. A blinding pain raced through my head, shooting stars into my vision from the bright lights around us. My palms dug into my eyes, not wanting to look at Amias now that he knew the secret I had promised to keep.

"You didn't know?" I asked incredulously. My voice was uneven and raspy from disuse. I had been in the Simulation for what felt like hours—days even.

My breaths came in short bursts, the air I took in doing nothing to satiate my starving lungs. My father had died to protect me as I stood watching, unable to do anything. And when I needed her the most, my mother had all but abandoned me in the wake of tragedy. I had been thrown out like garbage and was forced to find an entirely new family.

I was so sure Amias had known who I was, so it was shocking to find out that I had successfully hid something from the king of deception. Proud wasn't the word I would describe my feelings with, but satisfied would do the trick.

"I never watched your Simulation practice."

I looked up at Amias, blinking as my eyes adjusted to the bright, overhead lights. His jaw clenched and unclenched, clearly fighting back his rage. I quickly looked away, staring at my fists in my lap. Feeling more and more like that little girl trapped in her mountain home, her choices stripped away.

"We have nothing if we do not have trust," he said, baring his teeth.

"I couldn't tell you. I made a promise."

"You are a liar," he stated. I whipped my gaze to him, mouth dropping open to protest but he raised a hand to silence me. "A lie of omission is no less of a lie."

"I made a promise," I repeated. "One that I kept for eight years, and that I plan to continue keeping. I thought the Order valued loyalty?" I sneered. "Is this not a true testament to how loyal I can be?"

Amias had been angry with me before, but the way his rage was so blatantly displayed across his features was new. He did not often lose the mask of cool composure that he kept so carefully in place.

He moved with feline grace, so quickly that he crossed the room before I could blink. Gripping my chin between his fingers, he pulled it up until our eyes met. The strength of his grip was so tight I knew I would find fingertip bruises.

"You are to be loyal to *me!*" he shouted.

I tried to jerk my head back, but he held it firm in his grasp. Anger rippled across his face, his gaze boring into mine for only a brief moment but it felt like an eternity. Seeming to realize his error he dropped my face and crossed his arms across his chest. His muscles clenched with the last strand of restraint he was holding on to like a tether in a storm.

"You are to be loyal to me," he repeated, his words now soft and hushed, with a firmness I had come to expect.

Amias held my past, present, and future in his hands and it frightened me to think of what he might do with them. The man before me kept his emotions so tightly restrained that they roared from freedom when they snapped their leash. One wrong move from me could set him off and there would be no going back. No more secrets to keep, and no more future.

Fear was an ugly creature that sent chills down my spine. At this moment, I would say and do just about anything to keep Amias from ruining everything I could be. I nodded my head; just a slight dip of my chin in acknowledgment of his demands.

It was ultimately a lie.

I really was the liar he claimed me to be.

I did not want to be loyal, not to the Order, not to Amias, and certainly not to anyone but myself. I spent way too long locked away and I wouldn't let my father's sacrifice be for nothing. Just like the past eight years, I would do what I needed to survive. I would pass the Trials, remain hidden, and figure out how to get my magic back.

Coming to know the sound far too personally, I didn't flinch when Amias slammed the door behind him. His hasty exit left me only a second's view of the hallway where Cenric could be seen slumped against the wall in slumber.

Tears flowed hot and fast down my cheeks. By the time they had run out, exhaustion was threatening to take hold, but the Simulation room had become claustrophobic, the walls threatening to close around me. I felt like I was suffocating, trapped in the endless pit of despair my heart had become.

The memory had ripped everything from me, but it had also given me purpose, a goal beyond the Order.

Desma had torn apart families for the last time. I would make sure no other child had to endure what I did, that no other parent had to watch their child be dragged away like the woman outside Tully's. It had gone on long enough and I would see the end of it, even if I had to reignite the rebellion to see it through.

By the time I had composed myself enough to leave I had lost track of the time. Was it still the same day as before? Everything was numb, save for the guilt that rested like a sharp stone in my stomach. Guilt that I would carry with me, for my entire life, the edges rounding but ever present.

My legs shook beneath me as I pushed myself from the chair, my fingertips digging into the sturdy wood arms. Though the Time Keeper and the Record

Holder remained in the room, I had never felt so alone. I needed to get out of here before my thoughts consumed me, swallowing me whole.

Neither creature had acknowledged me after the Trial, both standing straight against the wall, hooded cloaks concealing their faces as always. I was grateful they had not spoken or tried to comfort me. What I had needed was the time to process the memory, and they had given me exactly that.

I reached for the door handle, looking at the hooded figures one last time, unsure if I would see them again now that the Trial was complete.

"Varine," the Time Keeper called to me, holding out their gnarled, boney hand.

Hesitantly, I held the creature's fingers in mine, too shocked by the motion to understand what was happening.

"For what you have given, and what you shall receive, we thank you." The creature's voice was like a wild wind coursing through the room, enveloping me in cold.

"What does that mean?" I asked. They squeeze once before dropping their hand and returning to the wall to stand silently by the Record Holder. I wanted to ask again what they meant, but I knew I would get nothing in return.

I had the distinct feeling that I had been shattered and pieced back together. That this was both the beginning and the end.

CHAPTER 20

C enric jumped to his feet and wrapped me in the warm embrace of his arms before I could fully exit the room. He smelled of sweat and citrus, the clothes he wore wrinkled and dirty from wear. I buried my face into his muscular chest, clinging to him as if I could be pulled back under at any moment. My fingertips dug into his back, likely marring his skin, but he didn't so much as flinch.

"You made it," he whispered into my hair.

The evening sun was low in the sky, casting shadows along the corridor from the few windows that lined the hallway. The day began and ended in a blur of emotion as I held onto him. He was my lifeline, a raft in the tumultuous sea.

He pulled back to look at me, one hand grazing my shoulder while the other smoothed the tangled strands of my hair. His eyes searched mine, filled with emotion that I couldn't recognize.

"Are you done?" I asked, eyes frantically searching his. "You've completed your Trial?"

"I did. Melba went in right after me." His eyes sparked with emotion, the light reflecting off his jade eyes as he watched me intently.

I sighed with relief. "Did Amias drug you too?"

"Ewelyn laced my water while we were sparring. It made the match even more interesting," he said with a half smile.

"Are you okay?"

"No," he admitted. "Are you?"

"No."

Pulling me back into his arms he squeezed me tightly, his chin resting on the top of my head. "Varine," he whispered, my name a plea on his lips. A sob caught in my throat, threatening to undo me once again. "Varine."

Here in his arms I could imagine what a life with him could be like. My friend who could be so much more if only I wasn't so afraid of what that meant.

If things had been different and we had met under different circumstances, our love could have been like the fairytales Melba reads about. If we hadn't chosen to pursue a future where nothing was certain, everything could be different. We were two pieces of a puzzle, fitting together despite the conflicting illustrations on our jagged edges.

Looking up at him, all I could see was sadness. Tear stains carved paths down his cheeks, eyes rimmed in red. His fingers traced a slow circle on my back, while one hand tangled in my hair. We stood intertwined until our breaths became one, our hearts matching the beat of the other in a steady rhythm.

"Would you tell me what you faced?" I asked, mumbling the words into his chest.

"What?"

Pushing back with my hands on his chest I looked up at him. "In the Trial. Would you tell me what memory you had to face?"

He pursed his lips together, staring wordlessly at me. A realization jerked me out of the haze that was his comfort. I knew nothing of his past or where he came from, nor his motivations for joining the Order. I knew barely anything about him. Maybe he would tell me what he faced someday, and I could find a pebble of courage to share a piece of mine.

"It doesn't have to be now," I added.

"Varine." He sighed. "Can this wait? You're putting a damper on the moment we're sharing."

"Excuse me?" I asked incredulously, pulling out of his arms. He grunted in annoyance at the break in our connection. "I wasn't asking you to spill your soul to me in this hallway."

"I didn't mean it like that."

I took a step back, searching his eyes for whatever his intent had been. "How did you mean it then?"

"Trouble in paradise?" a high voice asked. Gedeon and his lapdog Xarissa appeared from around a bend in the hall.

"Mind your own business," Cenric snapped. He reached for me but I danced out of the way. This wouldn't be the end of that conversation. I wouldn't force him to tell me, but I wanted him to open up, just a little, or this would never work. If we couldn't trust each other, who could we trust?

Xarissa stuck out her lip. "Awe, the honeymoon phase is already over before it could even begin. What a shame."

I turned on her, baring my teeth. "Fuck off, Xarissa. I don't have the time nor the patience to deal with you right now."

Gedeon stepped forward, trying to shield her from my words. "Don't you talk to her like that."

I rolled my eyes. "You can fuck off too."

She pushed him out of the way, stalking toward me. Cenric blocked her way, hand outstretched to keep her from coming any closer. "Now's not the best time for settling any grudges. Melba's still in her Simulation, and we all have a lot to process," he tried to reason.

Looking at the closed doorway that sat adjacent to the Simulation room I had escaped from, I knew Melba had to be inside. I looked back at the people in front of me and made a choice I hoped I wouldn't regret.

The door handle was cold in my hand for only a moment before a strong hand gripped my bicep, ripping me away.

My head whipped to see Cenric holding me firmly. The movement was so harsh compared to what we had just shared. "Don't, Varine."

"She could be trapped, Cenric! I'm not just going to stand here and do nothing," I spat through gritted teeth. "Let go of me."

He jerked his hand away as if my skin had caused him pain.

"Go on then, get yourself disqualified and Amias can kill you instead of me," Xarissa crooned with far too much delight twinkling in her eyes.

"She'll only get disqualified if she tries to wake her up," Cenric countered, turning to me. "And you're not going to do that, right?"

I threw my hands out wide in exasperation. "I'm not stupid. It's similar to a coma, just my presence should be enough to offer her support."

"That's unfortunate, I already had the wood ready for your pyre."

Cenric looked to Gedeon. "Can you get her out of here before it's *her* body that will burn? I'm not going to continue to hold Varine back."

Unsure if Cenric would prevent me from entering the room, I used the seconds of his distraction to my advantage. Without waiting for the conversation to end, I slipped into the Simulation room, shutting the door softly behind me.

CHAPTER 21

"How long?"

My eyes were trained on Melba, her unconscious body lay draped upon a plush chaise made of velvet. I received no answer from the Time Keeper or Record Holder of this room, their shrouded silhouettes remaining silent and unmoving.

"How. Long?" I demanded, stepping toward the towering figures. "Answer me, I know you can speak."

The door opened and Cenric slipped in, shutting it softly behind him. His eyes swept the room before focusing on me. "Varine," he whispered, reaching for my arm. "You're going to get yourself killed."

I ripped away from his reach, worried that he would try to drag me from the room if he got a good grip on me. Taking another step toward the creatures, I was mere inches from them, the closest I had ever dared to be.

Their shadowed faces were featureless beneath their hoods. The one windowed room, cast in near darkness, made it impossible to discern if they had a reaction to my proximity. There I waited, locked in a bizarre fight for dominance, wondering who would relent first.

"Varine," Cenric said again.

I grunted, debating ignoring him altogether. "I'm a little busy right now."

After what felt like the passing of a lifetime, the creatures nodded their heads in unison. A voice drifted into my mind, the sound trickling across my skin and reverberating in my bones. "Almost ten minutes."

Startled by the intrusion, I stumbled backward into Cenric's awaiting arms.

"Did you hear that?" I asked.

"Hear what?"

Mind-speaking was not something I was aware these creatures could do since the ones in my room had spoken outright. Did they have other powers we were uninformed of? And if so, what else were they hiding?

"They spoke to me, in my mind. She's been in the Simulation for almost ten minutes," I told Cenric.

"They did *what?*" he stammered.

Ignoring the question, I went to Melba's side. Taking her hand in mine, I traced my thumb over the back of Melba's icy knuckles. Her heavy, limp arm reminded me too much of the bodies that had littered my front yard. Of my father who never opened his eyes again.

The ground where I knelt beside her was just as cold as her skin. Though I found myself shivering, I wouldn't dare move.

That was a dangerous amount of time. Ten minutes was the longest anyone on record had remained in the Simulation, and successfully made it back to consciousness. Melba was dancing right on the edge. If she didn't wake very soon, I might never get my friend back. My heart pounded in my chest at the possibility, panic rising and threatening to take me under.

Slowly, I counted the dark colored stones that made up the floor, skipping over any rock that was not black. Finishing this task, I attempted to count the lines on Melba's palms. My panic slowly started to recede with each ascending number.

Sixty-seven black rocks.

Sixteen prominent lines.

When my heart rate began to slow, I counted each breath. Willing the fear to return to the little box I had made for it within myself.

One, breathe in.

Two, breathe out.

I looked from Melba to the creatures at the far end of the room, debating whether it would be worth it to interfere. But even if I did, I didn't know how to wake her. Was there even a way to rouse her from the memory? Would my punishment be in exchange for her life, or would she die as well?

Melba's eyes moved beneath her lids, her nostrils flaring with each exhale. I squeezed her hand, attempting to offer any support I could. She had often hinted through passing remarks that her home life before the Order had been anything but a fairytale. The passing comments about her father being the "most frightening man she had ever encountered," often led to her boasting that she could face anything.

Now that I had faced my own memory, I knew how terrible reliving something like that could be. It was lonely and soul crushing to face alone and I wanted nothing more than to take her pain away.

My fingers stroked her hair, outlining the curves and contours of her sleeping face. I committed each breath to memory. The way she smelled, the way she moved, I wanted to savor every last detail knowing that it would likely be the last time I could.

Ten minutes had come and passed, the seconds ticking on, her chances of waking up growing slimmer and slimmer. She let out a little whimper, her eyelashes fluttering. My heart leaped in my chest and began to race in hope. I squeezed her hand hoping it would lead her back to me, but she did not rouse. I sent up a silent prayer, hoping that if the gods truly existed, they would find me in their favor.

Please. Please let her live. Please.

Like I had known it would, it went unanswered and time continued to tick on.

"Would you like to see?" Amias's velvet voice asked from the doorway. He looked like a divine being, backlit by the bright hallway with a cape tucked around him. His eyes held a softness; a look I could only describe as pity. If I had not begun to grieve the loss of my friend already, I might have been angry at him for that expression.

Amias tapped the mirror wall and a blue-white light began to emanate from it, gradually becoming brighter until it filled the room.

"I can show you."

To view one's darkest memory without permission was, without a doubt, an invasion. Melba had never shared this with me in consciousness, and had very deliberately avoided it whenever it was brought up in conversation. I would be a thief to take that which was not freely given. But that did not stop me from wanting it—from wanting to know her better in what might be her last moments.

I wanted every last piece of her that I could tuck into a box in my mind, storing her away for the times when I needed her. But that didn't mean it wasn't wrong. Before I could stop my traitorous lips, I found the word leaving my mouth. "Yes."

"Varine," Cenric started, his tone a warning.

Amias waved his hand dismissively at him, his attention never leaving me. "Enough. I was not speaking to you." Cenric's eyes nearly bulged from his head, his mouth opening and closing in successions. He made a small noise of protest before thinking better of it and snapping his mouth shut.

A nod of Amias's head to the creatures had the room filled with light in one burst at the snap of their boney fingers. I shielded my eyes at the sudden brightness, the imprint of a bright flare visible behind my closed lids.

When I felt as if it would burn through me, it faded to a soft picture of the inside of a beautiful mansion. A small girl, not much older than five, sat crossed-legged on an ornamental rug, brushing the long hair of a doll that looked identical to her.

CHAPTER 22

A young Melba's hair was braided into two pigtails that draped on either side of her shoulders. She wore a lace-covered white dress that puffed around her shoulders and fell across her knees. In the large bedroom she looked like a doll in a playhouse, the room painted shades of pink and white, ribbons and ruffles adorning every surface.

Large crystals and flickering balls of light dangled from a large chandelier above her head. The bed was pressed against one wall, and was much too large for such a young child. While a dainty white vanity sat against another, the chair was still pulled out and trinkets were scattered across the top. The two large windows cast rays of sunshine around the room and gave way to sprawling greenery beyond them.

The courtyard was vast, consisting of sparkling water features and immaculately pruned gardens. If the room and surrounding grounds were any indication, the family residing in it likely had large amounts of wealth.

Despite the lovely home, Melba sat on her floor with nothing but sadness in her eyes and tears streaking her cheeks. Softly she sang, her voice rising and falling with each brush through the doll's curls.

> *"You're my sunshine when the clouds are gray,*
> *With you beside me everything's okay.*
> *Your love is my light, always shining bright;*
> *With you beside me everything will be alright."*

Crashing and yelling sounded from somewhere outside the room, her voice growing louder to drown out the noise. The movement of her hands on her doll became frantic as the noises grew closer.

She paused, tensing as her eyes darted toward the door and back to the doll. Fear was evident in her tiny features and in the way she now clung to the doll. She continues the song, more tears leaking from her eyes and staining her dress. Her voice wavered with each lyric she sang, the words doing nothing to comfort her.

> "In my arms, you'll be so safe,
> A love so warm, here in my embrace.
> As you grow older, I hope you know
> I'm the one who loves you so."

The last word caught in her throat, coming out choked. Her soundless tears turned to soft sobs that she tried to muffle in the fabric of her dress. A woman's screaming and a loud thump could be heard much closer than the noises before. She looked around her room wildly, presumably looking for a place to hide.

I could feel my own pulse racing as I watched her terrified form half crawl, half run, toward her bed and throw herself under. Draped fabric of the duvet shielded her small body from the view of whatever was coming toward her room.

This was wrong. I made a mistake and I couldn't watch any longer.

"I'm done," I told Amias, despite my inability to remove my eyes from the picture in front of me. The knuckles of my hand that gripped Melba's had turned shades of white.

Amias responded dismissively. "You wanted to watch, so watch."

The wooden bedroom door was cast open so harshly that it slammed into the wall leaving dents in the wood and reverberating through the room. The same markings that had been left many times before it seemed, as the deep imprints became visible as the door rebounded.

A gruff-looking man entered the room, grasping at the door frame with one hand while clutching a brown bottle in the other. Half of his shirt was untucked and the vest he wore over the top had lost all three of its buttons. His pant legs were coated in dried mud, pieces of which fell onto the carpet with each stumble. I could practically smell the sour and stale scent he looked like he would emit. As the man staggered around the room, his head swiveled, looking for something, or someone.

"I know she's in here," he slurred. His eyelids drooped slightly but his teeth were bared in clear anger.

A woman entered the room, reaching for him. Her hair partially covered what appeared to be a black eye, and her bare arms were dotted in fingerprint bruises. Melba peered through a tiny portion of open area where the bedding failed to reach the floor, her body shaking in fear at what she saw.

She cast a hand across her mouth, covering the sobs that racked through her body.

"She's not here. Come to bed, sweetheart," the woman said; most likely her mother, as they bore a similar resemblance. Her voice was laced with faux kindness, the kind that you used to entice a stray animal, or a small child. Though her tone remained calm, her eyes were just as frantic as Melba's.

The man stumbled into the vanity, knocking bottles and brushes to the ground. Glass containers shattered, and Melba let out a yelp as pieces nicked her cheek.

"My love," her mother called, pulling gently on the man in an attempt to lead him from the room.

He grunted, tripping over the doll that had been left in the middle of the carpet. He caught himself and stopped to pick it up.

Using two fingers he held up the doll, letting it dangle from his fingertips. Leaning against the wall, he took a swig from the bottle in his hand. Angry at finding it empty, it was cast away where it shattered against the far wall.

The woman flinched but continued her sickly sweet words in an effort to protect her daughter. "Come, sweetheart. Let's go to bed." She pulled gently on his arm, guiding him toward the exit.

For a moment, he let her lead him, but as he neared the exit, he ripped his arm away from her and dropped the doll back to the ground.

"Do not touch me, woman," he grunted, nearly falling over from the movement. "Come on out, Melba!" he called. "I know you're here."

Little Melba let out a soft whimper, her hands pressing into the soft skin of her face as she tried to muffle the sound. Her father's eyes turned feral with rage, sliding into a savage mockery of a grin.

Booted footsteps moved clumsily toward the bed, stopping just as the tips of his toes peeked under the skirt.

"Amias, please. I don't want to watch this anymore," I begged. I had a feeling I knew where this was going and I couldn't stand to watch but was completely unable to look away on my own.

Melba's fear was palpable, the terror of and for my best friend freezing me in place. He ignored me, leaning against the far wall by the creatures, and continued to let the scene play out before us.

Slowly, the man dropped to his hands and knees, moving the bed skirt away in a gesture that was far too gentle for the violence I'm sure was about to ensue. Melba screamed as his drunken, weathered face appeared in front of her. She scrambled for the opposite side of the bed, her body struggling to slide due to her frantic movements.

Clawing at the ground, her small body just couldn't move fast enough. Her father's large hand reached for her and tangled in the hair at her scalp.

"There you are," he crooned. She thrashed and clawed, drawing blood from the skin of his hands but he remained unfazed by her attack, slowly pulling her from safety by the hair clenched in his fist.

What had I done? "Turn it off."

He continued to ignore my begging even when Cenric jumped in. "She's seen enough, turn it off."

My eyes were transfixed on the horrible scene. I wanted, no *needed* to look away but my body continued to betray my screaming thoughts.

"Please! You're hurting her!" the woman yelled. She pulled on the man's arm, grabbing at the fabric of his shirt. He shrugged the woman off, refusing to release Melba.

Her terror had turned to soft whimpers, her face contorted in pain and fear. Tears stained her round cheeks, dripping to the floor below. The woman reached for the man again, pulling on anything her fingers could grasp. She begged him to release Melba.

"Sweetheart. Come to bed. Please. Leave the girl. Come to bed."

He shoved her away forcefully, her body hitting the ground in a crumpled mess. Despite his drunken haze, his large stature and muscle were no match for the small woman and child.

"Shut your mouth, bitch. I'll deal with you next."

Melba thrashed in his hands, her desperation raged anew at the sight of her mother's body, crawling toward them on her hands and knees. Melba's fingers dug into the underside of the bed and the wooden slats of the floor, her body contorting to grip anything that would keep her out of her father's hands.

When her small body came into view, robbed of the small amount of protection the underside of the bed had offered, he dangled her in front of his face.

She cringed away, the fight draining from her as she hung limply in his hands.

"There you are."

The mirror went black, plunging the room into familiar darkness. My panting breaths the only sound.

CHAPTER 23

An invisible grime coated my skin, marking me as a traitor to my greatest friend. My entire body felt dirty from the intrusion. I knew, without a shred of doubt, that I would regret the decision I had made to view the intimate parts of Melba's life without her permission. The parts she had kept so perfectly hidden from the world were never mine to take.

I was a hypocrite, having just done the exact thing to my friend that I had been so angry about—the loss of my autonomy.

Her perfect smile never showed the atrocities that she experienced. I often let my anger and fear leak into my interactions with others, taking out my emotions on anyone near enough when they overwhelmed me. But not Melba, no, she was never like that. She treated everyone as if their presence in her life was a gift given to her from the gods.

My poor, kind hearted friend was probably gone forever. Who knew how long that memory had been repeating before we witnessed it. I didn't know what to expect next. What did it look like for someone to be trapped in their own mind? I wondered if it might be better to kill her than to allow her to exist as an empty shell.

Bile rose in my throat at the very thought. Sobs threatened to break from deep within my chest. The Order was taking everything from me and I was nothing but a complicit victim.

The taste of salty iron flooded my mouth from where my lip had been chewed to a bloody mess. It should have been me that didn't make it out. Melba deserved so much more.

Amias broke what felt like a never-ending silence. Stretching and rolling his shoulders, he placed his hands into his pockets. "Have this be a lesson, Varine. Do not ask for what you do not truly want." His words were flippant, uninterested. "If I were you, I would say my goodbyes."

He was right, too much time had passed. Watching her memory, it felt like an eternity had passed in the span of five minutes. Fifteen minutes into a Simulation was too long, she was gone.

Cenric pushed off the wall he had been leaning against, taking long strides toward Amias until they were nearly nose to nose. He had been so quiet that I had nearly forgotten his presence.

His lips curled back to expose his teeth, hands clenched into fists at his sides. I thought he would strike Amias for a moment, and I'm fairly certain he thought so too.

"It would do you well to remember your place," Amias chided, refusing to back down from Cenric's approach. Amias stood taller than him by just a hair, but Amias exuded an air of confidence that Cenric lacked.

A confidence that only came with time, something Amias seemed to have plenty of despite looking to be barely older than us. Cenric's body shook with his barely restrained rage. Amias was as calm and poised as ever as he took a step toward him, a cold smirk on his face.

Cenric's fists opened and closed at his sides. Amias was taunting him, trying to get him to play into his little game of dominance. I couldn't lose another friend. Cenric was all I had left now.

My heart broke in my chest, the tiny shards lodging themselves into the walls of the vacant cavity. What was I supposed to do now? The idea of carrying on without her stung worse than being stabbed.

Cenric refused to release the glare he and Amias shared. Tension built through the room as we all seemed to await the first blow. He began to raise his fist, bracing his posture for the inevitable one he would receive in return. I opened my mouth to call out to him, to end the fight that would get us nowhere, but a voice came that wasn't mine,

"Don't." The word was raspy, coming out as if it had stuck to both sides of the throat.

My head snapped back to Melba to find her eyes open and blinking away tears that streamed down her face. Her voice gravely and weak as mine had been too.

I threw my body over hers, burying my face in her abdomen. A rush of relief brought new tears to my eyes, staining her shirt in puddled marks.

"Don't," she repeated when neither Cenric or Amias moved, both frozen in place by the shock of Melba's consciousness.

Cenric's face colored in relief, his clenched fists now loose at his sides. He took staggering steps toward Melba and dropped to his knees beside me. Amias didn't move his feet, but crossed his arms in clear dissatisfaction. "Time?" he asked.

"Seventeen minutes, forty-six seconds."

Amias made a sound low in his throat. "A new record, Melba. However, not a good one. I'm thoroughly unimpressed with the performance of all three of you." When none of us responded, too wrapped up in each other to bother, he left the room without another word.

Anyone waking up after ten minutes was unheard of. But after seventeen minutes? Incredible. Melba wouldn't be winning any awards for her speed, but a win was a win. She was alive, she made it out, and she would move on to the next Trial with us. I was so relieved I could dance and sing, but I would settle for holding my best friend for as long as possible.

We walked Melba to her room when exhaustion threatened to take hold of us all. I placed a kiss on her head, before softly closing her door behind me. Finding myself alone in the hallway with Cenric, I didn't have the energy to say much more than a quick "goodnight." He hugged me gently, releasing me just as fast as it began and stepping away.

With one hand on the doorknob, I nodded to Cenric, offering him a half smile before disappearing into my room. I waited until his soft footsteps faded before sneaking off to my favorite place, which no one knew existed in this world, but me. I couldn't think about sleeping, not at a time like this. I couldn't stomach the idea of closing my eyes, I knew what visions would haunt me, and the thought of reliving them twice in one day made me ill.

CHAPTER 24

The dawn was just starting to rise, threading gold shimmering rays down every corridor. This was my favorite time of the day, when the sun was not yet strong enough to create harsh light, leaving everything washed in delicate, muted tones.

I passed the dining room and thought of my father's face, the way he smiled and leaned in whenever I spoke. As I passed the study rooms, I thought of his last moments, of my mother's screams still ringing in my ears. Shaking my head, I tried to clear the vivid images from my eyes, but they fought to remain.

I walked down past the interview rooms in the first basement, and past the teaching rooms where I had been forced to poison myself. My footsteps echoed in the empty hallways, far too loud for the tunneled catacombs I entered through a secret passage at the end of a hallway.

This tunnel was built for emergency use, exiting to the forest that lined the property's perimeter. Cobwebs coated the walls, dust floating in the air on the breeze created by my movements. I ran my fingers over the jagged mismatched stones of the long tunnel, allowing my other senses to guide me in the dark.

I needed to get away, one never knew how stifled they were until they tasted freedom, and these tunnels reeked of my liberation.

Despite still being unsure of my future, I convinced myself that a few moments alone would be well worth it. When I returned, I could scour the library for information on magical creatures and the favors they could grant. There had to be information somewhere on how to undo a bargain with a dragon, and if any library would hold it, it would be here.

Veering right, I began to climb the crumbling uneven steps that wound upward in tight loops. The metal handrail swayed and groaned under my weight but I pressed forward, using it to propel myself up the steps at almost a run. The air in the tunnel had become suffocating, my lungs threatening to give up if I did not get out soon. Though I knew, deep down, there was plenty of oxygen, my mind began to panic from its endless turning.

The list of things I did not know was now far longer than the one containing my current knowledge. I didn't know the price of the magical block, or if it had been fully paid. I didn't know why Queen Desma wanted me, or what prophecy I was meant to fulfill. And I certainly didn't know if Amias would keep my secret, or if my death was imminent.

I did know three thing though, I was alive, I had survived, and I was going to burn this place to the ground so that no one else had to be subjected to this torture.

Cold wind pricked my skin as I exited the ramshackle hut that guarded the entrance. Stepping into the evergreens surrounding this side of the mountain range, the wards rippled blue when I passed through them. Unlike the ones that protected my childhood home, these were not designed to trap me within.

The sound of distant rushing water had me following the familiar path I had woven among the trees. My favorite spot in the world was calling to me like a siren in the sea.

I patted my side, feeling for the Dragon blade I had hastily tucked into a holster. Away from the keep was the perfect place to examine it without all the watchful eyes.

As I stepped through an especially dense thicket, I found myself rewarded with rushing water, cascading from the cliffs high above me. Three tiers of waterfalls flowed into pools at the base of each. Rushing whitewater tickled my skin before draining into the river below. The second tier was my favorite, just high enough that I could view the vast valley below, and the pool shallow enough that I didn't risk washing away.

Bright rays of light from the now risen sun chased the shadows across the distant farm lands. Chimneys began to fill with smoke, and farmers turned out their animals for the day. The thick spray of water obscured the view, but I had spent so much time here that I knew it all too well.

I cleared the loose pebbles from the side of the pool with my foot, creating an area for me to sit without rocks stabbing into me. Satisfied that I had sufficiently removed them, I sat and removed my boots. My toes dipped into the icy waters sending a chill up my spine. It was a welcome distraction, giving me something to focus on other than the thoughts in my brain.

Birds chirped in the trees and as they passed overhead. The last remnants of the evening's insects were finishing up their songs before turning in for the night. It was so peaceful here; a cacophony of noise that was somehow still unabashedly beautiful in its own way.

The rock at my back had been worn from the years I had spent pressed against it, becoming a resting place that fit me perfectly. The heat of the day and the cold swirl of water on my feet made my eyelids begin to flutter closed. Fresh mountain air filled my lungs and spirit, rejuvenating me while it weaved through the forest. All the memories of the Trial and what I would soon face left my head, replaced by a peacefulness I hadn't felt in some time.

In a few moments I would need to return to the keep. I would sleep in my bed, facing the horrible memories on repeat, and then I would wake and face another day. But for now, I could rest my weary eyes and relish in the freedom of the swirling waters and rushing wind.

Dangling on the precipice of sleep, I felt a sigh of contentment leave my lips. Just a few more minutes.

Fingers gripped my shoulder, jolting me awake and out of the deep, relaxing state I had been transfixed in. I ripped a dagger from its sheath and whirled to face whoever had dared intrude.

"Fuck, Cenric! You scared the shit out of me," I breathed, air whooshing out of me. I put my hand over my heart's rapid beating, feeling it race beneath my fingertips. It had been so long since someone had snuck up on me, catching me by surprise. Cenric stood still, watching me with a boyish grin plastered on his handsome face.

"It's a really good thing you're an assassin and not a spy. You would make a really shit spy, Varine," he taunted.

"Oh, fuck you." I grabbed the nearest handful of pebbles and tossed them in Cenric's direction. Not a single one hit him.

He spun in a circle, surveying my special hidden place, that was no longer my secret. He let out a sharp whistle before turning to face me again. "You've been holding out on me. Is this where you sneak off to?"

"I didn't *sneak* anywhere," I answer shortly.

Cenric laughed, a deep chuckle that was low and rough. Gods I loved that sound. It sounded like happiness. I couldn't help the smile that spread across my face in the wake of his laughter. "Then why did I have to follow you to find out about it?" he asked.

When I didn't answer he sat next to me, removing his boots as I had. He kicked his feet in the water, sending water droplets in the air that created a rainbow of light before splashing on my tunic.

I know it hadn't been his intention to make me feel poorly about hiding this place from him, but I could feel a swell of guilt building in the pit of my stomach anyway. I wanted one place in this world that belonged to nobody and nothing but me. But was it really fair to hide yet another piece of myself from this man that I claimed to care for? We sat in content silence, both watching the way the water traveled over our submerged feet and down to the next fall.

He opened his mouth to speak but I stopped him before any words could leave his mouth. I knew exactly what he was going to say and I didn't think I was ready for it.

"I'm not talking about it."

He shrugged, pressing his lips together. "Guess we'll sit in silence then."

Silence was the noise that filled every crevice of the mountain home after my father's death. Silence was the emptiness I felt after each life I took. And I couldn't stand it anymore.

That was why I loved my little waterfall spot. It was never silent. Nature itself was very rarely quiet—the rushing water, the chirping birds, the flying insects. Relaxing, but never silent.

I stumbled upon this mountain oasis early on. The first weeks in the keep had been overwhelming, so naturally I looked for a place to escape to. A place that had never been stained by my past, or brushed by my future.

Even now, the remnants of my glyph scribbling were visible in the disturbed dirt around us. Piles of dirt swept here and there to cover the distinct lines that were invisible to most, but were etched into the back of my eyelids, visible even as I slept. I had made sure that the drawings were erased by my boots before leaving each time, but now, sitting here with Cenric, I worried that he would notice my treachery.

Cenric threw his head back, whistling a tune that sounded oddly familiar but I couldn't quite place. His arms were braced behind him, supporting the weight of his body. He peaked one eye open, tilting his head to look at me.

I let out an exasperated sigh before conceding, just a little. "A secret for a secret?" I asked.

"Fine. But you're going first."

"Fine."

"Fine," he mimicked.

Sticking my tongue out at him only resulted in another of his beautiful, near musical chuckles. I searched my thoughts for something small that I could give. A tiny piece of me that wouldn't give away any real truth.

The truth that I wanted, almost needed to share with him. The thought was terrifying.

What if he decided that I wasn't worth the risk? That it wasn't worth the danger that came with being with a magic wielder? Especially one that Queen Desma had gone to great lengths to find and was likely still searching for.

On the other hand, how could I ever concede to the thread that was pulling us together if we didn't know each other fully? Cenric was as guarded as I was, keeping his secrets hidden behind the locked bars of his heart just as well as I did. Did it make me a hypocrite for wanting what I was too afraid to give?

"I'm waiting," he crooned in the melody of the tune he had been whistling.

"I'm thinking," I grumbled. "Stop rushing me." But I wasn't. I was stalling and he knew it. "My favorite color is yellow."

This was not the secret that he wanted, I could tell by the look of disappointment that flashed through his eyes just briefly, but it was still something I had never shared. Trivial facts, small intricacies of our beings, were never something we had the time or luxury to discuss.

"Yellow," he repeated. "Why?"

A wistful laugh escaped my lips at his question. "It's the color of the first rays of light as the sun greets the new day. It's the promise of tomorrow as the night takes hold." He smiled at me, mine matching his in return. "It's the color of happiness and good. It's the color of fire after a long winter day, warming my bones."

It was the color of the flowers that grew in my father's garden and the ribbon he once weaved into my long braids. A bright shade for a childhood that should have been matching.

He stared wordlessly at me, the biggest grin I had ever seen gracing his handsome features.

"What?" I asked.

"You're incredible."

"Oh—" I started to object, but he raised a hand to cut me off.

"You are, Varine. I've known it from the very moment I met you that you were someone special. You remind me of yellow. You remind me of all the beautiful things you just said." He paused, reaching to place his palm on my cheek. "I think my new favorite color is yellow, you've fully convinced me."

I blinked in surprise at his words and the soft touch of his skin against mine. His eyes bore into me with such intensity, my entire body heating from his stare.

Alone, I had been so alone for so long. I leaned into his hand, closing my eyes, savoring the touch. His touch. I could let myself forget for just one moment.

"I don't know how to swim."

The tender moment was lost in his confession. I bit my lip trying to hide the laughter I knew my eyes gave away. They were filled with tears from the effort of holding back my amusement.

He feigned hurt, throwing his hand to his chest. "Don't you laugh at me," he bantered. "I gave you my secret!"

"That is the most ridiculous thing I have ever heard. How can you not swim?"

He laughed then too, shrugging his shoulders. "I never had a reason to learn."

"We'll have to remedy that sometime."

"I'd like that."

The heat of the late summer day was now fully upon us. Despite the chill of my toes in the rushing water, sweat dripped down my back. I was debating heading back to the keep to finally rest after the events of the previous evening.

"How about a secret for another secret?" he asked. "Something real this time?"

My pulse quickened. "Are you finally going to tell me about your mysterious past?"

"Are you?" he argued.

I swallowed loudly. His hand found mine, our fingers intertwining, his thumb brushing the back of my hand. My stomach fluttered, turning over. The last of my reservations melted away with the touch. It was now or never.

"I'm a Witch. Or, well, sort of."

The circles he had been tracing on my skin paused for only a second before continuing again. He slowly digested the secret I had given him. A smile spread across his lips. "I know."

I shook my head, trying to pull my fingers free at his confession but he held firm. "You know?"

He acted as if my revelation was old news that he had just been waiting to hear repeated. "I mean, I've had a hunch for a while."

My mouth hung open. "And you never thought to say anything?"

"I figured if you wanted me to know, you would tell me."

"I—I don't know what to say."

"What family do you hail from? Do you have an extra gift or power?" he asked excitedly, leaning in to look into my eyes, his brows slightly raised. "Did you get elemental magic like the Conjurors? Or did you get the abilities of a Shifter?"

I wanted to break his stare. It was too intense and I didn't want to disappoint him with the truth, but I couldn't look away. "I don't have any. I don't have any extra power and I can't even create anything with a glyph. There's no magic in me at all."

"Bullshit."

"I—What? I'm not lying." I snapped. Snatching my hand away from him and drawing my knees to my chest.

His brow furrowed. "That's not possible. She said—"

"I do not have any powers," I interrupted, feeling a rush of anger within me. "This isn't something I would lie about. I'm not just saying I'm powerless so you won't turn me in, I have no magic. Do you want me to draw you a glyph right now to prove it? Because I will."

"I don't understand." His voice faltered, the wrinkle in his brow deepening.

I threw my hands up in exasperation. "My father made a deal with a Dragon."

"Excuse me?"

"A Dragon, Cenric. A Dragon."

"I know what a fucking Dragon is, Varine." He rolled his eyes. "Which Dragon?"

"Which Dragon?" I repeated

"Yes."

"Why does it matter?"

He got to his feet and began to pace. He shook his head back and forth as he stared at the ground beneath his feet.

"Answer the question."

"Do you truly expect me to somehow know the name of the Dragon that my father talked to before I was born? Should I just write it a letter and ask it nicely to return my powers? I. Don't. Know. If I did, this conversation wouldn't be happening," I stated flatly.

"That's not what I meant."

His lips pressed together. He remained silent as he continued his pacing. I wasn't sure I wanted to know what he was getting at. The headache that had laid dormant during the few peaceful moments I had was now roaring in my head. I rubbed my temples with my fingertips and closed my eyes just enough to dull the sunlight.

Cenric looked at me with wary eyes. He ran a hand through his hair, leaving his hand on the back of his head. "Do you know about the gods?"

I scoffed, offended that he thought I was so stupid. "No, Cenric, I've been living under a rock." I waved my hand in the air in dismissal. "Of course I know about the gods."

His pacing was dizzying, his movements near frantic as he tried to piece together all he wanted to say. "You know that the gods created magic, giving it to the wielders, correct?"

"Yes."

"And you know that they also created relics that each have some sort of power, yes?"

"Yes, Cenric. What are you getting at?"

He held up his hand. "Give me just one second." His eyes darted around the dirt covered earth around us as if it held the answers he was looking for. "You know that each god created a Dragon species to guard their relics?"

I stared blankly back at him. This, I didn't know.

"Okay. Um—" He paused, suddenly rushing into the bushes. He returned quickly with a long stick and drew three circles in the dirt. "Each of these circles is a god. Aradia, Helka, and Pilean."

He drew a line in the dirt extending from each circle but not touching each other.

"Pilean," he continued, "is the God of Shifters." He drew an X at the end of the line he had just created. "Helka, the God of Conjurors." Another X in the dirt. Cenric paused, locking eyes with me as he drew the last X. "And Aradia, God of Witches."

I shook my head, pressing the heels of my palms to my eyes. "I'm not really interested in a history lesson right now."

"Can you just shut up and listen?" he asked in annoyance. I clamped my lips shut and threw a hand over my mouth for good measure.

He continued, not giving me a moment to interrupt. "Just like each god gave wielders a special power, they also gave their Dragons certain attributes, let's call them, to assist in the protection of their relics. Endwen are just one type of Dragon."

Growing annoyed by the lecture he determined I was so desperately in need of, I couldn't help myself from chiming in again. "So you're a horse guy and a Dragon guy, huh? How did you even learn all of this?"

"I like to read. Now, as I was saying. Dragons can be broken down into Fates, Oracles, and Endwen. Do you know what your father gave in the bargain? That could help determine which type of Dragon."

"No, Cenric. I don't."

His lips pressed together into a line. "Hmm," he mumbled. "If he made a deal with one it was likely an Endwen. They tend to do whatever they please, especially when it comes to Witches. That would be ideal if so, I'm not sure if a Fate or an Oracle could be located."

"Well," I said hopefully. "How do I get my magic back then?"

"That's exactly what I'm saying. I think you're going to have to make a deal with a Dragon."

"How convenient," I muttered. Slipping my socks and boots back onto my now wrinkled and pruning toes. "I don't have time for this. We're in the middle of the Trials."

"Maybe Queen Desma could help? She would likely know quite a bit about magical creatures."

I knew this had been a mistake. I shouldn't have told him. He was going to turn me over to the one person that I had spent the entirety of my life avoiding.

My heart leapt into my throat. "She will kill me, Cenric."

"We don't know that," he insisted, eyes pleading. "She could help you get your magic back and then you might be free of this place. She would keep you in her castle, and you wouldn't have to do this anymore."

"I don't want to be free of this place. I want to be here, not some stupid castle."

"No, you don't."

"Then you obviously don't know me very well."

That much was true, he did not know me as well as one should after so many days and years spent in close proximity. I had trusted him too soon and the sinking feeling in my chest told me I would pay for it.

"Are you going to turn me in?" I asked after long moments of silence. "Make a few coins off of a Witch?"

He stumbled forward, reaching for my hands. "I would never do that. You have to believe me, I just want to help. This isn't about money."

I stepped back, away from his touch, and his arms fell limply down to his sides.

I waved my hand at him. "Go on. Your turn then. Tell me your secret now that you know mine." Guilt was a devil that continued to lurk on my shoulder. I had broken too many promises in such a short amount of time. If Cenric betrayed me, everything my family had sacrificed would be in vain.

"Varine—" His hands reached for me, trying to close the distance I had made between us. "I think I love you." He shook his head, strands of hair falling into his eyes. "I mean, I'm in love with you."

"No."

"No?" he asked. "Yes, I do."

"No," I repeated. "You don't get to drop this on me in the middle of the Trials, in the middle of everything. You don't get to decide you suddenly love me after all the years I have spent pining after you."

"This isn't something sudden, Varine."

"No," I repeated, turning to run down the worn path back to the keep, boots in hand. I ran until my breath was ragged and my chest burned. My heart ached from the words Cenric had spoken. I wanted him to love me, I even spent hours dreaming of what a love like ours could look like.

But now was not the time for silly feelings, it would do nothing but distract me during a time when I needed to be the most attentive. Cenric loved me, but after everything, I didn't know if I was capable of love. I didn't want to hurt him, but I might not be able to live without him.

I forewent the tunnel, heading straight for the front gate. Cenric's voice called to me from somewhere behind, but I didn't spare him a glance, letting my feet continue to carry me.

My secrets, like the Dragon blade, began to heat under my skin, the hollow promise of relief from the scalding truth of who I was had drawn me into breaking my vow. The heat of the dagger at my side burned as I skidded to a stop before the towering metal gates.

I stared upward, gaze transfixed on what laid before me. Cenric burst into view in my peripheral, nearly slamming into my back as he hopped foot to foot to put his boots back on.

He panted as he said my name. "Varine, please—" His mouth slammed shut when his eyes met what had caught my attention.

A beaten and bloodied figure was strapped and suspended to the front gates of the keep. The man's white hair hung limp around his face, dried blood coating every exposed piece of skin. My hand drifted to my throat in horror as I realized that the man's eyes had been plucked from their sockets. A four-pointed star branded the skin of his exposed chest. This was for me, but I didn't know whether it was a warning or a threat.

"That's the man you talked to in the market, isn't it?" Cenric asked.

The Shifter I had stolen the Dragon blade from dangled lifelessly from the iron bars, held to them with nothing but knotted rope.

Cenric's hand found mine, and I buried myself in his chest at the horror before us, his arms shielding me from the view.

"Inside. Now!" Amias yelled from the front door. His command snapped us from our stupor. We pushed through the side of the gate the man wasn't attached to, careful not to jostle his decaying body. Amias had stepped into the foyer, leaving the front door open to us.

The sun blinded me as we made our way to the entrance, I couldn't see through the doorway, the inside too drenched in shadows. Cenric gripped my hand harder as we stepped over the threshold to be greeted by Amias, the four Masters, and the other four Journeymen; all clad in fighting leathers with weapons strapped to their bodies.

My eyes were still trying to adjust to the now dim light. Amias's face was grim as he moved to the center of the half circle the assassins created. He looked at each individual before his gaze fell to me.

"Time for a family meeting."

CHAPTER 25

The keep was silent, all awaiting what Amias would say. He kept us waiting, surveying the room. With fists clenched, apprentices hopped from foot to foot in anticipation.

Cenric rested his hand against the small of my back, maintaining contact as if he was afraid I would run away again. Melba stood so closely to me that her shoulder brushed mine. I would have sighed in relief had it not been for the bloody body outside our doors, and the suspense we were all left in.

"Due to unforeseen circumstances," Amias started, "I'm going to be expediting the timeline of the Trials." He glared pointedly at me before looking around the room. I wondered if he somehow knew that I had contact with the Shifter. Had Cenric been suspicious enough of me that he reported what he saw?

Why was I now painting Cenric as the enemy? I had wanted this; I wanted him. Shaking my head at the thoughts, I reached for the hand that pressed into my back, linking our fingers. He smiled down at me and I clung to him. If he truly loved me like he said he did, I could trust him. He wouldn't have turned me in before finding out the entire story first. But then again, I didn't know everything that he saw. As if trying to remind me, the Dragon blade warmed to a scorching temperature, threatening to sear my skin through my leather pants.

I gritted my teeth in an effort to cope with the pain that accompanied it, I couldn't exactly bring out the secret knife I stole in front of everyone. Maybe this weirdly sentient blade had become angered that its first master had been killed and was now blaming me? And was trying to burn me like the burial the Shifter would soon receive.

Amias pushed open his black cape and tucked his hands into the pockets of his leathers. A casual gesture that I knew meant more when Amias did it. "Previously, the Trials have been completed in three-week increments, evenly spaced over the course of four months, which I had planned to continue. However, it is advantageous to the safety of the Order for them to be moved up. We will hold a Trial every two days until they are completed."

Hollow quiet filled the entryway, the weight of what the next few weeks would look like bearing down on us. Amias quickly swept away to his office, giving us no time to argue or object.

Gedeon looked around at us wide-eyed. "That's insane! We'll have no time to recover between Trials. What if we become injured?"

"If you're so ill-prepared, you can drop out now," Melba retorted, rolling her eyes at him. His lips curled, exposing his teeth like a rabid dog. He tried to advance toward her but was ripped back by Xarissa, her arm encircling his bicep.

"Now is not the time," she whispered harshly.

Unable to help myself, I mumbled under my breath. "That's a first."

Xarissa's eyebrows raised, and her free hand clenched. "What was that, Varine?"

Cenric squeezed my hand tightly, a warning. I cleared my throat, making sure my voice would project. "I said, 'that's a first.' Sorry that your ears didn't work the first time."

With a sigh, Cenric rubbed his free hand across his face. "When are we to begin the next Trial?" He asked no one in particular, a distraction technique to keep Xarissa and me from each other's throats.

A Master standing on the balcony above us called down. "Tomorrow."

Great. Ten days was all that stood between destiny and death.

CHAPTER 26

"This is going to be a shit show," Melba said, taking a swig from the wine glass in her hands.

After Amias's announcement, Cenric, Melba, and I had retreated to my suite. Both of my friends had run off to change into more comfortable clothing, giving me just enough time to stow the magical blade away. I looked into the mirror as I tried to wash away the grime of this morning and the previous night. Black and purple bags hung under my eyes, exhaustion threatening to overtake me, but I knew that sleep would be out of reach. I barely recognized the person staring back at me anymore.

Without knocking, Melba barged through the door and draped herself across the lounge by the fireplace. Cenric followed quickly after, tending the embers that burst to life of their own accord.

"You're going to break the mirror if you keep glaring at it like that."

"Melba, that was rude," Cenric chastised.

"What? You're telling me she doesn't look like shit these days?" She turned to look at me, our eyes meeting in the reflection. "Are you even sleeping?"

I turned away from the mirror, hands on my hips. "You look beautiful too, Melbs."

I hadn't been sleeping, not since I had begun practicing the Simulation, and now I feared I would never sleep again.

Cenric rummaged in a cabinet, bringing forth three glasses and a bottle of wine I kept hidden in there. When he offered me the flute I waved it away.

"Isn't it a little early to be drinking?" I asked.

"Maybe it's early for you, but I need this after the past few days." She looked in the glass, swirling the crimson liquid. "Could use something stronger, though."

"I'm sorry about that," I mumbled scooting in next to her on the lounge chair. I cleared my throat. "For the intrusion."

She sighed loudly and set her glass on the ground. "Honestly, Varine? I should have told you sooner." She placed an arm around my shoulders and rested her head against it, her head tucking perfectly into the crook of my neck. "I should be apologizing for not trusting you enough with that truth."

Tears welled in my eyes. How did I come to deserve such a friend as her? I leaned into her, breathing in her vanilla and citrus scent. Of course she would apologize to *me* after I was the one who intruded on her private, and very intimate memories.

I knew this was my opportunity to return the favor; tell her who I really was. Having already given that part of me to Cenric, it only felt right to tell her as well. The promise had already been broken, what was one time more?

"Thank you," was all I could think to say. Thankfully, soft snoring broke the silence, relieving me of the impossible decision. We both looked to the chair Cenric sat in to find him slumped over. His body was comically large compared to the seat, head resting awkwardly on the arm. We broke out in giggles at the sight of him. A loud snore interrupted us, causing another round of laughter.

Wiping my eyes, I took the glass from Melba's hands and took a sip, hoping it would help me relax as well. I scrunched my nose up at the bitter taste and handed it back to her. Wine should never be bitter; no wonder I never opened that bottle. To be enjoyable it should be sweet and smooth, a dessert to end the day with, or start it, in this case.

I rose from my seat, untangling myself from Melba. "If we're going to drink," I said, crossing the room to the small cabinet next to my bed and pulling a large crystal bottle containing amber liquid from it, "we're going to do this right."

"Yes! I knew you had been holding out on us," Melba cheered gleefully.

Pouring a small amount into the glass Cenric had gotten for me, I sipped on the drink, savoring the burn as it went down my throat. Melba poured a large helping into her own glass, gulping it greedily.

Awakened by our excitement, Cenric reached out a hand.

"You want some?" Melba asked.

"The bottle, please." He reached out a long arm, snatching the bottle that Melba had passed back to me, and drank directly from it.

I laughed in surprise at how enthusiastically he guzzled the fiery liquid.

"Hey!" Melba called. "Save some for the rest of us!"

The bottle went from hand to hand, forgoing our cups, until it had been drained to the very dregs. We talked about everything and nothing and anything but the Trials to come and the one we had just faced. Having barely had time to talk as a group in the past few weeks, I savored the company of my two closest friends.

Each of us got exactly what we needed: an escape from the reality of the past and the awful anticipation of the future. The idea of ruining our momentary peace with talks about my lost magic and Cenric's confession, seemed like a waste of the little time we might have left.

Night quickly approached, as the day spent together in a haze of laughter and alcohol faded. As the impending darkness consumed the sun, tensions grew, but we refused to acknowledge it, our conversations becoming tight and forced. The clock struck midnight and the time to part had arrived. A few hours rest before a Trial would in no way be sufficient, but I wouldn't regret it. Any time spent with them was time well spent.

Standing in the doorway, Cenric and Melba turned to say their goodbyes. Their rooms were so close to mine that we stood only feet from each other. "I love you. Both of you," Melba blurted. "Whatever happens, I just wanted you to know. I couldn't have done any of this without you two."

Tears rimmed my eyes at what might be the final goodbye. Cenric walked from his doorway and wrapped Melba in an embrace. I watched the way their bodies sagged in relief against each other. My friends. My family. I saw the single tear run down Melba's face before she could hastily wipe it away.

"Goodnight," I called, not waiting for a response before entering my room and closing the door. If I had stayed even a moment longer I might have broken down into sobs right there in the hallway for anyone to find.

Sleep did not find me easily. The angry, taunting words repeated in my head.

Liar

A lie of omission is no less of a lie.

Amias's words caressed me with icy tendrils of guilt. The guilt of my lies to Melba, the truth I had continuously withheld when she had given me every-thing. *Everything.* There was a very real possibility that we would die tomorrow, and all I had done was lie and deceive her. I had offered Cenric a part of me, but couldn't even give her the full honest truth about anything because of my cowardice. I wasn't ready to tell her that I was a Witch, but I could tell her the truth about something else.

Tossing the blankets from my body, I padded to the door, checking the hallway before making my way to Melba's room. I used our secret knock—the same one my father had taught me—that I had in turn showed Melba and Cenric.

Three knocks on the door, followed by one, and then a few seconds later another.

"Come in," called Melba's sleep-filled voice.

I pushed the door open and quickly shut it behind me. "Since when do you not lock your door?"

Melba rubbed sleep from her eyes, braids falling around her in an elegant waterfall. "I just had a feeling you might need me. Is everything okay? Are you hurt?"

"I need to be honest with you, Melbs. In case we die tomorrow."

She straightened, adjusting the nightgown that hung askew on her shoulders. "That's morbid as fuck, Varine. Give me a second to wake up."

I snorted and rolled my eyes. "I'm trying to be real with you. I can't sleep until I tell you the truth. I told you about my first errand, but that wasn't the first person I killed. I was too scared to tell you at the time because I was worried that giving a part of me away would make me crumble, but I know better now. I know that I can trust you—you and Cenric—and this is my way of trying; of making sure you know how much you mean to me . . ." I trailed off, averting my gaze.

She sat in silence for a few moments, and though I had already said too much, I needed to fill the emptiness. "I don't want to wake up in two days regretting that I was never fully honest with you. After almost losing you, I couldn't forgive myself if I didn't trust you. If I can't trust my best friends, who can I trust?"

My fingers hurt from how tightly I wrung them as I waited for Melba to make a decision. Would she let me explain, or would she send me away? She scooted over in bed and lifted the duvet, offering me a place beside her. "Well, on with it then."

Not giving her a chance to change her mind, I ran to the bed, crawling in beside her. Leaning against the headboard she waited for me to tell the story.

"Uh—" I paused, my voice catching in my throat. "Where do I even begin? I guess at the beginning; that was a dumb question," I rambled on before clearing my throat. "It was Loretta. My first kill, that is. My first errand was difficult, I didn't lie about that, but I didn't tell you about the most painful death. And I'm sorry for that."

Melba sucked in a breath but did not speak. She reached out a hand, laying it on top of mine. Her offering of support was something I didn't deserve, but wasn't that ultimately why I had come? I wanted to tell her the truth, but I also needed her comfort, acceptance, and maybe even her forgiveness.

My voice was shaky when I continued. "We had been traveling through the Delisan Pass with Amias to rendezvous with a contact, when something large flew overhead. It's body was so massive it blocked out the sun for only a few seconds."

Tears filled my eyes as the memory flooded back to me. "Loretta's horse spooked and bucked her into one of the stone walls." My hands covered my face, sobs breaking from my throat. "I can still hear the sound of her head hitting the rocks. It was horrible."

Arms wound around me, pulling me into her soft body. I had forgotten how painful this memory was—the entire reason I hadn't spoken of it since that day.

"Her limbs were bent at weird angles, and her head was bleeding." I sobbed. "There was so much blood. Amias told me to leave her, but I couldn't do it. I couldn't just leave her like that, she meant too much to me. She would have suffered, or been eaten by a wild beast. I owed her more than that. No one deserves a death like that."

"Varine . . ." she whispered, stroking my hair.

"I—I couldn't just leave here there," I repeated. "I killed her so that she wouldn't suffer. I killed her so something else wouldn't find her. But I still killed her. The worst part of it all is that I had to beg Amias for the blade to do it."

A sob broke from my lips. "At first he refused. He told me that if I was so desperate to kill her I could do it with my own hands. He said I was a coward."

"That's horrible. I know how much you loved her."

I nodded, the movement hidden beneath my hands. "He finally gave in, but only because night was beginning to fall and he was anxious to get back."

"Varine—" she started, but I interrupted.

"I don't want your pity, I just want you to understand a little about why I am the way I am. There's a lot of things in my past that are painful to remember, and after the Simulation everything is just so fresh and raw. I couldn't live with myself if I didn't open up to you after just witnessing your memory and everything you have gone through. I know our experiences are in no way comparable, but this is my way of making up for watching without your permission. Maybe you could one day find a way to forgive me, not just for invading your privacy, but for all the secrets I still haven't told you."

All the words I had been dying to say to Melba flooded out in a wave, and I had only brushed the surface of everything she did not know about me.

"Varine," Melba said. "Varine, look at me."

Looking at her between the space between my fingers, I fought the onslaught of emotion that wanted to break free as her silver lined eyes came into view.

"I have told you before, but I will tell you again. I am not upset that my best friend wanted to support me in my time of need. I am not angry with you that you know about my worst memory, and I am not upset that you withheld information. We are very different people and I have known you long enough that I have accepted you as you are. I will take any pieces that you willingly give me, but I will never, I repeat *never*, judge you for wanting to keep some of those pieces hidden."

I nodded solemnly, feeling a vast weight lift from my shoulders, nearly causing me to slump in exhaustion.

"But thank you, Varine," she continued. "Thank you for trusting me with this information, and thank you for being my best friend."

"Mmhmm," I mumbled, fearful that if I spoke, the sobs would begin.

"Do you want to sleep in here tonight?" she asked. Before I could answer, she lifted a hand, silencing any response. "Actually, that's not even a question, you're going to sleep in here with me tonight because I need you, and you very obviously need me."

She was right. I did need her. I needed her more than I needed air to breathe and I was so thankful to whatever god was looking out for me that they had brought Melba into my life. I don't think I could do this without her.

We settled in for the night, huddled close enough that our breaths mixed. Our hands clenched together tightly, both knowing that the rising morning would come too soon.

CHAPTER 27

Bells rang through the keep, summoning the Journeymen to our next Trial. I woke to find the bed I had shared with Melba empty, the sheets where her body had been now cold.

Five minutes; I just wanted five more minutes for this headache and nausea to pass. The unfortunate result of our avoidant behaviors yesterday. I threw the blankets over my head in an attempt to drown out the filtered light streaming through the window.

I needed time. Time I no longer had.

Sighing heavily, I threw the blankets off of me and sat up. The room was as empty as the bed, and I wondered where Melba had snuck off to so early. Trudging back to my room, I found clothing had been laid out for me.

A billowy, white linen shirt and slick, brown leather pants lay on my armoire. The outfit was close to what I would wear on a normal day. Matching boots laced almost to my knees, and a leather breastplate that offered very little protection cinched tightly in the back. I wondered what Amias had planned if he was leaving me so unprotected. If my suspicions were correct, I would need to bring any extra weapons I had.

With my daggers securely in the sheaths at my sides, I quickly tied my hair up, pinning it back in two braids that draped down my back. The bells chimed a second time, demanding my attendance.

Each Trial was deadly in its own right, but knowing Amias, each one would be more deadly than the last. I could be walking right into a bloodbath, wildly underdressed and under-armed.

The five other Journeymen gathered in the entryway awaiting Amias's order. As the third and final bell tolled, I was the last to arrive. Cenric and Melba both offered me tentative smiles, the motion doing little to hide their anxieties, as I slid into the half circle next to them.

Each of us were dressed in nearly identical clothing, differing only in shades of brown, black, and gray. Gedeon and Xarissa, as always, wore their ever present sneers. Tatton was as stoic as ever.

Amias descended the steps as he spoke, an ebony and ruby cape drifting behind him.

"Always a fucking cape," Melba laugh whispered to me. I pursed my lips to keep a giggle from escaping. He always was one for the dramatics.

Cenric glared at us. "Shut up. Both of you," he whispered.

"Intelligence is as important as any other trait. One can wield a weapon, but it takes a special person to wield their mind. An assassin is expected to do both."

Theatrical words for a dramatic entry. I had to fight the urge to roll my eyes at him, knowing it wouldn't win me any favors, especially today. As if sensing my inner struggle, Cenric reached out and placed a hand on my shoulder. I caught the flicker of Amias's eyes to that hand; distaste flitted briefly in his expression before returning back to calm neutrality.

My chest felt tight, arms crossed over it, as Amias finished his descent to stand before us. No one spoke while we waited. Every scuff of a shoe or shuffle of the body seemed too loud.

"We will reconvene in the first classroom on the right in the basement in ten minutes," Amias stated. "Do not be late, or you will be disqualified."

No one moved a step until Amias turned away, heading hastily toward his study. Just before he was out of sight he called back, "Make sure to say your goodbyes now."

181

A collective breath was released as he disappeared down the hallway.

Here we go.

"Think you'll make it out of this one, Melba? Or do you need Varine to bail you out again?" Xarissa jeered.

Gods, I hated her. She looked and acted like a rat, never content until everyone else was suffering with her. I couldn't imagine being so unhappy that I had to bring everyone down to my level just to make myself feel something.

Cenric took a step in front of Melba, crossing his arms. "Varine didn't interfere or she would be disqualified," Cenric stated. "We all know the rules."

"I don't need you to defend me," Melba chided, stepping around Cenric to lock eyes with Xarissa.

"Sure you don't," she mocked, taking steps toward Melba. "Cenric, Varine, and even your own mother can't protect you now."

Melba reeled back. "Who told you?" Her voice was just barely above a whisper.

Cenric never would have told Xarissa about the Simulation, and I obviously hadn't. Amias was the only other person in the room.

"You couldn't protect yourself then, and you certainly can't now. You're pathetic. If you survive one more Trial after your pitiful performance during the last, we'll all be surprised," she continued, her words dripping with disdain.

"That's enough, Xarissa," I commanded.

She turned her attention to me. "Oh, come on! You know I'm right. She's nothing without a big strong protector. No wonder her father beat her," she spat with a shake of her head. "Worthless."

"We're done here," I said, grabbing Melba's hand to lead her away.

"You better watch your back, Melba. These things have a way of weeding out the weakest links."

"You're worried about other people's weaknesses?" Tatton piped up. "So preoccupied with everyone but yourself that you don't even notice the knife to your back."

He did, in fact, have a knife poised to her back. Raising it so fast I hardly had time to blink, he sliced a shallow cut through the leather on the back of the breastplate.

Xarissa gasped and whirled on him, drawing a dagger from her thigh sheath. "Don't you touch me!"

Tatton let out a low chuckle and tucked his knife back up his sleeve. She bared her teeth at him, spitting profanities, but he turned on his heel and walked away, heading for the basement.

I didn't have the time to ponder why Tatton had stood up for us, but I was thankful, and very suspicious. Picking a side was uncharacteristic of Tatton who had made it abundantly clear that he wanted nothing to do with any of us. If we made it out of this I would have to find out why.

Melba's hand was warm in mine. I squeezed it gently as I pulled her away from the others and into the kitchen. "I need a glass of water. How about you?" I asked.

"Who told them?"

While the glass filled I pondered how to make Amias pay for what he had done. Was this yet another way to get back at me? "Truthfully, I don't know. Cenric and I would never, which only leaves—"

"Amias."

"Yes."

She wiped a hand down her face, dropping her hand to clutch the top of her breastplate. "He's such a prick sometimes."

I handed her the glass before filling one for myself. "Pretty much all of the time."

After finishing our water, we linked arms and proceeded toward the stairs. Xarissa and Gedeon made a point not to move out of the way as we approached, blocking the way to the basement. I shoved through them, making sure to hit Xarissa's shoulder with mine harder than necessary.

Arriving in the same classroom where I had my first Toxicology lesson, I had a sick feeling in the pit of my stomach that this Trial was likely poison-related. Four tables were set up, each covered in an assortment of ingredients—fluids of all colors, charcoal, and various leafy greens.

While I had become an expert in poisons, I couldn't help the residual uncertainty that came from that first experience with Amias. The way he had stayed straight-faced as he watched me poison myself; as he let me suffer longer than was necessary just because he could. Or the way he had laughed as he poisoned me two nights ago in anticipation of the first Trial. I was beginning to think he had purposefully left out information on certain poisons so that he could use them to his own advantage.

CHAPTER 28

Amias drifted into the room on an invisible wind, four Masters sweeping in behind him. Each of their hands contained a different colored vial of liquid, confirming my suspicions about this Trial.

As the bottles were handed out, seemingly without rhyme or reason, Amias launched into another speech. "Today, we will be testing your intelligence. Many of you have studied Toxicology for years and have become quite knowledgeable. Some of you have studied for years and have learned nothing. Today we'll be sorting that out," Amias drawled, an arrogant smile on his lips. "In each of your hands is a type of poison. Your task is simple. Ingest it, determine the type, and cure yourself before it's too late."

"Oh, that's all?" I muttered sarcastically under my breath.

Amias gave me a sly wink. "Don't let those be your last words, Varine."

I shook my head, embarrassed that he had heard me.

"Begin," he commanded. He wasted no time, giving us no chance to formulate a plan or converse amongst ourselves.

Cenric and Melba returned my wide-eyed stare as we all wordlessly popped the lids from the vials in our hands. Sniffing at the red-purple liquid in mine, I tried to determine what it could possibly be. The scent only giving away a hint of sweetness.

My eyes flicked to Amias and he motioned for me to drink. The shaking of my hands threatened to spill the liquid, but somehow I made it to my mouth. Looking around the room at the others, I was the last one to drink the poison.

I swallowed down the lump in my throat before downing the contents. There was no turning back now.

The smell of the poison gave way to a cloying taste. I racked my brain for the types of poison these characteristics met but found my mind drawing a blank. My breathing began to speed up but I didn't know if it was from the poison or my panic—or both. I had to remind myself to take deep breaths; hysteria would get me nowhere but dead.

Xarissa and Gedeon spoke in hushed whispers in the corner of the room, both of them throwing glances at the tables but not reaching for any substances. Cenric leaned against the wall, staring across the room, presumably in deep thought; or at least, that's what I hoped. Melba was sitting crossed-legged on the floor, head propped up on her hand. Tatton was crushing leaves in a mortar and pestle, once he completed that task he scooped up the paste he created in his fist and jammed it into his mouth.

No way.

There was no way that Tatton had already figured out how to cure himself when I still had no idea. Admittedly, I was spending too much time watching the others instead of trying to figure out my poison. Was distraction one of the symptoms?

"Tatton has completed the Trials." Amias's voice seemed to boom through the small room. "Please stand against the wall."

Fuck.

I began pacing in front of one of the tables, pausing every few seconds to stare at the ingredients. Sweet. Sweet. What poisons were sweet? Berries maybe?

The room was turning to chaos. Xarissa was beginning to retch, red liquid hitting the stone. Cenric lunged for the table, reaching for a clear bottle of liquid, knocking over several jars and bowls in his desperation. He ripped open the top and downed the contents. His knees were buckling and he swayed on his feet.

"Cenric, you may take your place on the wall."

Think, Varine, think.

Sweet likely meant berries, and berries meant either Moonberry or Spindle-lock. Unless Amias was throwing in something he never taught us. What was that poison we retrieved from Tully again?

Gedeon was mixing a vial of milky looking liquid with charcoal when Xarissa's body slumped to the floor. She lay unconscious as he kneeled at her side, his fingers frantically checking for signs of life. He swayed slightly and looked back and forth between the concoction in his hand and the woman that laid under his other. He downed the contents, tears streaking his face.

"Please," he begged Amias. "Please don't let her die."

"Gedeon, your Trial is complete. Move to the wall."

He didn't move from where he lay draped over her body. Melba and I exchanged panicked glances, afraid that what was happening to Xarissa would be our fate soon.

The effects of the poison were starting to become apparent. My racing heart failed to calm, and my palms began to sweat profusely. Melba didn't look much better, at least what I could make of her as my vision began to whirl and unfocus.

She began coughing, her movements turning jerky and uncoordinated. Bright colors swirled around the room, intertwining ribbons of purple, green, and red danced in my vision.

I was going to die if I didn't get my shit together right now.

Melba started to fade away. Just before I lost sight of her completely, I watched her turn to the side, showing two fingers down her throat to make herself retch. She clamored to her feet and mixed a colorful powder substance with what looked like water, and gulped it down.

"Melba, to the wall."

I swayed on my feet, using all my willpower not to drop to my knees. That's when my father appeared in the doorway. He was both solid and transparent at once, made of many colors and none. A perfect replica of the man that had stood in my bedroom as a child, brushing my hair from my face. "Father?" I whispered, taking a step forward and stumbling. My foot caught on the uneven stone floor causing it to slip out from under me.

My knees hit the ground hard, the jagged rock cutting into my skin through my leathers. Warm blood began to pool and drip down. Father whispered to me, calling my name, begging me to join him with an extended hand. I reached for him, but he turned and walked toward the door. He looked over his shoulder once, before stepping through the doorway and disappearing once again.

I felt like I was choking. "Father!" I yelled. "Don't leave!" The words were barely audible, no more than a whisper. "Don't leave me."

With my head hung low, I contemplated giving up. If I let the poison consume my body I could join him in death. I wouldn't have to fight, or compete. I wouldn't even have to find a way to get my magic back or confront Queen Desma.

Looking toward the door a final time, where my father once stood was now the image of my mother. She stood with her arms crossed across her chest. Her face was stern, and the silver metal of a sword peeked up from behind her shoulders.

"Get up," she demanded. "You're better than this."

"I can't."

"Get. Up."

My hands shook as I tried and failed to push myself up. "I'm going to die."

"You're going to give up so easily? Not even put up a fight? Your father would be disappointed in you. He died so that you could have better, do better."

Her voice was like ice against my skin, waking me up and giving me just a moment of clarity.

"Get up," she repeated just before she faded into a mirage of blue and green vapor.

Xarissa's agonizing screams ripped through the room.

If I didn't figure this out now, I would end up just like her. Silently, I ran through the list of poisons and their treatments. Both of the berries I suspected had very similar antidotes but one wrong decision would mean death.

I had spent most of the time since coming to the Order indifferent to whether I lived or died. Thinking that it wouldn't make a difference to anyone. But now, as I looked at Melba, her eyes welling with tears and to Cenric, who mouthed something I couldn't quite make out, I realized that I just might mean something to someone. If I couldn't do this for me, I could do it for them.

Taking several deep breaths, I pushed myself to my feet, muscle straining and legs shaking so badly that I stumbled, nearly falling into a table. The table was sturdy beneath my hands as I swept my hands blindly over the ingredients. I willed my vision to focus for just a few seconds so I could find the right ingredients.

Powders and leaves fell, glass broke beneath my hands, tiny shards embedding in my flesh. Upon finding a tiny bottle of dark green liquid, I nearly sighed in relief. The cork stopper refused to budge underneath my fingertips, blood from my cuts making it impossible to open.

I could feel my heartbeat slowing, and as death loomed closer, I realized that I wanted to survive, I needed to live. If I wanted to defend others from the atrocities that I had witnessed and endured by the hands of Queen Desma and her royal guard, I had to be strong. No one deserved to have their family ripped from them.

Gripping the stopper with my teeth, I ripped it from the top of the vial and gulped the contents down greedily. My body slumped to the floor, head resting against the cool ground in a desperate attempt to cool the fever that threatened to consume me. My vision went black and I wondered if I had died.

Only seconds had passed before my eyes flew open. The swirling colors I had come to know had faded, and I heard the best words ever uttered from Amias's mouth. "Varine, your Trial is complete. Please move to the wall."

Spindlelock it had been then. I knew I had recognized the multicolored hallucinations from my time spent practicing with Amias.

My body was now too exhausted to stand, and every part of me hurt from the pounding in my head to the ache of my feet. Crawling on hands and knees to Melba, I laid my head in her lap, eyes closing of their own accord as she gently smoothed my hair.

"Gedeon, move to the wall," Amias commanded. But no sound of scuffling feet or moving body could be heard.

"Gedeon. Your Trial is complete," he repeated, his tone becoming increasingly forceful.

"No. Please, gods, no," Gedeon sobbed. "Don't make me leave her."

In the mess of my own Trial, I had forgotten about Xarissa. Peeking my eyes open, I looked to where she lay. Her skin had gone pale and she remained motionless. Her eyes stared blankly up toward the ceiling and a line of red dripped from her mouth—she was gone.

Gedeon's large body was draped over her. His sobs caused both of their bodies to shake and shudder.

Amias stood over Gedeon now. "You all knew the risks. Move to the wall or you will be eliminated as well."

"Fuck you," he spat, the words coming out with no conviction. His head hung low as he reluctantly left Xarissa's body to sit against the wall. He no longer looked like a strong warrior, but a young child who had just lost their most prized possessions.

Head in his hands, he mumbled under his breath. "I won't forget this."

"You would be a fool if you did," Amias retorted. He threw the door open, motioning the Masters to exit before him. Once they had filed out he turned to address us. "This Trial is over. Congratulations, you all live to see another day. The next Trial will be in two days. Rest, recover, and be prepared." He turned to leave but stopped in the doorway. "And Gedeon, dispose of the body if you would."

The door slammed closed behind him; the silence it left was deafening.

CHAPTER 29

B lack smoke swirled around as the pyre burned hot and fast. The icy hand of grief silenced us, leaving the hours we waited for her body to burn in the wind whipped flames, a lonely, sorrowful affair. Gedeon wept, trails of snot dripping down his face, making the already dismal situation even more grim. My eyes turned glassy from the burn of smoke, not because I had tears to shed for Xarissa.

Tatton hadn't joined us for Xarissa's final reading—the words spoken for a soul to descend to the Afterworld. I didn't like Gedeon, and I certainly didn't like Xarissa, but at least I had the decency to show some respect for a fallen Journeyman.

I stared into the fire, the crimson flames licking up the branches and logs that were connected horizontally to a point. In the crackle of the embers I could hear Xarissa's screams, her last breaths, Loretta's last breath, Esmond's, the last breath of everyone who had died at my hands. I couldn't take it anymore.

At the time, joining the Order felt like a choice. As a child, I thought I knew exactly what I was getting myself into and chose to do so because I had no other options. I was no longer the same person, and I knew that the decision I had made had been built on lies and empty promises and was simply a disgusting distortion of autonomy.

If the Trials had taught me anything so far, it's that I so desperately wanted to make a change. The large organizations in power, like the Order and Queen

Desma, had gone unchecked for too long. Their morals had become perverted and we all had suffered in the wake.

I was just one person, but one person was all it took to make a difference. Determination fueled me like the fire burning before me. I would get my magic back, pay whatever price the Dragons demanded, and become a Master Assassin. And then I would rip this entire Order to shreds. Once I had freed everyone in this keep, I would fight for the wielders Desma had imprisoned. I wouldn't stop until everyone had the ability to choose for themselves who and what they would become.

Darkness swept in like an inky blanket, and the roaring flames dulled to glowing embers. Gedeon's wails had grown louder and more desperate, while the wind blew the ashes of Xarissa away. The chill of the night sent shivers up my spine, I tucked my cloak in tighter but it did nothing to ward off the icy hand of death that loomed over our heads. Unable to bear Gedeon's animalistic cries any longer, I turned and ascended the marble steps of the keep.

CHAPTER 30

Ditching my boots by the back door, I savored the chill of the stones beneath my feet, silently padding my way to the kitchen. The smell of freshly baked bread filled the air the closer I walked. The smell always reminded me of the times spent with my father and mother. The thought caused my heart to ache inside my chest. I rubbed at the spot, wishing I could erase the pain from my heart and mind but everything was too fresh and hurt just as badly as I'm sure the first time did.

Having vomited up the contents of my stomach shortly after the Trial ended, both from the poison I had ingested and the shock of having to face my parents for the second time, I was in dire need of food and a stiff drink. The angry creature inside my belly growled incessantly, demanding sustenance and who was I to deny it?

I arrived to an empty room. The hearth still glowed with embers, and I gently stoked them back to life. A loaf of bread and cheese were laid out on the large, bare wooden table. I grabbed a knife and cut into the cheese, savoring the soft, nutty flavor. Jumping up onto the table, careful not to hit my head on the pots and pans that dangled from the ceiling, I swung my legs back and forth as I hummed a tune and continued my little feast.

"I knew you would be hungry. I asked Brenla to make an extra loaf before she left for the night."

I looked up to see that Cenric was leaning in the doorway, arms crossed over his chest. He watched me with a smile that I gladly returned. Of course, even in times like these he would still be thinking about me, worrying about me. It was one of the many things I liked about him.

His smile faded the longer he stood in the doorway. He looked just as tired as I probably looked—the kind of exhaustion that is all-encompassing, and even sleep cannot heal the weary mind. Cenric has always carried too much weight—always taking others' worries upon himself and refusing to share his. Everything I knew about him I had to pry from his clenched fists.

"Where's Melba?" I asked, craning my neck to see around him. The hallway was empty behind him but I didn't feel sad that she was not there. I was finally getting a moment alone with him. There was so much to discuss and so little time.

"I walked her to her room. She was tired."

"Oh," I said. "That's probably for the best."

The corner of his mouth crooked up, a spark lighting his eyes. "Oh? And why is that?"

I bit my lip, butterflies seeming to migrate into my stomach, filling me with heat as they fluttered. "Because she's tired," I joked with a grin. I had come to crave the exhilaration that came with his nearness and was finding it increasingly difficult to differentiate between what was friendship and what was *more*.

He rolled his eyes and stalked over, hopping up onto the counter next to me. His knee brushed mine for just a moment, and my body mourned the loss of his the second he pulled away. Reaching out a hand, he silently demanded some of the bread I gripped in my hands. Reluctant to share my feast, I tore him off a small chunk of bread and offered only a thin slice of cheese.

Laughing, he threw his head back at the meager portions I offered him. "I had to barter a week's worth of laundry duty to get Brenla to stay late and bake for you, and this is all you give me? This isn't even enough for a mouse."

"Exactly, for me. Not *you*." I giggled.

Before I could move an inch, Cenric leaned over toward me, his face mere inches from mine. So close, I could feel his breath mingling with mine. As I studied his face, my gaze caught on a scar that I had never noticed before that ran from the top of his lip to the side of his nose. I made a mental note as I would likely soon forget to ask him about it. There was no way I was going to remember anything in the next few moments if he stayed this close to me.

Citrus and smoke is what Cenric smelled like, with just a hint of something spicy underneath. His gaze was intense as he watched me and before I knew it, I found myself sinking into his warmth. I breathed in deeply, allowing it to wash over me, and committed it to memory. Slowly, he reached a hand toward me. Just when I thought he was going to touch me, he snatched the bread from my hand and stuffed the entire slice in his mouth.

"Hey!" I protested, shoving his shoulder gently. We both fell into a fit of laughter, my amusement only increasing when he began to cough, choking on the amount of food in his mouth.

Our giggles began to trail off, and the tears that had fallen from my eyes rolled down my cheeks. Exhaustion was a fickle beast that left us but a hair's breadth from hysterics.

Sitting in the content silence between us, Cenric leaned back on his hands, bracing them behind him. With my belly now content and full, I did the same, allowing the crackling hearth to warm me from the outside.

"Can we talk about what I told you?" he asked suddenly.

My eyes darted to the door, contemplating how quickly I could make it out before he caught up to me. I didn't know why I wanted to avoid this conversation. I wanted to be with him, there was no doubt about it, but I think the word *love* was what was causing me trepidation. It had too strong of a meaning, a word so powerful it had changed my life many times before. First, when my father betrayed my mother because of it, and most recently when my heart had nearly shattered when Melba almost hadn't woken up.

As if he sensed the direction of my thoughts he added, "Please don't run away again."

I grabbed for a bite of cheese, anything to hide the panic that was probably evident on my face. "You barely know me," I choked out. "Until a couple days ago you knew nothing about my past and who I truly am, how can you say you love me? And this," I said, motioning back and forth between us, "is a bad idea."

A terrible idea that would only end in one or both of us hurt.

He jumped down from the table and stood before me, either to look at me or stop me from fleeing, I was unsure of which. Towering above me, I had to look up to see into his eyes. My hair fell down my back, having been released from the braids I had hastily removed earlier, as I looked up into his eyes.

"I am in love with you, Varine. All of you. I don't care about the magic you do or do not have. I do not care that you hid that secret from me. There is nothing in this world that could tear me from you now. You are like the first ray of sunshine as the sun welcomes me into the new day; bright, and warm, and everything I have ever dreamed of."

Sliding to my feet, I contemplated making a run for it, but Cenric was too close, blocking my path. "I don't know if I can do this," I said.

His hand cupped my cheek, and I didn't pull away. Instead, I felt myself leaning in.

"I'm an orphan," he confided. "My parents were very sick with some incurable disease." Each word was shaky with the effort it looked like it took to say them. Taking in a deep breath, he continued. "I ended up on the streets of Vahlten, doing whatever I could to survive. Begging, stealing, providing, uh . . ." He paused. "*Services* to those willing to pay. I did everything I could to make an extra coin."

"How old were you?"

"Too young. They died when I was seven. I was working before I hit my eighth birthday."

"That's horrible," I whispered. "You were just a child."

He raised his other hand to my face, cradling both of my cheeks in hands. "Amias found me on the day of my tenth birthday. I had been beaten and left for dead by a man who had used me and left me on the street like trash. I thought he loved me. I was so young and naïve that I thought I meant something to him." He shook his head as if he could clear the memory from his mind. "Amias promised me money, a home, and revenge. I couldn't turn it down. That's how I know this is love. This"—he motioned between us—"feels nothing like that. This is real and pure and comforting. Seeing you each and every day feels like coming home, like this place has truly become a home. Being with you makes me forget every terrible thing I have done and experienced. Being with you makes me want to be a better person."

I reached for one of his hands that still held my cheek with mine, placing it over the top and sliding my fingers through his. Bright eyes seemed to bore into me, burning me so thoroughly that I thought I might catch fire.

"It is not love, Cenric. This is just a reaction—" I started, looking away from the intensity of his stare.

"I would die for you!" he shouted, dropping his hands to my shoulders. "Look at me. Please. Varine," he begged as I continued to look everywhere but at him. "I would endure every misery, every beating, every despicable act I performed ten times over just for one moment with you. I would spend the rest of my life killing if it meant I could come back to you. If anything ever separated us, I would always find my way back to you. There is nothing I wouldn't do for those that I care about."

My mouth hung open. I was shocked at the words that had just come from his mouth, but I couldn't return his affection. I loved Cenric with all my heart, but I was not in love with him.

"I can't," I whispered.

His fingers tangled in my hair as one hand moved to the back of my head and the other to my jaw. He dragged my chin up gently so that our eyes once again met. "I can. Let my love be enough."

My mind waged a war against my body, screaming that this wasn't right, I barely knew him, he couldn't possibly love me. My body, however, craved him with every fiber of my being. I wanted to know what his lips would feel like pressed against mine, his hands on my skin. But it would be a terrible mistake, to get close to someone that would ultimately leave or betray me like all those I had loved before. Father, Mother, Loretta, Esmond, it all ended the same, in heartache.

The pad of his thumb ran over my lips, willpower shattering as shivers ran down my spine.

Fuck it. We were probably going to die anyway.

Our lips crashed together with such force that I swear the earth stopped spinning for a moment. He stepped into me, pulling me tight against his body. He tasted like mountain air, like the sunrise. He was all the things I loved, all the things that felt right. Being with him felt right.

He was soft and gentle at first, allowing me to lead, and matching my intensity. I reached up, intertwining my hands around his neck and pressed into him so tight that no air lay between us. He jumped at the invitation, deepening our kiss until we were both left breathless and gasping. His hands ran up my sides and played with the hem of my tunic, almost pleading for permission. Before I could grant it, he turned me so my hips dug into the thick wood of the table, his chest pressing into my back. He began ravenous kisses trailing from the soft spot behind my ear to the base of my neck.

Closing my eyes, I threw my head back allowing him better access. My head rested on his shoulder and I bit my lip to suppress the moan that threatened to escape. The desire, the need for him, building with each movement we made, the pressure of our bodies connected together not nearly strong enough. I let out a breathy gasp when he nipped the place where my shoulder met my neck. It was just a moment of pain before pleasure overwhelmed me.

"We shouldn't," I gasped out as his hands roamed under my shirt, tickling the sensitive skin of my stomach.

"You're right. You shouldn't," a deep voice said from the open doorway.

We jumped apart, both breathing heavily, and turned to see Amias standing in all black, his arms crossed and a look of rage upon his face. My face burned so hot I worried it matched the color of my hair.

"Go to your room, Varine."

"But," I started to protest.

"Go."

I looked to Cenric, where I thought I would see fear, I saw only sadness. He quickly changed his demeanor when he saw me looking, trading his raw honesty for a smug smirk and a flirtatious wink before turning his attention to Amias.

"It's alright. Go ahead, Varine," Cenric said without looking at me.

"I'm getting really sick and tired of men telling me what to do," I grumbled, pushing past Amias to exit the kitchen.

As I ascended the stairs to my room I looked down the long hallway to the underclassman's rooms, only to see the twins poking their heads out of their doorways. Rune shook his head at me, while Ella covered what appeared to be a giggle with her hand. I stuck my tongue out at them but fought back a laugh. What were the odds that Amias would catch us in a position like *that*? I had avoided scandal in the keep for so long, too long it seemed, and my luck had now run out.

CHAPTER 31

C enric had avoided me for the last two days, or at least it felt that way, as he was nowhere to be found. I spent most of the time at my waterfall spot, but he knew where to find me now, and he had stayed away.

My head had been pounding for what felt like an eternity, the tolling bells indicating the next Trial only making the pain worse. I had hoped soaking my feet in the crisp pools of flowing water would help and it did, but only just a fraction. My anxieties raged around me most of the time, causing the nauseous feeling in my stomach to build. I was a mess and I had no one to talk to about what had happened between Cenric and I. I didn't even want to think of what Melba might say.

As I wove my hair into a sleek braid I thought about the kiss we had shared. The way he had looked at me like I was the most precious thing he had ever seen. Catching myself grinning at the memory, I quickly schooled my face back into a cool mask of indifference. Cenric was becoming a dangerous craving I feared I would never sate.

The bells chimed again, beckoning me to the third Trial. I tossed my braid over my shoulder and patted my thighs to confirm my blades were still securely in their sheaths. The clothing Amias had provided this time was nearly identical to the previous Trials. The only difference being the addition of shoulder padding and reinforced knee plates. If the uniform was any indication, I feared this Trial might be bloody.

I nearly ran down the steps and through the front door. Amias stood next to a row of horses, Cenric close by him. Both men looked up when the door closed behind me, but only Cenric looked away quickly.

Amias looked just as angry as he had been two nights prior when he had found us together. I didn't understand his reaction to Cenric and I. It wasn't uncommon for members of the Order to have sexual affairs. How else were we supposed to meet someone when the only other people we interacted with were dead moments later?

He was not known to be the jealous type; could his reaction be for a different reason? Could Amias possibly care for me and want to protect me? It was ridiculous to think that he would see Cenric as a threat now when he had tasked him to look after me during Melba's errand, especially when we were far more likely to die than to end up together.

Cenric's confession, his secrets laid bare, and now our shared kiss only added fuel to my desire to destroy everything we had ever known. Kalahvin would be a much different place if the Order didn't prey on the weak with promises of strength.

Gathered in the courtyard with the other Journeymen, I clutched the reins of a chestnut colored mare. The air was rife with unease as Amias informed us that we would be traveling to the Delisan Pass. I hadn't returned there since the trip that had taken Loretta's life, and I had hoped that I would never have reason to again.

The pass was well known for its beautiful, ancient inscriptions and towering limestone cliffs that stretched toward the gods. Sheer walls were broken only to allow meadows and waterfalls to grow among weather-worn paths. It was also known to be a backdoor into the capital city of Eltris and was heavily guarded on the other side of the mountain range.

It was truly a sight to behold, but just the thought of returning made my stomach clench and ache with remorse. I would be thinking about Loretta the entire time when I should be focusing on staying alive.

Amias had explained that we would travel to the pass for the entirety of the day and perform the Strength Trial tomorrow at sunrise. The satchels on our horses' backs were packed to the brim with bed rolls, food rations, and medical supplies.

"Ready?" Amias asked, looking at us before climbing atop his horse. We all nodded and mounted in response. "Let us proceed then."

The road out of town was winding and bumpy. Amias led the way, the rest of us falling in line behind him. Cenric trailed him, so close I thought I would find a leash tethering him to Amias's side.

Melba pulled her horse beside mine, falling in step beside me. "That's weird," Melba blurted, unabashedly pointing toward the front of the group.

I looked at her out of the corner of my eye, careful to keep my attention on the root-laced path we had started down. "What is?" I asked.

"You know," she said, angling her head. "Cenric being up there instead of with us. That's weird."

"Hmm," I mumbled.

She narrowed her eyes on me. "Why do you think that is, Varine?"

"Probably something to do with two nights ago," I guessed, not realizing that I had said the words out loud until it was too late. Melba turned to look at me with wide eyes.

"What happened two nights ago?"

My cheeks flushed red. A Master who was riding behind us snickered. I drew my hood up so that it shadowed my face and hid my embarrassment. "Keep your voice down, Melba," I said, blowing out a stream of air. "We may have . . . kissed."

Melba squealed. "May have?" she demanded. "Oh my gods. I knew it. I knew it! Give me all the details, I have to know!"

"Melba," I hissed. "Lower your voice."

She threw a hand over her mouth. Removing it only to mouth the word, "Sorry" to me. I rolled my eyes and gripped the reins a little tighter. "Amias caught us kissing in the kitchen two nights ago," I confessed, locking my eyes on the trail ahead and refusing to acknowledge Melba as she released another high-pitched squeal. The noise caused Cenric to turn his head to look at us, confusion flitted across his face, his brows knitted together. Amias said something to him that caused his head to whip back to the front and stare straight ahead.

"So," Melba said tentatively, "you said kissing. Like more than one." She arched a single eyebrow at me, a half-smile gracing her face.

"Melba," I hissed.

She threw a single hand in the air in a defensive posture, the other hand held her horse's reins loosely. "No need to be so defensive. I'm just saying, this changes everything."

"This changes nothing."

She scoffed. "You can fuck who you want, but that person being Cenric changes everything."

My head was pounding in time with each step the horse took. I rubbed two fingers against the center of my forehead in an attempt to alleviate the pressure. "We're not having sex. Now drop it," I snapped.

"So touchy," she huffed, pulling the reins of her horse to nudge it forward and away from me.

We rode in silence for a long while. The muscles in my horse's legs strained at the increasing elevation gain, the imposing shape of the mountains still looming in the distance. This was going to be a long ride.

The terrain was growing increasingly rocky, jostling the riders along the narrow trail. The sun had risen to its peak, releasing heat in waves. I was silently thankful that we were traveling through a heavily forested area. The densely clustered trees provided a welcome reprieve to the blistering heat. It was late into the year, the leaves had just begun to change color, a promise that the weather would soon shift to colder temperatures.

I swatted at the flies that buzzed around me and listened to the soft chatter of conversation. Tatton was asking one of the Masters, Lilith, questions about the Trial, trying to get an upper hand. She refused to tell him anything, but I could hear her flirtatious giggle with every word he spoke. Two other Masters, Brodric and Ewelyn, discussed a recent errand.

With nothing to do but stare straight ahead, my thoughts once again drifted to the first Trial and the information Cenric had given me. For the first time, I wished that I could speak with my mother. She would know what to do, how to proceed. She might even know how to get my powers back. It had been so many years that I did not know what had become of her, or the mountain house.

If the guards had returned after my disappearance, there would have been nothing and no one left. I did not miss her, but I missed the idea of what could have been, the magic we could have shared. I knew now why she had chosen to send me away to the only place she could think of where I would be safe.

"Are you done being mad yet?" Melba asked, looking over her shoulder at me. Her words snapped me from my past like a knife had been run through my thread of thought.

"What? I'm not—" I started but was cut off by the abrupt stillness of the group in front of us. Amias had stopped us in an open field. The meadow was flanked on one side by brown and rust colored cliff walls.

A small break in the walls led to a narrow canyon. The walls were so tight inside the canyon, we would likely have to travel single-file. A small crescent moon drawing was carved into the rock at the canyon entrance. I hadn't realized we had traveled so far; we had arrived at the Delisan Pass, the back door to the Temple of the Moon.

The meadow we had stopped in was beautiful and fragrant. Lush green grass and colorful wildflowers swayed gently in the breeze. A winding stream meandered through the meadow, disappearing into the cliff wall and continuing into the thick forest we had just emerged from.

Amias dismounted his horse and led it to the stream to drink; we all followed suit. The silence in the meadow was eerie. The only noise was the rush of the wind through the canyon and the cries of vibrant fowl as they nested for the evening. Amias waited for us to water our horses and return our attention back to him before speaking. "We will camp here tonight. Night will be upon us soon. Prepare your sleeping quarters and get some rest. We will start at sunrise."

I looked down at myself to see the light green blouse I had tucked into my leathers was wrinkled and stained. Part of it had come untucked and my hair was falling from its braid in loose tendrils around my face.

Amias, however, was pristine, not even a rogue wrinkle would dare cross his clothes, and there was not a speck of dirt on him. Luckily, the other assassins looked similar to me. The blush that had been creeping up my cheeks cooled, relieved that I wasn't the only mess.

CHAPTER 32

D inner was the crusty bread, cheese, and fruit we had brought along in our packs. We all chewed softly in silence, looking at each other with wary eyes. Amias retired to his quarters shortly after we arrived and had not reemerged or joined us for dinner. The Masters who had accompanied us had erected a large tent for him. Even in the wilderness, Amias was a creature of luxury.

Our bedrolls were arranged in a circle; our view of the night sky unimpeded by canvas on what might be the last warm night of the year. Staring up at the stars, the galaxies swirling above us, was enough. We made small talk, avoiding any conversation that would lead us to talking about the Trial. Each Trial was more deadly than the last; we couldn't forget that.

We knew that it could be the end for us tomorrow, but for tonight our words would remain light and distracting, ignoring the devastation the sunrise would bring. Cenric and Melba lay next to me, using each other for body heat, thanks to the chill that had crept in when the sun went down. Cenric and I didn't speak, but I hoped we would get the chance before it was too late.

I slept fitfully, tossing and turning all night. Sometime in the night, Cenric had moved his bedroll away from me. I had likely been moving too erratically for him to sleep soundly. Melba, however, had slept like the dead.

The first rays of sun peaked out from behind the towering cliff walls, so tall that most of the meadow was still shadowed. Assassins were starting to stir and the smell of fire and oats hit my nose. My stomach growled and I rolled over to the sounds of Melba snoring loudly in my face.

No wonder Cenric had moved away. It was impossible to get some sleep when I was a mess of limbs and Melba sounded like an angry warthog.

"Rise and shine!" Tatton called, as he stirred a large pot over the open fire near the center of camp.

Melba sat bolt upright, ripped from sleep with a panicked look in her eyes. I looked at her, startled by her sudden movement. Before I could speak to her, her features changed, becoming calmer and more aware. She stretched her arms over her head and ran her fingers over her tight braids, ensuring they were still intact. "Even on the ground I slept well," Melba said cheerfully.

"I didn't." Cenric frowned at her. "You snore. Loudly."

"I do not! Varine would tell me."

"You snore," I said flatly.

Melba put a hand over her heart, feigning hurt, but she couldn't fight the smile that lit up her eyes from within. "Maybe that's why my lovers never stayed," she speculated. "Except for you, Varine."

Cenric looked back and forth between us. I scoffed. "We both know I'm not your type. You like your women sweet and gentle."

"They probably left because they were afraid you would kill them. It's not like most people want to bring home an assassin to meet their parents," Cenric chimed in.

"Lucky for you, I don't have parents," I said flatly.

Cenric and Melba stared at me as if I had multiple heads.

I shrugged. "I mean, it's true." I stood and prepared to roll my bedding back up.

Melba began to laugh, a deep chuckle that rose until she was wiping tears from her eyes. "I cannot believe you just made a dead parent joke."

"Don't encourage her," Cenric grumbled, watching my every move. Melba was just beginning to gain control of her laughter when Tatton yelled again from the fire. "Come eat! Or starve, that's on you."

I finished packing my belongings away, tucking them into my horse's pack, and hastily changed my shirt into a cream-colored blouse that hugged tight to my arms and stomach. I patted the daggers at my side, confirming they were in place and secure.

"No weapons," Amias said, looking down on me. I jumped at his proximity, not expecting him to be so close when I hadn't heard him move.

Now it was my turn to look at someone like they had multiple heads. "You're joking?" I asked. There was no way I was going into a Trial without being armed. Just because no one had intentionally killed each other yet, didn't mean it was unlikely to happen.

Amias simply stared at me and reached out his hand, palm up. When I did not move, he quickly flicked his wrist and lowered it again to the same position, indicating that he wanted my weapons. I drew both daggers from their sheaths, gripping them so tightly in my hands, my knuckles turned white. Amias cocked his head at me. We were locked in a contest of wills and I knew mine would wear out long before his. I sighed heavily from my nose before placing both daggers in his outstretched hand. I turned on my heel and began to walk away.

"Not so fast," Amias called.

I turned around to face him again, throwing my hands in the air. "What now?"

"The one in your belt too, please," he smirked.

"This is ridiculous. I hope you're doing the same to the others." I drew the small knife from my belt and hurled it at his feet, it embedded itself in the ground to the hilt.

Amias slowly bent, pulling it from the dirt in one smooth motion and casually tucking it into his pocket. Amias continued to smirk at me as if I was the most entertaining thing he had seen all week and not a caged animal ready to rip the world to pieces to protect myself and those I cared about.

"Worry about yourself, Flower."

Before I could stop myself I was stomping forward, advancing until our noses almost touched. I could feel Amias's breath on my face, we were so close. He did not back away or even flinch. "Do not. Ever. Call me that," I snarled.

How dare he take that from my memory and how dare he use the name that only my father had ever called me. Now using it to belittle and shame me. I never wanted to hear that moniker cross another's lips again. I stepped to the side, knocking Amias's shoulder with mine as I stepped around him and continued to the fire and breakfast.

We were far enough away that no one had noticed our interaction. Melba and Cenric both looked up at me with concern as I marched into the circle the assassins had created to eat. I threw myself into a sitting position next to Cenric. He handed me a bowl full of oatmeal decorated with honey and sweet berries, and I glared down into it.

"You okay?" Cenric asked.

"I'm fine."

Melba and Cenric exchanged looks before turning back to their own bowls. I shoveled the oats into my mouth, burning my tongue in the process. My pace didn't slow because of the temperature because I knew if I stopped eating Melba and Cenric would ask too many questions that I did not want to answer.

Amias returned to the group, striding to the middle of the circle and clapping his hands to draw our attention. "It is time." He shifted his posture so that his feet were braced and crossed his arms. "Approximately a mile into the canyon it widens. We will travel there on foot. That will be the location of your next Trial. Clean up your messes, we wouldn't want to attract any large animals."

The last words were a reminder for me and an unwanted distraction technique. He had already taken my weapons. Was he now trying to waver my confidence?

CHAPTER 33

T he camp was cleaned fast and thoroughly, our horses packed and ready for the journey home upon completion of the Trial. Storm clouds brewed overhead, casting the day into a sea of gray.

"I hope it doesn't rain," Gedeon mumbled from where he walked ahead of us.

Melba agreed, nodding her head. "Especially while we're in this canyon. Has no one ever heard of flash floods?"

Amias wasted no time leading us into the narrow pass. He turned abruptly and the walls around us tightened until we had to walk sideways, my shoulders bumping Cenric ahead of me and Melba behind.

Branching paths led every which way. It would be easy to get lost among the sandstone if we weren't careful. On my past trip in this pass I had only ventured along the large main channel—large enough that our horses had no trouble making it through. The side trail we had taken looked as if the walls would crush me at any moment.

When I felt like the air from my lungs had been wrung out, it opened into a spacious cavernous bowl. It was at least a hundred feet wide, with the only exit being the one behind us. Sand littered the ground, remnants of the towering cliffs shaved down to tiny granules. It sucked my boots into its soft surface, making each step more difficult than the last.

Built into the cavern wall was a towering wooden obstacle course that looked like a torture device from my nightmares. I wasn't a good judge of distance, but

I would say that it climbed up into "nope" and "fuck this" territory. A fall from anywhere along the course would likely result in severe disfigurement or death.

Circling to face us as the last assassin broke through the tight walls, Amias threw his hands out wide and smiled broadly. "Welcome to your third Trial! Above you," Amias stated nodding his head upwards, "is an obstacle course designed to test your physical strength. Listen carefully because I will only explain this once."

His voice dropped to a low tone, causing all of us to lean in to hear his words. His smile grew. The stupid asshole was enjoying this too much.

"You will climb the rope ladder, walk the balance beam through the swinging obstacles, ascend the rope, cross the moving steps, and swing across the metal rungs to the top of the cliff face. Easy enough for a well-trained assassin."

It did sound rather easy when he put it like that. But if it was, why was someone's breathing becoming erratic, nearly hyperventilating beside me? I turned to the noise to see Gedeon practically cowering against the wall.

"Don't tell me. You're afraid of heights?" I asked, leaning toward him without taking my eyes off Amias.

"Shut up," Gedeon grunted in response.

"We shall proceed in this order: Cenric, Melba, Tatton, Varine, and Gedeon. Once Cenric has completed the first obstacle, Melba will begin, so on and so forth. This is not a timed exercise. Your goal is to complete the obstacle course, or die trying." Amias spoke the last words with a grin on his face.

I clenched my fists, willing them to stay at my sides. Every once in a while, I could be tricked into thinking that Amias cared for me, but seeing the way he found humor in our untimely deaths reminded me that I had once again been deceived. I had once thought of him as a father figure; the perfect replacement for the man I had lost. But he was nothing of a father. He was not tender. He was not kind. And most of all he did not love me or anyone else but himself.

Amias did not give us time to say our goodbyes before beginning the Trial.

"On you, Cenric," he called, retreating to lean against one of the cliff walls. We formed a haphazard line in the order in which we had been assigned to compete.

"At least you get to go last," I said to Gedeon. "Gives you plenty of time to work up some courage."

"What part of 'shut up' made you think that I wanted you to talk to me?"

The one time I try to be genuine, and he's still a raging asshole.

"Get fucked," Cenric called to Gedeon over his shoulder, before tossing me a wink.

He rocked back on his heels and launched himself into a dead sprint, throwing himself several feet up the rope ladder. It swayed and rocked with his weight but he did not falter. He climbed with terrifying speed, ascending up, up, up. He had barely reached the wooden beam, throwing his leg over the top and using his muscled arms to push him, before Amias yelled, "Next!"

Small drops of water began to stain the ground around us, the clouds swirling above our heads in what could only be a warning. The course was undoubtedly becoming slippery, but there was no stopping a Trial once it had begun.

Melba ran for the ladder, not gaining the height in her jump that Cenric had but she moved just as quickly. I looked back to Cenric who had his arms spread wide as he crossed the balance beam, the wooden barrels swinging perilously back and forth. He took steady, sure steps, not stopping for even a second.

Cenric was almost across when I heard Melba shriek. I searched for her along the course to find that she had become tangled in the rope ladder. One of her legs had gone through a break in the fishing net-like ladder. She thrashed and fought against the ensnarement, but the rain-slick ropes made it difficult.

She made an uncomfortable noise as she freed herself, almost a laugh to hide the embarrassment she probably felt. Stopping for only moments to catch her breath, she swiftly crossed the beam.

Tatton didn't wait for the command before racing for the ladder. He launched himself upon it and climbed with a fervor. The muscles of his arms were visible beneath his tight black shirt, rippling with each movement. His speed was much faster than Cenric's or Melba's, suspiciously so, almost as if he had practiced this Trial beforehand. Lilith giggled and clapped her hands from where she stood next to the other Masters. Had she told him of the Trial to give him the upper hand? Worse, did she show him before this morning?

I took deep breaths in an effort to calm my nerves and wiped my sweat stained hands on my tunic. My turn would be here sooner than I had thought. Amias watched me, and I could see his smirking face from the corner of my eye. Crossing my arms across my chest, I tried to hide the evidence of my nervousness.

"Don't like heights," Gedeon grumbled behind me. Small rocks skittered past my feet and I turned to see him kicking at them with the tips of his boots.

I knew better than to speak to him or even try to comfort him. With the loss of Xarissa, he was on his own; she was the only one who could tolerate his insufferable attitude. They had been the perfect pair, both deserving of only each other.

In an effort to busy myself and take my mind off of the Trial, I reached down and touched my toes. My body was stiff from sleeping on the ground the night before and needed a good stretch. Tatton would reach the beam in seconds and it would finally be my turn.

Dirt and debris rained down on us as Cenric reached the top, the cloud of dust so thick I could barely make out his outline. Looking up at the sheer cliff face, I wondered how we were to get down. The walls extended down the canyon as far as I could see and there were no slanting downgrades the way we had entered.

I turned to face Amias to ask him just that, but the word "go" left his mouth before my question could leave mine.

My mouth hung open, the question still dangling from my lips. "What?" I asked.

"Go!" he repeated, taking care to enunciate the word in a louder tone.

I was slow to realize that my turn had finally come. My mouth went dry and I hesitated just long enough that Gedeon grew impatient behind me. He shoved me forward. "Go!" he growled at me.

My steps were stumbling, off balance from the push, but I quickly regained my footing and ran for the ladder. Above me, I could see Tatton with his hands braced on his knees. Pushing off my back leg, I propelled myself forward and up. What little momentum I was able to maintain would save me much-needed seconds and energy.

The rope was slick from rain and swayed in the wind. It was tethered to the wall at only two points so each step I took was impeded by its unstoppable movement. Coarse fibers bit into my hands but I held firm, clinging to it for dear life.

The wooden beam above my head neared; the rope ladder tied to it groaned under my weight. Had Cenric and Tatton not gone before me, I might have worried that it would snap. But if it held them, it could certainly hold me.

Tatton still hadn't moved onto the next obstacle and I found him staring down at me as I gained more ground. The ground below seemed to shift in and out of focus when I stopped to look down. What a stupid, stupid idea.

A loud "snap" had my eyes darting back to the beam, and Tatton who now crouched on it. In his hand, shining in the sun, was an iridescent blade that he was using to saw through the ropes.

Snap. The sound of another rope breaking as Tatton's blade sawed through it.

Fuck.

I was climbing with a renewed urgency. My muscles barked in pain as I pushed them harder and harder. I reached my hand up and hauled my body up. Again, and again. Tatton was so close now I could make out the white of his eyes. Seeming to realize that his efforts were in vain as I brushed my hand against the wooden beam. He quickly darted away, lodging himself in the break between two swinging barrels.

Both of my hands were placed, palm down, on the beam as I hauled myself up and over. Staying low in an effort to maintain my balance, I crouched down, allowing my breathing to return to normal.

"What the fuck, Tatton?" I demanded between clenched teeth.

"It's nothing against you. You just happen to be the unlucky one to go after me. Blame Amias for your death sentence." His figure went in and out as the barrels swayed.

Amias was certainly at fault. He had taken my weapons, leaving me nearly defenseless and allowed the other Journeymen to retain theirs. I thought the Order was all for equality. I scoffed at my own thoughts. I had been with the Order for eight years now, I should know better. The only equality they favored was when it benefited them.

Fuck.

I was going to have to kill Tatton.

"Move, Tatton. You don't want to do this," I grunted, rising to my feet.

Tatton grinned at me, a wild look in his eyes. "You might not want to, but I certainly do."

I flung my arms out wide, careful not to look down as I took slow deliberate steps toward him. We were face to face, a swinging barrel the only obstacle between us. His brown eyes had somehow grown darker, they narrowed in on me. "All's fair, right?"

He didn't give me time to respond before he pushed the barrel at me. I caught it with my hands only to find that the wood had sharp metal protrusions sticking out of it that embedded into my skin. They ripped free as the barrel swung back into its assigned place. The glyphs intricately drawn over its surface snapped it back to its proper swing pattern.

Crimson dripped down, coating my arms. In the distance my name was called from the top of the cliffs but I couldn't spare a second to acknowledge it. Tatton advanced on me, dagger in hand. I blocked his jab only to have my hands slip in my blood. His blade embedded in my side barely pierced my skin through the armor I wore.

In my attempt to throw him from the beam, I had brought myself closer to him, giving him the opportunity to push the blade in further. I screamed in pain, my vision becoming foggy and black around the edges. The taste of iron filled my mouth, my feet swaying beneath me. Trying to use the blade against him, I took it from my side and waved it in a way that I knew didn't look threatening but I had to try something, anything.

To my relief, Tatton danced out of the way. He turned, giving me a sarcastic salute before jogging past the remaining barrels and up the single rope. "Nice knowing you, Varine! Try not to take out Gedeon on your way down," he called back, laughing to himself.

I bit into my cheek, trying to bring myself back to the present and away from the spots dancing in my vision. I wouldn't give him the satisfaction of killing me. Pocketing the dagger, I limped toward the remaining barrels. I had no other choice but to continue on.

Barrels swung past me, too close for comfort. The pointed ends threatened to impale me as they knocked me from the beam. I limped, slowly, barely missing a tragic death on several occasions.

Finally making it to the other side, I paused to breathe, air leaving me in shallow uncomfortable bursts. Below me, Gedeon was still making his slow ascent, moving one hand and foot before stopping for several seconds and squeezing his eyes closed as if the height would suddenly disappear behind his eyelids.

Why couldn't it have been Gedeon? I thought bitterly. Maybe I was just the unfortunate victim of opportunity and Tatton would have gone after anyone assigned to follow him. Or, maybe this was a targeted attack that Amias had known about all along.

My shirt was soaked in blood droplets that were beginning to land on the wood below. I needed to finish this Trial before it finished me, and there was only one way: up.

Looking to where I needed to go, water droplets fell into my eyes momentarily blinding me as they descended to mingle with the blood staining my hands.

I reached up and gripped the rope with one hand, my side barked in pain and spots dotted my vision. Gritting my teeth, I reached up with my other arm, tangling my feet in the bottom in an effort to gain some purchase. Painfully slow, I lifted myself upward, putting one hand in front of the other, pulling, and sliding my feet. Pull and slide, again and again. For every one foot I gained toward the top it felt as if I lost two, the blood and rain making the journey to the top near impossible.

Clenching my eyes closed in an effort to keep the agony at bay, I continued moving, praying to anyone listening that I would reach the top. When I thought my arms would give out, my head bounced against the cylindrical swinging step.

I reached up, draping one arm over the step and then the other, leaning there for a breath while I mustered the energy to swing a leg up. A sharp cry escaped my lips as I hauled one leg over. Blood dripped down my sides, coating my leathers.

Slowly, I rocked back and forth, until I could throw my other leg over. Each breath became more difficult than the last, my lungs refusing to fill with air.

Fuck Tatton. Fuck Amias. And fuck this Trial.

I pulled myself into a standing position. "Come on, Varine," I whispered to myself. "You can do this. Two more obstacles. You can. Do. This." The sharp pain in my side caused me to wince with each movement. By now I was sure that Tatton had made it to the top and would no longer be another barrier for me to deal with.

Gedeon had started to catch up and was now staring at the single dangling rope I had just climbed. Smears of my blood lay in the fibers. Gedeon did not make a move to climb. He looked at the rope and then the ground below him.

When he cast his gaze up at me all I could see was pure panic. I could not and would not waste my energy to send encouraging words to a man that had never shown one ounce of kindness. If he couldn't complete the task, that was one step closer to me becoming a Master; and at least I wasn't trying to kill the other Journeymen to do it.

Stepping forward onto the swinging steps, my entire body swayed and threatened to topple. I gripped the ropes in my clenched fists hard enough to turn my knuckles white. Streams of blood cascading down the fibrous ropes. I latched onto the next set of ropes and stepped forward onto the swinging step. This was taking too long and I was losing too much blood.

I reached out to grab the rope in front of me, two steps from the last obstacle, when a *thunk* and a screech sounded from behind me. The noise startled me, causing me to lose my balance before my hand could reach the next set of ropes. I reared back, clinging to the rope still in my hands. The step swayed beneath me, bucking me back and forth due to my uneven weight distribution. I waited for the step to stop swinging wildly before reaching out for the other rope connecting to the step. I dared a quick look over my shoulder to see Gedeon dangling from the second step, barely keeping his head above the wooden bar.

"Help!" Gedeon yelled. "Someone help me, please!"

He caught my eye, the desperation clear and unfiltered. I quickly averted my gaze focusing back on the task in front of me.

"Varine," he begged, "Please."

I ignored him, keeping my eyes forward. There was no way I was going to risk my life going back for him. I was fading fast from my injuries. If I didn't complete the Trial in the next few minutes my body would likely fail. I didn't have time for this.

"Please."

Gedeon became more panicked by the second. He began sobbing and desperately trying to pull himself up. I watched as his fingers began to slip, his grip beginning to break as he thrashed.

"Varine!" he screamed. "I'm slipping. Help me. Help me, please!"

I bit my lip to keep it shut. If I went back to help him, I likely wouldn't survive. He looked me in the eye, tears streaming down his face.

"Please," he whispered.

I looked up at the metal rings, the last obstacle, and the cliff side with Cenric and Melba peering over the edge. Cenric shook his head at me while Melba wrung her hands and paced back and forth. But I couldn't block out his cries, his pleas for help.

"Fuck!" I yelled at the sky before reaching for the ropes and the step behind me. I knew I was going to regret this. Maybe my heart was too soft to be an assassin.

Careful to avoid his hands, I positioned myself on the step he hung from. It creaked and groaned under the weight of both of us. I cast a wary glance up to where it connected above us. "We have to be quick."

"Thank you. Oh gods, thank—" Gedeon sputtered, but I cut him off.

"I'm only helping you so that you owe me a favor. Got it? A favor of my choosing that I can call in whenever I want," I stated. "If you don't agree I will turn around right now."

"Yes. Yes! I'll do anything! Help me."

If he could grovel at my feet in his current condition, I knew that was exactly what he would do. Gods I hope I didn't regret this. I was saving someone I had hated for as long as I could remember. I lowered myself into a sitting position facing him. Squeezing my legs in between the bar and his chest.

"You're going to crawl up my legs until you can stand above me. And I swear to the gods, Gedeon . . . you betray me, and I'm taking both of us down," I promised.

He simply nodded his head and began to use my body as leverage to haul himself up. I ground my teeth, sucking in the scream that threatened to break from my lips. Finally, when I thought the pain would go on forever, it started to fade. Gedeon now stood over me, panting. He held a hand to his heart with one hand and the side rope in the other. He was covered in blood but I couldn't tell if he had sustained an injury or if it was all from me.

"Both hands!" I snapped. If I had endured that torment just for him to die, I would bring him back just to kill him again.

Gedeon gave me a sheepish look and quickly grabbed the rope. "Sorry!" He stood looking down on me. For a moment I was sure he would push me off.

"Get going," I grunted, nodding my head toward the three steps in front of us. My words seemed to snap him from his daze and he burst into movement once more. He quickly reached the step in front of him, then the next, and the next. He looked back at me as if deciding whether I needed help or asking permission to continue.

"Go. Now. Before I change my mind."

All of the adrenaline from Gedeon's rescue was draining from me, leaving me mentally and physically exhausted. I slowly rose to my feet, my legs shaking under me, causing the step to sway. Very cautiously I faced the other direction, hyperaware of my every movement.

I was going to regret saving him, I just knew it. His rescue had wasted precious seconds, seconds that may cost me my life.

Each of my feet felt like they had twenty-pound weights strapped to them; each movement took a concentrated effort. I made it onto the third step and did not stop. I immediately reached for the next set of ropes and lifted my feet to step again. I knew if I stopped, it would be the end. I reached and stepped, doing the motion repeatedly until I found myself on a solid wooden platform. One obstacle to go.

All that was left between me and safety was the metal rings that ascended on a slanted vertical angle. My hands reached up and gripped the smooth ring directly in front of my face. The smooth, thick metal in my hands was cold, sending a shiver through my body. Exhausted past my breaking point, I had no other options but to hold onto the slippery rings. A hinge allowed them to swing back and forth giving me the momentum to move.

"It's just like the metal play contraption you would play on as a child! You can do this!" Melba shouted optimistically from the top of the cliff.

"I didn't do this shit as a kid!" I shouted back.

"Well . . ." Melba trailed off, pausing to think of what to say. "You can still do this!"

"Shut up! I can't concentrate."

"Sorry!" she called back.

At least Melba believed I could do it, even though my faith in myself was dying out at a rapid rate. I reached for the second ring with one hand still firmly on the first. My wounds stretched and pulled, sending new waves of agony through my body. I panted through my teeth, my legs leaving the platform. A scream ripped from my lungs as I swung my body toward the next metal ring. The cold metal ripped into my oozing palms. Three down, six to go.

"Don't stop!" Melba yelled as if she could sense my momentum waning.

"Melba! Shut. Up," I shouted back. "I don't have the energy to yell and swing."

Every muscle shook, each swing of my body, every reach of my hand threatened to pull me into the blackness that was forming along the edge of my vision. I should blame Gedeon for this, I should blame Tatton, but we were all just products of what the Order made us—what Amias had made us.

I dropped onto the cliff face with a thud, my limbs circling my frail, broken body until I was no more than a pile of fabric, blood, and bones. Clouds of dirt and debris rained down around me.

The world was starting to tilt and spin, the blackness creeping closer. Tatton was above me, a smug smile on his lips, speaking words that the ringing in my ears drowned out. Cenric shoved him, his face filled with rage. Both men drew daggers but I lost sight of them when Melba pulled me into her lap. Soft, steady hands brushed the hair from my face.

I lifted my hand and pointed a single limp finger at Tatton. Blood rolled down my arm and from the tip of my finger. "I'll kill you," I swore as the entire world went dark.

CHAPTER 34

The sounds of birds chirping and soft cloth blowing in a breeze floated to me, my eyes still sealed shut. A fire crackled nearby and shoes scuffed on hard floors. I kept my body still, knowing each movement would likely cause me pain.

The bed under me was soft and comforting. I fought back a sigh as my weight sunk me farther and farther into the lavish comfort of silk sheets and a heavy duvet. My breathing shifted from the deep breaths of sleep to the rhythmic rising and falling of consciousness.

The bed dipped on the side of me, and a warm hand brushed my hair from my face.

"Varine?" the voice whispered. When I did not move or open my eyes, the hand that was brushing my hair stopped on my forehead and began tapping gently.

"Varine?" they asked again.

I swatted the hand away, feeling my wounds that had now been stitched pull in my side with the movement. I winced and returned my arm to its position beside me.

The voice, now sounding an awful lot like Melba as I propelled further toward consciousness, hastily apologized. My pain must be written plainly across my face.

"I'm really sorry, Varine, but you need to wake up."

The divot in the bed disappeared, indicating the person had moved away. Suddenly, flashes of gold and red dotted my vision as the drapes in the room were thrown open. I scrunched my eyes trying to block out the colors that darted in the back of my eyelids.

"Amias will be here any moment. If you don't want him to see you in this . . . umm . . . condition, you may want to get up."

Condition? What was she talking about? Amias had to be well aware of the extent of my injuries. The injuries that his ridiculous task, and Tatton, had caused. Tatton, who I would have thought was the least likely to betray me between the remaining Journeymen, save for Cenric and Melba. And Gedeon now of course, since I rescued him—jeopardized my own life to rescue. Gods, it had been an unpredictable day. I was even surprising myself by my own reckless stupidity.

Cracking an eye open, I was greeted by an overwhelming brightness. I slammed them shut immediately, a low hiss escaping my lips.

A snicker came from the voice across the room. I cracked my eyes open, slowly this time to see Melba staring at me with a mixed expression of concern and amusement. Her arms were folded across her chest, her fists clenched close to her body. She watched my every move as I began to sit up. My face contorted with the sharp pain that came from the movement. I pulled myself into a sitting position, the heavy fabric that had been pressed onto my body shifted and pooled around my waist.

I looked down to assess the damage and found my body to be undressed. So that was the condition she was referring to. I did not, in fact, want Amias to see me naked. I ran my fingers over the jagged cut that had been stitched with black thread; the wound ached and burned.

Melba cringed and averted her gaze. "Sorry," she apologized again.

I tilted my head to the side, confused as to what she was trying to atone for.

"The lack of clothing," she started sheepishly, as if sensing my train of thought. She cleared her throat before continuing. "I had to keep them removed so they didn't get stuck in your wounds."

I looked back down at my pale skin, which was dotted in purple and red, before looking back at her. "I have never been shy in front of you, and I don't plan to start being so now," I smiled. "Thank you. Thank you for everything."

Melba smiled back at me and began crossing the room to my side once again.

"But," I started, "I don't believe Amias has earned the privilege of beholding my body. So either help me up, or hand me that robe," I said as I motioned to the bathroom door.

As I finished those last words a sharp rap sounded at the door. I threw a panicked look to Melba who quickly tossed me the robe. I had barely shoved my arms through the holes and tied the sash before my door was opened. The soft silk fabric bunched around my waist, my bottom half still covered by the duvet.

Amias strode through and shut the door behind him. His quick movements alluded to him not wanting to be seen standing outside my door. Gods forbid he show concern for the assassins in his care.

"I didn't say you could come in." My nose scrunched with a look of distaste.

Amias leaned against the door frame, one arm folded across his chest, and examining the nails on his other hand. He apprised me with a quick glance of disinterest before returning to the study of his fingers. "I do not need your permission. How many times do I need to remind you that I am King and this is my house?" he asked flatly.

I knew his questions weren't rhetorical and that he wanted an answer, but I refused to move my lips, and instead watched as he picked a speck of dust from his buttoned jacket and flicked it off of himself. Why was he even here?

I opened my mouth to ask him just that, but Amias beat me to speaking.

"Melba, you are excused."

I had almost forgotten she was here—Amias's presence tended to fill the room. Melba nodded, throwing me a shy smile before striding to the door.

"No. I want her to stay."

My words caused Melba to stop mid-step and throw me a panicked look over her shoulder. She shook her head slowly, her gaze warning me to be cautious.

"I'm actually quite hungry," Melba stated sweetly, her eyes becoming daggers boring into mine. "I'll step out and return at a later time."

Coward.

My eyes glared daggers at her but she only shook her head. I rolled my eyes in return. Melba took the motion as my agreement and silently excused herself from the room. Amias pushed off the door frame and came to stand at the foot of my bed. He ran his hands through his hair before letting out a push of air with such force, he must have been holding it. Amias watched me, eyes roving over my body starting at the top of my head and ending where my robe pooled. No words were spoken between us and frankly I was annoyed that he had commanded my friend out of the room for us only to sit in silence.

"What do you want?" I snapped.

A look of hurt flashed across his face before it turned back to the cool mask he normally wore. "I came to see how you were doing," he answered.

"Why? Are you checking on all the Journeymen?" I scoffed. "Or are you just here to check out your handiwork since I'm in this condition because of you; which seems to be a trend."

A muscle in his jaw ticked but his expression remained neutral. I knew I was annoying him and could tell he was growing more frustrated, but I didn't care. I couldn't stop the words that spilled from my mouth. Each word pointed, as if sharpened by the tip of my tongue.

"Are you going to fake concern for all the other Assassins? Going to pretend as if you care about their wellbeing? You don't get to kill us and then pretend that we mean anything to you."

Amias's back straightened, all calm and coolness suddenly replaced by fury. "You knew what you were getting yourself into when you signed up to join the Order. Don't complain to me now that things have gotten difficult—now that the risk is mounting. You chose this," he snapped.

My lips pulled back from my teeth and I leaned forward, sending a jolt of pain up my back. "I was a child! I didn't have a choice."

He reared back as if I had hit him, anger lighting up his brown eyes. "You had a choice. You always have a choice."

"Some would argue that a child of fourteen is not wise enough to make that decision."

"I didn't come here to argue." He sighed, running his hands through his hair before crossing them in front of him again.

"Then why are you here?" I asked. He might not have wanted to argue, but I certainly did. I would pick a fight any chance I could with Amias—someone had to. Being King doesn't mean I was going to let him off for the horrible things he had put me and my friends through.

Amias turned and sat at the foot of the bed. "Like I said before you accosted me, I came to check up on you."

I rolled my eyes and leaned back against the fluffed pillows behind me. "I'm doing great. Thanks for asking. Are we done here?" I challenged.

"You are impossible," he said with a shake of his head. "I wanted to inform you that the fourth Trial will take place tomorrow as scheduled."

"I can't compete tomorrow!" I argued and motioned to myself. "I lost a lot of blood and I'm in no condition to proceed."

"The Trial will take place tomorrow."

I stared at Amias for a long moment, trying to read his expression. My mouth hung open in disbelief as I found no trace that this was all some cruel joke. "I never would have taken you for someone that would violate your own rules of fairness, but after the little act of taking my weapons and leaving everyone else armed, I shouldn't be surprised."

228

"Not that I owe you an explanation, but I took everyone's weapons before the Trial. Tatton must have been given one by someone else. We do not have time to postpone, even if I wanted to, which I don't. I know you are angry and injured but there is nothing I can do."

"Yes, there is!" Now, I was yelling. "You are the King. You make the decisions. Isn't that what you just told me?" I pulled myself onto my knees and crawled across the bed so that our faces were inches from each other. "If you want me dead so badly you might as well just do it yourself."

Amias did not pull back; did not move. I shook from rage and the effort it had taken to move my body from the lying position I had been in. "And my decision is to move on with the Trials as scheduled."

I wanted to punch him in his stupid, calm face.

"This is a death sentence."

Amias stood, the movement of the bed knocking me back. I winced but resisted the urge to grab my side. I wouldn't show weakness in his presence, not after he had just signed my death warrant. "I have done everything, *everything*, Varine, to protect you. Completing the Trials is the only way I will have full rule over you. Until that moment, the Queen will not accept my authority. You will complete the Trials and they will continue as scheduled."

"I will die."

He sighed heavily, clearly upset. "Then so be it," he replied. "I'm not going to sit here and argue with you, Varine. I have as little choice in this as you do, but with the discretion that I do have at this time, I have decided to push forward. There has never been an exception made and I will not be setting a precedent now."

With those words he left, leaving me alone in my room.

CHAPTER 35

Melba returned shortly after Amias's departure, bringing a tray of food and tea with her. Cenric slipped in the door right behind her and took the tray from her hands. Melba smiled up at him and walked to the hearth to tend to the fire that was starting to die, only embers now visible.

Cenric set the tray on the bed in front of me, walked to the other side, then lay down next to me, tucking one hand under his head and crossing his legs at the ankle. He reached out and grabbed my hand, interlacing our fingers and squeezing gently. "Are you doing okay?" he asked. His touch and kind words of concern sent a sweet and soothing burst of heat up my arm and straight into my heart.

I smiled up at him. He was even more handsome when he looked at me with concern in his eyes. "Never better," I lied.

What had Amias meant when he said this was the only way for him to have full authority over me? Would completing the Trials protect me from the Queen?

He smiled back and tilted his head to the side, his dark hair now falling into his eyes. "That's the Varine I know and love," he said with a wink before turning his head to watch Melba struggle to reignite the fire. She was obviously struggling so much because she was trying too hard to listen to our conversation instead of focusing on the task ahead.

Love. A word that I was still not used to hearing even though Melba had told me often how much she loved and cared for me. But Cenric meant love in a different way. He *meant* the word love. He meant it in a world shattering, life altering way that I didn't know if I could ever reciprocate. So I remained silent, rolling the word around on my tongue like the sharp taste would dissipate the more I tried it.

Cenric let out a yawn, not even bothering to cover his mouth. I pulled my hand from his to reach for the steaming cup of tea on the tray in front of me. The heat from Cenric's touch retreated as fast as it appeared, sending a chill up my spine and leaving me missing him even though he hadn't moved from my side. I sipped the tea, the spicy and sweet flavors hitting my tongue in a delicious burst that ripped a small moan from my throat. Cenric's predatory gaze whipped to mine. His eyes quickly dipped to my lips as I licked the drops of tea from them.

"Make that noise again," he commanded.

A blush formed over my cheeks and my stomach clenched. I wanted nothing more than to make that noise again, to have him pull that noise from me.

"Eww, gross. I'm right here." Melba cringed, still stoking the fire. She threw an obscene gesture toward the logs that refused to ignite.

I jerked my head away from Cenric's deep stare, trying to hide the lust and now guilt that likely flashed across my face. I was never good at hiding my thoughts. Every emotion clearly written across my face like a book ready for its next reader. I could see Cenric from the corner of my eye. He continued to watch me, a smirk on his face. Not an ounce of guilt showed in his expression at the intimate moment we had just been caught in.

"Need help with that fire, Melbs?" Cenric asked smugly.

Melba turned, pointing the poker she was holding in her hands at Cenric. "Not from you. I don't know where your hands have been."

Cenric smirked, raising his hands in a defensive position, palms out.

"Melba!" I chastised.

She snickered, turning back to the embers that finally roared into flames. Cenric reached over me, removing the cover from the plate of food that had been brought to me. He brushed against me so gently the sensation caused my breath to hitch. Cenric stiffened, noticing the change in my breathing. His gaze once again caught on my lips. Gods, was this what it was going to be like anytime he was near now? Like there was a thread linking us together, stretching taut anytime we shared the same space? Melba had moved slowly across the room, watching every move between Cenric and I. She sat gingerly on the edge of the bed in front of me, careful not to jostle the tray.

"I know that whatever is going on between you two is important," Melba said, gesturing between Cenric and I. "But what is more important is that Varine eats something before she passes out."

Somehow Melba had noticed my pale face and the slight sway of my body before I did. I was hungry, ravenous even. The smell of slow cooked beef and vegetables wafted from the plate causing my mouth to water. I nodded eagerly, reaching for the fork and stabbing a large piece of juicy beef. I popped it into my mouth, biting off a piece too large. The second it was gone I chewed another, and another, only slowing down when all the beef had been consumed.

"So, what is the likelihood you'll die tomorrow?" Melba asked, averting her eyes and placing her hands in her lap.

I responded, "Likely," around a mouthful of carrot, while Cenric answered, "That's not going to happen."

I finished the food in my mouth and took a swig from the water cup next to the plate. Cenric and I turned to look at each other.

"That's not going to happen," he repeated.

I rolled my eyes and turned back to Melba. "The likelihood of me dying tomorrow is very high. Every movement I make hurts."

"I tried asking some of the Masters what to expect, but because of the vow of secrecy, they wouldn't tell me anything," Melba admitted.

Her hands were warm in mine, the squeeze I gave them more for me than it was for her. "I appreciate you trying to cheat for me, but I would rather face the Trial without sacrificing my honor. Unlike Tatton," I added.

Cenric let out a low animalistic growl at the sound of that name. "Don't even get me started on Tatton. I'll kill him for what he did to you."

"Me too!" Melba added, her face suddenly fierce.

"Get in line," I said with a wink. "I have first dibs."

Cenric and Melba shook their heads at me, slow smiles spreading across their faces. "That's our Varine, always so tough, even in the face of sure death," Cenric mused.

Melba nodded, looking down at my now empty plate. "You done? I'll take care of your dishes before I head to bed. Busy day tomorrow, I need to get as much rest as possible."

"Oh yes, thank you. It was delicious."

Melba stood, grabbed the tray, and gently placed the tea cup and water cup on the table next to the bed. "Don't stay up too late," she called with a wink as she exited the room, shutting the door behind her.

"I should probably go too."

I looked at Cenric with wide eyes, suddenly worried that I would never see him again. I did want to love him, even if I didn't feel it now. Maybe if I tried hard enough it would come. I didn't want this to be my last opportunity to try, to spend the night with him at my side. Maybe that's all it would take to click into place for me. I had been so alone for so long and I didn't want to be alone anymore. He stood to leave, his long legs stretching out as they slid from the bed. I frantically reached out, grabbing his hand and gripping it tightly. "Stay," I blurted.

"What?" he asked.

"Please—" I started. "Please stay."

"For you, I would do anything."

I smiled, letting my cheeks warm with the heat of his words. He slid his shoes off, leaving them on the floor next to the bed and pulled the duvet back slightly. I quickly tucked my robe lower, suddenly remembering that I had not put clothes on after my conversation with Amias. Cenric marked the movement, his eyes grazing over the bare skin of my thighs. His eyes filled with hunger as I watched them take in every curve of my body, twice, before rising to my lips and then eyes. He slid in bed next to me, turning his body so that his head lay on the pillow, facing me.

Turning toward him in return, I tried to hide the wince of pain that crossed my face but he noticed it. His hands bracketed my cheeks, cupping my face in a tender gesture. My whole body felt like it was on fire. It burned and tingled with every movement of his skin against mine.

Agonizingly slowly, he leaned in, giving me every opportunity to pull away, but when I didn't he brushed a kiss lightly to my lips. The kiss a faint echo of the ravenous passion our last ones had been filled with.

When he pulled away, a sound of protest left my throat. He chuckled, tracing a thumb over my lips. "You can barely move. I'm not doing this when you can't enjoy it."

I opened my mouth to protest but was cut off by his sudden movement toward me. His lips were on my ear, each breath sending sweet tingles down my spine. He sucked the lobe into his mouth, biting down with enough force to make me jump before releasing it again. "I don't want to worry about your injuries when I make you scream my name."

I sucked in a sharp breath, willing my heart to stop racing, but his proximity made that entirely too difficult. He rolled, moving on to his back, the warmth from his touch leaving. A smile was plastered on his face as he stared up at the ceiling.

He knew exactly what he was doing to me and he didn't care. I shivered, the room suddenly too cold without his hands on me. I scooted my body nearer to him, trying to keep my torso from being jostled. His head leaned to the side, appraising me with his gorgeous jade eyes. He watched me struggle for a moment before turning once again to his side, moving his body to mine, and pulling my head to his chest. One arm draped lazily over my side, his fingers trailing up my back.

"Goodnight, Varine," he whispered, placing a tender kiss to the top of my head. "No matter what happens, I need you to trust me."

"What?" I asked. His words didn't make sense as I was already more than halfway to unconsciousness.

"Shhh," he whispered. "Everything will be okay. I'm here. I'm here."

CHAPTER 36

Warm sun beat down on me, but unlike the previous morning, the calming birds chirping were now accompanied by large flapping wings that seemed to grow closer and louder.

Rolling onto my side, I expected to feel the soft blankets and the warm embrace of Cenric. My fingers ached to run along his bare skin, trailing every line and angle of his body. But there was nothing but cold, solid, ground around me.

Something wasn't right.

Wet leaves and dirt embedded themselves under my fingernails as I blindly reached out. My eyes immediately snapped open only to find I was in the middle of a wooded forest, alone. Sitting upright, my wounds stretched and pulled, sending waves of burning pain through my body.

I slowly looked around, searching my surroundings for a clue as to where I was and what I was doing here. First, I saw the grove of long and slender trees, their bark as white as the snow that would arrive to signal the changing of seasons. The white tree's proximity was interrupted by round, thick trunks, covered in needle-like leaves. These were the same trees we encountered near the Delisan Pass, I recalled. However, this area of the forest was far denser than I remember the Pass being. While the genus of tree was important for location purposes, it could only indicate I was somewhere along the mountain range.

Large insects buzzed around my head. I swatted them away with a hand absentmindedly as I continued to look around. Beneath me were lush, green, mossy forest floors. The beginnings of falling leaves littered aimlessly about. I was brushing my fingertips across the soft moss I had just been sleeping on when my fingers snagged on the sharp edges of paper. I spun around, reaching for the parchment. I ripped open the ruby seal, an onyx raven pressed into it to find a formal letter addressed to me.

Varine,

For a trained assassin, who claims to have mastered poisons, you sure are shit at identifying when you have received a dose. I thought I had trained you better, but it's good to know that the poisons I kept hidden you didn't discover on your own.

Welcome to your fourth Trial—Determination. Your task is to locate the Yilane Pass, cross through without getting caught and await further instructions. As always, the hardest part of the Trial will be to stay alive.

Good luck.

-Amias

I sighed and folded the letter before tucking it into my pocket. Amias, always one for the dramatics. *Let's send the illegal assassins to the forbidden pass. Great idea.*

The sun was now high in the sky, the canopy above sheltering me from the majority of the heat, but rays of warmth still reached me, forcing beads of sweat to begin dripping down my back. I ran my tongue over my dried lips; I would need water soon.

"Think, Varine," I muttered to myself, needing to hear a sound to fill the void of silence. A silence that was never truly silent. Twigs crunched nearby, the wind whistled through leaves, and small animals scurried around collecting their next meal. I had been emotionally alone for a very long time, but I had not been this physically alone in some time.

My arrival at the keep and my submission to the Order meant that I was always a breath away from another person. I was frightened to be alone, but I wasn't scared of the animals, or inclement weather. I was not even frightened by the prospect of locating another unfriendly Journeyman. The fear stemmed from what my mind may bring forth in the absence of all else.

The bugs continued to swarm me, crawling onto my exposed forearms. At least Amias had the decency to change me into actual clothing. The robe I wore to sleep would not have been sufficient in these conditions. I hoped that Brenla had been the one to clothe me and not Amias himself.

I was dressed in thick, black leather pants that were tucked into my riding boots. A ruby colored blouse, made out of what I believed to be cotton, was rolled to my elbows. The fabric was smooth and airy; it brushed softly on my skin as a breeze floated through the trees. An ebony corseted breastplate covered from my beltline to the edge of my shoulders and down my back, dipping low in the front to mirror the blouse. A dark cloak etched in silver rested on my shoulders, the hood draping almost to my mid back.

A sudden realization dawned on me as I examined my attire, swiping away yet another bug. Insects meant water, and based on the amount swarming near me, there was likely a large body of water nearby. My stomach growled at that moment. I reached out a hand, placing it on my now hollow stomach.

"Water first, then food," I said to no one. Out of habit, I patted my sides, searching for the daggers that I had given to Amias during the last Trial. To my surprise, they were sheathed at my thighs. I reached to my belt, a smile spreading across my face as my fingers brushed the hidden dagger I always kept there. At least I would not be defenseless when a monster, be it human or animal, found me, if I didn't find it first.

The sounds of a trickling stream nearby perked my ears as I wandered toward the path the sun was following across the sky. The mountains were west, they had to be. The vast mountain range cut through the entirety of the continent, dividing us in two.

Desma frequently sent out guards into these woods, and the many passes that bordered her home, looking for anyone that may possess a spark of magic. Shifters, Conjurors, Witches, creatures, she didn't care what, as long as they had even a drop of magic in their blood.

The young Conjuror's face as he was dragged away from everything he knew flashed across my mind. I didn't want to end up like that. I couldn't end up like that. There was still so much I had to accomplish, not just for me but for the sake of the people of Kalahvin—forced to live in the shadows, hiding the most intrinsic parts of themselves. I would be the one to help them, I had to.

Tree branches whipped at my face as I continued west, toward the sound of moving water. Lost in my thoughts, I didn't notice a large, distended root that had grown up from the path I weaved through the trees. My foot caught under it, twisting on my way to the ground. A scream ripped from my mouth, the sound echoing among the branches. Birds flooded the skies, trying to escape the commotion that had disrupted them from their peace. Multicolored leaves fell around me, half burying my prone body as they twirled on the wind.

I was so incredibly fucked.

Not only were there prior injuries from the other Trial, I had barely made it a couple of hours before reinjuring myself. I sat up, tucking one leg under me and bringing the now injured ankle into my lap so I could examine it. I prodded it with my fingers, twisting it lightly around the joint. Sore, definitely sore, but not broken, thank the gods. The palms of my hands were scraped and weeping from trying to stop my fall. I was lucky I didn't break an arm trying to catch myself.

"Fucking idiot," I grumbled. Testing my weight on my sore ankle, I gingerly rose to my feet. Every part of my body ached, feeling like I had been trampled repeatedly by a rogue stampede. Every breath, every step, every movement, sent new pain through my body. If I ran into an animal or another Journeyman, I would be wildly outmatched. Amias had really sent me to die.

Thinking about the time spent with Amias, I often thought he was fond of me. That he might even care for me in his own way. He spent his own limited time teaching me new skills and concepts and frequently gave me coveted errands. But I was foolish to think that he would do anything to benefit another.

Slowly continuing down the path, the sound of running water grew louder. The sun was high in the sky by the time I reached a small clearing in the trees that opened into a grassy meadow. A pond, or a swimming hole, I realized, had a river running into it on one side that immediately flowed out the other. The hole must have been deep, as when I peered over the side, I could not see the bottom.

The water was clear enough that I didn't fear sickness as I bent to drink, cupping the icy water in my hands. It slid down the back of my throat and coated my parched lips, tasting incredible. Running my fingers through it, I watched the ripples move across the pool. It was enchanting, hypnotizing even. I was so tired, what was one moment of rest next to this serene pool?

This must be what people feel like when they return from the Alrezian Desert. A mere handful of water could bring someone to their knees. While it soothed my thirst, it did nothing for hunger. A growl emanated from my stomach, reminding me that the last meal I had eaten had drugged me.

I patted the pockets of my cloak and looked around, trying to locate anything that could hold water. I didn't know when I would find fresh water again, especially not water as delicious as this. I found nothing that could be used as a makeshift container. All around me was soft, supple grass, waist high in some places. I could just rest my head on this soft moss-covered bank for a few moments. The sun was high; I had plenty of time.

I knew I was wasting time, but I didn't care. I wanted to lay in the warm embrace of the sun's rays. Each lick of warmth on my face was like a gentle caress. There was something so calming about this little meadow. I could lay here forever; I *wanted* to lay here forever, if the risk was not so great.

My reflection was distorted in the pool of water, and I watched as it bent and shifted at my fingertips. I pulled my hand back, preparing to stand, but a slight tug pulled me back. An invisible force was begging me to stay. I leaned in closer to see a small scaled creature no longer than my palm.

Its body shone silver in the light and its webbed four-toed feet moved back and forth in a silent tread. It had long tendrils of patchy black hair that floated around its tiny body. Sharp pointed teeth grinned at me.

Something about this little creature intrigued me. It pulled again on my fingers, beckoning me to drink again from the plentiful water source *"Stay with me,"* a voice inside my head said. It sounded like a whisper of wind, caressing over my skin, promising relief from the pain I felt—a sweet embrace of nothing. I was tempted to listen, to stay with this tiny creature.

A twig snapped in the distance, then another one closer. I jerked my hand from the pond, looking around frantically for the source of the noise. Another twig snapped, and another. It sounded like something large was moving through the forest at an incredible speed, heading directly for me.

Panicking, I looked around for somewhere to hide, I could barely defend myself right now. All around me was the tall grass with no shelter in sight, not even a boulder. I would be too slow to make it back into the tree line. The creature making the noise would be upon me before I could move ten steps in my condition.

Stupid. Stupid. Stupid. I knew better. I knew better than to stop in a wide open field with no shelter. I knew better than to waste time lying next to a pond contemplating jumping in, when I should be completing the Trial. There was no safety until the Trials were complete—isn't that what Amias had told me?

The silver creature whipped its tiny body through the water, swimming deeper and deeper until I lost sight of it in the darkness. It moved with such speed as if it too was frightened by whatever was approaching.

Twigs snapping and leaves crunching grew louder with each passing second. I drew my dagger and rose to my feet. With nowhere to run and nowhere to hide, I had no options but to retreat backwards and put distance between me and whatever was approaching. I wouldn't go down without a fight. It might be pathetic, but at least I wouldn't die a coward. I had worked too hard and survived too much to have *this* be the end.

The crunching had reached deafening levels. I raised my dagger, holding it loosely in my hand so that it could leave my fingers with just a flick of my wrist. The blade was a second from leaving my grip when the figure crashed through the trees and into the meadow. It was caked in mud and bleeding from scratches on its arms.

I dropped the dagger from my hand, the blade embedding in the soft dirt, and ran.

CHAPTER 37

My heart raced, threatening to jump from beneath my skin.

The dirt-coated creature stumbled toward me, tears running down its cheeks. "I found you," Cenric panted, gripping my face in his hands. "Thank the gods. I found you." He paused to catch his breath, nearly choking on his words. "When I woke up in the middle of the forest I thought something terrible had happened to you. I heard a scream. I knew in my heart was yours. I didn't think, I just ran."

He collapsed to his knees and I followed, throwing my hands around his neck. "Are you okay? Are you hurt?" I asked, my voice laced in panic. My fingers found the shredded arms of his shirt and gently prodded the angry wounds beneath.

He shook his head, leaning forward to rest his forehead against mine. "I thought I lost you, Varine. I thought you were dead. I wouldn't be able to live if I had come upon your body."

"I'm right here. I'm okay. You're okay," I murmured, gently smoothing his face with the palms of my hands. "We're okay."

I couldn't remember a time when someone had cared so deeply for me. I never had someone who would run through the forest searching for me. Someone that would put injury and pain aside to find me. I brushed my lips gently against his cheek, pulling on his hand as I stood.

"This was a lovely reunion, and I know neither of us have had time to process this Trial, or what's happened in the past couple of days—what's currently happening between us," I said, trying to force down the lump rising in my throat from his actions. "But we need to find food and shelter before it gets dark or we're really going to be in trouble."

"And we need to find Melba," he added.

"And find Melba."

Cenric carried most of my weight, arm draped across his shoulders. Our movements were slow, a trek that should have taken an hour took many. The forest was dense, making navigation substantially more difficult than I would have preferred. My injuries, and Cenric half-carrying me caused us to take several breaks, both of us needing to catch our breath.

He never once complained, though he did grunt a time or two when I stumbled over loose rocks, or protruding roots. I was growing weaker by the minute, a trail of blood left in our wake. Darkness was coming too soon, worsening our vision and causing me to stumble more often. We needed to find somewhere to camp for the night or my injuries would be the least of our worries.

The temperature began to drop, lacing the air in a cold that threatened to chill to the bone. If we had been trekking through these woods even a month later, the impending winter would have been deadly.

Game was scarce, but we were able to corner small animals in between boulders. We worked together in unison, the perfect team. Small rodents with long silken ears and short stubby tails were the easiest to catch, but it would take several to fill us up.

Cenric built a small, smoldering fire, the flames only dancing a few inches from their embers. A large, roaring fire sounded incredible but we couldn't take the risk knowing it could draw anyone, or anything, to our location. We roasted the creatures until confident they were heated through. Each eating our fill, we sucked on the marrow in the bones, trying to capture any liquid to sooth our dry throats.

Warmth filled my body but not from the meager fire, but from the proximity of Cenric. We sat so close, our shoulders nearly bumping and touching with each movement as we consumed our dinner. Sparks sang through me with each brush of skin and cloth.

That night in the kitchen, the bed we shared, my mind raced with what could have been if we had not been interrupted. I swallowed audibly, quickly ducking my head so that I would not see his face if he turned to me. My cheeks burned as hot as the fire in front of us. Now was not the time or place to be thinking about such things. I knew that Cenric was interested in me, *loved me,* but since we reunited in that meadow, he had been stern and serious. He set a devastatingly fast pace, insisting that we needed to get to the pass and complete the Trial as soon as possible. I didn't disagree but I wished that he would talk to me, look at me like he had before. Was he feeling the same warm feelings every time we grew near, or was this just my stupid body reacting of its own accord?

Pain blossomed in my head from the dehydration, and my throat threatened to shrivel up from the dryness. We had passed no other water source since the meadow where I had downed my fill, regretting that I had no way to bring even a drop back with me.

Sitting before the dying light of the burning embers, I ached for the comfort and peace I had felt sitting next to the watering hole. Each drink I had taken was more intoxicating than the last. I wanted more, *needed* more, craved it like an addict thinking about their next fix.

"You should get some rest. I'll take the first watch."

The words startled me, causing me to jump. I had been wildly distracted lately, struggling to grasp how quickly my life had turned on its head. Within the span of a few days, everything I had known to be true was no more.

Cenric laughed at my jumpiness, gently pushing my shoulder. He grinned at me, "Aren't you supposed to be a trained Assassin, aware of your surroundings at all times?"

I pushed his shoulder back. "Oh shut up. I know you're watching my back, I trust you."

His smile faded, his eyes suddenly serious, if not stern. "You need to watch your back and keep an eye out. There are dangerous things in this forest." He paused. "And people."

The words sounded oddly like a threat, like he was almost warning me that he was the dangerous thing lurking here. I tilted my head, scrutinizing him as I started to scoot away.

"There are all sorts of dangers everywhere," he quickly added, his features changing from serious to near nervous as he surveyed the treetops above us.

Leaves and dirt fell from my pants as I stood, wiping them away. "I'm going to get ready for bed."

The leaves were soft, only a few cracking and breaking when I scooped them into my arms, depositing them into a pile, a makeshift bed. My cloak would have to be a blanket. I settled in, worming my way deeper until my body was nearly covered by the leaves. Gods I wished I had a blanket and warm sheets right now. I could already feel the ache in my back tomorrow would bring.

I repeated Amias's words to me: "We have nothing if we do not have trust, right?"

"Trust." Cenric nodded, staring down at his hands before looking off into the now dark forest. "I'll wake you in a few hours."

Despite the precarious situation we remained in, I drifted off into a deep sleep the moment my eyelids closed. A welcome reprieve from what was to come.

CHAPTER 38

The sound of whispering voices drifted to me. Dawn was still hours away but there was enough light to let me see the outline of our camp. Our fire had long since burned out, the embers reduced to nothing but ashes. No smoke emanated from them and I was sure they would be cold to the touch.

A bed of leaves lay directly across from me, containing the imprint of a body that was no longer there. I looked around but was met only with the sturdy figure of the towering trees surrounding me. The whispers continued to carry on the wind from a location I could not determine.

"I must still be dreaming," I murmured to myself.

The whispering instantly stopped. I looked around again at the forest, furrowing my brow in confusion. Nothing but trees and their shadows greeted me once again. I must be dreaming and imagining people were talking, or the wind was playing tricks on me as it blew through the branches. Maybe it was a hallucination from my injuries or the blood loss.

Where was Cenric, anyway? I began to stand, shaking the leaves that clung to my clothing. The crunch of the leaves echoed loudly among the branches. I made it only a few steps toward Cenric's bed before he came stomping out of the woods, buttoning his pants as he walked toward me.

"Who were you talking to?" I asked.

Cenric looked up at me, startled that I was suddenly awake and standing in front of him. "What?"

"I heard voices. Who were you talking to?" I repeated.

He shook his head, pushing past me to lay on the pile of leaves he had made into his bed. "I wasn't talking to anyone. I went to relieve myself."

"Oh."

"Yeah," he replied, tossing a hand over his mouth to cover his yawn. "Your turn to take watch."

Cenric turned over, facing away from me and preventing me from reading his expressions. Sitting upon my bed of leaves, I stared at his back until the rhythmic rise and fall of his breaths deepened and the sun began to peek through the trees.

Had I truly imagined the entire thing? No voices greeted me in the early morning light, the forest remaining silent, almost too much so. No birds called out, the insects were even surprisingly muted, giving the fog rolling through the trees an even eerier feeling.

The night had passed without incident, other than Cenric's self-discussions while relieving himself. When I woke Cenric, the sun was still low on the horizon. We couldn't risk staying here any longer; we needed to find Melba and complete the Trial.

Cenric laid face down on his pile of leaves, arms propped underneath his head. My presence above him startled him so thoroughly that they rose in a cloud around us as he jumped to his feet. His hair was plastered to his head, his clothes were rumpled and his eyes looked tired as if he had tossed and turned all night. The stance he took, however, told me that he was ready for a fight. A walking contradiction, that's what he looked like, a body so at odds with itself. The incredulous look he gave me told me that he was not nearly as amused as I was.

"Let's get going," I said through my smile, trying and failing to hold in the laughter threatening to escape.

"Stop laughing at me. You know you have leaves in your hair?" he challenged, sounding more like a statement than a question.

Throwing my head back, I shook my long hair back and forth until the leaves and stem fragments cascaded down around me. Confident that they had all fallen, I looked at Cenric over my shoulder to find him smiling at me. He shook his head at me when I crooked an eyebrow at him. "What?" I asked.

His long strides made his movements sleek and efficient, eating up the distance between us in what felt like a single moment. The calloused skin of his fingers trailed softly against the side of my cheek, filling my body with heat and sending a shiver down to the base of my spine. I leaned into the touch, closing my eyes.

"You're just so beautiful."

My cheeks flushed at the words. Melba had been right. Since that night in the kitchen, everything had changed between Cenric and I. Every brush of our fingers, every accidental touch of our shoulders as we walked, every look we exchanged, set my body on fire and I was fully ready to burn with it. Allowing my entire being to go up in flames if it meant that I could hold onto this feeling.

Thoughts of the strange noises from the night before, the whispered voices, the odd way Cenric had reacted, everything left my brain, like a fog rolling in, blanketing everything. Hallucinations were common when people were seriously injured or suffered large amounts of blood loss.

Cenric thought I was beautiful.

He loved me.

CHAPTER 39

"We've been walking for ages," Cenric complained after several hours of trudging through the forest.

The trek today was surprisingly easier than yesterday. It was still slow going as I limped along, but we had made it a significant distance, or so I guessed. Rogue strands of hair that had escaped my long braid were plastered to my forehead and neck, the building humidity causing sweat to trickle everywhere it could. I tossed a glare over my shoulder at Cenric, who followed closely behind me, having traded places guiding after insisting that he needed to watch behind us and that having "the weakest link" in the back was asking for trouble. My glare was returned with a pout that spread across his face into a grin.

We had been walking for most of the morning, stopping only to pick berries and hunt the little creatures we had eaten last evening. The hunt hadn't been nearly as fruitful, my stomach protesting and bellowing its rage. My throat was parched and burned with the thirst that now consumed my every thought. Finding a water source was priority number one.

"We can stop once we find water," I promised, turning forward and quickening my steps. Cenric's hand reached for mine, pulling me slightly backward and to a stop, the corded muscles of his arms trembling slightly while they wrapped around my body.

"Hey!" I protested. "Now's not the time—" But I was cut off mid-sentence by a hand covering my mouth. The hard lines of his chest pressed into my back, holding me in place. The other hand, not gripping my mouth, reached for a blade at his side. My eyes darted around, looking for the threat that Cenric believed was upon us, but I saw nothing but trees. I swore my breathing stopped when he pressed the blade into my hand and lowered his head to whisper in my ear.

"Without making a sound or any sudden movements, look at the grove just east of us."

Cenric released the hand covering my mouth, sliding it down my body to grip my hip in a protective manner. The shift of his hand allowed me to turn my head slowly, in search of anything out of the ordinary. I pressed my body further into his, leaning back so that he could hear me. "I don't see anything," I whispered.

"Look again. The grove where the soil looks disturbed."

I looked around, achingly slow, trying to keep as still as possible, when my eyes caught on movement. My gaze snapped to an opening of trees where three creatures stood over what appeared to be a dead animal.

The forest had gone quiet, the only sounds were the tearing of flesh and the ragged breaths Cenric and I tried to stifle. I had never seen anything quite like these creatures. They were the things of childhood bedtime stories, told to keep children from leaving their beds in the middle of the night. I had hoped that these creatures were just rumors from the past, but before me they were like living, breathing, nightmares.

The creatures were humanoid in shape but their skin was a sickly shade of gray, as if their essence had been sucked from them. Their round heads contained no hair, and neither did the rest of their body. The movements of their limbs were erratic as they fought for pieces of the carcass.

Sharp, jagged teeth protruded from their mouths at odd angles tearing through the thick fur and bones of what appeared to be a type of deer. Where a nose would be was an empty, gaping hole, as if it had been torn from their bodies. Their clawed hands contained only three bony, finger-like protrusions. Each claw was curved slightly downward and dripped with green ooze that hissed and sputtered as it fell onto the animal's body below them.

One began to walk away, growing to its full height as it moved away from its feast. It stood so tall that its body nearly folded in half to avoid the lowest branches. The beast's spine was twisted and protruding in multiple places along its back. Its clawed feet dragged across the ground with each step, leaving deep gashes in the earth.

The creature's movements were jerky, giving the appearance that it would topple over at any moment. My body involuntarily shivered and I sucked in the gasp that escaped my lips as I realized that each of the creature's extremities were facing the wrong way. The joints in its arms and legs were pushed to their breaking point with each step it took.

My gasp had been quiet, barely a whisper, but it was loud enough to alert the creatures to our presence. The one moving away stopped walking. Their heads snapped to us in unison, showing sunken eyes as black as pits of tar. Cenric and I held our breaths and remained motionless, hoping that if we didn't move they would move along.

One of the creatures raised its head to the sky, the green ooze dripping from its mouth and eye sockets. It sniffed the air once, and then again. Cenric began walking us backwards, my body still pressed tightly to his. Our feet slid over the ground, never leaving contact with the dirt, as silent as the forest around us.

A loud, high pitched, blood curdling screech rang from the creature's pale lips. In unison, the creatures began to move toward us. They were much quicker than I had expected, and gained on us quickly. I stood frozen, unable to move, and unable to take my eyes off the certain death in front of me. Their arms and legs were synchronized together as if controlled by only one brain—right extremities moving together, followed by their left, in perfect sync with each other.

The forest filled with the sound of screaming—the sound of my screaming, I realized. Cenric was pulling on my hand, urging me to run with him, but I stood transfixed by the creatures.

"Varine!" Cenric yelled, ripping me from my trance. His eyes were wide with panic. Sweat dripped down the sides of his face and the front of his shirt was wet, where my head had been pressed to him.

"Run," I screamed. "RUN!"

We took off through the trees, moving with a swiftness I was shocked I could muster due to my injuries. The creatures were gaining on us still, crashing through every branch we had ducked under or thrown aside. Their large stature ripped limbs from trees in one movement as they ran after us.

We were so incredibly fucked and it was all my fault. Some incredibly trained assassin I was. More like an incredibly trained fuck up. That's what I had been lately. Maybe I didn't deserve to become a Master if I couldn't maintain my silence. I pushed the thoughts aside, my self-pity would do us no good.

Branches ripped at my face, opening new scratches and stinging my eyes. The creatures bellowed behind us, much closer now than before. Their joints creaked and crunched in a deafening cacophony. The sound made my teeth clench and chills run down my spine. They were disgusting, unnatural.

How anything could move like that was beyond me. The simple fact that these creatures existed defied nature. Their bodies were built backward, as if they had been ripped apart and put back together by a child.

Cenric launched himself into the river, vaulting across stones in the middle before jumping to the other side. His foot hit the edge of the bank, almost toppling him into the water before he righted himself. I had been right on his heels and nearly crashed into him as I followed his steps. We quickly righted ourselves, our boots slipping and sliding in the mud.

The closer they got to us, the more the scent of death and decay floated to us on the breeze. The putrid smell filled my nose, and I resisted the urge to gag, throwing a hand over my mouth. Cenric reached for my other hand, pulling me faster. The sound of all three creatures screeching behind us drew my attention. I dared a glance over my shoulder, allowing Cenric to guide my body in my sight's absence.

I pulled on Cenric's hand, urging him to stop but he continued to pull me along. I dug my feet into the soft dirt. "Stop!" I yelled. "They didn't cross the stream."

"What?"

"They didn't cross the stream," I repeated, panting through my teeth.

Cenric braced his hands on his knees as he tried desperately to catch his breath. I placed a hand on my ribs, trying to soothe the pain that ripped through my side. "Why? Why didn't they cross?" Cenric asked, eyebrows knitting together in confusion.

"I don't even care. Thank the gods they didn't." I breathed each word through my gasps for air. "What even are those things?" When the pain in my side began to subside, I removed my hand, only to see it covered in my own crimson blood. The exertion of running must have reopened my wounds. This day just kept getting better and better.

Cenric shook his head, eyes fixed on the path we had created through the brush behind us. "I have no idea, and I'm not going to wait around for them to find a way around the stream. We need to get out of here."

I nodded my head in agreement. He looked at me and then down at my hand. Concern laced his features, and he suddenly lunged for me, holding me at arm's length. His fingers were so long they wrapped around my biceps completely, almost touching. His eyes roved over my body, inspecting me from head to toe.

"Are you hurt?" he asked. His voice had gone deep and gravely.

My breath caught in my throat. The fatigue I was feeling from our sprint left my body, and a new wave of adrenaline filled my blood at the way he was looking at me.

"I'm fine."

"You're bleeding."

"Not from them. Really, I'm fine."

His gaze roved over my body again before locking on my eyes. They moved rapidly as if searching mine for the truth.

"I'm fine, Cenric. We need to move."

Cenric nodded, the reluctance visible throughout his features as he dropped his hands from my shoulders. He laced his fingers with mine, holding my hand so tightly I feared the bones may break, but I didn't mind.

The creatures continued to bellow in the distance, their screeching growing louder with their frustration. We moved quickly, not quite running as before but certainly not leisurely walking. A loud crunch sounded, and I feared they had caught up to us without us knowing.

The noise sounded again, louder and seemingly from above us. Cenric pulled me into his chest, his blade once again in his hand as we both looked up toward the canopy of trees. The sound of breaking branches continued above us as we were showered with leaves. I palmed a dagger, raising it slightly to defend against whatever creature was now coming for us.

Suddenly, a face appeared, breaking through the lush, overgrown leaves.

"Get in the trees, you fucking idiots," Melba snapped.

She lowered a rope down, the end of which I could not see above us. She disappeared back into the security of the trees as fast as she had come, leaving me to wonder if I was starting to hallucinate from dehydration.

The rope remained, forcing me to believe that this may truly be reality. I gripped it with both hands, tugging lightly to confirm its sturdiness. I tried and failed to climb the rope. My body strained and ached. I looked up in the trees, at the distance that remained between me and safety but my injured body refused to move. The pain was too much.

"I can't do it!" I yelled into the trees before turning to find Cenric with a hand over his jaw. He rubbed at the stubble that had accumulated over the past couple days, appearing to be deep in thought.

Cenric reached for the rope, pulling it from my hands. "I'm going to try something, okay?" I nodded in response. At this point I was willing to try anything to get off the ground and further away from those terrible creatures.

He moved quickly and with certainty, wrapping the end of the rope into a near perfect circle and knotting it so it stayed in place. "I'm going to climb up the rope first. You're going to stick your feet in this loop, and I'm going to pull you up."

"That would be incredible," I admitted.

"Let's be quick now, just in case." Cenric climbed the rope swiftly. I watched as he disappeared into the branches as Melba had. The silence of the forest was eerie, like the moment of calm before a storm struck. The hairs on the back of my neck prickled, and I suddenly prayed that Cenric would move faster.

Both of my feet were confined in the loop of the rope. Just when my imagination was starting to run wild, and I swore I saw movement in the trees near us, I was moving upward.

My head broke through the first wave of branches, but the rope continued on. Each tier of limbs brought me closer and closer to the top of the mountainous trees.

I reached the limb that held the rope and climbed onto the makeshift platform made of interwoven vines that sat to its side. Melba descended another rope that climbed higher into the trees and dropped onto the platform beside me.

"Melba," I breathed, reaching my arms out and pulling her into them.

The tears poured down my face, leaving clean streaks among the dirt that stained my skin. Ragged sobs escaped my lips, even as I fought to push them down. Melba's tears joined mine, our foreheads pressed together. We sat like that for several moments, holding each other until our breathing calmed and our eyes dried.

Cenric broke the silence as he tentatively tested the platform before crawling over to us.

"Did you see those creatures?" he asked Melba.

She let out a shudder. "Yes. I'm assuming neither of you know what they are?" She looked back and forth between Cenric and me, but we both shook our heads.

Melba wrung her hands in her lap and sighed loudly. "Well, I guess we'll camp here for the night. It appears that they can't climb or cross water."

"Have you ever seen anything like that? Where did they come from?" I asked.

"There are a lot of things in the forest that we likely have never seen and don't understand. The closer we get to the Pass, the stranger things may become," Melba stated, shaking her head. "I'm just glad I'm faster at climbing trees than they are at running."

Cenric nodded and quickly changed the subject. "We need food, and water. You two stay here and I'll see what I can find."

"You're kidding me, right?" Melba's voice filled with fury. She looked back and forth between Cenric and me. "A big strong man is here to save us," she mocked. "You think I'm incapable of fending for myself? I've already gathered enough supplies to last us weeks." She gestured between Cenric and me with an accusatory finger. "It's you two who seem to be woefully unprepared."

"That's—" I started, trying and failing to clear my dry throat. "Fair. You're not entirely wrong."

Melba scoffed and shook her head before pulling on a second rope that hung behind her. A large woven basket filled with berries, leafy greens, and skeins of water lowered in front of us.

"You seem to forget that while I spend a vast majority of my time in the library, I still train. Just not always with a sword and dagger like you brutes." Melba rolled her eyes at us before throwing a water skein at my head. "Drink this. You sound horrible."

I snatched the container out of the air before it could hit me or fall to the ground below. The water was cold and sweet, soothing my aching throat.

"Bless you, Melbs," I said with a grin after finishing off the entire skein.

"It's not that I doubted you," Cenric said as he tossed an arm around Melba's shoulders. "I just didn't want Varine to be alone in her current state."

I frowned and tossed him a glare through narrowed eyes. "I'm feeling much better, thank you for asking."

"Don't lie," Melba chided.

It was both a lie, and it wasn't. I was feeling better than I had when I woke up two days ago, but I was in no condition to complete this task unassisted—but I wouldn't tell them that. They had their own lives to worry about; they shouldn't be worrying about mine.

The intertwining branches on which we sat seemed sturdy enough as we moved about, consuming the rations Melba had gathered.

Dark began to fall, the scorching day once again turning into the soft, cool fingers of night. The chill was even more evident due to the altitude. We all huddled in close, using each other's body heat to retain even a fraction of heat.

"I'll take the first watch," Cenric said flatly from my right side. His breathing was already becoming deep and even. I knew he would be out within minutes.

A small whispery laugh escaped my lips, and I reached out with a hand to hold his. "I'll take the first watch, you're almost asleep anyway."

A light humming noise from between his lips was his only response before he drifted off into sleep.

The stars shone brightly above us, peeking through the dense canopy. Bright emerald, ruby, and sapphire lights jumped across the sky, causing me to suck in a breath. I had spent many sleepless nights out in the forest staring up at these exact stars, but I had never seen anything as incredible as the ribbons of light that now danced across the sky.

"Melba?" I whispered. "Are you seeing this?"

"It's incredible."

The lights seemed to dance of their own accord. "I've never seen anything like this." I didn't dare look away, afraid that they would disappear before I had gotten my fill. Melba reached out, grasping my left hand in hers as her breathing began to slow and deepen.

Laying there, gripping the hands of the two most important people in my life, sent a calm through me that I didn't know I was capable of feeling any longer. These two people made me feel like anything we would face in the future, we would do so together. We could conquer all as long as we had each other.

Melba switched me out of my watch a few hours into the night, and I drifted off peacefully, my head tucked into the crook of her shoulder.

CHAPTER 40

Gentle fingers wove through the strands of my hair, using the ends to tickle my nose until I stirred into consciousness to blinding sunlight and chirping birds. It was the same each day.

I was getting really sick of their cheerful noises, and I was really wishing that I had my bow so there would finally be some peace and quiet.

Melba smiled down at me before offering me a handful of plump berries. I pushed my hands behind me and moved to sit up. The injuries in my abdomen stung, but they hurt less than yesterday.

"We have to keep moving. We're only about half a day from the Pass." Melba's eyes crinkled as she poured the berries into my outstretched hands. "I wanted to make sure you got some before Cenric eats them all."

"Hey!" Cenric called around a mouthful of berries, the juice dripping down his face and staining the collar of his white shirt.

I laughed and popped a berry into my mouth. It was sweet and perfectly ripe.

"How do you know where the Pass is?" I asked.

A soft smile graced her lips, and she looked up at the sky as if she could see the Pass from here. The light's rays reflected off her face and danced in the thin lines of silver scars on her cheeks and neck.

"I actually grew up not far from here." She paused as if trying to recall a far-off memory. "These woods were my playground. I spent many nights in these very trees. Hence, the woven branches we used for safety and the extra supplies I left hidden here," she said, patting the branches we sat upon. "I've seen many strange things near this Pass, but never those awful gray creatures."

"So those lights we saw last night, you've seen them before?"

"What lights?" Cenric asked, interrupting our conversation.

Melba and I both glared in his direction. Cenric tossed both of his hands and went back to greedily eating the food supplies from the basket.

She shook her head. "Never. That was incredible."

"I wonder what it means."

"It means that this forest is fucking weird," Cenric interjected.

Melba grabbed a berry out of my hand and tossed it at Cenric, who caught it in his mouth and grinned. "Will you shut up? We're trying to have a conversation."

"We better get going before those creatures decide they also need breakfast," I warned. I quickly ran my fingers through the knots in my hair, braiding each side and weaving the ends together so they flowed in one long braid down my back.

Flat on my belly, I peered over the edge and saw nothing but an empty forest floor below me.

"Anything?"

"Nope, let's go."

My pockets were stuffed to the brim with the edible greenery Melba had foraged, and a water skein was clutched in my hand as I slid down the rope. My feet hit the ground with a thud, and I quickly looked around to confirm that no creatures had been alerted to our presence.

When I was sure we were as safe as we could be in these woods, I looked up to the other two. "All clear!" They had finally let me go first after a lengthy argument. In the end, I somehow convinced them that the most logical person to check our surroundings should be the easiest to kill. That would give both of them a better chance to get away. They obviously didn't like that plan, but I didn't give them much of a choice.

Melba and Cenric's boots hit the ground in quick succession. We dusted ourselves off and straightened our clothes as best as possible, but we all looked ragged and worn down—exactly how Amias likes his obedient disciples.

"This way!" Melba called over her shoulder, leading us west through dense foliage and towering trees.

We stopped only to refill our skeins and eat a hasty lunch of what remained of the rations Melba claimed would last for weeks. It didn't matter anyway, by this time tomorrow we would be well into the Celestial Territories.

"I didn't expect Cenric to eat so much," Melba said bashfully when he was out of earshot.

I patted the hand Melba had looped through my arm. We both knew that she had done so to give me somewhere to lean on when I became tired. But I refused to do so. If Amias wanted to see determination, I'd show him determination.

"We'll find more if we need it. I'm not worried about it at all."

Melba smiled down at me. Though she was only an inch or two taller, I had always felt like her personality towered over me. Melba was the most incredible woman I knew, and not just because I was severely lacking in female role models.

She has never let her past change the kindness she shows to everyone. After witnessing just a small glimpse of what she experienced, I wouldn't fault her for being angry. I was almost jealous that she was able to shove aside what had been done to her and move on with her life while I wallowed in the anger and deceit that had been my life.

"You remind me a lot of my mother," Melba confessed.

My brows knit together. "Your mother?" I asked warily.

"For one, she was short, like you." Melba laughed and winked at me.

I swat her away, pulling my arm from her. "Ha. Ha. Very funny."

We walked side by side for a few minutes in silence, with Cenric trailing behind us. The only sound was the crunch of our boots through the underbrush. Towering in the distance were large, red and brown sheer cliff walls. We were getting close.

"But really," Melba continued. "She was feisty and determined just like you. She never showed fear, even—" She paused. "Even when my father would hit us."

I sucked in a breath but remained silent.

She watched the path in front of her, no longer looking at me. I wanted to reach out and hold her, tell Melba she was just as fierce as me, as her mother. But I kept my other hand swinging at my side. If that was what Melba needed, she would ask.

"Mother never once backed down," she continued. "She never raised a hand to my father. She would take the beating and silently plan our escape. She worked little jobs sewing dresses. Father called it a ridiculous hobby, but what he didn't know was that she charged minuscule amounts and tucked the money away each time, hiding it in the floorboards."

Tears were sliding down Melba's face now, threatening to leave tracks in the dirt. I tucked my hands into my pockets and quickly looked over my shoulder to find that Cenric had retreated a few steps to give us some privacy.

"The day we were supposed to leave—" Melba's voice caught and a sob broke through her lips. "He came home early and caught her packing my bag and he killed her right in front of me. Leaving her to bleed and call out to me from the rug in my room, while he tossed me into the cellar and locked the door."

My fists clenched in my pockets, and I bit my lip to keep from interrupting her.

After a few moments of silence, and a few deep breaths, she continued. "He told me that I wasn't his daughter and that I had two options. I could join the Order, or I could die in the cellar." She let out a dry laugh. "Both options sounded terrible, but at least I'm alive."

Her words sent a stab of pain through me. I knew what it felt like to be unwanted and left to fend for myself. To be forced into an impossible choice and stripped of your discretion. My hand reached out for her, but I didn't touch her, allowing her to touch me only if that's what she chose.

She looked at my hand and offered me a small smile before interlacing our fingers together.

"You are more than the actions of others. You are smart, kind, and funny. You are the fiercest and most determined woman I know. And I know that I never met your mother, but I would bet she would be proud."

The tears dripped from Melba's cheeks as she looked me in the eyes. "Thank you."

I smiled at her and squeezed her hand gently.

She raked the back of her hand across her face, wiping the tears away. "Sorry, there's just something about this forest that brings back so many memories."

I bumped her with my shoulder. "Don't you ever apologize for feeling. It just means you still have some humanity left in you." I hitched a thumb over my shoulder. "Unlike Cenric back there."

Muscled arms draped over our shoulders moments later and squeezed us into Cenric's hard body. "I know all this making fun of me means you like me, so I'll take it."

The edge of the forest loomed ahead of us breaking the impenetrable barrier of trees to a view of sandstone walls standing so tall they kissed the sky above. Even with my head craned back, I couldn't see where the cliffs ended.

Melba pulled away from the group, walking at a pace that was nearly impossible for me to sustain. "Now we travel south along the cliff walls," Melba called, leading the way once again.

"That leaves us out in the open," I called out, but she was so far ahead that she either did not hear or chose to ignore me.

"It'll be fine," Cenric promised, throwing me a smile that made my heart flip in my chest.

Cenric began to walk past me, but I grabbed his hand and pulled him back to me. Melba was now out of sight, having disappeared around a corner. I knew this was a mistake and that now wasn't the best time for me to rehash my complicated emotions, but I wanted the feeling of that first kiss back. I wanted to spend one more moment with him before we completed this Trial and were cast into another.

His eyes darted down to my lips as he moved back toward me. I retreated until my back hit the hard stone of the cliffs. My teeth dragged over my bottom lip, and his gaze heated and narrowed in on the movement.

The hand that didn't hold mine clenched and released as if it was taking all of his willpower to remain calm. A thrill ran through me as I realized the power I had over him. This was what I needed: a little something to break the tension and a little bit of relaxation in the midst of all of this darkness.

After what felt like agonizingly long moments, his body pressed into mine. He brought the tangled fingers of our hands up to rest on the top of my head, pinning my body to the wall.

Every place our bodies met was like kindling to the fire deep inside me. My hand raked over his chest, gripping the unbuttoned collar of his shirt. He braced his other hand on the wall beside my head, leaning just inches from my face.

"This is a bad idea," Cenric murmured, his eyes darting from my lips to hold my simmering gaze.

I gripped his shirt tighter in my fist, pulling him in close to me. "I know," I agreed, seconds before his lips met mine.

All my thoughts were drowned out by the feeling of him. His hand dropped to my waist as his body pushed into me, pinning me fiercely into the hard rock behind me. The cuts all over my body screamed in protest, but I ignored them. I would take a little bit of pain for the pleasure.

His teeth brushed my bottom lip, and a moan escaped me. Cenric's eyes flared wide with desire. He kissed me again, harder than before. Hands met the backs of my thighs, and I wrapped my legs around his waist, grinding myself forward into his body. He groaned into the side of my neck.

My fingers rushed to his hair where they slipped through the soft strands. His lips kissed a trail down my neck, leaving sparks of heat in their wake.

"Uh, guys! We have a problem!"

Cenric snapped his head up, meeting my eyes with the same panic I knew was visible in mine. He slowly lowered my legs to the ground. The moment they hit the dirt, I was already mourning the sensation of his nearness.

"You need to see this. Now!" Melba yelled, her voice nearing as she sprinted toward us.

I knew she noticed the flush of my skin as she approached but ignored it.

"Guards," she panted. "The Queen's Guards, and lots of them."

Cenric grabbed her by the shoulders, a mockery of the position he just had me in. "Where?" he demanded.

"Heading north, they're just south of the Pass."

There was no place to hide. The further south we traveled, the more sparse the tree line had become, leaving us few options. Frantically, I searched for something, anything, but we were out of luck, and I was running out of ideas.

"We're going to have to make a run for the Pass," I said with as much calm as I could muster, though my pulse hammered in my veins.

"Can you even run?" Melba asked, looking down at my abdomen and eyeing me suspiciously.

Cenric mumbled under his breath. "She can do more than that."

"I don't think now is the time for this," I said flatly.

"That's not what you said a few minutes ago," he retorted.

Melba covered her face with her hand. "I swear, the second we're done with this Trial you two better get a room. I can't take any more of the sexual frustration wafting off of you two."

My cheeks were tinged in pink, hands clenched at my sides. "Can we just go, please?"

Melba took off at a full sprint, Cenric close on my heels. Our feet pounded the dirt, sending up clouds of dust in our wake. The closer the Pass entrance became, the closer the sound of the guards did in return. They hadn't noticed us yet, their heads still turned away from our direction deep in their conversations.

Slowing down to a brisk walk, each movement was silent that only our training would allow. One of my hands trailed along the sandstone while the other gripped a dagger.

"I'll go first," Cenric offered, leading us. Melba took up the rear, sandwiching me between them. Every few feet we stopped to listen, but their boisterous voices indicated we hadn't been caught.

Without looking behind him, Cenric whispered to us, "There's six of them, standing just south of the Pass entrance."

Fuck.

What were they doing sitting at the mouth of the Pass? They had to be looking for something, or someone. Was this part of the Trial? Surely Amias wasn't stupid enough to alert them.

Hooded figures stood in a small clearing filling containers with water from a stream that trickled from the side wall of the Pass and ran down the hill away from the entrance. Large jeweled swords were laid between the shoulders of each guard. They softly spoke to each other, so quietly that I could not make out their words.

Our backs pressed into the cliffside just as one looked over their shoulder in our direction. He narrowed his eyes, but looked back to the group to join in their conversation. Water dribbled from his canteen down his face and neck. I ached to waste water the way he was. After days in the wilderness, a bath, no matter the temperature, sounded incredible. And here we were, just hours from that becoming a reality, if we could just make it past these guards.

"Maybe if we sit here silently for a few minutes, they'll move on," Melba speculated.

Cenric shook his head. "Doubtful. It looks like they're looking for something."

"I bet they're looking for us," I hissed through clenched teeth. Amias had probably tipped off the guards, informing them that a group was attempting to travel through the forbidden pass. If we got out of this, I would make Amias pay.

Panic was written across Cenric's face, an emotion I didn't understand. Was he truly that worried about the guards? Though we were outnumbered, we were better trained.

"Why do you say that?" he asked.

"Amias probably wanted to make this more difficult," I stated flatly.

Realization flashed in Melba's eyes. "We're screwed."

"Completely." Cenric nodded in agreement.

We watched the guards like hunters watched their prey, even though I felt more like the animal than they probably did. A branch snapped from behind us, and echoed against the canyon walls.

"Shhh," I whispered.

"That wasn't me," Melba argued.

"Will you two shut up?" Cenric demanded.

Another branch snapped, this time closer. My eyes darted back and forth between the guards but they didn't seem to hear the noise. I was growing more annoyed by Melba's inability to sit still. The crunch of leaves and the snapping of twigs grew louder.

"Stop moving, Melba."

"It's not me," she insisted.

I rolled my eyes and glanced over my shoulder. What I saw crawling through the underbrush stopped my heart, and my blood ran cold.

"Move. NOW!" I screamed, grabbing Melba's hand and sprinting toward the Pass, leaving Cenric to run after us. She glanced behind us and when she looked back toward me, her eyes were as wide as saucers.

Two giant gray creatures were running toward us with unnatural speed. The guards' heads whipped up at the sound of our bodies crashing through the trees. They drew their swords, and looked directly at us. The one appearing to be the pack's leader had a sinister smile on his face.

Our only hope was to make it to the narrow portion of the slot canyon before the creatures got to us. They were likely too large to fit through, and they'd take care of the guards for us if we could just be quick enough.

Once we entered the pass, there were no trees for us to climb, and no stream of running water to stop the creatures. We had to be fast.

Cenric drew his sword and passed us. I expected to hear the clang of metal hitting metal as Cenric intercepted the guards, but there was only the crashing of the monsters behind us and the frantic pounding of our feet. He disappeared into the Pass moments before we reached the edge of the opening.

One of the waiting guards tried to grab Melba but she sliced into his hand with her dagger.

"You little bitch," he snarled at her with yellow teeth bared.

The next guard didn't see me before there was a dagger in his ribs. I pulled it out quickly, looking for another, but it was as if they had faded into the trees. The disgusting gray creatures were almost upon us, green-tinged saliva dripping from their maws.

Fear sliced through me. There was no way to win this battle.

"Run!" I yelled, pulling on Melba's arm. "We have to get into the Pass."

Our feet sunk into the deep, sand covered ravine as we ran. Clanging swords thundered in the distance. As we turned a corner we found Cenric fighting off several guards in a round outcropping in the rock. A trickle of sand slid down the wall, pooling with its like at our feet.

Backed into a corner with nowhere to go, the guards fought zealously. Cenric was bleeding from a cut to his cheek and forearm but otherwise looked unharmed. Jumping into the fray, my dagger met flesh, and crimson stained the ground. I listened for the sound of the creatures following us into the Pass but they seemed to have stopped. Were they afraid of confined spaces as well?

"Surrender to us, or die." The man I fought sneered. My eyes narrowed to slits as he circled me like a hungry shark looking for his next opening.

"You're the ones backed into a corner. You surrender."

Three guards looked up toward the top of the canyon walls while the one who had ordered our surrender smiled. "Are we?" he asked. A crooked finger pointed up to the sky, and at the same moment, a horrible screeching noise emanated from above us.

I glanced upward to see three gray creatures scaling the cliffside, crawling head first toward us. Gnarled claws dug into the sandstone, sending sand and debris skittering down the sides.

My mouth hung open in horror at what loomed before and above us. A green drop of their saliva hit my cheek, blistering the skin and burning like acid. I frantically swiped it away with my forearm but the sting lingered.

All my confidence that we would complete this Trial had disappeared. We were so incredibly, absolutely fucked. If we made it out alive it would be a gift from the gods.

Upon hearing the clattering above us, Melba, Cenric, and I, exchanged panicked glances. I inclined my head back the way we came, hoping they would follow me as I made a mad dash away. There was no way to fight the guards and the creatures without one or all of us dying, but we could possibly outrun them.

Exhaustion was a wave threatening to pull me under its depths. Adrenaline was the only thing keeping me upright as my wounds threatened to unstitch. "Run!" I yelled before taking off into the pass.

Gripping the sides of the cliffs, I launched myself through the winding slot canyon, using each turn as a way to fling myself further. Footsteps and heavy breathing followed after me, and I could only hope it was my friends.

I turned a corner only to find my path blocked by a towering boulder field. In the few moments I had paused, the clang of armor and the sounds of screeching creatures had caught up.

Cenric grabbed my hand as he ran past, pulling me toward the rocks and the exit far above. "We have to go up!" he yelled over the deafening noises. He clambered up, sending loose rubble tumbling down onto Melba and me.

The jagged rocks cut into my skin, leaving small cuts in their wake. I pulled myself up and over a boulder, only to be knocked down as my feet slipped in the shale. I looked over my shoulder to see the guards and the creatures enter. Turning back, I realized I could no longer hear Melba below me. There was no sound of rocks crashing or grunting as she pulled herself up.

Melba stopped mid-stride. Looking up at me, she smiled sadly before turning to make her way back down.

"Melba!" I yelled. "We have to go now!"

She shook her head, tears rimming her eyes.

"No! Please don't do this!"

Turning away, she ignored me.

"Melba!" I screamed, desperate. I wouldn't let her do this. I wouldn't let another person die for me.

"Go, Varine!"

I began to climb down the boulder, but she yelled back, "Varine, you have to go! I'll hold them off until you can get to the other side. Go. Now!"

Tears were streaming down my face, and I moved to brush them away, leaving my cheeks tinged in pink from the blood that lingered on my hands.

"I'm not leaving without you."

"You have to," she begged.

My breathing was coming in ragged gasps, all semblance of calm having left me long ago.

"Varine!" Cenric screamed from the top of the boulders.

I looked up at him, the tears clouding my vision, and then quickly back down to Melba just in time to see the first guard run toward her. She watched me, waiting for me to abandon her, but how could I?

"My one regret is that I did not share my truth with you sooner. That we didn't trust each other enough to find comfort with one another. I hope you live, Varine. I hope you find everything you are looking for, and more."

"Melba," I sobbed.

She drew the sword from her back, turning to block the attack of the incoming guards. The creatures seemed to linger in the back, watching and waiting until we were at our weakest. Dancing from his path, Melba blocked the blade and slashed her sword through the guard's abdomen. His body crashed to the ground as he tried desperately to staunch the wound. Melba turned just in time to dodge the next attack, metal whined against metal, her grip slowly starting to slip.

"Varine! Now! You have to climb!" Cenric yelled from somewhere out of sight.

I watched in horror as the creatures lurched forward, crawling toward us with unnatural speed. The thought of leaving Melba to die alone ripped me apart. She was an exceptionally trained warrior, but there was no way for her to survive this.

Melba had claimed that I was like her mother, but it was actually Melba that was like her mother—fierce and unyielding, and protective to a fault. That was the memory I wanted to be seared into my brain as I scrambled away from the bloodbath below. The last memory I would have of her. I reached the top of the boulder field just in time to hear Melba's scream pierce the air.

Cenric was in front of me in a flash, grabbing my arms and pulling me down the far side. My feet slipped in the loose rocks, but he held me close; his arms were the only thing keeping me upright.

"Melba," I blubbered, my shoulders heaving.

Cenric cradled my face in his hands but there was no sympathy or love on his face. "We have to go now or that will be us. Do you understand?"

Before I could respond, his grip on my forearm tensed, his fingernails digging into my flesh hard enough to draw blood as he jerked me through the rubble. I demanded he release me but he held tight, pulling me along. Exhaustion made it difficult to fight him, my head drooped as I stumbled behind him.

Once on solid ground, our pace slowed and the vast opening to the canyon loomed before us. The sounds of fighting and the creatures had ceased behind us. I wondered how long we had before they caught up. I wondered where Melba's body would lay for all eternity.

Silently, I mouthed the words that would allow Melba's soul to pass into the Afterlife, hoping that the gods would accept her even if they weren't being done correctly. A sob built in my chest when we finally broke through the opening and witnessed the green valley below us, and the city in the distance.

Pulling Cenric to me, I noticed his body had gone rigid, but I didn't care. His shirt was clenched in my fists as hot, wet tears streamed from my eyes. Finally, his arms wrapped around me and he whispered something into my hair over and over that I couldn't seem to make out. His fingers brushed the back of my head, soothing me until the sobs became hiccups.

Something hard dug into my back where his hands gripped me, but I didn't mind as long as he held me.

"I'm sorry," was the words he had been repeating that he now said louder. "I'm sorry," he said again.

I cupped his cheek reassuringly. "It's not your fault."

"I'm sorry," he whispered into my hair. His voice had taken on a different tone than his words before, something harsher, most insistent.

I looked up into his beautiful green eyes, tears had rimmed his eyes, spilling down into the sand that covered his cheeks. But where I expected to see sadness, something else was gleaming, something I couldn't recognize. One of his hands raised and I could just make out an object in my periphery. I pulled back, using my hands to shove away from him, desperate to understand what was happening but he tightened his grip, holding me firmly to him, painfully so.

"What—" I started but was cut off by the sharp sting of a heavy stone hitting my head.

I'm sorry, is all I heard as my body slumped and blackness consumed me.

CHAPTER 41

D arkness.

Never-ending darkness.

No beginning and certainly no end.

There was no counting the amount of times I drifted in and out of consciousness. No way to determine how many, if any, days had passed. I remembered nothing after Melba's screams had rang through the canyon. Had we made it out? Or had she sacrificed herself in vain?

Water dripped from somewhere above, the spray of droplets splashing against my burning forehead. My head pounded in my skull, and even behind my closed lids, colors danced and swirled in the all-encompassing black.

The stones beneath my stomach chilled the heat that ran through my blood, a welcome reprieve from the burning that seemed to fill me. Was this death, or was I just on the pathway there?

Whispered voices drifted to me on an unseen wind. The words were soft and rushed though I couldn't even begin to make out their meaning.

Each blink of my eyes was met with more of the unseeing night. I was beginning to wonder whether I had gone blind. Where was I?

My hands were tucked beneath my body, pressed so tightly to the ground that if I could see, I would likely witness stone imprints on them. Trying to push my body from the floor, I was met with screaming pain that radiated through the bones in my right hand and wrist. I flipped over onto my side, cradling what appeared to be a broken arm to my chest.

An agony-filled cry threatened to break from my lips, but I bit down on it to keep it at bay. I didn't know what enemies lurked here, and I certainly didn't want to find out in this condition.

Using what strength remained in my good arm, I pushed myself up and back, only to be met with more stone. My back hit the wall hard, and I struggled to bring in what little air my lungs would allow.

Solid walls and metal bars began to appear, and my vision finally adjusted to the darkness. A relieved sigh shuddered through my body at the knowledge that I had indeed not lost my vision. On either side of me was nothing but thick stone walls, and then a single door was cut in the metal before me. My body had grown so weak, rampant with fever, that I couldn't bring myself to test the door. A small voice in my head was telling me that even if I summoned the strength to do so, I would find it locked.

How long had I been in this cell? Where was Cenric? Was he alive?

I tried to rest my head against the wall behind me but was met with a sharp burst of pain radiating in my skull. Raising a hand to touch the tender spot, my finger came away slick with what could only be blood. At this point I was running out of body parts that had not been injured, and the ones that were, caused so much agony that the individual places couldn't be counted. Everything hurt, *everything*. But especially my heart.

Flicking my tongue out to wet my dry lips, I wondered how long I had gone without food or drink. My body was getting weaker by the moment, unconsciousness threatening to pull me under once again. My body began to shiver even as sweat poured down my forehead.

In the silence of my cage, I began to rock back and forth, trying to soothe the thoughts of Melba's death and the ache in my soul. My eyelids began to droop, and I raised my hand to pry them open, scared that if I were to fall asleep, I might never wake again. But the urge was too tempting. My arm dropped to my side as my eyes slid closed.

And just like Melba had, I wondered if I would die alone.

CHAPTER 42

My eyes fluttered as strong hands lifted me, cradling me to a hard chest. Jingling keys, tapping footsteps, and warm breath were all I knew.

But I was cold.

So cold.

I was awake for only moments before oblivion dragged me back under.

CHAPTER 43

L oud snoring jarred me awake, my eyes flying open, only to be blinded by the harsh floating lights above my head. I was no longer in the dark cell, and metal bars no longer confined me.

I lay in a soft bed in a near-sterile white room. No decorations adorned the walls, and there were no windows—only a single door. Staring up at the ceiling, I took stock of my body without moving. Nothing hurt any longer, and the pain in my hand had gone.

Had someone healed me?

The snoring grew louder next to me. Slowly, I turned my head, afraid that any sudden movements might bring back the pain or alert someone that I was awake before I was ready for them to know.

A figure was curled up on a chair next to me, their large body nearly falling off. Dark hair hung in their eyes, making them look boyish.

"Cenric," I breathed. He was here. He was okay. With my memory missing of the events that transpired, I had worried that something had happened to him—that he might have met the same fate as Melba.

At the sound of his name, his eyes snapped open. He scanned the room before looking back at me, his eyebrows drawn together in a look of concern.

I smiled back at him, tears sliding down my cheeks. His demeanor immediately changed; a look of relief passed over his features. Reaching out a hand, he caressed my cheek, and I leaned into his nearness.

Cenric was here. He was safe. We would figure out how to get out of here together—wherever *here was.* I attempted to raise a hand to stroke his cheek in return but found that I couldn't move. Pinning my arms to the bed were metal shackles. Chains rattled at my feet, preventing me from moving my legs. I was trapped, no longer in a cell but a prisoner all the same.

"Cenric?" I asked, panic racing through me. My heart felt like it was going to beat out of my chest. "What's going on?"

I ignored the ache in my wrist as I tried to rip the shackles from my arms with sheer force. Frantically, I scanned the room for a tool to use to free me, a pin, a weapon, anything, but found that the only objects in the room were the bed I was confined to and the chair Cenric sat in.

I narrowed my eyes at his ability to sit freely. He wasn't in chains.

"What's going on?" I repeated when he didn't answer me.

Cenric lunged for me, his hands frantically caressing the sides of my head, sending strands of my hair cascading in multiple directions as he attempted to soothe me. "I'm sorry. I'm so sorry," he whispered, refusing to meet my eyes.

Those words hit me like a lead weight in my chest.

The events of before came crashing back to me. My head spun with the weight of those words.

I'm sorry.

A blunt object raised above my head.

I'm sorry.

The darkness that consumed me.

I'm sorry.

My wrist shattered as I was tossed into a cold cell—infection running through my veins.

I'm sorry.

Melba was dead and Cenric had betrayed me.

He wasn't sorry. I had been taken as a fool, trusting a man I knew nothing about. My body jerked back from his touch, the chains tethering me rattled with the force as I tried to escape him.

"Do not touch me," I enunciated through clenched teeth.

He immediately dropped his hands but continued to stand over me and searched my eyes. Where I saw pain in his eyes, I'm sure he found only rage in mine.

"Where am I?" I demanded.

He opened his mouth and closed it again. Remorse washed over his face, and he clenched his fists to his side. "I think you already know."

Though I had a feeling I knew exactly where we were, I needed to hear it directly from his lips. To hear the exact level he had dipped to in his betrayal. "Where am I, Cenric?"

He exhaled loudly. "You're—we're in Eltris. We're in the castle."

"Why?"

I was met with only silence. He turned his head away, downcasting his eyes.

"Why are we in the castle? We got away! We made it through the Pass! Why are we here?"

He continued to stare wordlessly, a muscle in his jaw clenching.

"Answer me, Cenric."

"Because your friend here sold you out."

A figure stood in the doorway—one of the guards from the Pass. His putrid yellow teeth grinned back at me.

He was short and wide. The pale skin on his cheeks was flushed as if he had been exerting himself. Greasy tendrils of hair hung in his face and stuck to the skin behind his ears. His features were flat and squished together as if he had spent too much time with his face pressed against the panes of a window. He was absolutely revolting, and the way he looked at me like I was his next meal only made it worse.

Red-rimmed eyes grazed over my body, every muscle stiffening to keep the shudder that passed through my body at bay. He stepped closer, and I involuntarily cringed backward, trying to put as much distance between us as possible, but I was held firm by the chains. I thrashed against them, though it did nothing but cut into my skin and burn the energy I needed to conserve.

Amusement lit the man's eyes, his laughing filling the room at my discomfort. Cenric reached a hand for me, but I cast a glare that could turn a man into stone.

The disgusting man walked toward me, a golden set of keys jingling from the ring at his waistband with every step. I looked for anything that would cover me from the man's greedy gaze, but when I looked down, I noticed that I was no longer in my fighting leather and tunic. In my panic, I had missed entirely that someone had changed me into a nearly sheer shift that barely met the tops of my thighs.

Whipping my head to Cenric, I threw him an accusatory glare. "Did you dress me?" I demanded.

He threw his hands up in a gesture of surrender. "I didn't touch you," he swore, eyes wide. "Someone else changed you. Your clothes were soaked in urine and vomit, and you were burning up with fever; we—they had to do something."

"Why?" I wasn't quite sure what exactly I was asking. Why did he betray me? Why did he let them touch me? Why was I the only one in chains?

He shook his head, looking at the open palms that lay in his lap. "I—" he began but didn't finish. With a shake of his head, his lips formed a solid line, and I knew that he wouldn't give me answers to any of my questions.

I shouldn't have been surprised that Cenric was unwilling to give me the truth. This had been a pattern for as long as I had known him, having only given me information when it furthered his agenda. Had telling me he loved me been a ruse all along?

"My sister," he blurted, eyes wide. "It's my sister. They took her."

"Your sister?" I questioned.

"They were going to kill her unless I gave you to them."

The short guard laughed, but I didn't care to look at him right now; my eyes were glued to Cenric.

He continued. "I received a letter that they had found my sister and would kill her if I didn't do as they said. I didn't even know she was still alive, but they gave me so many details about her and my life that they wouldn't have known otherwise. I couldn't refuse." He sucked in a breath. "What was I supposed to do?"

"You betrayed me for a sister you believed to be long dead? Have you even *seen* her since you arrived?" I didn't know whether to believe him or not. His words screamed truth, but the delivery lacked sincerity.

"Please, Varine. You have to believe me."

"How much did they pay you?"

His mouth hung open wordlessly.

"That's what I thought. I never want you to touch me again," I spat, lacing each word with venom. "Don't even look at me. If you do, I'll gouge your eyes out like they did to that Shifter."

The guard rattled the keys in front of my face, and I blinked in surprise. "Now that we've settled this lover's quarrel, we have places to be and the Queen to see." He held up his other hand, finger extended. "Here's how this is going to go. First, I'm going to release your shackles, and you're not going to fight me like the good little girl you are." He paused, a yellow toothy grin spreading across his face as he raised another finger. "And second, if you do, I'll just kill you, sound fair?"

I looked to Cenric, his gaze still downcast, and then back to the guard. My body felt better than it had in weeks; I was confident that I could take both of them. The guard had a sword sheathed at his side, and while it was not my weapon of choice, it would have to do.

But where would I go once I disarmed him? How was I supposed to get out of here? How many more guards would be waiting for me outside these doors?

There was no time for the answers to all my questions. I had to act, it was now or never.

I nodded my head, doing my best to look sincere.

"She's not going to be compliant, Morton," Cenric warned.

Pasting a smile on my face that was more near a grimace, I spoke through my teeth. "Shut the fuck up, Cenric. You lost the privilege to speak about me."

At least I now had a name for the vile, sniveling face in front of me. *Morton.* An ugly name for an even uglier man. I dropped my shoulders in feigned defeat and lowered my eyes, doing my best to appear meek and timid. "I'll behave," I promised Morton.

Morton ran a clammy, possessive hand over my face and neck. I had to resist the urge to turn and bite him. His hands felt slimy and wrong against my skin. My eyes stayed glued to my lap, making sure I came off as submissive to this man.

His fingers started to trace the low neckline of the shift, his eyes glazing slightly. My hands clenched at my sides, but I remained still. "She doesn't look dangerous to me," he crooned.

Cenric cleared his throat, which snapped Morton back to the task at hand. He moved to the end of the bed and braced a hand on my bare ankle. "Remember what I said. Fight me, and I'll kill you."

I remained still as the key entered the lock, and the shackle sprung open. My feet were released first before he moved on to my wrists. I waited patiently until he moved back to my side.

Just a few more seconds.

When the last lock clicked, I changed my plan.

Lunging forward, my fist connected with Cenric's nose. Startled, he reared back, clutching it as blood began dripping onto the floor.

"You bitch! You broke my nose!"

Sharp pain ripped through my scalp as Morton dragged me toward the door by a fistful of my hair. "Ask them to fix it so I can do it again!" I screamed at Cenric. My fingers dug so deeply into the flesh of my captor's hand that crimson embedded itself under my nails. I thrashed, ripping at my hair, but he didn't release me. He was surprisingly strong, much more so than I had anticipated, easily dragging my flailing body toward the exit with ease, barely pausing to open the door. "That was for Melba, you piece of shit!"

If I ever got out of here, I was going to kill him. Rip him to pieces the way I'm sure the creatures had done to Melba, and when I was done, I would burn every piece of him with the discarded trash.

The door was thrown open when Morton kicked it, and two large guards waited for us, shackles in their hands. They secured the chains to my ankles and wrists; short loops of metal connected them together, allowing me to walk but not move much otherwise.

"I told you!" Cenric called to Morton, voice mumbled from where he still clutched his, hopefully broken, nose.

He snorted, fully handing me to the other guards. "I'm not stupid; I just wanted to see what she was capable of. And I knew she hated you enough to give me some entertainment." He smirked at me. "Honestly, I'm a little disappointed . . ."

The two guards grasped me under either arm and began to drag me away. I let them, not bothering to fight back, as I knew there was no way out now. I had used my one chance at escape, and it had been worth it.

Before the door shut behind me, I turned my head and spat toward Cenric. "I'll kill you, if it's the last thing I do. You better pray to the gods that if I ever get out of here, I won't find you, because if I do, I won't stop until you're dead. I hope your sister was worth it, you filthy traitor."

CHAPTER 44

T wo turns right, one turn left, a long straight down a hallway.

I counted each turn in the maze-like castle, the shackles rubbing the skin on my ankle and wrists raw with each step. Every exit, every window, doorway, and every face, or lack thereof, I memorized.

None of this was what I had expected. No wielders walked the hall; no Conjuror, Shifter, or Witch practiced magic or lingered in alcoves. We passed three young females cleaning floors and just a handful of other guards, but there weren't any full corridors of magic users stolen from their families.

The only magic-possessing creatures that dwelled anywhere around me were the ones holding my chains. I could feel it radiating off of them, a strange tingling sensation that pricked the hair on the back of my neck.

"Where is everyone?" I asked, craning my neck to the side to look at one of the guards, and then at the next when he didn't answer me. "Isn't this castle supposed to be full of people?"

The men guiding me were nearly identical. The one on my right had light red hair, not nearly as dark as my own, and the other had hair the color of mud. They were both tall, broad-chested, and apparently very annoyed with me, if their facial expressions were any indication.

"Why is it so empty?" I questioned, rephrasing what I had asked.

Instead of giving me any information, the muddy haired guard sharply yanked on my arm, causing me to stumble forward. My knees hit the ground, crimson blossoming from where they had scraped. "Hey! Watch it!" I hissed, clamoring back to my feet.

He stopped suddenly, turning toward me as he violently released my arm. I backed up a step, bumping into the other guard. My mouth hung open, ready to loose the words to defend myself.

"You will be silent before I cut your tongue from your mouth. We are not here to give you answers or even to speak to you, so close your gaping lips before I close them for you."

When my mouth slammed shut, his tugged up at the corner with a smug, self-righteous smile.

"That's what I thought. Keep moving."

Instead of holding me under my arm once again, he tugged on the chains at my waist, pulling me along by the small chain that connected my hands to my waist and feet. Each turn, every winding hallway, felt like I was getting sucked deeper into the belly of a beast. My palms began sweating, knowing each turn might be my last.

One left, three right, seventy-two windows, eighty doors, no exits.

The hallways were lined in gold—gold paintings, gold flowing tapestries against stone walls, and gold statues depicting the Queen. Even the stones on the floor were lined in speckles of gold. Through the stained glass windows, a rainbow of light covered the walls in bursts of color.

The closer we grew to our destination the more formal the decor became. Ornate rugs covered the ground, and glass chandeliers filled with floating orbs dangled overhead. Another left turn led us to large double doors at the end of another long hallway.

Though I had never been here, somehow I knew that what lay behind those doors would either be my savior, or my doom. Would Queen Desma keep me as part of her collection, or would she kill me when she found out that I was not only powerless, but also a trained assassin who had spent nearly half of my life killing her citizens? Or would she do with me whatever she had done with the other wielders, because they certainly weren't here.

Thousands of people had been ripped from their families and now just appeared to cease to exist. This castle couldn't contain their numbers; where were they?

My captors paraded me down the hallway, the walls lined with depictions of wielders locked in battle with soldiers bearing the four-pointed star. The paintings told a gruesome story, each one bloodier than the last. As I stopped in front of the closed doors, I beheld the final image of a soldier holding the bloody decapitated head of a Witch. A Witch who wore a golden crown upon her head.

I was no stranger to death and destruction, but seeing what was most likely my grandmother's death was disturbing on an entirely different level. Even after I had looked away, the image was still burned into my mind.

We waited behind the closed doors, the men standing beside me. I began to grow restless in the silence and decided to try speaking to them again now that we had reached the end of our journey. Looking back and forth between them, I noted that they shared similar facial features and appeared close to the same age—long noses and the same look of disdain.

"Are you two twins?" I asked tentatively.

"No, we're cousins," the red-haired one answered.

The rude one only glared at us, red hair throwing him a sheepish grin.

"Could have fooled me." I smiled smugly at the tiniest bit of information I had obtained. While it did nothing for the tension brewing, I knew information was like currency, and if everyone talked as easily as him, I would be bathing in riches soon enough.

"What part of shut up do you not understand?"

I ignored the question, knowing it was meant rhetorically. "How long are we going to stand here?"

The deep ebony of the doors in front of us starkly contrasted the white etched symbols on its surface. I recognized some of them, the whirls and jagged lines meant to ward a place from unwanted visitors. That was one of the best and the worst parts about Witch magic. Because they channeled magic through glyphs, they were far more capable of creating just about anything and harnessing objects that others couldn't even dream of. That's what made them so dangerous: the ability to create and destroy by a simple brushstroke.

Reaching out a hand to trace the symbols, I was made painfully aware of my inability to move freely, the chains restricting me from raising my hands much higher than my waist.

"So," I asked. "What do you guys do for fun around here?"

Before they could answer or yell at me to be quiet again, unseen hands slid the doors open, showering us in blinding golden light.

Like the rest of the castle, gold greeted me inside the expansive throne room. Three large golden pillars flanked each side of the room. At their tops were metalwork feathers, reaching for the ceiling like the fingers of a hand.

The room was long and wide, extending back to a rounded wall of windows with a throne in the middle. Three large round skylights illuminated the golden room from the entrance, center, and above the throne.

Arched floor-to-ceiling windows were strategically placed between each pillar, giving the feeling that the entire room was open to the air. The base of each pillar was surrounded by greenery. Plants of every kind, most of which I had never seen, even in a book—large thistle-leaved ferns, and blooming dark-petalled flowers.

An intricately designed collage of four pointed stonework stars graced the area directly below the dais. A rug of red was cast the length of the room, looking like a pool of blood on the pristine floor.

The dais was pale white, with golden stars etched into the sides of each of the three steps toward the main platform. It was large, encompassing the length of the back window. The golden high-backed throne sat in the center.

Feathers arched out from the back, like magnificent wings ready to take flight. Seated on a cushion made of crimson was a tall, thin woman, with hair so devoid of color it looked to be made of ice. It fell in waved sheets around her face and pooled onto her lap. Atop her head was a crown made of the darkest ebony. Eight points rose from the base in sharp dagger-like spikes, and a large jewel sat in the center—an amethyst so dark it nearly blended in with the crown.

The woman's thin lips were pressed into hard lines, and her copper-colored eyes followed my every movement as I was led into the room. To her right stood a towering man with pale blonde hair pulled back by a strip of leather. His jawline was sharp, and his features cruel as he turned to face me.

A small part of my brain screamed of his familiarity, had I seen him before?

The tan skin of his arms was etched in glyphs similar to the ones on the doors we had passed through, but from a distance I couldn't quite make out their meaning. He towered over Queen Desma, a look of cool disinterest plastered on his face.

Simple black pants and a white, near sheer tunic, were all he wore. Nothing like the deep purple uniforms with intricate stitching that the two guards next to me were dressed in. His large hands were weapons enough, but he still carried a sword at his side and two daggers strapped to either side of his muscular thighs.

I was tugged forward until I stood at the base of the dais. A sharp jerk sent me almost to my knees. Fresh blood trickled from the sores on my extremities, marring the once pristine floor.

"Asshole," I mumbled under my breath and cast a glare at the brunette guard.

Since the doors opened, I had counted every door, every window, and every weapon. If I could get free of the chains holding my hands I would have a fighting chance of escape. What was below me if I were to toss myself through one of the nine windows?

The guard to my left, the talkative redhead would be the first to go. The dagger at his side would be my weapon against the others. Then, the other guard would likely put up a fight, but I knew he would be no match for me. How sad his death would be at his cousin's blade.

The tall blond currently glaring at me might cause some issues, but despite his large stature, and apparent strength, I had speed on my side.

And then there was the Queen. She was a woman feared and lethal, but her appearance was that of fragility. Her limbs looked like they would snap as easily as a twig. I knew better though; I was often underestimated due to my size. My strength and ruthlessness however was shown in my errand streak. Maybe I was wrong to think less of her. After all, she had murdered my family, indirectly, but still, the blood remained on her hands.

"Bow before your Queen," the brunette hissed.

Desma raised an eyebrow at my defiance, looking me over from head to toe. A flicker of amusement brushed across her expression before turning to stone again.

I refused to kneel before a false ruler—the woman who had ruined so many lives.

Another sharp pull of the chains sent me sprawling onto my hands and knees. A surprised gasp left my lips as I looked at the smirking face of the guard. I pushed up to stand but found I couldn't move a muscle. I tried again, grunting with the effort but it was as if an invisible hand was holding me to the ground.

A wave of energy hit me, pushing me to the ground. I fought, straining against it but it didn't cease until my arms gave out beneath me. The sharp crack of my head hitting the tile rang in my ears, accompanied by spider-webbing pain. Fear raced through me at the power that had taken hold of my body.

"He said *bow*," Desma's sing-song voice stated.

Any thoughts I had of escape were now solid lumps in my throat. Was this how my mother had felt when she was paralyzed by magic and forced to watch the last bit of light leave my father's eyes?

"*Cursed.*"

"*Shameful.*"

"Useless."

"Dangerous."

The words she had used that I had come to know better than I knew myself. Their meaning rang true despite how hard I had tried to triumph over them.

My mother's worst nightmare had come to life. I was defiling my father's grave, his death meaningless as he had tried and failed to save me from this very moment.

The pressure of Desma's magic held me tightly to the ground, building until I felt my lungs begin to weaken and my bones threatened to break. She was far stronger than any wielder had a right to be, and I hadn't known she even was one until now. How had she kept something like that hidden for so long?

I was going to die here, I just knew it.

Pressure was building in my head, threatening to rupture with each passing second.

"Did you like my present?" she asked, releasing the holds of her magic just enough to allow me to lift my head.

She descended the dais to stand before me, her pale green gown brushing against the floor with each step and pooling around her like ripples in a pond.

Her voice was childlike, but the sneer upon her lips and the fire in her eyes was that of an aged and battle-hardened woman.

"What present?" I ground out, clenching my jaw. Whatever she believed she had given me was no gift.

"Your little Shifter friend from the market," she stated flatly, circling my useless body—a shark searching for prey. "He had wonderful things to say about you, my little thief."

Images of his destroyed body, hanging from the gates of the keep flooded my mind. His blood dripped into puddles that stained the soles of my boots. Had he been the first betrayal? Did he tell her who I was?

My lips pulled back from my teeth as I watched her dance around me. She smiled before turning on her heel, heading for her throne once again.

"I thought so."

When she turned to sit, the bounds of magic released me. A huff of air poured from me as my body went from taut to limp. I scrambled to my feet, the chains around me falling in an echoing clink.

"Say 'thank you,'" she commanded.

"Fuck you," I retorted before lunging for the red-haired guard's weapon.

My fingertips brushed the hilt of his dagger, and the guard's eyes widened in surprise for only a moment before I found my body immobilized once more. Searing pain built in my toes, racing through my bloodstream as it traveled upward, my skin burning from the inside out.

She tsked. "Now, that just won't do."

Pain, blinding, hot pain ripped through me, and a scream built in my chest. The organs in my body clenched and released in spasms in time with the pulse of magic.

"Are you going to behave?" a deep male voice asked from the dais.

I couldn't turn my head to see who had spoken but knew it must have been the tall, cruel-looking guard. I gasped out a "yes," unable to do much more. The pain continued, and I wondered if everyone in this room could hear the lie in my voice.

Death meant nothing to me unless I could take the worthless beings before me into the Afterworld as well.

A bucket of magical cold washed over me, the pain retreating as fast as it had come. Crouching on the ground, I watched the guards retreat to stand by the door. This must have been what a wild animal felt like when captured and brought to the market for entertainment. All I could think about was ripping out the throats of everyone in this room.

"I know who you are, Witch, and I am in need of your services."

I shook my head. "Unless you're wanting someone to be assassinated, I'm not entirely sure what you mean." Waving a hand to the men in the room, I looked at her skeptically. "I'm sure anyone else here would better suit your needs."

She threw her head back, a sharp laugh echoing through the room. "Not those services, dear. I am in need of services from the Crestin line."

"Hmm, you should have thought about that before you had my grandmother murdered."

Anger was a rose blossoming inside of me. I tried to collect my features into a cool mask but rage was not an emotion easily hidden. I'd rather die than help this bitch.

A chalice appeared from thin air at the snap of her fingers. She stared over the top at me as she took a long drink. Her body seemed to glow as whatever she ingested trickled down her throat. With another snap of her fingers, it was once again done.

Her lips pouted out, making a show of feigning disappointment. "You haven't even heard what I wish of you and you already reject me? What if I could promise you power beyond your wildest dreams and freedom to roam the continent, or any continent you wish, unburdened?" she asked. "Would you refuse me then?"

"I am marked as the property of the Order. I do not have freedom," I repeated the words Amias had drilled into us blandly. The guard at her side noticeably tensed, his hands clenching and loosening at his side. His face gave nothing away, all his features remaining in the neutral cold stare he seemed to have perfected.

"How naïve to think that the only forces that control you are that of the Order." She laughed. "My task is quite simple, dear. I just need you to retrieve an amulet for me." She paused, waiting for me to speak. When I didn't, she continued. "In case you didn't quite understand, that is an order, not a question."

"Why? What do you want with an amulet you can't get yourself?"

"It holds something taken from me, and I want it back."

"Like I said"—crossing my arms over my chest—"get it yourself then."

She had been examining her nails but she looked up sharply, her eyes narrowing to slits. "You will refuse my promise of magic? Of power? Of everything you've dreamed of in your little mortal life? Do not think that I know nothing of your desires. We are one and the same, you and I. You wish to destroy the very thing that gave you freedom, and I wish to destroy those that took mine away."

I scoffed. "You know nothing of me."

"You think that I have not been watching, Witchling? You truly believe I have let you live this long and don't know you? My spies are all around you, I even know what you hide in the bottom of your trunk." Another snap and she twirled the dragon blade on her fingertips. "If you refuse, you are of no use to me."

My mouth hung aghast at the web of betrayal she was weaving. Not even the place I had called home was safe—the enemy was merely biding its time. Even without saying the words I knew what they meant. If I refused, she would kill me.

She was right, I had dreamed of magic, of tearing down the controls Amias used to bind me. Surely this task was more than simply retrieving a necklace.

Sensing my hesitation, she continued. "Once you retrieve the amulet, I will reward you with magic beyond your wildest dreams. We will have more power than we ever imagined and I will be free of this shell of a body."

I laughed at her words. "I'm not naïve enough to believe that you won't kill me the moment I return this amulet to you."

"That's certainly a risk you take. How much do you value your magic?" She tilted her head to the side. "What would you do for even a hint of power?" Blue fire danced at her fingertips, she held it aloft so I could witness as the flames grew until they wound like a serpent around her outstretched arm.

I shook my head, fighting my soul's longing for the magic it craved. "Why me? Send your little pet." I nodded toward the guard.

The twitch of a muscle in his jaw was the only indication that he was listening to the conversation. His eyes bore into me, and while I couldn't make out their color from where I stood, the edge of familiarity struck again. I searched his figure but found nothing that would lead me to believe I knew this man in this life or another.

Her face turned down in a frown. "You see, that is the problem and why I need *you*. The terms of your father's bargain seal you and any of your blood to the relics."

How could she possibly know about that? Who was this woman?

To my surprise, she laughed—a sound I was beginning to hate as it grated on my last nerve. I had never felt so in the dark about my own life before, and it was wearing on my soul.

"*A protector of the relics in exchange for a magical block,*" she mocked, eyes near bursting with rage. "Those stupid Dragons laughed in my face when I came to claim what was rightfully mine." As if catching herself, a smile returned. "Unfortunately, the spell they cast means only you can retrieve it."

I looked around the room, waiting for someone to shout that this was just a cruel joke. "This is ridiculous. What are you even talking about?"

> "*In long days before, a mystical charm,*
> *A long-held secret, a potent arm.*
> *A gem so rare, with magic might,*
> *In daylight dulled, in shadows, light.*
> *Once adorned, the gods, in battles raged,*
> *Harnessed its strength, foes to cage.*
> *Through incantations and spells it weaved,*
> *A shield of protection, never to be cleaved.*
> *A family legacy, a sacred trust,*
> *To safeguard the treasure from forces unjust.*"

The words filled my mind like nails, scratching my brain. They were spoken to me, but my ears did not hear them. I covered my head to block them out, the ending trailing into a girlish giggle. Desma had just spoken directly into my head.

"What the fuck was that? How did you do that?" I demanded. The touch seemed to linger, scratching at my mind with its claws on its way out.

She ignored my question, waving a hand. "There's much more to it than that, but you get the jist."

The wheels in my mind turned, attempting to untangle the web of information. I replayed her words, wondering if the amulet she was after was the one that had sealed the god Zylah's magic inside. Either way, I wasn't about to help.

"Ask someone else. I won't help you, and don't do that weird mind-whispering thing again."

"There is no one left to ask. If I had known of this deal, I wouldn't have disposed of Mathilda so quickly. Ursa, while living, is useless."

"My mother is alive?"

I had thought she was long dead, never bothering to write or visit when she knew exactly where I was.

She shrugged. "Driven mad by the death of your father, but very much alive." She rolled her eyes as if my father's death was a great inconvenience to her. "She is useless for my desires, though she does make a decent housemaid."

Clenching my fists, I fought to rein in the temper that was brewing in me at the disgusting way she referenced my mother—my mother, who was somehow still alive and here in this castle. I could see her after so many years apart, ask her all of the burning questions that ate at me, and finally get some answers. Would she remember me if she was truly as damaged as Desma claimed? Could she give me answers, or were they now lost?

I crossed my arms across my chest. "Won't stealing the amulet anger the gods? I'm sure even someone as powerful as yourself wouldn't want that wrath brought down upon you."

Her eyes seemed to alight with fire; she leaned forward, bracing her hands on the arms of the throne. Her fingernails dug into the plush sides. "You stupid girl. Do you not understand? I *am* a god. And once you retrieve Aradia's amulet, I will be made whole again. You will return to me that which has been stolen."

My mouth opened and closed in rapid succession. Desma was not the name of one of the gods. I shook my head back and forth, looking down at my feet as my head filled with confusion. It wasn't that she wanted Zylah's power, she *was* Zylah.

The god so bloodthirsty for power the others had cast her out in fear of what she would do. The feeling of sharp nails once again entered my mind, caressing the ridges of my brain and sending a tingling sensation through my body. The hand took its time holding and taunting me as if deciding what to show, or take from me next.

As if reading my thoughts, she waved her hand dismissively at me before placing it again on the arm of her throne, leaning fully into the back of the chair. "Names mean nothing. Desma, Zylah, Queen, God, Goddess. Call me what you wish. Who I am cannot be defined by one name alone. When I am reunited with my power I will be returned to my former glory, I will become a god once again, and I will make them pay for what they have done to me."

"How?" I demanded between labored gasps, the hand slowly retreating.

"Though the gods have stolen my power, locking it in that wretched amulet, I am anything but powerless." She sneered as she angrily spat the words. "I could sense their treachery in my very bones. So, I created a backup plan." With a snap of her fingers, the chalice was back in her hand. She held it up, letting the light reflect on the bronze cup lined with black stones. She swirled the liquid inside before taking a sip.

The red liquid stained her lips before she could lick them clean. "I might not have any of my own magic, but through this chalice, I can siphon the power of any wielder simply by drinking their blood."

By drinking their blood.

I repeated those words in my head until they caught a foothold in the waves of my brain. That was why there were so few wielders living in this castle. She was not collecting them, she was feasting upon them. I stumbled back, my hand unconsciously raising to my mouth to stifle the horror of what she was doing.

She grinned at me, her teeth coated in the remains of the crimson blood she had devoured. "Do we have a deal? You will retrieve the amulet, and I will let you live in return."

I no longer had a choice, she would keep murdering innocent people until she got what she wanted. Doing as she asked was the only way to stop this horror.

"But what of my magic?" I protested. I wouldn't enter into a deal where she only provided half promises.

She shook her head. "Those Dragons can be so tricky with their wording. The enchantment I spoke to you is only part of it, the other portion holds the answers you seek."

"Tell me it then! I would be much more useful to you if I had magic," I pleaded, considering throwing myself at her feet.

For so long, all I had wanted was to escape the confines of the mountain house—the confines of my parents. When I promised myself to the Order, I thought that would be my escape toward the life of adventure and quests I had always dreamed of, but it was a prison. Magic is what would bring me freedom, I just knew it.

Each choice had a conscience, discretion being a powerful burden to carry. My father's choices, my mother's choices, and ultimately, my choices led me to this complicated decision. It was an amazing thing to have so much power over the fate of the continent.

"I am not stupid, Witchling. I'm not giving you the answer just to have you run away with it. No, I need you to do just a simple task for me, and then I'll give it to you."

Even though I was afraid of the answer, I still asked. "And what will you do with the amulet once you have it?"

Her smile turned cruel. "I will become the most powerful being of all."

A sick feeling twisted in my stomach. Something about how she smiled down at me from that golden throne, the blood of magic on her lips, sparked defiance within me. I couldn't let her get her hands on that amulet. She had killed my family in her quest for power, and I knew, without a doubt, that she would not stop with her revenge until she had cleaved the world in two and sucked the marrow from the bones of the galaxy.

Here it was, everything I had ever wanted, within my grasp, being offered to me on a platter and ripe for the taking. But it wasn't enough.

I had been stripped of my very being. I had my autonomy taken time and time again by those I thought I had trusted. Amias had held me and so many other children prisoner, trapping us in servitude. Zylah had done the same thing to hundreds, if not thousands, of wielders. She stole them from their homes and bled them dry.

A smile formed across my lips, the beginnings of a plan forming in my head. I waited for the icy kiss of her mind touching mine, but nothing happened. Hopefully, she wasn't reading my thoughts right now because I would be eternally screwed.

Her teeth were bared in a mockery of a grin. "Do we have a deal?"

Satisfied that she had no idea I planned to betray her, I agreed. "I will retrieve the amulet, but what of the Order? The tattoo on my back marks me as theirs. It is inked in magic that cannot be broken."

"Amias is still hiding that secret? You are not property of the Order until you complete your Trials. The spell is incomplete until that moment. Luckily, we caught you just in time—two Trials left, right?"

"I was about to complete one when you so rudely interrupted."

This revelation was unsurprising. Amias had never been forthcoming with information, so why would this be any different?

"And what of Cenric and his sister? I demand as part of the deal they be released and unharmed."

She smirked. "He does not have a sister."

"Excuse me?"

"He does not have a sister," she repeated. "The Oracles spoke to me, not having the same reservations as my family's other pets. They told me exactly where to find you, which is why Cenric was there. The son of one of my trusted advisors makes for an excellent spy, don't you think?" She giggled.

"No," I said, unable to believe her. Cenric had sworn he loved me, and though I didn't love him in return, I thought it was true. I trusted him, but he sold me out long before I knew it. "No, Amias would have known."

"It was a gamble, I'll admit, but that old bastard has lost the ability to discern over the last hundred years. He would be surprised by what was happening right under his nose. My lovely guard, who retrieved your blade, practically walked through the front door to do so." She ran a possessive hand over the arm of the guard next to her, licking her lips as if she were trying to taste his blood through the air he breathed. "The Order has become quite the embarrassment; that's why I don't imprison any of you; it's far more entertaining to watch you all become your own tormentors."

Staring down at my hands, I shook my head and wished I was anywhere but here. Nothing made sense any longer.

"If we have a deal, we will seal it in our blood so neither can break the terms." She picked up the Dragon blade from where it rested on the arm of her chair, raising it so it shimmered in the light.

She sliced her palm with the blade, letting a thin line of blood well from the shallow cut. She held it out to me, but she ripped it back before my fingers could graze it. "Don't even think about going back on the deal. If either of us dies before the deal is complete, the other's life is forfeit."

Wincing in preparation for the pain, I sliced into my palm but was surprised to find that it didn't hurt. As beads of crimson welled, the blade turned frigid to the touch. The sensation was so jarring I nearly dropped it.

"Here are the conditions of the deal. You shall retrieve the amulet of Aradia and bring it back to me unharmed. In return, I will allow you to live and assist you with the block on your magic. Do you still wish to add in that part about Cenric?" Her tone was mocking.

I had been so stupid to trust him and to think that I almost believed that he had done it for his sister. I would give anything for my father to be alive, to just speak with him one last time. If that had been Cenric's motivation, I almost couldn't fault him, but he truly had a heart as dark as the night. I had been mistaken to let the appeal of his loving embrace suck me in.

"No, but I swear to you that if he comes near me again, I'll slit his throat with this blade."

"I do not care what you do with mortal lives, nor do I truly care what you do with those of a Wielder; I just ask that if you wish to sully the hallways of my home with blood, you bring the magical ones back for me to drink." She paused, waiting for a response from me that did not come. "Now, if there are no additional terms to be added, it shall be done."

Oaths were binding, so I carefully sifted through the words for any hint of deception. The last thing I wanted was to be trapped in a half-truth, in a loophole that would end in my death. Finding none, I repeated her words back to her. "It shall be done."

As the oath sealed, the Dragon blade sent icy crystals training up my arm. When I tried to drop it, it clung to my frozen skin. As our blood dripped to the floor, steam rose and melted away and remnants of ice.

I had just made a deal with a god.

Zylah clapped with glee. "Now that's been settled, Waylon, can you show our guest to her room?"

The guard next to her nodded, striding quickly from his position toward me and straight past. I watched as Zylah disappeared from the dais, leaving nothing but wispy tendrils of shadow in her wake.

Waylon moved quickly, heading for the double doors at the end of the room. He moved quickly, hurriedly even, but not fast enough to avoid me seeing the black ink tattooed on the skin of his back. The near sheer fabric of his shirt nearly blurred the tattoo that I knew so well.

A dagger, wreathed in beautiful, deceptive clematis. A scale hanging from either side of its guard.

Branded on his skin, right between his shoulder blades.

Marking him as the property of the Order of Assassins.

CHAPTER 45

"**Y**ou're supposed to be dead."

Waylon, the Journeyman that was supposedly poisoned and long dead, was here. Alive, unharmed. Seeing him reminded me of that first day, the way I had been crudely beaten. How he had stood by and watched, his hands crossed across his chest, seemingly amused by the sight of my pain. I felt no relief in his familiarity. I felt nothing but anger and hatred for this man.

"And yet, here I stand." He smirked mockingly.

Waylon was still as arrogant as ever. I haven't missed his company in the keep, and I wanted nothing to do with him now. I stared intently at his back, the tattoo between his shoulder blades as he tried to motion me from the throne room.

"How?" I asked. "How did you do it?"

"That's none of your business."

I still hated him. "I would have preferred you stayed dead."

He smirked, looking at me from head to mud-crusted toe. "And I would have *preferred* you died during the Trials. It looks like we're both disappointed."

"I hate you." The words flew from my mouth. I wish they had the sting I wanted them to carry, but they felt childish.

"Get in line."

I glared at his back as he led me through the palace. We winded through lengthy hallways and climbed three different sets of stairs. By the time we reached the top, I was sweaty and weak with fatigue.

He led me down a long hallway until we reached a large wooden door. The walls were empty in this part of the palace. All the windows were shrouded, leaving the hallways in near darkness, save for the floating lights that moved with us.

"So, you're going to lock me in a tower and hold me prisoner?"

"You're not a prisoner; you're just not free to leave," he said flatly, reaching around me to open the door. He was too close, the proximity making me back up until I was a few steps into the room.

With my hands on my hips, I stared at him incredulously. "That's what a prisoner is."

"Semantics."

"I'd like to see you locked in a tower, and then I can call your freedom *semantics*," I grumbled. Of course he had no sympathy for my position; he got out. He left the Order, and he chose to join the Queen. Here, he stood in a position of power and authority. Everything this pompous asshole ever wanted.

I would be locked away in this dirty tower until the Queen decided to send me on this ridiculous quest. That's how my life had progressed, consistently trading one prison for the next.

"Can I see my mother?" I blurted, suddenly remembering that the Queen had said she was here, living in this castle.

His eyes, a soft golden brown, searched mine. His face softened for only a fraction of a second. I swore I had imagined it before it returned to the icy indifference he must have learned from Amias. "I'll come get you first thing in the morning. We'll begin training then."

"I don't want to train," I snapped. "I asked to see my mother. I'm the best assassin in Kalahvin. There's nothing you can teach me that I don't already know."

He took a step toward me, his frame towering over me. "You would not survive a minute in Tinuag. You have no idea of the creatures that lurk in the forests. You have been sheltered and are just as naïve as you have always been."

He was trying to intimidate me, but I wouldn't be afraid. I had trained for almost half of my life to be a force to be reckoned with. I wouldn't be intimidated by some man because of his brute strength or his empty threats. I stepped toward him, looking up to see into his eyes.

"I want to see my mother," I repeated. His jaw clenched, and I savored the thought that I was getting to him.

"I did not ask you what you want; frankly, I do not care." He shook his head and stepped back, closing the door in my face.

The floor was cold beneath me, but I didn't mind, my back resting against the sturdy, gnarled wood of the door that I slid down against it the second the door shut behind me. I couldn't hold it together any longer. A rush of tears swept from my eyes and blurred my surroundings. Nothing was ever going to be the same again; everyone I knew and loved had been ripped from me, and I feared that my heart would never recover.

I was terrified of the position that I had found myself in—still no magic, and now I had yet another person to control me. I needed to figure out a plan and a workaround for this deal I had entered into. I wiped my eyes and surveyed the room before me.

Small, yet cozy. It was large enough to contain a bed big enough for at least four, a vanity with a small mirror, and a roaring fireplace. A soft, cream-colored rug spanned most of the stone floor. No windows or tapestries graced the white walls; the only illumination was the fire and twin floating lights above the bed.

A door to the right led to a small washing room. I wanted to stay barricading the door, but despite my questionable safety, I needed to use the washroom. My bladder was full, and I was sure I could be smelled from several doors down. I wiggled the door handle of my room to find that it had been locked from the outside.

Letting out an exasperated sigh, I left my position on the ground and investigated the bathing chamber. There was no use in barricading the door; nothing in this room was heavy enough to keep out an intruder, and it seemed like they were more interested in keeping me in.

Maybe it was for the safety of the castle occupants. A smirk crossed my face at the thought.

Emptying the contents of the small jars that lined the edge of the tub, the sharp, sweet scent of vanilla and amber drifted through the air. A knock sounded from the main room. I quickly looked for anything that could be used as a weapon but found nothing. I gripped one of the jars in my hands; maybe the sticky soaps could blind someone enough to aid my escape.

Peering around the washing room door, I found a tray had been placed at the entrance to the room. Whoever had entered had quickly left, and I wondered if it had been Waylon.

The thought was quickly dismissed. Surely, in a palace this large, a warrior would not need to do the work of a maid.

Steaming piles of meat, fresh vegetables, and seasonal fruit greeted me. But despite the hunger that rumbled through my empty belly, I couldn't bring myself to sample even a scrap of what they had provided.

I let my sore body soak in the washtub until the water had turned cold and my skin pruned. When exhaustion finally dragged me from the tub, the large bed welcomed me like an old friend. I buried myself deep into the fur-covered blankets and let the crackling of the embers in the fireplace lure me into sleep.

CHAPTER 46

Sweat dripped down my back, and the loose strands of my hair were plastered to my face and neck. "I'm done," I panted from the ground that Waylon had once again slammed my back into. "You've proven your point."

Waylon grunted his disapproval. "I'm not trying to prove a point. I'm trying to help you."

His fists pounded on my door early this morning, startling me awake. I had no concept of time in the windowless room, but I knew it had to be the next day as I had felt more rested than the previous days. He had tossed black leather pants and a white linen shirt to me before slamming the door shut again.

I quickly changed, donning my dirt and blood-covered boots. I ran my hands over where the daggers should have been sheathed at my sides and sighed in their absence. I hadn't felt so powerless since my first days at the keep. Seeing Waylon had brought back all the memories of how frightened I had been.

Wordlessly, he led me down hallway after hallway. I marked every twist and turn, hoping that I would soon memorize the entirety of this expansive palace. We entered a long room on the second floor; it was empty save for the soft mats layering the floor and a rack of weapons in one corner. Large windows filled the room with sunlight, and I resisted the urge to push my body against the warm panels.

I pushed the strands of hair from my eyes and debated what weapon I could sneak out of here unnoticed. Waylon caught my line of sight and scolded me.

"Don't even think about it. I know every weapon in this room, every speck of dust. You move a single object, and I will know."

How confident of him. I had trained longer and harder with the Order. But he progressed too quickly, not learning his lessons fully. I would be sure to use that against him.

The morning had been spent with Waylon, proving time and time again that his strength outmatched my speed. Every time I landed a quick blow and danced away, he would push forward until I had nowhere else to go. I was no match for him in hand-to-hand combat; he was too strong and much quicker than I would have anticipated.

If I couldn't beat him, maybe distraction would work.

"How did you do it?" I asked.

"Do what?"

"Fake your death." When he ignored my question, I pressed on. "How did you trick Amias? He had to have known, right?"

He extended a wooden sword out to me. "We're going to move on to weapons. Your lack of ability in hand-to-hand combat bores me."

"Did Amias help you?" I pressed. "What a strange turn of events that would be." The tick of his jaw was the only sign his annoyance was growing. That seemed to be his tell. A smile grew across my face at his reaction.

"Where did you even come from? Before the Order?"

His eyes narrowed into a glare. "If you're looking for a tragic backstory, you're not going to find it. I don't have any flaws for you to exploit, so you might as well stop looking."

"Aren't you full of yourself?" I mocked.

"You're awfully thorny for a girl with no other options," Waylon said with a smirk. "Maybe your father should have called you 'Bramble' instead of 'Flower.'"

I was annoyed that he knew the nickname my father had given me, but it didn't surprise me. I didn't know what my mother had told them. "I do have options."

Waylon folded his arms across his chest. "You can either complete the quest and train appropriately," he said, regaining his composure. "Or you'll die."

I rolled my eyes, crossing my arms in a crude imitation of him. "Sure sounds like options to me."

It did. Options were options. I didn't have to like them, but I had some semblance of a choice in this, whether they liked it or not. I stared at the sword Waylon was holding out to me.

I didn't like the way he watched me. His eyes glinted with amusement, and I swear the end of his lip twitched up in a smile for just a fraction of a second before his face once again turned to stone. He thought this was a game, huh? I'd show him how to play.

I lunged for his leg, hoping to leave him sprawled on the ground like he had done so many times to me this morning, but he simply swatted me away like a bothersome fly. I looked up at him from my back. "Why are you so fast," I grumbled.

He stood over me, his fair hair shining in the rays of the sun. It had been tied back, secured by a thin band of leather. As we trained, strands had escaped, and now, as he looked down on me, they framed his face like a halo. He was no angel, though he was nearly as handsome as one. I couldn't think of him like this. I couldn't let myself think of anyone like that ever again.

"So," I said lightheartedly. "You rummaged through my things. If I find any of my underwear missing, I know who to talk to."

"If you're not going to take this seriously, we're done for today."

"Aww, did I embarrass the big tough warrior man?"

He strode for the door, throwing it open. "You're going to get eaten alive in the Forbidden Lands. We only have a few weeks before leaving, and you are in dire need of training." He paused, looking over his shoulder. "Good luck finding your way back to your room."

The door slammed behind him and I was left alone to my thoughts. With nothing to do now that my teasing had upset the kill-joy warrior, I wandered the halls in search of something, but I didn't know what.

Everything looked the same, a maze of identical rooms and hallways.

A library, that's what I needed. Surely, there were books on the subject of Dragons and how to alter or break deals. Maybe I would even get lucky and find an entire section on them.

I grew frustrated as I wound around and around through unmarked hallways, peeking into empty rooms. There was never anyone for me to ask for directions; there was just endless emptiness. I turned a corner and found myself at a dead end. Nothing but a table with a floral vase sat at the end of the hall. I sighed in frustration and looked at the ceiling, beseeching the gods to assist me.

"Library's on the bottom floor. If that's what you're looking for."

I turned to find who the soft voice belonged to but found only an empty hallway behind me. Completing my turn in a full circle, I found myself utterly alone.

"Down here."

I looked to my feet, where a plump, tawny tabby blinked up at me. It looked at me with knowing eyes that struck me as familiar. Had that cat just spoken?

"Caylina?" I asked. There was no way my cat would be here; too many years had passed. She would have been long gone, but the resemblance was uncanny. I missed Caylina; I missed her companionship and the normalcy of home.

Before my eyes, the tabby's form grew. Where claws extended were now long bronze fingers. Her back arched and grew, her spine extending until it resembled my own. Short, spiked brown hair protruded from a short, squat woman who now stood in place of where the cat once did.

I stumbled backward, in awe of what I had just witnessed. I had met many Shifters but I had never watched them actually shift into another form.

309

She wore a brown dress that was wrapped with a cream-colored apron. She smiled up at me. As I looked down at her, worried that I would see the sharp canines of the cat, she looked utterly ordinary.

The woman wrapped me in a hug before I could move, burying her face in my abdomen. "It is so nice to finally get to introduce myself to you, Varine." I placed my hands on her shoulders but made no move to return the embrace.

"Caylina?" I repeated. My childhood cat was here and was somehow a flesh and skin person.

"It's me, child. I have so much to tell you."

CHAPTER 47

I slammed another book shut, startling Caylina, who had returned to her feline form and now rested on the window sill, basking in the midday light.

Sighing, I rested my head on the long wooden table and closed my eyes. We had been at this for hours, and I had no more information than when I started. Caylina had led me to the library and I had gasped when she flung open the large wooden doors.

The library was massive, spanning two full levels of just books and several more containing quiet studying tables that ascended into one of the castle's spires. The room was illuminated by large windows and a dangling chandelier full of floating light orbs. It was both beautiful and morbid as it had obviously fallen into disuse.

A thin coat of dust coated everything in the room, causing my nose to crinkle and my eyes to water. There were books of all ages dating back hundreds of years to almost recent. Every genre imaginable filled the shelves, from history to romance to mystery and adventure. Melba would have loved it. The room, though ripe with grime, smelled exactly as I had remembered her.

If she was here, she would know what to do. She would hold me in her arms and tell me everything would be okay. I needed her. I needed someone to tell me that everything would work out, even if I knew it was just a lie.

"I'm going to find more books," I called to Caylina. Her furry head rose, blinking at me before she rested it again on her paws and closed her eyes. It was surprising Waylon hadn't come to find me after I had left so abruptly. He seemed

311

to think he was my keeper, and I was beginning to wonder if the Queen had appointed him to watch me or if he was doing it out of his own suspicions.

I ran my fingers over the dusty spines, savoring the feeling of the old paper on my fingertips. Everything reminded me of what I had lost. I let myself cry within the walls of my room, but I wouldn't show that weakness now, not when I didn't know who was watching. I fought the sting that threatened my eyes and steadied my breathing.

Winding through the stacks, I willed the information I needed to call for me. I begged the gods to guide me and lead me to the information, but no beacon in the night was found. Everything looked the same, each book bound identically to the next in emerald green covers that resembled the book my father had gifted me.

My eyes swam from the words I had read, everything from the history of Kalahvin to the history of magic itself. But there was no record of my curse or how to remedy it. Having a library this large was arbitrary if it didn't hold useful information. I was growing frustrated and worried that I would run out of time and the Queen would run out of hospitality.

The farther into the stacks I traveled, the darker it became. An alcove appeared in front of me, but I couldn't figure out what it contained in the blackness. My curiosity got the best of me, and I continued toward it, noting the silence of the library. A few steps from the alcove, I paused, listening for any sounds of approaching footsteps, but I heard none. I silently reprimanded myself for sneaking around. I was allowed to be here; I should be acting like it.

I let my next footsteps smack the stone floor louder, laughing to myself.

"There's nothing in there," Caylina said, stepping out from the side of a book stack. Her sudden appearance startled me, and I threw a hand to cover my racing heart. "It's just empty shelves," she continued, trailing off when she noted the look of shock on my face.

She smirked at me, looking me up and down. "Are you sneaking around?"

"I'm allowed to be here," I said defensively.

Her lips were drawn into a line, humor dancing in her eyes as she tried not to laugh at me. I narrowed my eyes on her. "And you shouldn't go around sneaking up on people. You're much too quiet in your feline form. Announce yourself by knocking a book from a shelf or something a cat would do."

She laughed now, throwing her head back, letting it move through her entire body before it was liberated from her mouth. "I'm headed to get us some lunch. I'll leave you to your—" She paused. "Exploring," she finished with a wink.

"My exploring," I mocked as I continued toward the alcove. The darkness had begun to seep around me; I extended my hand to make sure I did not run into anything. The last thing I needed was to arrive back to my room with a book-sized knot on my forehead.

I shuffled forward and stumbled as my foot hit something hard. The sound of an object sliding on the floor resounded in the quiet. I dropped to a crouch, searching for what I had tripped over. My fingers trailed over a velvet cover, lifting it close to my face, I sighed deeply when I couldn't make out a title. I tucked it under my arm to read in the light.

My hands brushed the shelves of the alcove, using touch where my sight failed. I found them disappointingly empty despite the way I seemed to be called to them. Maybe the dust and mold were getting to my head. I could quite possibly be imagining the pulse of energy that seemed to emanate from that direction.

Returning to a better-lit bookcase, I snatched two interesting-looking books from the shelves, briefly looked at their titles, and tucked them under my arm with the other.

The table I had been working at was strewn with a cluttered array of parchment, quills, and miscellaneous books. The three new ones only added to the mess. I opened the first and found it to be a memoir of a Witch from a small village in the Temple of the Sun. Skimming through the pages, the only useful information I found was a glyph shaped like a serpent biting its tail that allowed water to suspend without a container. That would have been useful during the last Trial.

I closed the cover and added it to the pile of the others I had discarded. My stomach growled, and I knew Caylina would likely be returning with a tray of lunch soon. Reaching for the second book, my fingers brushed velvet. Suddenly remembering the strange book that had nearly caused me to fall, I picked it up and examined the cover.

It was entirely black with no markings on the spine or covers. A gold band of fabric held it closed. Moving the fabric away and opening it, my breath caught in my throat at my recognition of the words on the front page. This was a diary.

In elegant, sweeping writing on the first page was the name *Ursa Crestin*. My mother.

Each entry was dated, the first of which was nine months before my birth.

I wrote to Mother today to inform her that our bloodline would be carried on. Even if she is not excited, Odell and I are. A little girl! I can hardly believe it. The Oracles confirmed it just a few hours ago.

I am overjoyed to be bringing a life into this world. For as long as I can remember, I've wanted to be a mother. My only hope is that I can be a better example to my little girl than my mother was. I can just picture our nights spent by the fire, a brush in my hand as she sits before me. I love her so much already.

The tiny life inside me is going to do incredible things. With the Crestin power passed onto her, she will be a force to be reckoned with. I can't wait to see all that she accomplishes.

The tears I had been fighting threatened to spill from my eyes. Where had that mother been when I needed her? Where was that woman when I grieved all alone?

Breathing in deeply through my nose and out my mouth, I willed the tears to remain stagnant until there was no risk of being interrupted. The last thing I needed was my weakness to be the talk of the castle.

Flipping through a few entries, I found one from shortly after my birth.

My beautiful Varine arrived safely into the world this morning. She is perfect, from her fingers to her toes, absolutely perfect. My labor lasted longer than I thought it would, but thanks to a pain reliever from Monet, it was relatively painless.

The pain truly came after when Odell admitted to me he had made a mistake. Several months ago, he beseeched an Endwen and bargained away the magic in Varine's blood. I didn't even think to question the extended trip he made to visit relatives—had that all been a lie?

Worry had often consumed my thoughts over Odell's acceptance of me and my powers; his actions have now confirmed that he never will. I should have known better. My mother even warned me against our union, but I do love him so much.

Devastated doesn't even begin to describe how I'm feeling; the pure bliss of this morning has been overshadowed by the grief of what could have been. When Varine turns thirteen, that will be the true test; in the meantime, I'll try to find a way to see them restored.

No one can know what he has done. If my mother finds out, she will disown both Varine and me, and we desperately need her protection. Something is brewing in the West, and I'm afraid of what might come of it.

I do not know what to do other than to wrap my sweet baby in my arms and hope for better news.

This was the love that I had dreamed of receiving from my mother. A love that did not admonish me for what I didn't have but instead accepted me as I was. Hope swelled in my chest like a rising tide. If she had found a way to break this cursed block on my magic, it would likely be in this diary. If I was lucky, I wouldn't even need Zylah's help.

Skimming the next several entries, I looked for anything that indicated she had found an answer. I vowed to myself that I would return to read the diary in its entirety. The craving to know my mother, truly know her, was overwhelming. The person I remembered was nothing like the one writing, and I worried that I might never come to know her this way. If Zylah was telling the truth about

Mother's fall into her grief, this would be the closest I would ever be to knowing who she was before.

After thumbing through several pages detailing my eating habits and bowel movements as an infant—I'm still not entirely sure why she needed to write about that—the word "Endwen" caught my attention.

I left my baby for two weeks only to have those vile creatures give me nothing but a mindless riddle. Baldwin and Monet stayed with her because Odell was unwilling to let me travel alone.

Tinuag was every bit of a barren wasteland as it has been described to be. Most days were difficult, not only because of the travel but also because I was so far from my precious child. We barely spoke for almost the entirety of the journey. Thankfully, we ran into few creatures that would force us to communicate. I almost made him sleep in a separate canvas until he reminded me that it was unsafe. Though we are bonded both in body and soul and by voice and by fate, the anger I have only grows.

Will this anger ever recede?

Will I be happy with my husband again?

I do not know if I can remain with a man who would make such a rash decision without consulting me.

Mother writes that Desma is growing with power, seemingly siphoning it from some source. She grows worried that the Queen's abilities are what will bring darkness, as the prophecy states. Mother believes Varine to be the prophecy's savior and advised me to train her well and shield her from the world so she is not used against us. Would they still come to claim her if they knew she was powerless?

Luckily, bringing Odell did have one advantage. He was able to identify the Endwen he had made the deal with. A gangly looking red Dragon, who looked much too young to be granting such powerful and reckless favors. Such powerful creatures with unlimited power and no consequences for their actions.

Everything has a price, something I now know more than ever, even if the price had no bearing on those monsters.

No matter how long I stare at the words the filthy creature spouted from its disgusting maw, I cannot yet understand their meaning. I cannot fathom why they must speak in riddles when they are perfectly capable of speaking plainly.

I plan to continue my research, though I do not know where to begin now.

It was an unpleasant surprise to return home and find that Mother had sent her friend for a visit. I am worried that the Shifter is a spy for Mother, and I pray to the gods that she will take her leave quickly.

Frantically turning the pages, I searched for the riddle she spoke of. Could this be the other half I needed to break the bargain? The second to last page had been torn from the diary, but the imprint of the words had been left behind.

Finding a piece of slate across the table, I dove for it, knocking paper and books to the floor in desperation. Brushing the soft rock across the last page, bits and pieces of words began to appear. I was disappointed to find only three lines were legible, the rest having been covered by the pressure of entries before it.

The halves of a whole now cleaved into two

A missing piece, a sacred heart,

Joined together shall never depart.

I repeated the words, feeling them run over my tongue. "The halves of a whole now cleaved into two." What could they mean? Was I a broken soul, condemned to search for my other half?

The pounding of blood in my ears drowned out my thoughts, silencing the chime of a bell somewhere in the castle. I was so close I could feel it. Distracted by my own excitement, I didn't notice the heavy footsteps coming from behind me.

"Learn anything new?" a deep voice asked.

Afraid that they might see what I had discovered, I slammed the cover shut and hid the diary in a stack of parchment and books. Would discovering the entirety of the riddle make me no more than a liability to Zylah? Could a god go back on a bargain?

Waylon walked toward me, a silver tray in his hands piled high with an assortment of foods. "Caylina sent me; she had other matters to attend to."

I pushed away from the table. "I'm not hungry."

"You didn't even eat breakfast. A dainty flower like you will begin to wilt." His voice was mocking, lips turning upward when he received the reaction he wanted.

"Don't call me that," I snapped. Grabbing an armful of books, careful to keep the diary hidden between them, I pushed past him.

"Suit yourself!" he called before the thick library doors slammed shut behind me.

In my haste, I left a trail of parchment drifting down the hallway that I didn't stop to retrieve. They didn't matter anyway. It took double the amount of time it should have to find my room in this stupid maze of a castle, but when I finally did, I barricaded the door with the small vanity behind me.

I guarded the diary like a lifeline even though I was unsure if it would even help. However, after seeing the side of my mother that I couldn't remember, I didn't want it taken away.

Flipping back to where I had last stopped reading, I realized some time had passed between entries. I only skimmed it, not caring to read about my first teeth or how many steps I took—that was heartwarming information that could wait.

Finally, I found what I was looking for.

I went to visit the Endwen again, but this time, I did not bring Odell. He refused to accompany me, accusing me of hating powerless individuals. What he doesn't understand is the danger he has put our family in, and he no longer listens to my pleas.

The Endwen wouldn't answer my questions about the riddle, but despite it, I believe I have figured out what "The halves of a whole now cleaved into two" means. Before the mess Odell put us in, I had often believed the old fable that mates were just two parts of a whole cleaved into two, cursed to wander the world alone until they found their fated mate. Odell, was that for me, so maybe that was what Varine was missing?

Surprisingly, when I asked if she had a mate and who it was, they gave me a name and a location. I plan to visit as soon as I can, though my heart breaks to continue leaving my baby like this. I know she will understand as she grows older that everything I do is for her.

I also asked the Endwen what had been promised in exchange for the magical block, but this only angered them. The cavern I convened with them in was filled with heat, and I had to run from it to not be burned alive.

If I am right about the riddle, Varine might have her magic back in time to come into her power, and then we can try to stop the prophecy from coming to fruition before it becomes a problem.

Upon my return home, I found that Caylina was still lingering. I am worried that Varine is growing attached to her. Though she chooses to remain in an animal form most days, she still whispers to Varine, but only when I am not listening. The only benefit to having her around is that Varine has someone to chase through the hallways. If she would at least hunt the mice that have invaded my home, I might want to keep her.

My baby girl grows more every day, a flourishing flower in our garden. My little flower.

Hungry for more, I turned the page, searching for the next entry. In my excitement, I ripped the thin paper, but when I held the two halves together, I could still make out the words. Several years passed between entries. I wondered why she had waited so long before writing again. What was happening in our lives during that time?

Canlere is beautiful in the spring. I haven't had the opportunity to spend much time in this area, but the inn where I will stay for the next few days is lovely. I visited a market and found a dress for Varine. They were selling one that matched, but in my size, but I could not justify spending that amount of gold. I plan to try to recreate it with material around the house. Though they won't be identical in pattern, it will be close enough.

The farm the Endwen had given me the location to was really just a mansion in disguise. A strong Witch had warded the entire area to give the illusion of a small working farm. When I gave the name of the boy I was looking for, I was told that Amias Ronin would speak with me tomorrow. With nothing to do but wait, I wandered the trails near the area. I could make out a waterfall on one path, but unfortunately, I was spooked by an animal among the trees, so I quickly retreated.

Hopefully, I will get answers in the morning.

This must have been how Mother had found out about the Order.

I would rather die than have another assassin be my mate.

When I met with Amias, I was shocked to find a young gentleman instead of an elderly male. The woman I spoke to at the door told me he was the King of Assassins, so I naturally suspected someone elderly, not a young and very handsome man. In fact, he reminded me quite a bit of the portraits I had seen of my great-great-grandfather, Lief.

He led me into his office and then brought in the boy's parents, whom I had provided the name of. They were very understanding of my plight and agreed to let me meet the boy. He was very polite and seemed well-mannered enough for such a young child. I hope he ages well and that the Fates have provided my daughter with a good match.

Upon explaining the precarious situation unfolding and the prophecy, the boy's parents and Amias swore a blood oath not to tell a soul. Amias even offered to take in Varine if anything were to happen to Odell or me, though I wouldn't utilize his help unless I had exceeded all options. Gods forbid that day ever comes.

Frantically searching through the diary, I found nothing more. No name of my bonded. No steps to remove the curse. Nothing more. I lay in the pile I had haphazardly scattered, letting the feel of paper scrape against my skin. This changed everything and nothing. My plan was still the same.

Still bound by the oath I had sworn, I would still need to find the amulet. But if I could restore my magic without Zylah's help, could I find a way to keep her from it?

I needed to find whoever my "missing piece" was. If we were truly fated, I'm sure I would be able to feel it in my soul.

Everything felt so overwhelming, the levy of my heart and soul was mere seconds from breaking. I needed time, the only thing I seemed to be in short supply of lately. Tears poured from my eyes; everything was happening too quickly, and I was struggling to find the way forward.

I grieved for Melba, for the loss of my father, for the time I had lost with my mother, but most of all, I grieved for myself. I had lost everything in a span of hours, all the expectations I had for the life ahead of me crumbling in a matter of seconds.

Deep in my heart, I knew that I could defeat this magic block and even a god.

That was the power of choice, and I wouldn't sit idly by and let it be taken from me once again.

Tomorrow was a new day, but just for tonight, I would let the tears flow and the words in my mother's diary repeat over and over until they became a jumbled mess.

The halves of a whole now cleaved into two
A missing piece.
My missing piece.

EPILOGUE

The Prophecy

Upon the decline, another will rise,

A universe kept as an unhidden prize

When the dawn breaks but only darkness walks the land,

A voice will entice, seduce, and demand.

For under the rubbles lies power untold,

A burden to carry that cannot be sold

Turn not away from those you held dear,

For they have carried the very same fear.

Marrow will be drained, we must carry on toward,

Rebuild, not regress, is the only way forward.

Beware the promises that light the air,

Together, not separate, fates perfect pair

To allow the deceiver to stand unopposed

Just by her will shall lands decompose

When all has been lost and evil has won,

A curse unraveled a spell undone.

A Witch will rise, a god will fall.

A failure to choose shall condemn us all.

Acknowledgements

How do I even begin to thank everyone for the mountain of support I have received? Self-publishing has been a daunting, whirlwind of uncertainty that I decided to jump head-first into. The people in this community are some of the most incredible, kind-hearted, and helpful people I have ever had the pleasure of meeting. I would have given up long ago without the support of my friends, both new and old, and my family.

First, I wanted to thank YOU the reader, for taking a chance on *Trials of the Order*. Thank you for reading the little idea that popped into my head one day and never left.

To my husband, who didn't bat an eye when I said, "I think I'm going to write a book." Thank you for the support, the gifted laptop, and for listening to me talk on and on about the writing and publishing process despite having no idea what I'm talking about.

A huge thank you to my Alpha Readers: Sherri Vogelesang, Anna Swift, S.E. Urel, and Suz who read the very first draft and didn't run away. This story wouldn't be half of what it is without your valuable insights and encouraging comments.

To Yogi's Mom (Courtney Hanan) for making me laugh as you absolutely ripped my draft to shreds. Thank you for your friendship and your support. I'm so glad to have met you and I can't wait to base a character on your dog.

To my Beta Readers: Miranda, Allie, Chelsey, Liz, and Jessica, thank you for giving my book a chance. Thank you for your valuable comments that made this story so much better. From the plot holes to misused words, you all helped me far more than I can ever express. You all make the book world a better place and I'm so lucky to have met each and every one of you.

To my lovely editor, Caitlin, who I might be paying but who also became a dear friend. Thank you for the all the late nights spent commiserating on the trials of motherhood. Thank you for being an ear to listen when I needed it the most. Most of all, thank you for spending countless hours slaving over your hot laptop, to edit my book baby. You're a great person, a fantastic editor, and an even better friend.

About the Author

S.E. Schaefer lives in Utah with her husband and two children. She has a house full of pets: two dogs and three cats. When not reading or writing, she likes to spend time in nature while hiking, boating, or on an OHV.

From a young age, S.E. Schaefer would write fantasy and adventure stories. She once won an award for submitting to an essay contest on "The Best Place to go on a Field Trip." She said the best place was to visit an animal shelter where the class could volunteer and then take a pet home (hence having three cats now, one of which was a foster failure).

Growing up, S.E. Schaefer's favorite types of books were dystopian and fantasy. She loved getting lost in far-off places that she would never visit. Now, she likes to think up her own and make her readers long for those worlds as much as she does.

Follow S.E. Schaefer on social media at @seschaeferwrites to keep up to date on their writing and adventures.